praise for
The Devil Makes Three

"A spine-tingling, entrancing read. *The Devil Makes Three* is the perfect blend of supernatural horror and contemporary gothic, with each page as heart-pounding as the next. Tori Bovalino is an absolute master at atmosphere."

— Chloe Gong, *New York Times* bestselling author of *These Violent Delights*

"Bovalino's debut crackles. Dripping with dark atmosphere, *The Devil Makes Three* is perfect for fans of Leigh Bardugo's *Ninth House*. Make sure to read this with the lights on!"

— Erin A. Craig, *New York Times* bestselling author of *House of Salt and Sorrows*

"With its magical library, brooding British boy, and haunted heroine, *The Devil Makes Three* is as darkly compelling as the grimoires of Jessop. A thrilling debut that cast a spell on me from page one!"

— Mara Rutherford, author of *Crown of Coral and Pearl*

Content warning:

This book contains instances
of self-harm, child abuse, and
parental illness.

THE
DEVIL
MAKES
THREE

TORI BOVALINO

PAGE STREET
PUBLISHING CO.

PAGE STREET
PUBLISHING CO.

For my parents,
who are significantly
better than the ones
I write about.

one

Tess

TESS MATHESON WAS ONE OF THE FEW PEOPLE ON CAMPUS who didn't think that the Jessop English Library was haunted. This wasn't because of a lack of belief in the paranormal. Tess, who'd grown up under the watchful presence of a host of ghosts that haunted her family's central Pennsylvania farm-house, considered herself to have a particularly keen sixth sense. The Jessop Library never gave her any hair-raising or spine-tingling sensations beyond the regular chills from the abnormally forceful air conditioner.

If anything was haunting Jessop, it was Tess Matheson herself. And for the first time in her employment there, she was late for work. A miscalculation on her part: too long spent playing her cello, stealing whatever time to practice she could.

She considered her options as she power walked up Dawson Street and took a detour through the alley between her favorite Indian restaurant and a frat house. It was possible she would get there in time—but no, she couldn't vault over the chain-link fence of the parking lot in her favorite pair of white lace shorts. Another miscalculation.

It was also possible that Aunt Mathilde wouldn't notice that Tess was late. Possible, but unlikely.

Mathilde—or Ms. Matheson, to the rest of the students at

Falk—had a reputation. There used to be three other students working at Jessop before they violated Mathilde's strict code of conduct. One, a sophomore, had accidentally spilled coffee on some printouts that belonged to Dr. Birch. The second, a junior, was let go after he let a student check out books from a senior's research carrel. The final student was released the first week of summer after showing up late.

Just like Tess.

And that wasn't counting the students who'd been fired before Tess even got to Falk, the ones Regina was all too happy to tell her about. Part of Tess wondered if the only reason she'd managed to get a work-study there was because they couldn't keep anyone employed at Jessop for very long.

Tess threw open the heavy door of the English building and rushed through the hallways to Jessop. It was early enough in the morning that she was the only one in the halls. The building smelled of lemon-scented cleaner and pencil shavings. Normally, this was one of Tess's favorite times of day, when the building was quiet and clean and deserted. But today, when she punched her ID number into the keypad outside of the door, the clock read 9:07.

Everything was terrible.

"Theresa?" she heard, barely before she had the door open. No matter how many times Tess had asked Mathilde to call her by her nickname, her great aunt always used the same incorrect pronunciation of her full one. It was always "Tur-eh-sa" to Aunt Mathilde, never "Tess" or "Tar-ee-sa" or even her sister's personal favorite, "Tessy."

"Sorry I'm late," Tess said, pulling open the other door until it clicked into place. She knew Mathilde hated excuses more than anything, so she didn't bother offering any. Instead,

Tess took the velvet display case covers from Mathilde's pale, withered hands and set to folding them.

Mathilde sighed. There was something unspoken in that small noise. A warning. A *you-know-what-strings-I-had-to-pull-to-get-you-here*. And worse, the stern look at Tess that said *if-anyone-else-was-here-I-couldn't-ignore-this*. She wrapped her ever-present cardigan around her thin shoulders and shuffled towards her office. "I have a stack of requests for you to find. I'll bring them out."

It was only when Mathilde was out of sight that Tess felt her shoulders relax. She slipped her bag off and stowed it under the circulation desk, taking a deep breath of dusty air.

The Jessop English Library was the undeniable golden child of Falk University Preparatory Academy's campus. The reading room was paneled with shining wood and lined with five floors of balconies. Each floor had fifteen offices, which seniors used in their last year of studying as they put together their final projects. If Tess was still here for her senior year, she'd claim one on the fifth floor, where she could spend all day looking down at the reading room instead of bustling around it.

"Theresa?" Mathilde called again, as if Tess had run away in the time her great aunt had spent walking to her office and back. Mathilde walked halfway into the reading room and abruptly stopped, like going any further would mean spontaneous combustion. She held a book in one hand and a nauseatingly large stack of requests in the other. "Can you find these?"

"Okay," Tess said, taking the papers. It wasn't like she had a choice. Usually, someone requested a couple of books at a time, maybe as many as ten. This stack, though... Tess thumbed through the papers. She gave up counting when she got to twenty-five.

"It's a big one," Mathilde said. Her voice was as thin and frail as old paper. When Tess was younger, Mathilde always made her think of a story her mother used to tell her, about a woman who died and became a butterfly. In Tess's eyes, Mathilde, who'd never been young for as long as Tess had been alive, was half butterfly wings herself.

"Do your best not to be late again, dear," Mathilde said, giving Tess another significant look before turning back to her office. She didn't tell Tess she got special treatment. She didn't have to.

Tess counted more from the stack of requests. This many would take her hours to locate, if not days. And the stack was another reminder that she'd be spending her summer here, in Jessop, or at Emiliano's, where she waited tables.

This was not a comfortable home, no matter how much she tried to rearrange herself into a Falk-shaped box, no matter how much she worked to act like she loved this, if only to convince Nat.

On days like this, when she still had the memory of the scent of dewy grass in her nose and the sun shone vividly through the windows, the idea of sitting in the library was unbearable. It was one of those thick, rare mornings that flung itself right into summer, made for spreading blankets on the quad and rolling her tank top over her ribs to catch some sunlight. It didn't help that today was a Wednesday, which meant that her library jail time would be followed by an extended probation at Emiliano's.

And now, she couldn't even sit in a patch of sunlight and pretend she was outside—because she had to go to the stacks and find those books.

She grabbed a cart and steered it back to the staff area. Jessop was a closed stack system, which meant that patrons weren't allowed past the reading room. The seven floors of books were only accessible to staff, who had to pull everything. Even so, the stacks were a little too secure. To get back there, she had to use a staff key to unlock the door to the stacks and another key if she needed into the cages.

The smell of dust, faded ink, and old paper immediately surrounded her. There was no metallic tinge of technology back here, no hair-and-skin scent of other humans. In the stacks, Tess was alone, surrounded by ink and paper.

She was in a sour mood by the time she keyed herself into the cage on the first floor. This was her second-least favorite part of the stacks. On the first floor, there was barely any Wi-Fi and never any people. It was impossible to tell what noises were from the old building shifting and what were from a potential axe murderer coming to kill her in the depths of the library.

On the bright side, it wasn't the basement. The basement cage was even worse.

Instead of focusing too much on the noises, Tess put in her headphones and flipped to the concerto she was practicing for Friday. She could wall herself off, imagine the movements of her own hands over the body of her cello as she worked. When she couldn't hear any of her thoughts over the sound of Barber, she flipped to the first of the requests and began to search.

All the books were for the same patron: Birch, Eliot. Status: FUFAC. Really, it was unfortunate, Tess thought, that Falk leaned into the F-U branding.

It was like this. Person: Where do you go to school?
Tess: Falk. FUA Prep.

Person: Well, FU too!

Tess: *withers in exhaustion.*

The same thing, repeated over and over again. It didn't matter that Falk was one of the best high schools in Pennsylvania. That nearly every graduate got a full ride to college for either academic achievement or from the trustees. It was always just FU.

And to make matters worse, Tess knew *exactly* who Eliot Birch, FUFAC, was. She could see the cruel curl of his thin upper lip and the glint in his brown eyes. Though she'd never heard his first name, Eliot Birch could be none other than Dr. Birch, the headmaster.

Unfortunately, Dr. Birch was one of the first people she'd met at the school. Tess and her sister Nat's enrollment at Falk was the result of years of favors to Mathilde called in at once. Their presence broke multiple rules: no students admitted midterm, no students admitted without entrance exams, no scholarships awarded for the year past January. They were only here because of Mathilde's flawless thirty-year record at the school and the board's general respect for her.

It also wasn't a secret that Tess didn't fit in. She and Nat weren't wealthy, like the regular kids. Nor was Tess anywhere near smart enough to be a scholarship student, even if Nat was. If anything, Tess scraped by here and would've been out of luck if her roommate Anna hadn't tutored her.

Based on her brief, tense meeting with Dr. Birch, it was clear no matter what Tess or Nat did to prove themselves, he would never think them worthy of places at his school.

But that was the arrangement they had. Tess and Nat were admitted to Falk based on nepotism alone—not that they didn't have good grades back home, which they did, Nat especially. But grades were such a small factor in the decision of who was accepted into the school.

It was not a comfortable agreement, and she was reminded of that every time she had the misfortune of running into Dr. Birch. But she cared about Nat's future, and so she dealt with it.

At least, this time, she could take some enjoyment in the easy insult that was already there. Every time she added to the ridiculous Dr. Birch's stack, who she considered to be one of the authors of her misery, she was rewarded with FUCK YOU FAC. Book one: *Magyc and Ritual*. Birch, Eliot. Fuck you too. Book two: *Witches of Southern Wales*. Birch, Eliot. Fuck you again, Birch. Book seven: *Alchemy of the Stars*. Birch, Eliot. Fuck you a thousand times to the edge of the Milky Way and back again.

By book twenty-three (*Rituals of the British Isles*), she was pretty certain the headmaster could feel the force of her annoyance from whatever hellhole he occupied around campus.

And she wasn't even a quarter of the way through the request stack yet.

There were a million things she could've been doing: practicing the concerto for Friday, conducting in front of a mirror, checking in on Nat. All these options were more desirable than being in this cage, where she felt more trapped in this dull life than anywhere else on campus.

"Theresa?" Mathilde's thin voice floated down the stairs in the silence between the concerto ending and beginning again.

Tess abandoned the books half-loaded into the dumbwaiter and ducked out of the cage. She could just see Mathilde's thin, wrinkled ankles and orthopedic flats at the top of the stairs above her.

"I'm coming," Tess called, pulling her headphones out and looping them around the back of her neck. She hurried up the stairs, stopping a couple of steps below Mathilde. "What do you need?"

"Are you busy?"

It took all of Tess's effort not to roll her eyes. Of course she was busy.

"I can make some time," she hedged.

"A few requests came in." She had another unbearable stack of papers in her hand.

It was one of those moments when Tess fantasized about quitting. She'd done this a few times, mostly during spring semester, when the sting of turning down her music scholarship and choosing Falk instead was still searing on her skin. But in the end, she'd made this choice months ago. Coming to Falk was the only way to make sure Nat's future was taken care of.

Tess held her hand out for the stack. Mathilde passed it to her, saying, "Take your time."

She glanced down at the name on the pages. Birch, Eliot. FUFAC.

Hopefully, Dr. Birch would find some sort of protection charm in the magical books he was requesting. Because if not, Tess was fairly certain that she was going to murder him.

She had to send the first round of books up the dumbwaiter to the cart so they wouldn't be in an ungainly pile in the cage. Tess darted up the stairs to the cart and was passing the office supply closet when she noticed the boxes full of sticky notes.

Tess considered the closet. It would make her feel better to write down what she really thought, especially since she could just crumple up the notes and toss them later. And she had her favorite pen tucked behind her ear, already inked with California Teal.

She hated how awful she felt, both because of her job and her tenuous position at Falk. She hated even more that Birch had power over her—that *everyone* had power over her, and that she had so little of her own.

It would eliminate some of the tedium, at least. One reckless, wasteful thing that she would obviously clean up before there were consequences. Tess grabbed a stack of sticky notes.

When she got back down to the stacks with the notes, she didn't hold back. Every few books got a bright yellow square with a new, horrid thought about Eliot Birch.

Eliot Birch is a fuckmonkey.

Eliot Birch's family tree must be a cactus because everyone on it is a prick.

Eliot Birch's birth certificate is an apology letter from the condom factory.

When she had Wi-Fi, she googled one-liners. When she didn't, she entertained herself by coming up with the crassest insults she could imagine. By the time Mathilde called down to tell her that it was nearly 4:00, the carts of books were peppered with sticky notes of insults.

When Tess changed for Emiliano's, she had a trace of a smile. She almost felt better about Dr. Birch as a human being.

Almost.

two

Eliot

It was the sunniest afternoon Eliot Birch had ever seen in Pittsburgh, and he detested it. Eliot shuffled down the escalator towards the tram that would take him to baggage claim—really, what airport needed a goddamn dinosaur greeting people?—and tried to imagine he was back amidst the gloom of London.

Eliot joined the other dead-eyed travelers on the tram. As he leaned against the doors, he closed his eyes and shrugged off British Eliot like a worn coat. Tried to imagine smiling wider, talking louder. Walking taller, head high. He tried to stifle the magic in him, thrumming like a crackling of static just under his skin; to push it back into dormancy. Turn his sardonic humor into something lighter, less self-deprecating.

When he opened his eyes, American-passing Eliot was slipping not-so-neatly back into place. A disguise. A survival instinct.

He wanted to be home. He wanted to get on a plane and never set foot in America ever again. Instead, he dropped his headphones around his neck, shuffled off the tram and down two more escalators to baggage claim, and waited for his beaten gray luggage to appear on the belt.

Eliot had taken a tincture in the airplane loo before descending, and he felt even odder because of it. He'd found it just before leaving his mother's house, squirreled away in the back of a forgotten cupboard in what was once her workroom. This one, simply marked *Awake* in his mother's careful handwriting, did make him feel more energetic. Unfortunately, it gave his right eye a terrible twitch and made his mouth taste awfully of sulfurous boiled eggs.

The only relief was that his father wasn't here. He had a meeting or a dinner or a murder and couldn't come to scrape his son from the airport, even though it was on his orders that Eliot spend the summer in Pittsburgh. Instead, Eliot was to hail a cab or take a bus or walk. The details were fuzzy. Sunshine made Eliot's thoughts more jumbled than usual.

He had no desire to go back to his single dorm on Dithridge Street, a luxury he'd demanded for the sake of his sanity and his father had begrudgingly agreed to, so he asked the driver to take him to Jessop. The library was Eliot's favorite place on campus—not that any of the staff knew. He usually only went there at night, when his insomnia was thick and vicious, and he could safely key in with his father's passcode and no spectators.

Today, though, he'd deal with other people.

He leaned his head against the cab window and watched the trees along 376 East rush past his window. The first time he'd come, it was a surprise how the city materialized out of the tunnel. London was too big, too sprawling to simply hide behind a mountain. But here in Pittsburgh, it was this: trees, tunnel, and then, after a moment of breathless sunlight, river and city. He was fourteen that first time he saw it, but still, he was awed for only a moment before he went right back to hating it.

"You in college, kid?" the cab driver asked.

"No," Eliot said, and the answering silence was so awful and interrogative and American that Eliot cleared his throat and said, "I'm going to be a senior in high school. I go to Falk."

"Ah, Falk," the cabbie said, immediately disinterested. And Eliot couldn't blame him. Falk kids weren't from around here, as was clear as day from Eliot's accent. They came, they stayed for four years or until they failed out, they terrorized the city with their wealth and temerity, and they left.

Eliot leaned his head against the window and waited for the river to turn into Forbes and Oakland. Or for the cab to crash and deposit them both into the Monongahela.

He didn't feel any sense of homecoming as the cab pulled around Jessop and Eliot unloaded his bags. There was dull resentment and a tinge of hatred directed towards his father. No peace. No relief, even though he'd spent the last twelve hours traveling and this was his first time on steady ground with the promise of food, shelter, and Wi-Fi.

He tipped the cabbie more than he should've, both because he had the money and because the cabbie knew he had the money and didn't expect Eliot to use it.

Eliot stowed his suitcase under a stairway—nobody was going to steal it, not in the English building, and especially not in the English building during the summer—and started towards Jessop. When he was halfway down the hall, a girl dashed out of the library, eyes on her watch, and stalked off down the stairs.

He stopped. Watched her go.

It wasn't peculiar to see a girl in Jessop—after all, this was a school, and girls did go here. But it was unusual to see a girl he didn't recognize.

Eliot had been going to Falk ever since he was a freshman; ever since he'd become less of a son and more of a bargaining tool. He knew every person from every class from the time he was fourteen until now. There were no strangers at Falk—but there she was. He watched her blond ponytail swing against her back as she ducked out the door and disappeared.

He didn't know what to make of this. The girl was as unfamiliar as contentment, as unwelcome as a gunshot, and made him feel even more unbalanced.

If he could just get his hands on a book and his mind out of the present, he'd feel more cemented. Rubbing his temples, Eliot went into Jessop. He did know the girl behind the circulation desk, which was a welcome reassurance that he hadn't been transported into an alternate universe. Her name was Rebecca or Rylie or something like that. She looked up when he came in.

"Hi," she said, recognition lighting in her eyes. "Can I help you?"

Eliot shifted, unable to shake the sense of being a little unmoored, a little uneasy, as if the entire library had shifted and resettled in the week he'd been away. He wished his eye would stop twitching. "Do you have the offices assigned yet? For seniors?"

"Uh, yeah." She slid down the desk and pulled out a clipboard. Eliot withered a little when he saw she wasn't in her school uniform. It wasn't that he cared what she wore, but it was another one of those little shifts that made this library unfamiliar. During the school year, everyone was so tidy: khaki pants and plaid skirts and pressed white shirts and sweaters and ties. He'd blend in, even in the non-uniform black jeans and shirt and cardigan he wore on the plane. But now he was overdressed in his own territory, a remnant from a not-so-distant past in the face of the girl's modernity.

"You're 354," the girl said. She pulled a key out of one of the desk drawers, double-checked the number on it, and slid it over to him.

The key was heavy, solid, real. If only he felt the same way. "Do you know if my books are already upstairs? I requested some while I was away."

The girl blinked at him, and for one stomach-flipping moment, he wondered if his requests hadn't gone through. The sooner he could get to work, the sooner he'd feel better.

"One sec." She grabbed a legal pad and squinted down at it. "Tess has some notes about a lot of faculty requests..." She trailed off, looking him over. Maybe even daring him to correct her.

Trying to remain smooth, Eliot said, "That's me. I have faculty permissions for the summer." It was a simplification. Students were only allowed to take out fifteen books at a time, but faculty had unlimited access. It had only taken a quick talk with the IT team and some gentle bribing to get the faculty permissions added to his computing account. Not that anyone needed to know that.

She seemed satisfied with his answer. After all, why would she doubt him? "Fair enough. Tess is halfway through pulling them. They're in the cage."

The locked cage he had no access to. All of this would be so much easier if he could pull his own books, but not even his father's passcode or the IT team could get him into the stacks, which required a real key. And there was no way he'd convince the half-mummified pissant of a librarian, Ms. Matheson, to let him go off on his own.

"Is there any way I can get them tomorrow morning?" Eliot asked, keeping his voice smooth and neutral. He forced his eyes to relax, forced his lips into a smile. If there was anything of his father's he needed to use, it was his charm.

It worked. The girl smiled back. "Yeah, of course. I can finish those today and have them in your office before I leave."

"Thank you," Eliot said, feeling his smile relax into a real grin. It meant he couldn't start any of his work today, but maybe it would be best to go home and sleep off the jet lag and try to remember what contentment here was like.

And the conversation yielded another victory: the identity of the girl from the stairs. It only made sense that the girl he saw on the stairs was Tess. It didn't erase the oddity of not knowing her, but at least he had a name to put to the face, and that made him feel like his kingdom was once more within his control.

Eliot retrieved his suitcase and left Jessop's cool darkness behind. The streets were still sunny and awful, but he had a plan now. He'd call his mother—maybe call his mother, considering she might've been sleeping—and eat something that wasn't served on an airplane, and then he'd ignore his phone when his father remembered Eliot was back on this side of the Atlantic.

And tomorrow, the fun would begin.

As Eliot walked to Dithridge, he turned over his requests in his head. They'd been unconventional, to the say the least; grimoires and books of magical history, things that other students would probably sneer at. And it was lucky he had the cover of a senior project—he was Eliot *Birch*. No matter what he wrote about, one of the English teachers would be happy to supervise. He could take all his work and turn it into something academic and worthy of study.

None of them needed to know that Eliot was not conduct-ing his project for academic purposes, nor that this was a ritual of self-discovery. As he walked, Eliot ran through words, tast-ing the magic of them on his tongue: *ita mnitim jusre,* a spell for minor healing; *kirra istra moine qua,* one for basic tidying; *mannitua critem mag,* for a clearer head. Nothing happened with the words alone, but the shape of them was a comfort.

It was one thing to read about witchcraft. Learning to use it properly was another thing entirely. And this time, Eliot was on his own.

three

Tess

"THIS TASTES LIKE FEET. IS IT SUPPOSED TO TASTE LIKE FEET?"

The spoon hovering in front of Tess's nose did vaguely smell like feet. She glanced at Anna Liu, her roommate and closest friend, on the other side of the spoon.

"Believe it or not, footy soup is not the first thing I want to put in my mouth after work."

"Sorry," Anna said, pulling the spoon back and giving it an experimental lick. Her lips quirked into a frown. "We're all out of dick."

Tess rolled her eyes and pushed past her into the living room. The scent of whatever Anna was cooking had permeated the entire dorm. It only smelled marginally better than Tess, who'd spent the last six hours at Emiliano's. There was a dining hall, open during regular hours for anyone left on campus, but it kind of sucked. Tess would have to risk the soup if she was hungry.

She threw herself down on the couch. In her room, her cello called to her, half-unpacked across her bed where she'd abandoned it. There was a concerto she needed to record, and she had to email her cello instructor, Alejandra, and the program director of the camp she usually attended over the summer to explain why she wouldn't be going this year. There were a dozen other emails to send, *Sorry I can't attend*s and *I'm afraid I won't be able to play for*s, things she'd been gradually canceling since she moved across the state months ago.

She also needed to call her parents, even though she dreaded the tense, silent, blame-filled conversations.

Asked: "Did Aunt Mathilde give you and your sister grocery money for the month?"

Unspoken: We'll do our best to help, but we barely have enough for the bills.

Asked: "Did you talk to your sister today? Can you ask her to call us?"

Unspoken: It's killing us to have you both so far away for so long. If this was up to us, we wouldn't have chosen it. We would've figured something out.

Asked: "Have you had time to practice?"

Unspoken: I'm sorry. I love you. This isn't what we wanted for you.

"You okay, buddy?" Anna asked, crashing down on the cushion next to her.

"Fine," Tess said, leaning her head back and closing her eyes. She could fall asleep right here, shoes on her feet and apron still double-knotted around her waist.

"Anything happen at work?"

Tess opened one eye. "I'm going to kill Dr. Birch," she announced. "He requested 147 books. I spent all morning in the stacks, and I only got through half."

"Make Regina do it."

"You know as well as I do that Regina doesn't do anything."

"Back to the first plan, then. Kill him."

"I'm strongly considering it."

"Well, it certainly wouldn't make the school any more of a hellscape," Anna said. The couch creaked as she got up and padded back to the kitchen. "Oh, hey. Package came. It's on the table."

If Tess didn't get up, she was going to fall asleep like this, and there was far too much work to be done tonight to let that happen. She heaved herself up, ignoring the ache in her feet, and shuffled to the kitchen table.

The package was nondescript: a plain brown box the size of a toaster, the only label handwritten in gray ink. She picked it up immediately when she saw the return address was to the Matheson Pen Company. Her father. She hated how it made her stomach lurch with equal measures of anger and hope. Tess tore off the tape to reveal two bottles of ink and a slim navy box nestled among the bubble wrap.

She pulled out each item and set it on the table. Two inks, azure and deep amethyst. Inside the navy case was a new pen and a note from her father.

Tess,

I had a canceled order and thought you'd like the colors. Let me know what you think of the pen. New model. Nib feels dry to me.

Xoxo,

Dad

The letter was written on paper she recognized from the short-lived and disastrous Matheson Stationery, a brick-and-mortar extension of the pen company. Even the faintest reminder of the shop made her immediately angry. Tess crumpled the note into a ball and tossed it into the trash.

It was more likely that there was no canceled order, that her father had merely been thinking of her and put this together himself. Maybe it was a sign that he was trying. Which...okay, but it didn't count for much.

Tess Matheson had sprouted out of a childhood drenched with ink.

Her father, owner of the Matheson Pen Company, taught her from an early age how to change nibs and fill cartridges until both of their hands seemed to be permanently lined with a rainbow of pigment. Her mother, a teacher, corrected papers in careful red and slashed through incorrectly spelled words with bold purple. Tess was watered by fuchsia and turquoise, nurtured by emerald and onyx.

Ink was malleable. It did what it was told, unless there was too much of it and it bled through the paper. But Tess was too good, by now, to let it bleed.

Unlike the internet, information on paper wasn't forever. It could be burned, consumed, never seen again. Love letters could be forgotten. Secrets could be destroyed. Stains could be scrubbed away. Ink was not forever.

And neither were businesses, apparently.

But unfortunately for her parents, Tess's grudges outlasted ink. She frowned and shoved the samples back in with the bubble wrap.

"Pretty," Anna remarked, looking over Tess's shoulder. Another relic of Falk, Anna would never fit into the scattered and messy life of the Matheson's farmhouse. She was too perfect, too polished, too real instead of a smudged mixed of uncertainties. Anna reached down and touched the nib of the fountain pen. "Seems sharp. Could be a secret weapon. Birch would never see it coming."

The idea satisfied Tess for only a moment. "I don't think Aunt Mathilde would be too fond of me shanking someone in the library. Especially not Dr. Birch."

Anna shrugged. "She'll never know if you hide the body well."

Tess rubbed her eyes. "Maybe," she said, and she was so, so tired of it all.

"What did he request, anyway? It's not like Jessop has math books."

Tess wrinkled her nose. That was another oddity. Dr. Birch had a special focus on astrophysics or something else Tess herself could never bring herself to care about. "Occult books, actually. Grimoires."

Anna snorted. "You've got to be kidding me."

Despite the dozen times she'd washed her hands since leaving Jessop, Tess could still feel the dust of the books pressed into the lines of her palms.

"Maybe he's trying to put a spell on you. On us. To rid the world of scholarship students for good."

Tess rolled her eyes. "He's such an entitled dickhead." She could spend all night here with Anna, complaining about Dr. Birch, but her cello called to her from her room, no matter how exhausted she was. "I'm going to go practice. Let me know if it's too loud."

She gathered her stuff and went to her room. Tess had an odd, fierce love for the upperclassmen dorms at Falk. They were set in converted rowhouses, with each floor housing two suites and a dorm sister. Anna and Tess technically shared the suite with two other girls, but since it was summer, their rooms were deserted and their doors were locked. Even the dorm sisters, as the college students who were paid to supervise the girls were called, were more relaxed than Tess had expected—and fairly nonexistent during the break, though she wasn't sure if that was a result of loosened school policy or because the girl who was supposed to be watching over their accommodations was more interested in bar-hopping than checking in on the few residents who stayed for the summer.

When they first arrived, Tess was worried she and Nat would be sent to Mathilde's home in Squirrel Hill, but her great aunt decided they would adjust better to Falk if they lived in the dormitories.

Living in the dorms had the added, unexpected perk of Anna. Tess and Anna were too self-contained on their own; they never would've gotten up the nerve to talk to one another and become friends if they hadn't been forced into a living situation.

Tess loved the muffled noises of the other girls in the dorms during the school year, and the odd quiet during the summer. She even loved her bedroom, though it was more of a broom closet, with space for a bed and wardrobe and very little else.

The room looked even smaller due to the fact it was cluttered with assorted pens and inks, sheaves of sheet music, clothes, and books. Luckily, growing up the way she had, Tess wasn't bothered by untidiness. She was most comfortable in a stable state of clutter.

Alone, she sat on her bed and flipped the new pen over and over in her hands. Tess rarely allowed herself to feel homesick. It was a weakness she couldn't afford, not with everything else she was trying to keep in check. Besides, *homesick* wasn't the best word for what she felt. She could go home, probably, but it wouldn't be the same.

It wasn't just home she missed. It was a mix of things: trusting her parents; practicing her cello whenever she wanted; not worrying about money; being able to breathe without feeling like the walls were falling in on her.

She flopped back and closed her eyes. There, on the slippery underside of her thoughts, was the ever-running mantra. *Jessop at 10:00, sleep, cello, concerto for this weekend, but Jessop in the morning and Emiliano's. Work, sleep, did you talk to Nat?, sleep, don't sleep, you need to practice, you need to practice, you need to practice.*

Sleep.

Don't sleep.

Don't think of home, don't think of home, don't think of home.

You'll never become anything if you just lay there, if you don't practice.

You'll never become anything.

Tess opened her eyes and glanced at her clock. It was late, both too late and not late enough to make excuses. Though every muscle ached, she got up and retrieved her cello. As the rest of the city quieted down and settled into sleep, Tess pushed aside her crowding thoughts, raised her bow, and began to play.

Nothing, she thought with each down-bow. *You will become nothing.* With every up-bow, she tried to fight it, tried to remind herself how far she had come and how far she could go. But in the end, it was *nothing, nothing, nothing,* until every stroke dissolved into discord.

four

Tess

Thursday was Regina's day to open the library alone, so Tess went in at 10:00. She would've killed for five more minutes of sleep, and the sky outside was just as gray as her mood. To make matters worse, Regina started talking as soon as Tess was through the doors of the library.

It wasn't that she hated Regina. Tess's feelings towards Regina were similar to her feelings towards small dogs. Both were fine enough, but rather useless, and made far too much noise.

"But anyways," Regina said, finishing a story about some senior Tess didn't know. "I finished that big request and delivered the books for you."

That *for you* was enough to get Tess's attention, since it implied both that Regina was doing Tess a favor and that she didn't believe doing work was her actual job, but the rest of the sentence sent Tess's heart hammering. Her eyes snapped away from her laptop screen to Regina's face. She looked too helpful, and there was something cruel in her eyes.

"What books?" Tess asked, fearing the answer.

"The ones in the first-floor cage. I put them in Eliot's office."

As Regina prattled on, a vein of icy dread opened in Tess's brain and leached throughout her body. Part of her thought it was odd that Regina was calling Dr. Birch "Eliot," as if they were friends, but then again, it was like Regina (and most of the students at Falk, really) to suck up like that. But worse: All those sticky notes. All those insults.

"Did you, uh, happen to take the sticky notes off of the covers?" Tess asked.

Regina blinked at her for a second. "No…should I have?" Tess would've thought Regina was innocent if she hadn't caught the smirk at the end of the question.

Regina knew *exactly* what she was doing.

Tess swore and pushed away from the desk. "I have to go… Are they in his office?"

"Yeah," Regina said, "but he already came in and grabbed some of them, and I think he locked the door."

What, was Regina just camped outside Dr. Birch's office? Either way, this was bad. Very, very bad. There was no way to get those books back now. Tess's face glowed hot with shame.

Maybe he hadn't seen them yet, but he was going to. And Tess doubted very highly he would keep his mouth shut about it, especially since he had already decided to hate her.

But there were still books to shelve, and Tess found she wasn't past hiding in the stacks for the rest of the day. Perhaps the rest of the year, if it meant avoiding Dr. Birch entirely.

"Okay," Tess said, fumbling for her headphones. "I'm going to, uh, finish up that stack of books. Let me know if you need anything."

Regina only smiled. Tess wanted to punch her.

Tess's crisis continued past Mathilde's office, down the stairs, and into the cage. *I could lose my job for this*, Tess thought. Or, even worse than losing her job: she could make her great aunt regret she'd ever gotten Tess into Falk in the first place.

After all Mathilde did for them, this was how Tess paid her back. Hot shame curled in her veins.

Maybe he wouldn't notice. Or maybe he wouldn't know it was her. For one piercing second, she considered pinning it on Regina, but she immediately knew she couldn't do that.

One thing was certain, though: She had no idea how Dr. Birch would react. And until then, she could only wait.

Though they were creepy, Tess felt oddly comfortable in the stacks. The smell of paper, the loneliness of it, reminded her of her father's short-lived shop.

When her father had owned the shop, Tess spent weekends there when she didn't have gigs to play. It was her favorite thing, to curl up in the beaten window seat and read or listen to music. She loved the stationery shop with a deep, intrinsic part of her, the same way she loved her cello. And more than anything, it symbolized so much for her dad: his own dream come true.

Tess reached the bottom cage and rested her forehead against one of the shelves. She curled her fingers against the cold metal, rubbing her thumb against the leather binding of one of the grimoires. She breathed in deep, taking in the dust and paper and ink, the horribly unsettling feeling of being isolated underground, the awareness of just how alone she truly was.

Maybe she liked it in the stacks because these books were set aside and forgotten. They meant nothing to anybody, and yet they continued to exist.

five

Eliot

ELIOT WAS FEELING SIGNIFICANTLY BETTER BY THE TIME HE made it to Jessop. He'd had nearly twelve hours of sleep and successfully managed to avoid his father for the entire time he'd been back on American soil. The sky was back to dismal clouds, which was a relief, and he knew when he eventually got to his new office in Jessop, there'd be books inside.

Things were looking up.

He walked to Falk as the first drizzle of the morning broke through the clouds. He had an umbrella but chose not to use it, welcoming the fat, lazy drops splattering the shoulders of his sweater and dampening his hair.

He'd always been partial to rain. Anytime it rained when he was younger, his mother, Caroline, would wait until his father went to work and then pull Eliot out into the garden. She'd turn the music on loud in the house, and the sound would float out to them. She would take one of her tinctures and charm them both to be water repellant. They'd dance and spin and fling water droplets off leaves at one another. They'd hide in the dry place beneath the willow, still shimmering with the tingle of magic, and listen to the pattering drizzle mix with the drums of whatever song she put on. Under the willow in the rain, they'd talk about magic. Those were the times he liked best.

The R-named girl (bloody hell, he really had to do a better job remembering people's names—it made him seem unobservant) was in Jessop again when he entered, staring at her phone, book unread and pushed to one side.

"Good morning," Eliot said to her, and she flashed him a smile that was too perfect for spontaneity.

"Good morning," the girl said. "I finished those books and put them in your office."

"Ah, wonderful. Thank you."

"Of course." The girl paused, and Eliot had the weighted feeling she wanted to say more, so he pretended to examine a flyer at one end of the desk while she decided whether to keep speaking. "I didn't know that Tess disliked you so much."

Eliot frowned. "I'm not sure what you're talking about. Who is Tess?" He had an idea of who she was—the specter on the stairs yesterday—but that wasn't enough of an explanation.

"Tess Matheson? She works here?" The girl must not've seen the recognition she was looking for in Eliot's eyes, because she continued, "She's Ms. Matheson's niece. She moved here, like, right after spring break with her sister. You know, she's that prodigy cellist or whatever?"

This story sounded familiar, but Eliot couldn't pick apart the details. Spring break was rough for him; he'd gone back home, only to find his mother was doing worse, and then he had to come back so quickly after. He'd spent the rest of the spring semester in a haze of anxiety, worrying that each buzz of his phone would be a call from his mother's caretaker. It was no wonder he hadn't been involved in the gossip when Tess and her unnamed sister arrived with the spring sunshine.

"Why don't you think she likes me?" Eliot asked.

"The notes," she said. "You'll see them."

Eliot waited for clarification, but the girl went right back to her phone. He climbed the stairs to the third floor and unlocked the door to his office.

There were floor-to-ceiling bookshelves on one side, already stocked with anthologies and dictionaries and ethnographies that Eliot would have to pick through later. A huge desk and comfy chair stood in front of a window that looked out over campus. And there, next to the radiator, were two carts full of books.

It was everything Eliot wanted.

He set down his bag and ran a hand over the wood of the desk. It was smooth, polished by years of use.

Not even being in Pittsburgh could crush his spirits now.

The first order of business was unpacking. Eliot fumbled through his bag, awkwardly heavy with his trove: a bone he'd managed to take from a forgotten crypt in the English countryside; a variety of crystals acquired both from his mother's collections and shops around the world; small vials of dirt from Hyde Park and Frick Park and the Himalayas and a handful of other places; a feather from a crow; three scales from a long-dead viper; a collection of other bits and bobs that would hold no significance to anyone else, but to Eliot were sources of power. Carefully, he unwrapped the leather-bound notebooks of his mother's spells and notations she'd written over the years. Though Jessop was full of grimoires, none were as precious to him as these.

If only they held the answers he needed.

He sat down at his desk and reached back for a book. It didn't matter which one—they were all important; they'd all come across his desk at some point. He had the pleasant sense of focus that came with the beginning of a job, that signified there was work to be done and one way or another, he would accomplish it.

There was something there, on the cover of the book. A Post-it note. Yellow against the black cover, teal writing boldly slashed across it in a slanted, uneven cursive.

Eliot Birch is a bland, wrinkled, crap-coated mailbox flag.

He read it once, then again. It didn't make sense for a few reasons. First and foremost, he was not bland. When he was actually trying, Eliot thought he was quite an interesting person.

He also wasn't wrinkled. After all, Eliot was only seventeen. He had none of his father's worried creases or his mother's laugh lines.

And lastly, *what* was a crap-coated mailbox flag? He didn't understand.

Out of the corner of his eye, he noticed the other yellow squares. They were all over the first cart of books, written in the same hand, inked in the same teal color. He pulled them all off, scanning them, tossing them to the ground. By the time he reached the last of them, the notes blanketed the carpet around him like crisp autumn leaves.

Who even had the time to insult him this much?

And who *cared* about Eliot enough to write what had to be dozens of sticky notes about the finer points of his breeding?

Tess Matheson. That was her name—the girl who'd done this. Who had some sort of problem with him. If only he had any idea what that problem was.

Eliot sat down heavily. Something that bothered him more than any of the questions was how he felt. Because Eliot, who'd spent enough of his time with horrible, angry, malicious people, never considered himself to be one of them.

The puzzle of his thoughts was a constant nuisance into the afternoon. He tried to do work, to pull the grimoires and scan the contents, to check the spells, but he kept getting distracted by some new turn of phrase that stamped the sticky notes near his feet. He stared down at his hands. His mother's wedding ring was around his pinky; he usually twisted it when he was upset or anxious, but he couldn't bring himself to touch it now. It was like the metal was conductive, and touching it now would transfer all of those bad things someone had written about him straight to his mother's brain.

He had to know why Tess hated him, and he was going straight to the source. Eliot got up and shuffled through the sea of Post-its, back to the door. He peeked out over the reading room. The girl's dark hair from this morning was gone, replaced by blondish-brown that he recognized from the staircase.

Tess.

He stepped back to compose himself. Eliot straightened his tie and pulled at his sweater, making sure his shirt was fully tucked underneath. His father never taught him much, but he did beat one thing into Eliot: when cornered, it was imperative to remain as charming as possible. Eliot ran his fingers through his hair, taming the dark curls, and pulled out an award-winning smile from his back pocket, slipping it on like sunglasses to disguise the thunderstorm in his eyes. Tess Matheson had no idea who she'd decided to battle.

SIX

Tess

BUT REALLY, TESS MATHESON HAD *NO IDEA* WHO SHE'D decided to battle.

She'd hidden in the stacks, shelving books for nearly an hour before Regina summoned her to watch the desk while she went on lunch break. It was absolutely the last place Tess wanted to be, but the rules required someone to be within shouting distance of the reading room at all times, and Mathilde had some sort of meeting about funding.

So Tess sorted through her email and studiously thought of anything other than Dr. Birch. She had a few requests for private engagements in her inbox, forwarded from Alejandra. It was something she was trying. Except the first one was a wedding offering to pay in "exposure :)" so Tess shut her laptop and dragged out a book instead.

It was ten minutes past the time Regina should've been back when the boy walked out of one of the upstairs offices. He surprised Tess for three reasons: first, because nobody came into Jessop during the summer and second, when they did, they were almost always curmudgeonly old men either looking for the bathroom or there to recount tales of Falk's glory days, back when it was an all-boys school. This boy did not fit into that category. And third, because she'd thought she was alone. The unexpectedness of his appearance set her on edge immediately.

He looked to be about her age, with a navy sweater over a collared shirt and a smartly patterned yellow tie. He had the kind of nose Tess's mother would've called stately and dark brown eyes Nat would've cut from a magazine and pasted into one of her "Painting Inspiration" scrapbooks, which she kept because she was too hipster to have a Pinterest. His curly hair was arranged like he'd tried to tame it a few times and had been only marginally successful. In short, he looked like he'd stumbled into Jessop on accident—or, maybe more fittingly, like he was meant to be in Jessop when it was something else, when it wasn't just summer and no students were here.

"Hello," the boy said, striding across to the circulation desk. "Are you Tess?"

She felt disarmed. She'd never seen this boy before, she was sure—or had she? Her first couple of months at Jessop were a blur of faces, mostly sophomores that shared her classes. The longer she looked at him, the more uncertain she became. There was something in the twist of his mouth, the glint of his eyes, that looked familiar, but out of place on his face.

"I am," she said.

"I think you and I need to have a chat," he said. His voice was pleasant, kind, and distinctly British. Falk did have a variety of international students, but it wasn't often she encountered accents like his in Pittsburgh, Pennsylvania. In fact, Dr. Birch was the only Brit she could recall running into at Falk.

"Sure. How can I help you?"

"I'm missing some books I requested," he said, and his voice was a little more clipped, his eyes harder. Over the collar of his shirt, his neck was bright red.

Something was not right here.

"What name are they under?" Tess asked, voice thin. She hated the fact she thought he was attractive even though he was rude, hated that he was acting like every other Falk boy she'd had the misfortune of talking to.

"They could be under lazy douche canoe or witch-hunting fuckface. I would suspect either."

Oh.

Oh no.

Tess looked up at him. The boy's dark eyes were cool as he appraised her. Now, she saw, he had a crumpled ball of yellow notes in his left hand, with a curl of California Teal ink in her own handwriting.

There was nothing she could say. By the look on his face, she knew the rush of blood to her cheeks proved her guilt.

But *who* was he? Because he sure as hell wasn't Dr. Birch.

She had to play it cool. Not act until she had more context on the situation. "I'm sorry, can you repeat the name?" she asked, fingers poised on the keyboard as if she needed to look it up.

The boy rolled his eyes. "My name is *Eliot*," he said, nearly spitting the word at her. "Eliot *Birch*. But I suspect you knew that, considering you wrote it all over these notes."

Another Birch. Oh hell almighty, how had she not known that there was another Birch at Falk?

"I'm...sorry?" she said, testing it out. It sounded too much like a question. Eliot's frown deepened. But then again, why was she the one apologizing here? "It's not like I meant to insult you."

The flash of red spread up the boy's neck and dotted the high points on his cheeks and darkened his ears. He looked younger this way. Younger and combustible.

"You called me a fuckmonkey!"

"It wasn't supposed to go to you!"

She had to keep her voice down. Between being late the other day and insulting a student to his face... She could certainly lose her job for this. Her job and her scholarship, and Nat's on top of that. The only silver lining to this mess was that the notes hadn't gone to Dr. Birch after all, though she couldn't be sure Eliot was much better.

Eliot must've seen her furtive look towards the back offices because he took a step away from her and a deep breath. His voice was somewhat more level when he said, "Well, then, who were they supposed to go to?"

To lie or not to lie, that was the question. If he was just like Dr. Birch and Tess told him that she thought the books were meant for his dad, she had no doubt he'd be back to tell Mathilde before she'd even taken a breath to apologize. But if she said it was for someone else...maybe she could get away with it.

Except. If he was like Dr. Birch, then she doubted either route would lead her to safety. If she lied, she could be caught, or he could tell Mathilde anyway.

"Well?" Eliot pressed.

"I thought they'd be going to Dr. Birch," Tess blurted.

There was a silence. She couldn't keep looking down, not when he was standing there, arms crossed, frozen in silence. His mouth was twisted, but it was somewhere between humor and annoyance, and there was a light in his eyes that hadn't been there before. And suddenly, he didn't look quite so angry.

"It seems that you don't like my father very much," Eliot said.

"I meant to take the notes off before delivering them," Tess insisted. She needed to explain herself. She didn't want to start the next year being known as the girl who called the headmaster's son a fuckmonkey. "It was about the volume, really, not the—"

"What has he ever done to you to make you hate him?" Eliot interrupted, and he sounded like he was being strangled or holding back a laugh.

She couldn't say. She couldn't speak of her embarrassment, of the brief conferences they'd had when he'd called her intelligence into question, of his sarcastic inquiries into her family's financial situation, of the awful sensation of him leering at her back whenever she passed him in the halls.

She couldn't relay any of this to Birch's son while Eliot stood in front of her wearing a younger version of his father's face, sounding like he was going to laugh at her.

She hated him. Tess glared up at him, choosing not to answer his question and resorting to silence instead.

"I don't like him very much either," Eliot said, keeping his voice low, like he was telling a secret. He opened his fist and dropped a shower of torn-up Post-it confetti on the circulation desk. "Tess, is it?"

He had her name. He had power. She cleared her throat. "Yes."

"I sent in some requests this afternoon. Just a couple, shouldn't take long. And be careful who you trust here." Eliot's eyes flicked to Regina's empty seat and then back to Tess's face. "Not everyone is quite so forgiving as I am."

Eliot Birch turned on his heel and stalked across the library, back up to his office.

She had no idea what to make of him. He had his father's

awful, sharp charm, his father's handsome features. And apparently, his father's library request credentials, because no *student* could request over a hundred books at once.

Tess bottled up her shame because it wouldn't help any-thing—except it was rapidly turning into anger. Yes, she'd insulted him, but it was entirely unintentional. What business did he have reserving books under faculty permissions? What was he even going to *do* with that many books?

Even more distressing, he hadn't actually *said* what he was going to do about the incident. Tess still had the sinking sen-sation that her scholarship was on the line, and the only way to save it was to get off of Eliot Birch's shit list. So even though it really was Regina's turn, when she returned from lunch, Tess went back to the first-floor cage to hunt for the last few books in Eliot's haul.

The worst part of the entire experience, the part that left a bitter taste in her mouth, was this: Eliot Birch had done noth-ing wrong. It had been her actions, her words, that brought him storming out of the clouds and into her atmosphere. She had summoned her misfortune herself.

seven

Eliot

ELIOT'S HEAD WAS FUZZY AS HE TUCKED HIMSELF BACK INTO the office and lit a candle in the window. There was something about Tess Matheson, something he couldn't quite put his finger on. He couldn't tell if it terrified him or enchanted him. Or both.

But for now, the mystery of the Post-it notes was sorted. He hadn't done anything particularly *wrong*, minus requesting a ridiculous number of books, but this was basically all he'd need for the entire summer, so he thought it was a forgivable sin.

With renewed focus, he picked up where he'd left off. He'd already put a few books into his pile of discarded items because, to be honest, they were useless. They only had simple cantrips and spells: cleaning and brewing potions and small healing, things like that. Nothing big. Nothing that he needed.

He paged through another book, tracing his finger down the contents of spells. The page was dusty on his finger, and some of the ink rubbed off, staining the pad of his pointer finger a dull, dingy gray, as if he'd grabbed one of the cheap papers to take onto the Tube and had sweat on the ink. In a strange way, it was a familiar sensation, like if he closed his eyes and rubbed his fingers together, he'd open his eyes to find himself on that massive escalator in Holborn Station, rising up towards gloomy sunlight.

Tidying spells, easy healing spells, summoning spells. Things he already knew and already had in a more accessible form in his mother's notebooks. Another book went into the discard pile.

It was difficult to define what Eliot *was*—but much easier to explain what he *wasn't*. He did not think of himself as a wizard or a practitioner of Wicca. His mother called herself a witch, but every time Eliot used the term on himself he felt as if someone would appear immediately to assess if he floated when tossed into water or burn him at the stake.

He was a boy who believed in things; a boy who had power, when he wanted to. He thought of it as magic, even though it was far too ordinary to be anything spectacular or impossible, and he used it for small tasks: spells and herbs for waterproofing boots while traipsing around the countryside; a short incantation he used on his mother's garden whenever he was certain he was alone, one that kept her cabbages and aubergines and courgettes growing nicely even through her illness; an herby smoke and spell for every hotel room, on the off chance he encountered bedbugs.

No, Eliot knew the truth of his own magic. It was a small thing, a simple thing. But it could be more, if he let it.

His mother, though… She was powerful. It was in a way that scared him, if he thought of it too much. Not as much as it scared his father, but his father didn't share their magic.

Their magic was rooted in the world around them, most powerful when he tethered himself to the earth and channeled it with soil and sand and crystals. Herbs clarified the magic, signaling his intention. Fire activated his incantations. If he was better able to channel the power, he would only have needed his own blood.

Eliot could manage minor incantations and healing, spells to make his life marginally better. But his mother could heal illnesses and mend broken bones with a tincture, three words, and the touch of her hand. She could grow wild roses with the snap of her fingers and a smile, or shape a tablecloth into a full suit by burying the cloth with a needle and thread, tossing a handful of herbs over it, and stamping on the ground four times with her left foot.

If only she were strong enough to heal herself.

A self-proclaimed wizard in Whitechapel had told Eliot once that it wasn't so much the spell that mattered. A person didn't have to be *magical* to use magic. Only one thing mattered in the successful completion of a spell: conviction.

Eliot didn't think he had the conviction that he could read a few words and a toad would appear. But he did have conviction, when it came to his mother. He had conviction to…to…

Another grimoire. This one was older, stained with usage and water damage, binding cracked and barely holding. He ran his fingers down the table of contents, and there it was. It was a spell of reanimation, of renewal. For Eliot, it was a spell of hope.

He hungrily flipped through the pages, searching for 132. Page 115, 126, 128, 131…148. A gasp caught in his throat. Where page 132 should've been, there was…nothing. Blank space. A whole *section* had been cut free from the volume, leaving only ragged edges behind, close to the binding.

He sat back in his chair, running a finger over the paper's edge. He doubted the exclusion had been done by an employee of Jessop: nobody at the library thought the grimoires were dangerous, let alone cared enough to cut out potentially harmful spells. Except for Ms. Matheson, maybe, but he doubted that a librarian would maim a book, even if it meant keeping dangerous spells away from reckless teenagers.

No, this was probably the work of someone else. Maybe someone who worked at the university before Jessop Library became a part of Falk's campus, maybe whoever had donated the book to the library in the first place.

But the realization sent a sick fear crawling through Eliot's stomach. He spun around to the cart and pulled down grimoires two or three at a time and easily deemed which were potentially useful. But every time he was close, every time he found a spell that was a higher working and not just a simple enchantment, every time he felt the thrill of a lead, he turned to find the pages missing.

Every grimoire. Every single bloody book was dissected like an autopsied corpse. They lay scattered across his office, missing their guts.

Eliot sat back and closed his eyes. Of course this was happening. The destruction was too thorough to be coincidence. It had to be the work of Ms. Matheson. If anyone believed the grimoires had power, it was her. She wouldn't let students get ahold of the most valuable of the spell books.

He tugged his laptop out of if its case and went to the student portal. There was another place where grimoires were stored. He had enough basic knowledge of the library to know this: the first-floor cage held the grimoires. Not maximum security, but bad enough. But the basement cage, the one that held the special collections… Maybe there were grimoires there. Dangerous ones.

His fingers paused on the keys. But if there were grimoires down there, would he be able to request them, even with faculty permissions? Probably not. He'd heard of books not being in the system because they were too valuable. Eliot pulled out his notebook and traced over a list of books he'd thought were in the library. A few were uncrossed—ones he hadn't been able to find in the databases, but that he'd thought were shelved here.

Maybe.

Except there was a problem. He had no way to get into that cage.

He sat back in his chair, crunching against a Post-it that had fluttered down from a shelf. *Eliot Birch was conceived on a highway, because that's where most accidents happen.* If he wasn't so devastated, he might've smiled. He crumpled the Post-it in his hand and tossed it across the room, into the rubbish bin.

Was it ridiculous to admit that he was *jealous* of Tess Matheson? She worked here. Maybe she hated being the one that pulled all his books, but at least she had the option to go into the stacks and get them herself.

His hand froze halfway through replacing a book on the cart. Tess Matheson could go into the stacks. It was a long shot, but maybe she could get into the lowest cages.

Maybe she could access the books he needed.

He sat back, considering the idea. She didn't like his *father*, but he suspected that she didn't particularly hate *him*. Maybe if he asked nicely…

It wasn't much, Eliot thought as he thumbed through his notebook. No, the fact that he had to ask Tess for help wasn't much at all. But it was a lead. It was a plan.

And despite what those damn sticky notes said, he was Eliot Birch. This summer, he was going to do something impossible.

eight

TESS SPENT HER WEEKS LOOKING FORWARD TO FRIDAYS. NOT because they were the beginning of weekends, since that didn't mean much when she doubled at Emiliano's, but because she Skyped her cello instructor from home for a private lesson. Tess missed her former schedule of three lessons a week, but that just wasn't feasible anymore.

So when Alejandra texted Tess as she was leaving Jessop, *Sorry hon—I have to reschedule this week. I have to fill in for a show in Philly. Send me a video when you have time, and we'll have a double lesson next week,* Tess found herself staring at the magazine wall in Jessop for a few self-deprecating minutes. This week was continuously getting worse.

Alejandra had been Tess's cello teacher since she was seven, since Tess first insisted that she wanted to play the large instrument and refused to touch the piano downstairs or any vegetables until her parents gave in. And give in they did, with Mom rolling her eyes at Tess's stubbornness and Dad laughing as he insisted that Mom deserved Tess as a daughter because they were exactly alike.

She was the best in the area, and she fascinated Tess. Little Tess watched Alejandra's slender, brown hands draw the bow across the strings. She was about thirty when Tess first started lessons, and she always had her shiny black hair tucked into a French twist and wore dark, fitted dresses. Tendrils of her hair slipped as she played, eyes shut, lips moving, slender shoulders bowing and flexing.

Tess sighed and took another moment to contain her frustration. There were plenty of instructors here, and the orchestra was fantastic, but Tess was too loyal to Alejandra to find someone else. Besides, Alejandra understood the situation. She hadn't been happy about Tess turning down her acceptance to an elite music high school in Boston, but she'd understood. Tess wasn't sure a teacher here would be the same way, and a part of her felt ashamed about explaining it all over again.

It didn't hurt that Alejandra gave her lessons at a reduced price, either.

She was frustrated enough that the idea of playing her cello tonight sounded more like a chore than a relief, so she picked up a last-minute shift at Emiliano's and dashed home to change.

Weekends at Emiliano's were busy enough to pass quickly, even though the college town had mostly emptied out for the summer. It was a good social experiment to prove that tequila was always in season.

By now, Tess knew how to set her brain to only consider the work she was doing while time wrapped around her like a blanket. One moment it was 4:00, and then one tucked wrinkle later it was nearly 6:00, and then before she knew it, happy hour was over and done.

It was nearing 8:00 and she had just been double-sat, and there was this needy couple at table 106 that kept asking for something different every time she went over. She was going back to the kitchen for the extra cup of ranch for them when she nearly ran straight into someone who had stepped into the aisle.

It only took half a second for Tess to realize it was Eliot Birch.

"Uh, hi," he said. "Tess, right?" He said it like he knew her name but the assurance was more to remind her of who he was than to make sure he knew who she was.

As if she'd forgotten.

Immediately defensive, she crossed her arms over her chest. There was no way around him; he stood between the wall and the bar, blocking her way to the kitchen.

"What, are you stalking me now?" With a little discomfort, she remembered all the grimoires he had in his office. All those spells, all those enchantments, there right under his fingertips, if he had the need to use them.

No. Tess didn't believe that. Eliot Birch was a lot of things but he was *not* a wizard. There was no such thing as magic or sorcery. These grimoires all around her were just paper and ink, the futile attempts of people long-dead to change their fates or disrupt processes they didn't understand. To believe anything else, to believe in *magic*, was foolishness.

"No, of course not," he said, and he sounded even more flustered with his accent. Eliot mirrored her posture, crossing his arms over his chest, and Tess did not look at the way his forearms stood out when he did. He'd rolled the sleeves of his button-down to the elbows and something about that made him look less evil. "I meant to apologize. I was brusque earlier."

Tess's eyebrows shot into her hairline. *He* was apologizing to *her*? Of course, Tess knew she was the one who should've been saying sorry again, and he had done nothing wrong, but she was still committed to disliking him.

And who casually used *brusque* in conversation?

"I shouldn't have requested that many books all at once, or I should've done something to help you," Eliot continued, "but I was coming straight from the airport the other day and I wanted to get an immediate start. I'm sorry you had to lug around all of my books for me, and I'm immensely sorry for whatever it is my father did to you to make you hate him so much."

"Apology accepted," Tess mumbled, too shocked for anything more. She couldn't begin to wrap her head around even half of what he'd said, but one thing was clear: nobody else at Falk had apologized to her or ever would.

"And I was wondering," Eliot finished, "if you would be willing to help me find one more book."

Of course he was asking for something now, a caveat to the apology. She fought the urge to roll her eyes—or better yet, to turn around and walk away and never speak to him again. But one more book wouldn't break her, and after all, it was still her job. "I can find it for you."

"I don't want you to find it, though," Eliot said. "I want to come with you into the stacks. Into the special collections cage."

Tess stopped. This was forbidden. Strictly forbidden. The cage Eliot wanted into, the one in the very basement of the library, was overly protected. Some of the books in there weren't in the library logs, open to be requested, because they were supposed to be dangerous.

Which was exactly why, Tess realized, Eliot wanted to go down there. The special collections cage was where they kept the worst and rarest of the grimoires.

But. "Why didn't you tell your dad about me or report me to Mathilde?"

Back to silence as Eliot considered this. Tess's entire

section could see her, 106 included, and the worst thing she could possibly do here while serving was look idle. Because customers always assumed the worst—assumed laziness, that was, even though this short conversation with Eliot was the first time Tess had actually stood still since she clocked in that afternoon.

Finally, Eliot answered, "I prefer to make allies over enemies. So do you think you could help me?"

And even though Tess didn't want to think of him as a friend, even though she didn't want to think of him at all or help him with what he wanted to do, she knew that Eliot Birch had power over her. That made *two* Birches who could make her life miserable.

"I could lose my job if I take you into the cage," Tess said, measuring her words. Maybe she was testing him. How much he was willing to risk for this, how much he was willing to push.

Eliot was quiet for a moment, and she wondered if he was thinking of the same thing she was: yellow Post-its with teal ink, probably still scattered over Eliot's office. If Eliot wanted Tess to lose her job, she already would've. And even worse, if she didn't take him into the cage, he could take all those notes right back to Mathilde. Or his father.

"Please," Eliot said. It was a weighted word, coming from him.

Tess squeezed her eyes shut. What choice did she have? "Okay. I'll meet you in your office on Monday at closing time."

Eliot tipped his head and went back to his booth, and stunned, Tess went to the beverage station to catch her breath. One of the other girls threw her a wink, which she chose to ignore. When she went back into the dining room, Eliot Birch was gone.

Anna was laying on the couch, watching a movie, when Tess got home from work. She threw off her shoes and apron and stretched out on the floor.

"How was work?" Anna asked.

Tess groaned and threw an arm over her eyes. "You'll never guess what happened. That request, the big one. It wasn't from Dr. Birch. Apparently, the bastard has a *son*."

"Eliot," Anna said automatically.

"You know him?"

Anna rolled her eyes. "Tess, there are only like fifty people in each grade. Everyone knows *everyone*. And everyone especially knows Eliot Birch."

Tess turned this over in her mind. If Anna knew Eliot, then she probably knew if he was a total prick. "What do you think of him?" she asked.

Anna cast her a glance. "He's too pretty for his own good," she said. Tess thought of his dark brown eyes, his sharp cheekbones, his curly hair; she couldn't disagree. "But nice. He keeps to himself. I can't say for sure that I know anyone who is *friends* with him, but enough people are friend*ly*."

That didn't entirely align with the version of him that Tess had seen, but then again, didn't Dr. Birch himself come off as charming, too? Maybe they were both nice on the outside and terrible, rotten people on the inside. "There's also the fact he requested all those grimoires."

Anna snorted. "Maybe he's trying to cast a spell on you. A *luuuurrrrvveeee* spell."

Tess rolled up to hit Anna with one of the couch pillows. "Bullshit," she said. "He's probably trying to grow enchanted weed in a dorm room."

"Or," Anna said, raising the other pillow to block Tess's, "he's trying to curse his father. Apparently, they don't get along too well."

The way she said it was enough to stop Tess. There was that glimmer in his eye earlier, when he was talking about Dr. Birch, when he asked why Tess didn't like him. As if he had enough resentment on his own.

"What are the rumors?" Tess asked.

Anna shrugged. "It's impossible to get them straight. Like I said, he keeps to himself. But he goes to England a lot. Like a lot a lot. Henri Bleauchard—one of the seniors—told my chem partner that his mom is dying, and she's still there."

A rush of unwelcome sympathy hit Tess square in the stomach. Okay, so maybe she didn't know enough to hate him. Maybe he wasn't so bad after all. But he was still trying to blackmail her. Maybe. Probably. Family aside, Eliot himself was proving to be a questionable sort of person.

"Well," Tess said, getting up. She should practice, even if she didn't want to. "If I start having really, really bad luck, we know who to blame."

Anna snorted. "And if you bang him, I expect a full report."

Blood rushed to her cheeks, and she managed to hit Anna one last time with the pillow before she retreated to her room.

She had just started to run the bow over her cello when her phone buzzed on top of her desk. Tess debated ignoring it. It could've been any number of people: her mother or father, calling to run through scripted responses; Regina, asking her to cover a shift; Anna, calling from the living room. But it also could be Nat.

And because it could've been Nat, Tess set her cello down.

Even though she needed to practice. Even though she was exhausted. Even though she couldn't imagine dredging up the mental capacity necessary to hold a coherent conversation.

And it was worth it, because it was Nat, after all.

"Hey," Tess said, falling back into her desk chair.

"Tessy," Nat said, and even though she was thirteen now, the way her voice sounded when she said it always reminded Tess of her younger sister as a small child. In the background, she could hear the chatter and squeals of some of the other girls who'd stayed behind for the summer. Nat must've been in the common room of the dormitory.

"What's up?"

"I have a proposition." This was always how Nat started conversations. She could never say exactly what she meant without an introduction.

"Go for it," Tess said, because the second thing about talking to Nat was that she had to be urged forward.

"I want to go home," Nat said, "and I hate it here."

Tess snorted. She wasn't expecting that, not from Nat. It wasn't Pittsburgh Nat hated. It was that she hadn't been given the choice to be here, couldn't choose to be somewhere else, and didn't understand the choice in the first place. She couldn't.

Nat didn't hate Falk, either. Above all things, she was happy here. She *had* to be happy here.

"We can't exactly go home," Tess said, feeling the repetition of the phrase on her lips.

"Hear me out," Nat said. Tess could just imagine her curled up in the corner of the common room, angled away from the other girls. "We take a bus back. It'll be what, like four hours? And then we surprise Mom and Dad, and they can't send us away."

Nat was right, in a way. Mom and Dad wouldn't send them back here to Mathilde, but that was mostly because Mom and Dad hadn't *sent* them here in the first place. But responsibility weighed heavily in Tess's chest.

"You know that won't work," Tess lied. She wished she could protect Nat from everything, but she couldn't. At least, for now, she could protect Nat from the truth. "Next summer, we can spend it at home again. Okay?"

Nat's sigh was withering and betrayed. Of course she'd expected Tess to agree, to go along with it. This was one thing Tess couldn't explain, one reason she couldn't give in: Nat loved their parents to a fault.

"Please?" Nat tried.

"I'm sorry," Tess said.

The line went dead without Nat saying goodbye. Tess wasn't sure she could blame her.

Everything was too quiet and her body ached and all she wanted to do was curl up and sleep. But she had to make the best of being here, and the guilt of running away like a child was beginning to seep into her veins, just like it did every time she spoke to her sister. There was only one way to dissolve completely, to stop being Theresa Matheson, displaced and angry, and become nothing more than the space between her hands, the emotion in her heart, Tess to her very core.

She settled her cello between her legs and began to play. And still, she was distracted in a way she usually wasn't. All she could think about was Nat, over and over: *I hate it here. I hate it here. I hate it here.*

You can't hate it here, Tess thought, a little desperately. She remembered what it was like in that odd month of time when they were at the same school in Gettysburg. A montage of Nat's misery: tear tracks and faked stomachaches to miss school; jibes from upperclassmen bullies and dropping grades and excuses.

No, Nat didn't hate Falk. She was happy here. She was *thriving* here. Back to being her smart, happy self.

Things hadn't always been this hard. This tense. And if she was being fair—though Tess didn't generally feel *fair* these days—it wasn't entirely within her parents' control.

Like so many other teachers across the state, across the country, Tess's mom was laid off. Which would've been fine if Tess's dad hadn't been secretly throwing money at his failing business for the better part of the four years the stationery store was open, if the family wasn't already at the edge of bankruptcy.

The savings account. The business account. The girls' college funds. All of it was gone, put into rent and renovations and stock that never even left the shelves.

When Matheson Stationery opened, Tess thought it was the best day of her life. She saw her father accomplishing his lifelong dream, and she swore then she wouldn't give up until she accomplished hers too.

It was a stroke of bad luck that Tess uncovered her father's debts herself. A few days after Tess's mother had lost her job, Tess went into a joint account to pay fees for music camp, which she deposited her gig money into.

The account was empty.

Though they managed to keep it from Nat, Tess was there for the big blowup between her parents. The argument went on for days and days, escalating when the notice from the bank came: they were at risk of having the house foreclosed upon. Nat was pulled out of private school to save money and unceremoniously dumped into Tess's school.

While her parents argued one night, Tess ran out of the house. She could barely breathe, her chest was so tight with anxiety. Her college fund was drained, but she had a full scholarship to performing arts school. If she persisted, she'd get a good scholarship to college too. She was good enough. Hell, she was the best in the state.

But there was Nat.

Nat, who was the smartest kid Tess knew. Nat, who after only a few weeks was struggling terribly at her new school. She was skipping meals and slamming her door and shutting Tess out, and she could not let it go on for years and years.

It wasn't that there was anything inherently *wrong* with public school. The greatest flaw was in its funding, or lack thereof. The teachers and administration tried their best but there were no resources: no money for extracurriculars, nothing for new books, barely enough to keep the building safe.

Truly, it wasn't about the school. Attending Falk was a means to an end: above all, Tess needed to get Nat out of this house. She would protect her at all costs, even if that meant protecting Nat from their own parents.

With shaking hands, Tess had pulled out her phone and called Aunt Mathilde.

"Oh, Theresa," Mathilde said breathily into the phone. "I haven't heard from you in ages. How are you doing?"

Tess squeezed her eyes shut. *This will be the worst part*, she thought. *Just get through this, and you can get through the rest.* "Hey, Aunt Mathilde. So I've been thinking a lot about, uh, your offers. To try to get Nat into Falk."

There was a long silence on the other end of the line. Tess

wasn't making it up: Mathilde had been talking for years about the school, how great accommodations were, how well Tess and Nat would do.

"Well," Mathilde said uncertainly, "I think...I think they're past the time to consider new students. Definitely not for this year, and I think next year might be full as well. And then there's the problem that they don't take on seniors... But of course, I could speak to the board. You have great talent, Theresa, and I'm certain someone would like to see you join our student body."

Tess's heart plummeted. She had somewhere to go already. "I'm fine. I'm just asking for Nat."

Another long silence. "They're very selective. I'm sure Nat is brilliant, but if she doesn't have anything to set her apart from other applicants, I'm not sure I can get her a place in general, let alone in odd timing."

"Can you talk to them?" Tess asked. "I mean, it's around spring break, right? Maybe we could—"

"It'll be difficult," Mathilde said.

Difficult. But she hadn't said impossible. "Please," Tess asked, leaning back against the wall, staring up at the stars. It smelled of rain. Distantly, she could still hear her parents shouting.

"I'll do my best."

The answer came the following day. Tess's phone rang as she was leaving her lesson with Alejandra, and she ducked into a side hallway before her mom could see her. With shaking hands, Tess opened the phone. "Hi, Aunt Mathilde."

"Theresa," Mathilde said, and her voice was weighted with sympathy. "I'm sorry. But the board does not see a reason to admit Natalie, especially so late in the semester. There was some interest in you, of course, given your talents. You'd be accepted, despite the lateness in the year. But smart girls are everywhere. I'm sure Natalie will be fine if…"

She kept going, talking about how Nat would do well anyway, how she'd be the top of her class, how her parents had been saving for ages to get her through college.

But Mathilde did not see the way Nat had changed in the last month since changing schools. It was like something just…switched off inside her. She spent long hours in her room. And twice in the last few weeks, Tess saw yellow slips tucked into Nat's bag and knew what they meant: her sister had failed something.

That had *never* happened before.

And Mathilde didn't know the money was gone.

Tess slid down the wall, knees tucked against her chest. The admissions letter to school was tucked in her cello case. Nat did not have a similar future.

Tess would be good at cello no matter where she went. It would be hard, of course; hard to keep practicing through school; hard to be competitive if she wasn't going to performing arts school; hard to keep up and even harder to set herself apart.

But she'd do it for Nat. She'd put it on the line.

"What if we were a package deal?" Tess blurted. "Nat and me. I'll go and add to the student body or whatever, as long as Nat gets a spot, too."

Mathilde hesitated. "I'll run it by the board. They were certainly interested in you. But Theresa… I'm not sure about funding, especially this late in the year…"

"I'll figure it out," Tess said hastily. Already, she was ~ lating in her head.

The second call came later that evening, when Tess was doing dishes. This was the arrangement Mathilde had fought for: Full scholarship for Nat, who was too young for a work study. Half scholarship for Tess and a job at Jessop to cover room and board. It left a few thousand in the air, but Tess had done the math and figured she could cover it with a few gigs and another job.

She had then called the Boston Academy of Arts to decline her place at the school. Every word tasted bitter in her mouth.

For Nat, she reminded herself. *For Nat.*

When she proposed the plan to her parents, she was already packed. She hadn't told them about the money still needed for her tuition, or how miserable she was to give up what she'd worked so hard for.

All she could see was the pain in her father's eyes as it set in all over again that he'd gotten the one thing he wanted, and let it break him. Let it break his family.

In her tiny room at Falk, Tess closed her eyes and drew her bow over the strings. She was not a failure, not now, and she refused to be one. She'd cling onto any success she could grab. She'd grit her teeth until they shattered.

nine

Eliot

Over the summer, Jessop was closed on weekends, but that didn't stop Eliot. It never had.

He used his father's passcode to key into the English building, and then into Jessop itself. He could've used magic to get in, maybe, but magic was always risky and fiddly when used on technology.

He loved the nighttime library. It was formidable in daylight, but at night, the shadows made everything mysterious and claustrophobic. The tall windows of the reading room were shuttered and locked for the night, but nobody bothered to close the shutters on the windows past the third floor, so thin light streamed down to the reading room floor.

He closed the doors behind him and just breathed for a moment. When he was little, his mother was finishing her education at Oxford. Those were the years his father taught in France and was rarely home to bother them. If Eliot promised to be quiet, she took him with her to the library. They would sit at the long tables, and he'd watch her read or scribble magic words on scrap paper. Jessop reminded him of that, sharpening his homesickness from a dull ache to a jagged point.

He followed his usual ritual. Eliot checked all the magazines in the back racks to see if any interested him; they didn't.

He thumbed his way through the volumes of encyclopedias in the reading room to see if any were out of place. The blame didn't fall on Tess, possibly, but many times, they were out of order during the school year and that bothered him. It wasn't hard to organize things alphabetically and keep them that way.

Once the encyclopedias were sorted, he did his final—and most forbidden—rite, before going to his office. He keyed into the offices and made his way back to the stacks.

As usual, Mathilde's office was locked, as were the entrances to the stacks. And all the keys were in here, but inaccessible behind Mathilde's office door.

It was hopelessly frustrating, Eliot thought, to be standing in this room, only a couple of floors above the grimoires, and to be unable to access them.

He left the offices and shut the door behind him. It clicked locked automatically. Once, during his freshman year, just after he'd stolen his father's passcode, he'd been caught in Jessop by an aging security guard named Brooks. Eliot had bought him lunch, though, and continued to eat lunch with him a few times a month, so nobody ever came if Eliot tripped an errant alarm during his nightly roamings.

But Brooks couldn't get him into the stacks.

Eliot trudged up the stairs to his office. At least he had books in here. As he pulled one off the carrel, he saw fingerprints in the dust on the cover and imagined Tess's hands pulling it off of a shelf. She had small hands with short, slender fingers. He'd caught himself staring while she was at work, marveling that she could carry three cups at once with those small fingers.

He was still uncomfortable about running into Tess at Emiliano's, both because he knew he'd acted poorly and out of character and because it removed the sanctity of the place. Eliot went there most Fridays with Henri, a French student from down the hall who also wasn't fond of talking to other people. But now that Eliot knew Tess haunted Emiliano's in addition to Jessop, his two favorite places, the prospects of him being comfortable there dwindled.

It was an odd coincidence he'd run into her, though he couldn't yet decide if it was fortuitous or not. He *had* wanted to catch Tess outside of Jessop, away from Mathilde's ears, but his half-baked plans to do that involved hanging around the lobby of the English building to catch her before or after a shift, which did feel stalkerish. He couldn't tell if their unplanned meeting at Emiliano's was *more* stalkerish, but he hadn't planned on approaching her until his feet were carrying him across the restaurant's dining room and then there he was, sputtering while she glared up at him.

Eliot stopped himself. Why was he thinking of Tess? She was nothing to him, and a dark part of him knew he'd forced her hand. She was only helping him because she thought he'd tell his father or Mathilde about the notes, but there was no way he would do that. He'd already gotten rid of the notes, except for one, because he liked the curve of her f's.

He took the book to his desk and opened it. It was a grimoire with all the usual, meaningless spells: beauty, love, health. Nothing to catch his eye.

And yet, Tess could go into the stacks whenever she wanted, pull whatever she wanted, read whatever she wanted. He tasted bitterness in his mouth and realized that it was jealousy. She had so much freedom here and she didn't even know it.

Eliot's father would never allow him to work in the library

or hold a job—apparently, it was below his class. Eliot suspected it was more about the library's contents than anything else.

His father knew what Eliot had inherited from his mother, and it wasn't just his nose. There was a *reason* her grimoires and crystals and herbs and other necessities were locked away, where Eliot's father could not find them. And a reason why he hated Eliot spending so much time in Jessop, when they both knew what sorts of books were shelved there.

He called his mother. Thousands of miles away, a voice said, "Hello?" It wasn't his mother, but her caretaker, and Eliot's heart fell a little bit.

"Josie. Hi, it's Eliot."

"Eliot dear." Josie's northern accent warmed immediately. "How was your trip back?"

"Good," Eliot said, drawing circles on the page of the grimoire with the tip of his finger. "Or, bearable, at least."

"And you got home safely?"

"I did, thank you. Is Mum awake?"

There was a hesitation, and Eliot read a thousand things into that pause: his mother was worse, they were at the hospital, his mother was dying, his father had served divorce papers after all.

Josie said, "She's awake, but she had a rough night."

Eliot closed his eyes and released a breath. He could deal with bad days as long as they were days. "I'd like to talk to her for a little, if I could."

There was a shuffling noise and then the sound of labored breathing, and then someone said, "Eli. Baby. How are the stars there?"

This was his mother, all breathy-voiced and velvety. He tilted his head back to the window and looked at the swollen, yellow moon.

"Oh, they're there," Eliot said. He cleared his throat. It was odd to talk at full volume here in Jessop at night, when he was so accustomed to silence. "Light pollution from the city makes them difficult to see."

"Ah," his mother breathed. Eliot glanced at his watch. It was nearly 2:00 here, so it was 7:00 in the morning there.

"Have you eaten?" Eliot asked.

"I can't stomach it," his mother said. "Josie is cooking something, aren't you, Josie? It smells wonderful, but I can't bear the idea of it."

"You should eat."

No answer. Eliot thought, for a moment, that she'd hung up. He checked the screen. She was still there.

"When are you coming home, Eli?"

He sighed. "As soon as I can, Mum," which was the closest to a truth he could come.

"But I haven't seen you in so long, darling," she said, like she'd completely forgotten that Eliot was home only days ago. Which she probably had. "I want you to come home."

"I want to come home, too," Eliot said.

"How is school?"

Eliot frowned. School was out, and had been for weeks. "I'm done for the summer, Mum," Eliot said, and his mother's withering sigh on the other line made him wish that he hadn't.

"I want you to come home," she said again. "I miss you so much." There was an edge of tears to her voice, and Eliot had to take a moment to get himself under control so she couldn't hear the agony in his own voice.

"If it was my choice, I'd be there already."

Thin and frail, she called, "Josie? When is Eli coming home?"

In the background, Josie answered, "He was just here, Miss Caroline."

"Did I miss him?" And then, louder, into the phone, "Eli. Did I miss you? When you were here?" Like he was a ghost, able to appear and disappear at will without an eight-hour flight and connections, as if he'd passed through the walls like air.

"You saw me," Eliot said, and he regretted this phone call. Was it possible to grieve someone who was still alive? Because he did. He grieved the soft curve of her hands on the grand piano in the living room and the bubbling sound of her laugh. He grieved the woman he'd known his entire life, who taught him everything he'd ever known, who'd given him her magic, because she would never be that woman again. She had moments of clarity, here and there, but they were becoming few and far between.

"But I *didn't*, Eli," she said. "I didn't see you. Where have you gone? Why aren't you back? It's nearly bedtime, Eli, and you shouldn't be out past curfew."

He closed his eyes, recognizing the slip in her memory, yet another side effect. There was no way to explain to her that he wasn't coming back anytime soon, that he might never see her again. His voice was ragged when he said, "I'll be home before you know it, Mum. Can you get Josie for me?"

Almost immediately, like she was waiting, Josie's voice took over. "I'm sorry, Eliot," she said. "I told you it wasn't a good day."

"It's okay," Eliot said, even though it very much wasn't. He rubbed his eyes and leaned back in his chair. "What did the doctor say when you went yesterday?"

"It's not looking any better," Josie said. "The medicine keeps her from feeling too much pain, but it's not helping her mind. You're certain you can't come back this summer?"

Eliot wanted to spend the whole summer with his mother, but there was nothing he could do when his father insisted he be here. And the thought of his father, at home with his girlfriend, Lucille, made Eliot's blood boil.

But maybe. Maybe, he could beg, bargain to have the summer. Maybe. But he who paid for the treatments controlled wherever Eliot was at any given moment, and his father liked Eliot within reaching distance at all times.

"I'll see what I can do," Eliot said. He'd never felt so powerless.

"And I'll call you if anything changes," Josie said.

They hung up. Eliot leaned back, back, back in his chair, until the window was upside down in his view and the moon hung heavy in the sky.

Once, at the beginning of it all, he'd asked his mother about her magic. They'd been sitting at the hospital for her treatment. She was flipping through a magazine on knitting and Eliot was curled into the corner, reading a book he'd found in the back of Harrow's library, covered in dust. He kept getting distracted by the constant beeping and the squeak of nurse's shoes in the hallway. And by his mother: her bony fingers, looking more frail by the day; the way her hair was becoming brittle and thin.

"Mum?"

She'd barely looked up from her reading. "Eliot?"

"Why don't you heal yourself?"

She didn't look at him, but her eyes stopped traveling over the page. She let out a long breath, and after a moment, set the magazine aside. "That's not how it works, love," she said. "Come here."

Even though he was too old to be cuddled against her, Eliot crawled into the hospital bed beside his mother. Her bony hip pressed into his side. She took his hand and placed it on her head, over the place where the tumor grew. "I can't heal this," she said. "It's too big. It's too much. My own magic won't work to heal something so significant in my own body."

Eliot took his hand back and laced his fingers through his mother's. Her hands were so, so cold. "What if I did it?" Eliot asked. "Would my magic work?"

"My sweet boy." She kissed his knuckles, like she used to when they were playing together in the yard when he was much younger. "I don't have the spells for something this big, Eli. I don't know where to begin looking. And it would take so much energy... I can't ask that of you."

But Eliot knew what she really meant. That she didn't have the spells because his father had purged their home of anything magic related, and he wouldn't be able to access any grimoires elsewhere without his mother's guidance. And if he tried and wasn't able to save her, she didn't want him to live with the guilt of failure.

Except Eliot knew where to look. And worse, he knew that the guilt of failing to save her would not be as bad as the guilt of not trying at all.

These grimoires were useless. His father was useless. For his mother, even modern medicine was useless. And when he took stock of his life here, the only one person he could find who was not useless was Tess Matheson. Eliot wasn't at all sure how he felt about that.

ten

Tess

EVEN THOUGH SHE KNEW SHE WAS WANTED, KNOCKING ON the door to Eliot's office seemed forbidden. Tess hesitated outside, fiddling with the edge of her sweater. Every day after Tess or Regina closed the doors to the library to the public, Mathilde took a short break to get coffee. It gave the girls time to shelve the remaining books without worrying about watching the reading room or patrons before Mathilde came back to complete a final walk-through of the stacks and lock up for the night. For now, the library was hers and hers alone. Well, and Eliot's.

She had to get this over with. They had to be out of the stacks before Mathilde came back. Tess knocked.

Almost immediately, as if he'd been waiting just on the other side, Eliot opened the door. "Tess," he said. "Are you ready?"

She didn't like the way he said it, like they were going on some sort of life-changing adventure when really, they were just going down a few flights of stairs.

"Of course," Tess said, plastering on a fake smile. He had that confidence again, the brand that was missing when he'd spoken to her at Emiliano's. It was clear that this—libraries, academia, the book- and paper-filled office—was Eliot's domain. Maybe Falk in its entirety. She idly wondered if he was self-possessed in his own home, or in a park, or a grocery store, or if he was tight-shouldered and uncertain.

"Come into my office," Eliot said. "I'll explain what I'm looking for."

Tess followed him inside. The office was small but felt enormous, as if the books around the walls were layers and layers deep. To her vague annoyance, the room reminded her of her father's office.

Eliot gestured to the chair across from him and she sunk down into it. His office smelled of leather, paper, and vanilla; he had a candle burning near the window, which accounted for the vanilla. Part of her realized she could scold him for this, since candles were strictly forbidden, but it seemed like a petty and vindictive thing to do after he hadn't reported her.

"You might've noticed," Eliot said, "that I'm doing my research on the occult."

Of course she'd noticed. Tess took another look around the room, taking in the bundles of herbs on the bookshelves, the crystals that lined his desk, the smudges of a chalk pentagram partially obscured by the rug.

"You're in a good place to do it," she observed. Before, she'd just thought that Eliot was preparing some sort of academic takedown of the language of occult books, or some other dry and boring research paper that would get him good grades and scholarships and be unendurably dull to everyone else. But here in his office, she couldn't fight the sense that he was actually *practicing* the magic. She didn't believe in magic— couldn't believe in magic—but the bizarre things scattered around Eliot's office gave her the impression that he did.

Eliot inclined his head. "Exactly. But none of the books I

requested have what I'm looking for, and I imagine the ones that do are meant to be kept under lock and key, out of the records, and I haven't the foggiest idea of how to get them."

Which meant that all the books he'd requested were useless, and she'd done all that work for no reason. Tess bit the inside of her cheek to keep any scathing words from leaving her mouth. "What *are* you looking for?"

"Do you know what a grimoire is?"

She did, and not because she had any personal interest in the occult. The rumors of ghosts in Jessop Library didn't exist just because the library was old and creepy at night. Jessop held a *massive* collection of occult manuscripts. Grimoires, satanic texts, wiccan books, voodoo guides—all were accounted for. So Tess had seen more than her fair share of grimoires: magic books containing spells, charms, and instructions on how to summon demons and the like. In fact, it was a running joke for students to find the most graphic spells in the Jessop grimoires and attempt to perform them in their dorm rooms.

If any of them worked, Tess was pretty sure she would've heard about it.

"I do," she said. "I saw you requested quite a few already."

Eliot nodded. "Yes, but they're all too…light for my project."

Tess thought of commenting on this—after all, if spell books were too light for what he was trying to do, what the *hell* was he looking for? And also, *why* was she getting herself involved? If he burnt Jessop down trying to do some ridiculous, impossible spell and Tess had something to do with it, Mathilde would be pissed.

But. There was also a sort of odd, distant curiosity. She didn't believe in magic, not in the same way she believed in ghosts. Perhaps that was just because she'd never seen magic with her own eyes. At least for ghosts, she could claim the proof of the specters that floated from room to room in her family's farmhouse, cold spots that showed up without warning and vanished a few minutes later.

Maybe magic was a little bit like that. And maybe, Tess thought dangerously, she *wanted* to see what Eliot Birch was planning to do, if only to see him fail catastrophically.

He ruffled through the pages on his desk, uncovering a slim notebook. Eliot flipped through the pages to a list of crossed-off titles. But no—when he passed it to her, she saw that a few were missing strikethroughs.

The Book of Shadows. Death Spells. Secrets of the Undying. The Glencoe Grimoire. Margaret's Spells. The Book of Truths.

"Oh, I've definitely seen some of these before," Tess said. "In the basement cage."

"That's what I suspected," Eliot said.

"But when we talked, you only asked for one book?"

Eliot didn't meet her eyes. "This is a general list, but I doubt we have all of them here. I only expect we have one or two."

She could've argued the point further, but that would only prolong her interaction with Eliot. He was still a bastard, and she was still breaking the rules. The longer they sat, the more likely they were to be caught.

She'd brought the keys to the stacks with her. Going back through the main reading room made her nervous. What if Mathilde forgot something and came back just in time to catch Tess taking Eliot through the offices to the stacks? But there was another way through the lounge on this level.

"Come with me," she said.

She led the way through the lounge and the locked door to the stacks, past the dumbwaiter to the stairs, down to the basement floor. This floor was different from the rest of the stacks: colder, mustier. Older, too, if the rumors she'd heard were true: Jessop was built on top of a university building that had been damaged in a bizarre fire. Casualties unknown. Half of the basement was set aside for the sprawling special collections cage, and shelves and boxes climbed the walls. She used the smaller key to unlock the cage and pulled open the creaky grated door to let them in. Eliot watched with silent fascination.

"What?" she asked, feeling self-conscious under his gaze.

"There's just so much protection for these," he said, running a finger down the side of the cage. "For books."

Tess shrugged. "They're dangerous, apparently," she said. Out of the corner of her eye, she barely saw Eliot grimace.

Eliot followed her inside. He'd brought the notebook with the titles on it, and they both set to looking for the grimoires.

"So, how long have you been working here?" Eliot asked suddenly, startling Tess out of the silence.

"Uh, a couple of months. Since spring break." And then, because she felt like she had to tell him, she said, "Mathilde— Ms. Matheson—is my great aunt. That's, uh, one of the reasons I go here." It was a simplification, but she wasn't turning out secrets unprompted.

"Ah," Eliot said, but something about the way he shaped the word made her feel like he'd already known. "She seems... dedicated."

That was one way to put it.

"And what exactly is your project on?" Tess asked.

Eliot's smile thinned to a line, and the fact that she noted it made Tess register that she was spending more time examining his face than she was examining the shelves. As if he came to the same conclusion, Eliot looked away quickly. "I've always been fascinated by the occult—ghosts and witches and magic and all."

He was leaving something out, she could tell, but just as she wasn't telling him her secrets, she didn't expect him to tell her his.

To her surprise, he continued. "This," he said, sweeping a hand towards the books, or maybe the entire library itself, "almost makes Falk bearable." He wasn't even pretending to look for the books anymore, so Tess gave up the charade as well, and leaned against a shelf with her arms crossed.

"And it wouldn't be otherwise?" Tess asked.

"I hardly think being close to my father is a comfort," Eliot said quickly, and that blush immediately crept up his neck to his ears and over his cheeks. "I'm sorry. It doesn't matter."

"No, it's okay," Tess said, looking away from him. It made her feel odd to fully meet his eye. "So you're not here for your father then."

"I'm not here for him," Eliot agreed, "but that doesn't mean I'm not here *because* of him."

"At least the grimoires are here," Tess said, because she had to say something.

Eliot nodded. "To answer your question," he said, "I'm doing my research on death and resurrection and magic." He caught her eye for a moment too long.

What the fuck, Tess thought, but she had the sense not to say it out loud. And then, *Am I about to be murdered by Eliot Birch?*

"Well," Tess said, trying not to show her surprise. Eliot seemed like such a practical, unenchanted sort of person—not even close to the type interested in something like raising the dead. She'd be less surprised if he said he was studying intergalactic squirrels or something of the like. It was even more unlikely when she held up what she knew of his old, harsh-tongued father. "That sounds like an interesting project."

Eliot nodded, but he looked disappointed, like she hadn't said what he'd expected—or like she'd said *exactly* what he'd expected, and that was even worse.

They lapsed into an awkward bit of silence. Tess moved down a shelf, nearly tripping over a dusty box. She opened it to find it full of withered pages with jagged edges that looked like they'd been cut from the middles of books. On the lid of the box, Mathilde's scrawl read *Level 3 Dangers*. Tess had no idea what to make of that or the danger scale that was being alluded to. She bent down to investigate the contents. The first page she picked up was wrinkled on the corner, as if it had been ripped straight from a book. It contained a list of things—dirt, blood, herbs, other random objects—and a sequence of words that looked to be in another language. She was testing out the shape of them when Eliot cleared his throat. Tess dropped the page.

"Hey, what's—"

The sound of Eliot's voice was cut off by a bizarre jarring sound, like metal grating against metal or stone, or a mechanical bit that hadn't moved in decades. The sound grew louder, and Tess realized that there was *movement*, too—a bottom section of the shelf between Eliot and her was moving, sinking into the ground, and taking the books down with it.

The shelf descended until it was flush against the ground, revealing a dark square in the wall.

Silence pressed between Eliot and Tess. Tess looked over her shoulder, certain someone had heard the noise and would come running, certain that this was a prank.

Finally, breathlessly, Eliot asked, "Was that supposed to happen?"

Tess looked between Eliot and the hole. Now that her eyes were adjusting to the darkness within, she could make out stone steps leading down, further into the pits of the library. She had no idea what could be down there—and it wasn't like her orientation tour of the stacks had included a discussion of the secret, creepy passageway.

"No," she said, certain that this was far, far outside of her job description. "No, that was not supposed to happen."

eleven

Tess

ONCE, WHEN TESS WAS MUCH YOUNGER AND NAT WAS BARELY taller than her knee, they found an abandoned tree house in the woods behind their house. It was the same kind of surprise: the woods were familiar, like the library was to Tess now, and there wasn't supposed to be anything like that there. There shouldn't have been anything…structural.

But even when Tess was eight, the tree house didn't feel foreboding. Abandoned, yes, and maybe a little sad because of it—a reminder that children grow older and leave their tree houses behind—but it did not feel dangerous.

That was the main difference, Tess thought. Thick, cloying dread made the hair on the back of her neck stand on end and goose bumps erupt on her arms. She felt the thrill of danger from the newly exposed staircase. So when Eliot turned on the flashlight on his phone and moved towards the door, she could only watch in horror.

"Well?" he said, turning to look back, like he expected her to be on the step behind him. "Are you coming?"

"Um, no," Tess said.

He cocked his head. "Why not?"

There were a million things she could've said, but all moved too quickly through her thoughts for her to grasp one. "I'm not just following you into a hole in the ground," Tess stammered.

"Tess," Eliot said, and again, she noticed the way he said her name: less like a word, more like a promise. If only she knew what he was promising. "What are you afraid of?"

It was exactly something a serial killer would say. "I'm not afraid," she lied. "I just have a sense of self-preservation. Unlike you, apparently."

Eliot laughed, and his mouth did a smooth little flip into a smile. "It'll be an adventure," he said, reaching out a hand toward her.

Tess weighed her options. Obviously, she could *not* go in the hole, order Eliot back out, shut the passageway, and drag him back up to his office where she would never have to acknowledge him again.

Except she couldn't fight the curiosity herself, even though she was somewhat terrified. There was still time before Mathilde came back, and the thought of looking like a coward in front of Eliot rankled her. He just looked so confident, even standing there in the gaping hole to nothing, smiling at her. Tess groaned, kicking the box of dusty pages. She knew what her decision was, and she knew she was going to hate herself for it later.

"Okay," Tess said. She turned on her own phone flashlight and took his hand as more of a precaution against falling down the stairs than anything else.

"Okay," Eliot repeated, like he hadn't been expecting her to come—but Tess had the suspicion that he had.

They started down the steps. The walls were hewn in rough stone, porous and cold when she reached out for balance. The whole thing smelled like a damp basement, which wasn't too surprising considering that was probably what it was. Tess didn't look too closely at the walls because the bits she did see looked to be draped with cobwebs, and spiders topped the list of things she was afraid of. She considered dethroning spiders in favor of creepy staircases that randomly appeared, but so far, this staircase hadn't done anything too malevolent.

The staircase flattened into a narrow hallway made of the same stone. Shadowed indentations stood in the walls, filled with stone and rubble, as if other tunnels had once existed and been filled in. It was far colder down here. When she shivered, Eliot turned back to check on her. His face was all shadows.

"Are you okay?" He spoke barely above a whisper, and Tess wondered if he felt the same disquiet she did, now that they were underground. There was no trace of a smile on his face.

Tess nodded. She was glad for the darkness and how it masked the goose bumps creeping up her arms. Eliot turned away, and they pressed forward.

It was then that Tess noticed the buzzing in her ears.

It was less of a buzzing and more of a humming. Or maybe a whisper. She couldn't hear it well enough to say. A discordant tone, somewhere far along the tunnel or deep within her head.

"Do you hear that?" Tess whispered. Her voice sounded too loud.

"Hear what?"

"*That.*"

Eliot stopped moving and cocked his head to one side. He didn't let go of Tess's hand, she noticed, and she wasn't sure what to make of that. As Eliot listened to the humming, pulsing darkness of the tunnel, his hand tightened on hers.

"Maybe?" he said. "Is it…like a ringing?"

Maybe it was a ringing, maybe it was a hum, or maybe it was a faraway, sustained scream. "We should go back," Tess said.

Eliot pointed the flashlight forward. The darkness seemed to swirl and press closer, and the light of the flashlight was no match for the gloom. "I think it opens up a few feet ahead," he said, squinting into the tunnel. "Only a bit farther. And then we'll go back."

She didn't want to go farther. Her brain was clouded with everything that could be up ahead: rotting bodies and giant spiders, abandoned and forgotten things. Everything inside of her was screaming to turn back. But Eliot was already moving forward.

Tess bit back her fear and followed him down the tunnel. It was too narrow for them to walk side by side without brushing the walls. Instead, she let him lead her like she was a child, clinging to his hand. A large part of her knew she didn't have to go, that she could turn back and leave Eliot alone in this godforsaken hole by himself. But there was a bigger part of her that felt a dangerous sort of thrill going on like this. There was something heart pounding about the press of his fingers and the sweat of his palm, and she knew that even though he looked composed, he was scared too.

"What do you think is up there?" Tess asked. Both of their footsteps were slowing, whether it was out of fear or excitement.

"I don't know," Eliot said, and that small part of her relished the edge in his voice. He paused at one of the blocked off passages. Wordlessly, Eliot handed her the light. He dug his fingers around one of the bits of rubble and pulled. Pebbles shifted and dust rained down, but the blockage didn't move. Tess just wanted him to quit touching things. She pushed the flashlight back into his hand before he could cause some sort of collapse.

It was like the sleepovers she'd been to in middle school, where they had turned off the lights and shut the bathroom door and spoken "Bloody Mary" three times in front of a mirror, or like the ghost stories told around a campfire, or even like the way those students who took out grimoires and recited spells felt. It was terror of the unknown, of the unknowable, and the realization that maybe, there actually was something there in the dark.

As Eliot had predicted, the tunnel opened into a small room. The room had high ceilings and dirt floors and the same stone walls as the tunnel. It was damp and cold, like they'd left the modern day behind and walked directly into a medieval crypt. Tess imagined she could go to the walls, breathe a spell from one of the grimoires upstairs, and reveal an entire court that had long since been forgotten. Or the corpse of a banished king, full of magical vengeance. She shuddered and turned away, back towards Eliot, with his warm, human heartbeat and his broad-shouldered certainty.

Tess and Eliot shone their lights around, and Tess half expected something to jump out of the darkness to grab them.

Even though they weren't moving, Tess didn't let go of Eliot's hand. A safety precaution.

"What's that?" Eliot said, and the echo of his voice made her jump.

"What's what?"

Eliot dragged her closer to the far wall of the room, and Tess realized what he'd seen. There was a small alcove cut into the stone wall with a shelf in the middle. On that shelf was a book.

She shouldn't have been bewildered to see it there. After all, in a library, a book was about the most likely thing that could be found. But here amongst the dust and cobwebs, Tess was intensely surprised to see it.

Tess picked it up. It was cool, like the air in the tunnel, and dry, which she wasn't expecting, since the air decidedly wasn't. The cover didn't feel dusty like every other abandoned book she'd found. It was bound in something black and porous like skin—and maybe, Tess realized, it really *was* skin.

Even worse was the clingy feel of it: there was this effect as if the book wanted to stick to her skin, as if it was begging her to open the cover and reveal the contents. *Let me tell you my secrets*, the book whispered inside of her. *Let me give you what you desire.* She shook it off, shuddering. Books didn't whisper inside people's brains. It was only her own fear, Tess decided, like the sensation of her name being called in a dark, silent room, on the edge of sleep.

She dropped Eliot's hand to aim her flashlight at the cover. There was no title.

"What do you think it is?" Eliot asked.

"I don't know." She opened the book and flipped through the pages. There were no words, no illustrations, nothing. The pages inside were blank, except for one short line on the very first page: *Ex Libris Infernorum.*

"What does this mean?"

Eliot squinted down at the book between them. "I think… well, *ex libris* is 'from the library of.' *Infernorum* could be, well. I think hell, or more generally, those below."

"From the library of those below," Tess repeated. Something sounded in the tunnel behind them. Fear prickled up Tess's spine. Was there someone else in the tunnel?

Tess glanced back, but there was nothing else. They were alone.

"Does it say anything else?"

Tess shook her head, flipping through the pages again. All blank.

"Maybe the ink is too light, and it's too dark to see it in here?" he suggested.

"Maybe," Tess agreed, but she doubted it. There would at least be a trace of something, if the book was full of writing.

"Oh," Eliot said, running his hand along the upper edge of the alcove, wiping away years of dust. "There's writing here."

Tess looked up as the inscription revealed itself, carved into the stone above the place the book rested.

Let the righteous burn.

They were quiet for a moment, Tess trying not to think about how they were underground, trying not to think of the sound of Eliot breathing, trying not to imagine the tunnel collapsing around them.

"Let's get back," she said.

He took the book from her hands and started back towards the stairs. "I couldn't agree more."

"Wait." She hadn't been expecting him to take the book with them, and the idea of daylight on that hide-bound cover made her uneasy. "Don't you think we should leave that here?"

Framed by the mouth of the tunnel, Eliot looked at the book, then back at her. "Why?"

"It gives me the creeps." Though she couldn't say for sure whether she considered herself righteous, the warning in the alcove was at least enough to give her pause.

Eliot blinked slowly at her, and she could tell by his face that he had a million responses, some of them nice and most of them not, and he was deciding which was most appropriate for the situation.

"Just spit it out," Tess snapped.

"Isn't it a little ironic to be afraid of books if you, you know, work at a library?" Eliot swept a hand out as if they were standing in the stacks rather than in this horrifying, dead-end room. "Especially a library like this. It's not entirely conventional, you know."

Tess did know, and the fact he pointed it out made her even more annoyed. "Lending out grimoires and finding creepy-ass blank books in secret tunnels are two entirely different things."

Eliot was still absorbed by the book. He tilted it to and fro, as if writing would magically appear if he shone the light on it just right.

She could understand him being interested in the book—judging by the books he already had and his research project, this was right up his alley—but Eliot had a smile on his face. Down here, in the awful death tunnel, he looked positively gleeful.

"Let's get out of here before Mathilde comes back," Tess said with a little more urgency. Time tugged at her: if Mathilde returned and found Tess and Eliot in the deepest part of the library, Tess would be in huge trouble.

"We won't get caught," Eliot said, tucking the book under his arm. "And if we do, I don't see how that would be a problem."

Tess blinked at him. Of *course* it would be a problem. "Why is that?"

Eliot answered like it was obvious. "Because even though my father is terrible, he's useful. I don't mean to be *that* kid, but Ms. Matheson won't do anything to me, even if she finds me in the stacks. She can't."

Tess sputtered for words, but there weren't any she could find to fill the steely, fiery, anger-filled second. Maybe she was actually going to kill him. Eliot was mistaken. Maybe he had power, or his father had power, but this was Mathilde's domain.

"It's not you I'm worried about, Eliot," she spat. Before he could say anything else, she spun on her heel and stalked back down the corridor. If he followed her, then whatever. But if he didn't, she wasn't going to stand around waiting for him, waiting to get caught by Mathilde. A few hours locked in this creepy dark hallway would do him good.

At the very least, maybe it would make him stop smiling.

His footsteps sounded behind her. Eliot didn't extend a hand to her this time, which was good, because there was no way that Tess would've taken it.

The light from the library barely penetrated the darkness as they went back towards the stairs. It was as if the square of empty space between the stairs and the library was a wall.

Relief rushed through her the second she stepped out of the staircase, back onto the familiar, drab carpet of the special collections cage. Eliot leaned against a shelf, examining the book in the light.

"Hey," Tess said, and then when she failed to get his attention, the insufferable, self-centered bastard: "*Hey*. Eliot."

"What?"

"We need to figure out how to close this." The only thing Tess could think of that was worse than Mathilde finding Eliot Birch and her alone in the cage was Eliot Birch and her alone in the cage with a gaping hole to hell replacing one wall.

She wasn't going to be fired for discovering a secret passageway to nowhere, and she wasn't going to be fired on account of Eliot. "How did you open this in the first place?"

Eliot set the book on a clear space of shelf and joined her at the hole. "There was a...a switch thing."

Tess dragged over a box to stand on and peered between the books on the shelf, shifting them here and there. In a crack between two books, she caught sight of something along the wall. Why Eliot had reached through the entire shelf to the back wall was beyond her.

She flipped the brassy metal switch. Instantly, the mechanical groaning started. Beside Tess, the displaced section of books ascended back into position, securely blocking off the tunnel once more.

"That's curious," Eliot noted, as if he were watching a squirrel eat an acorn or examining an impressionist painting. He traced along the edges of the shelf where it had connected back to its space. "And you've never seen that before?"

Tess crossed her arms over her chest. "Don't you think I would've been less surprised if I'd seen it?"

Eliot shrugged. "Or you're easily frightened." It sounded like an insult to Tess, even though he didn't say it like one. Or maybe, right now, every word that came out of his mouth felt like a slight. "I think I'm going to take this up to my office."

Clearly, the books they'd come to special collections for were no longer important to him. "And *The Book of Shadows*?"

Eliot shrugged. "I'll come back."

Tess's eyebrows shot into her hairline. "I did you a favor! I won't bring you down here again. It's now or never."

At the far end of the room, Tess heard footsteps coming down the metal stairs. If Mathilde was back, and she stumbled upon Tess and Eliot in the cage, holding a book that shouldn't have been in the cage where Eliot was not permitted to go…

"There's a back staircase," Tess hissed, pushing Eliot out of the cage. She locked the door as quietly as she could. "Around the corner. The door next to the dumbwaiter."

Eliot kept to the wall and Tess slid behind him. Down the line, she could see one frail, sweater-clad shoulder sticking out from an aisle.

She pulled open the door and shoved Eliot inside. The small, square room was there for electrical purposes. The closet-sized space held the workings of both the building's elevator and the dumbwaiter in the stacks.

Eliot moved to ascend the stairs—which was more of a spiraling metal ladder, with landings both to the hallway and stacks on each floor, and would be *very loud* under his weight—but Tess grabbed him by the tie and put a hand over his mouth. She pushed him back against the wall, pressing a hip into his thigh so he wouldn't move, wouldn't make a sound. Eliot's eyes flew wide.

Tess peeked out the grated vent set into the middle of the door. Mathilde came around the corner of the stacks, mouth twisted up at the corner. She frowned at the special collections cage, coming close and running her fingers against the lock. Tess said a quick prayer that she'd locked it properly.

Her aunt's shoulders relaxed. Mathilde darted another glance around the stacks and moved back towards the main stairs.

Tess let out a breath. Except, suddenly, she was very aware that one hand was still pressed firmly against Eliot Birch's mouth, and the other was wrapped around his tie.

The silk of it was very, very soft.

Eliot raised an eyebrow. "Comfortable?" he asked, voiced muffled as his lips brushed against her hand.

"*Go*," Tess whispered, pushing him away. Tess started up the ladder, scampering breathlessly all the way up to the third floor. She didn't bother to check if he followed, but she could feel him shaking the metal behind her.

Tess grabbed his hand and dragged him up the last few stairs, through a row of shelves, and out of the stacks to his office. Floors away from Mathilde, she let herself relax.

"Well, that's a good thing to know about," Eliot said.

"No," Tess said, shutting Eliot's door behind her. "No, no, no. You are *not* going down there again."

Bewildered, Eliot blinked back at her. "But why not?"

He was insufferable. She shouldn't have to explain this to him, considering he knew how Mathilde was, but apparently this Birch thought he was above everyone else here too. Besides, the door they went through was always locked in the reading room and only opened from the stacks.

"I have to get back to work," Tess said.

Eliot didn't move for a moment. He looked at her, and she hated the way he did it, like he was stripping away each layer of her to find the center until she wasn't even sure what was left behind.

"Why do you hate me?" Eliot asked.

As if he didn't know. As if it wasn't obvious. Because she had done something impulsive—*again*—and put both her and Nat's scholarships at risk. "You literally blackmailed me. I could've lost my job. I still can. And you're just standing there in your fancy tie with your fancy book, looking at me like *I'm* the one who's being unreasonable."

"I would never actually go to Mathilde or try to get you in trouble, even if you didn't want to help me," Eliot said, immediately defensive. "I asked for a favor, and you agreed."

Tess wanted to scream. It didn't matter what he *intended* to do. "You have power here, whether you want to admit it or not," she said, struggling to keep her voice level. "You had the notes. Information that could get me fired."

Eliot threw his hands up. "You couldn't have actually expected me to turn you in. I'm not *cruel*."

What else was she supposed to assume?

He was like every other rich boy at Falk. And like the rest of them, he didn't understand what it meant to work so hard for something and end up a failure anyways. After all, there was too much of her father in her. No matter how much she pushed, how much she tried, she would amount to nothing.

The silence stretched uncomfortably. Tess watched him, angry and unflinching, as Eliot stared back. Gradually, the resolution in his eyes turned to realization, and then to sadness. Perhaps she'd actually gotten through to him.

Eliot closed his eyes. "But it seems I've acted cruelly," he admitted, as if he read her mind. "I made a mistake. You're right. I do have power, and it's something I should be more aware of. I'm sorry. Truly."

"You can be as sorry as you want," Tess snapped. "You were still a dick."

She wouldn't have been surprised if he ordered her out of his office right then and there. But Eliot studied her face for a moment. She had that feeling again, like he was searching for something below the layers and was left wanting. Finally he sighed, and it released all of the tension he'd been holding in his shoulders.

"Alright," Eliot said. He picked up the book and looked down at the cover. "I was a dick. And in the future, I'll work on that. But I want you to know that if you said no, if you told me you wouldn't take me into the collections, I wouldn't have questioned you or pressed. That's not who I am. And I'm sorry. I see now I gave off the impression that I *am* that person."

If only she knew who Eliot really was.

Not that it mattered. After today, after this moment, Tess would return to her desk and Eliot would stay in his office and they would probably never speak to one another again.

There was something *odd* about Eliot Birch. Something that didn't quite fit in with his scholarly persona. She'd never sensed it in another person; it was as if a shimmer clung to his skin.

"Let me see that book," Tess said. If it really was important, she figured she'd be able to tell.

Somewhat reluctantly, Eliot handed it over. It was heavier than it looked, but these old books usually were. The fabric cover was black with gilded edges, and the pages were also gold when the book was closed. Tess balanced it on one arm and flipped through. Just like before, they were blank—or, no. No, they weren't.

There, in the middle, Tess could only just make out words written in gold ink.

"Hey, did you see this?"

Eliot moved behind her, looking over her shoulder. "No," he said. "What does it say?"

Tess squinted down at the words. They were faded, barely there against the eggshell-white page. "May the Earth belong to the damned and forsaken. Let the righteous burn in the burden of their ignorance. For he who looks inward for guidance trusts only himself, but he who seeks knowledge trusts all ink that has come before him."

The words felt hostile as they left Tess's lips and poured into the room.

She looked up just in time to see Eliot's clothing ignite.

Tess gasped, stumbling backwards. She hadn't seen the

source of the blaze; she could only watch in horror as flames licked over Eliot's tie and sweater, as his skin blistered and blackened. His mouth opened wider, wider, cracking and bleeding. Tess reached out to do something only to see that her own hands were aflame.

Time stopped. Adrenaline spiked in her veins.

The pain came in one furious blast, sharp and devastating.

She shrieked, falling to her knees and beating her hands against the carpet. The flames would not go out, nor would they catch on anything else. She tucked against herself, trying to smother it, but her whole body burned and ached and cracked and this would never end, *it would never end*, and she was meant to die here in this moment, in Eliot Birch's office, probably because of his *fucking* candles and Nat, and Nat, and Nat—

Let the righteous burn.

"Tess!"

Tess?

Her heartbeat echoed in her ears. She opened her eyes. The room rolled and spun but, deliriously, she realized she was no longer burning.

Eliot was curled up on the floor next to her, one hand poised next to her cheek as if reaching out to touch her.

He was not on fire. In fact, he looked as if he'd never *been* on fire. Aftershocks of phantom pain roiled through Tess's body, but as she looked down at herself, she bore no evidence of the flames either.

Eliot moved away. He stood up, breathing hard. "Jesus," he muttered, examining his hands. Probably searching for burn marks. *"Jesus."*

The office stopped spinning and righted itself, and across the room, she heard Eliot sigh. A light sheen of sweat glistened on his face. He rested his hands on his desk and leaned over it, trying to gain control of his breathing, watching Tess as carefully, she suspected, as she was watching him.

"Are you okay?" Tess asked, once she could find her voice again. She expected her throat to feel raspy and smoke-burned, but it was normal as ever.

"I think so," Eliot said, rubbing his stomach. "Are you?"

No, Tess thought. *No, I'm not okay.* But she was not going to tell Eliot that, so she nodded. She wanted out of this room, out of this library. And she wanted out *now*.

Something here was changing. Shifting. Waking up.

Let me show you, it crooned in the back of her mind. *What you are. What you can be.*

She ignored it. Tess Matheson was what she was, and no grimoire was going to tell her otherwise. No fear-driven invasive thoughts were going to force her into a panic attack, and she was not going to reveal yet another vulnerability to Eliot.

Eliot was moving, going to the shelf. He grabbed a bundle of herbs, and with a self-conscious glance in Tess's direction, lit them on fire. Fragrant smoke curled from his hands and he whispered something under his breath.

Already, Tess's head felt clearer. She couldn't be sure... couldn't be certain...that quickly, the whole thing seemed like it had been entirely imagined.

"What are you doing?" she asked.

Eliot shook his head, blowing out the smallest bit of flame and setting the herbs aside. "Sage. Smudging. It's meant to clear the air. Whatever happened just then... It needs to be cleansed."

"I... We have to go," Tess said. She was done with this whole thing. "Tomorrow morning, you and I are taking that book back where it belongs."

Eliot frowned. "We can discuss that tomorrow. When we've had time to think."

They had just been *on fire*. This was not a negotiation, no matter what Eliot Birch thought he was entitled to. There would be no time to think. She did not understand what had happened, what they'd been through, and she refused to believe in magic, except she could not deny the feeling the grimoire had something to do with the imagined flames.

That book was going back as soon as possible. But she wasn't going to argue with Eliot right now, while they were still in the library, at risk of being discovered.

Tess led the way out to the reading room and down the stairs.

"Theresa?" Mathilde called from the offices. Half of the lights were off, casting her skeletal body in shadow, making her look even more jarring. "Where were you?"

Tess stopped, and Eliot bumped into her back. He cleared his throat and stepped away, pretending to examine a shelf nearby.

She swallowed hard. "I was in here, on the fourth-floor balcony, shelving. Didn't you hear me say hi when you came in?"

Mathilde squinted at her, not quite believing, but almost convinced all the same. "You didn't leave the reading room while I was gone? You weren't in the stacks?"

"No," Tess said quickly. "I went as far as the office, but that's it." Mathilde still seemed to be thinking through this, and more thought could lead to more doubt, so Tess said, "Well, I'm going to close up out here. Do you need anything else?"

"Actually..." Mathilde looked at Eliot over Tess's shoulder. She raised an eyebrow. "The library is closed, Mr. Birch."

Eliot opened his mouth, and Tess was certain that he was going to say something infuriating, but he just pursed his lips, nodded once, and said, "Right. Thank you for your help, Tess."

Tess winced. It was too much.

She was relieved when he went, but maybe it was because his absence made it easier to forget the strange book and all it did or didn't contain, or the feelings of illness in his office—or maybe, because she could forget the feelings that were more surprising, the ones related to Eliot Birch himself and the way his mouth looked when he smiled.

Mathilde watched Eliot go, waiting until the door shut behind him before she turned back to Tess. Her eyes were softer now, almost like Tess's father's, and that horrible tenderness made her feel even worse about what she'd done.

"What did you help him with?" Mathilde asked.

Tess shook her head. She couldn't bear to lie outright, so she settled for a half-truth. "I helped him organize his books by call number so I can return them easier. There were a lot. That's all."

Mathilde nodded, but she didn't look convinced. She set a hand on Tess's shoulder and the motion was uncomfortable, unprecedented, until Tess realized her great aunt was just swiping a cobwebby bit of dust off her sleeve. Mathilde's hand fell, and Tess's guilt rushed right back again.

"Boys like that scare me," Mathilde confessed, and Tess was unsettled by the statement. Mathilde rarely had anything nice to say about the students, it was true, but she was never so forward about her dislike.

"Why?"

Her frown deepened, darkening the creases around her eyes. Mathilde's hands cupped her elbows as if she was chilled.

"Because," she said, "they want to know everything."

Tess felt oddly unmoored, lost in time. For the first time since moving to Falk, Tess longed to know more about Mathilde and how she'd become...this.

"Is that a problem?" Tess asked.

Mathilde frowned, shuffling back towards her office, back towards the stacks. "Only when they go too far."

twelve

Eliot

During his seventeen years of life, Eliot had had more than enough time to practice avoiding his father. But there was his phone, most of yesterday and all day today until he'd turned it off, buzzing away in his pocket.

Finally, it was too much to bear. Eliot's breaking point came at almost seven-thirty, a few hours after he'd left Tess behind at the library. Eliot would've still had his phone off, but there was always the chance of his mother calling, and he couldn't risk missing that.

"What?" Eliot nearly snarled into the phone. He stopped before saying more. He had to keep control of himself, had to keep his voice steady, had to keep his tone in check. There was too much at risk to upset his father.

"Eliot," his father said on the other end of the line. "Why haven't you answered my calls?"

"I've been busy," Eliot said. It was a lie, but not a difficult one. It was the kind of lie that slid out easily, naturally—a half fib, if anything.

"Doing what?" he asked, voice dripping with derision.

For anyone else, it would've been a polite inquiry and nothing more—a check-in, maybe, or a checkup. But this was his father asking. Eliot would not answer that he was doing something athletic or mathematic or scholarly, so the answer would not be worthy.

"Working," he said shortly. It was enough of an answer to fulfill the demands necessitated by the question, but not too much of an answer to give his father any idea of what he was doing.

"As if you know what that word means," Birch said, a touch icier now. "It implies that you're actually accomplishing something."

Eliot hated talking to his father. He sat back and stared at the ceiling, waiting for it to be over.

"And thank you for calling to tell me you're back," Birch said. "I love knowing when my son is gallivanting between continents on my money."

Soon. It would be over soon.

"Did you receive my invitation to dinner?"

Eliot hadn't, because he hadn't checked his voicemail, but he could only imagine what a dinner with his father would entail. "I won't be able to join you, I'm afraid." He wasn't afraid, he wasn't sorry—but he definitely was not going.

"Now, Eliot," his father started, and there was that blade of warning Eliot recognized all too well. It was the tone he'd used with his wife regarding their separation and medical bills, the one he'd used with Eliot about Falk, the one he'd used when they'd boarded a plane to America together three years before. It was a tone that left no room for negotiation. "You know what we discussed."

Eliot did know what they discussed. He wished there was a way to *un*-know what they'd discussed. It was like this: Eliot's father traipsed around America while his wife withered away from advanced brain cancer that took away more of her every day. But without his father's money, his mother could not pay for the experimental treatment that kept her alive, and a divorce would force her out of the country home she'd haunted in her illness. Birch denied her comfort and dignity. And now, he denied her her only son and put an ocean between them.

He closed his eyes. He had to keep control of himself, for his mother's sake. Eliot was the only reason his father paid for her treatments in the first place.

"I remember," Eliot said, running his pointer finger along a frayed bit of the couch. Maybe, if he made the hole wide enough, it would swallow him whole.

"Sunday night," his father said. "You will be there."

Eliot didn't answer. He didn't want to go to dinner, and he didn't want to be beholden to his father. But he had to go, and they both knew it. He couldn't say no if he cared about his mother at all.

"What time?" Eliot asked.

"Eight. Lucille will be so happy to see you."

Eliot hated the fact his father could feign flippancy, that he could turn the switch to that cordiality he used so easily. It was not an ability Eliot himself had inherited, and he almost hated himself for it. Only almost, though, because he couldn't be truly mad for finding himself unlike his father in any way.

The line went dead. There were no parting words, no "Goodnight, son," no "I love you," or anything of that sort. But he had never been that sort of father. Most times, Eliot wasn't sure his father even liked him. Eliot the son was a forgotten trophy from his younger years, there to pull from the shelf and polish when company was over, only to be a reminder that he was awarded for second place, a consolation prize of a child.

Eliot preferred to stay on the shelf, covered in dust. It was safer there.

He stared at his phone for a moment, certain it would begin ringing again and there would be even more demands on the other line. But instead, there was just his home screen: a picture of his mother as he saw her last week, sitting together on the porch swing in the garden, taken by Josie in a moment of clarity. Those moments were getting rarer and rarer, and he didn't know if he'd see another one from her before the end.

He couldn't bear the thought of it, even though they all knew it was coming. For a moment, Eliot considered calling her. But no, it was nearly 8:00 here, so it would be almost 1:00 her time, and she would be sleeping.

Eliot got up and grabbed his car keys.

He had to get out, away. He couldn't stay here, in this room. Maybe he could go to the library, but the thought of it curled horror in his stomach like sour milk after the events of earlier. The book was in his office, and he didn't want to be anywhere near it right now. He wanted to talk to Tess, but there was no way to contact her, and she wasn't the sort of person he could just casually speak to.

After all, Tess and Eliot weren't friends. They were accomplices, maybe, complicit in the same crimes. And besides, Tess was not a viable candidate for his first true friend: she was prickly and hot-headed. She did not seem like the type who wanted to be confided in. And she hated him, which seemed like an important fact to weigh against any potential for friendship.

So he grabbed his keys and drove off into the darkness of the night. Far above, the stars glimmered in a clear sky. There was all that bullshit about them being the same stars he could see from England, the same stars that watched over his mother, but that was not the way he felt now. He couldn't get to his mother any easier than he could get to another planet. For all intents and purposes, they were in separate solar systems.

He drove.

Back in the UK, where he didn't have his license, he didn't understand how people could think that it was relaxing. Relaxing was the sway of the Tube or the rickety speed of the train. Here, with the night air screaming through the open windows and the radio blasting, he got it. It was getting out of his own head. It was existing only in the black spaces between the headlights of other cars. Here in the city, it was so hard to be alone, so he drove until the buildings became cornfields and he was surrounded by darkness. Pennsylvania was good this way: isolation was so close, so present. He could be nobody from nowhere in less than half an hour.

Eliot drove until he was nothing but the pounding of his heart, the leather of the wheel between his hands, a disturbance in the wind. He drove until he didn't know where he was and had no clue how to get back, and then he drove even farther. He drove until his jaw hurt from clenching his teeth too tightly and he didn't recognize the names of the places on the exit signs.

Originally, he wasn't meant to move to the States with his father. When Birch got the job at Falk, Eliot was starting his second year at Harrow, a posh boarding school in North London. He was meant to stay at the school during the week and escape to the country house in Hertfordshire when he could, to visit his mother.

His father had been home for break, trying to muddle something through with Eliot's mother, even though there was no love left between them and even Eliot knew it. They were in London. His mother had an appointment with a specialist and an overnight stay, so Eliot and his father returned to the flat without her. Eliot muttered something about a shower and went into the bathroom, then crawled out the window to sit on top of one of the dormers outside.

In the cool springtime air, he'd emptied his pockets: the foot of a rabbit, a book of matches, a vial of his own blood, some chalk, a crumpled piece of paper, and a crystal from his mother's stash. He'd set his treasures in a line and started working.

The blood, spilled into the shape of a circle with dots in four places. A streak of blood on the hare's foot, then a lit match to set it on fire. The fur smelled awful as it caught.

He'd found the spell in a grimoire in the British Library. Intended for growths and cysts, but possibly, it could be used for tumors.

Eliot set the foot in the middle of the circle, watching it smolder. He unfolded the spell he'd scrawled onto the paper. "*Itaska mulitae, matskna—*"

"Eliot Julian Edward Birch, what do you think you're doing?" A firm hand had clasped onto his shoulder, and Eliot was dragged firmly back into the bathroom, smelling of burnt fur.

"I—"

But it was too late. His father had seen what he was doing, seen the things on the dormer, and his face filled with vicious rage. He slammed Eliot into the wall so hard that Eliot's teeth went through his cheek. He tasted blood.

"What did I tell you?" his father seethed. "What did I *strictly forbid you from doing?*"

How much you must hate me, Eliot thought, *because of my magic.*

Eliot did not answer. His father shook him firmly by the shoulders. "Do you think this is a game?"

"No," Eliot said, looking at the place over his father's left shoulder, focusing on a chipped porcelain tile.

"No more of this foolishness," Birch snarled. His eyes were still furious, blazing with anger. He pulled his hands away, and without meaning to, Eliot rubbed one of his shoulders. He was certain it would be bruised tomorrow.

His father stalked away, and Eliot thought the argument was over. Except, it wasn't. The next week he was pulled out of Harrow and his father made some grandiose claim about his mother being unfit, too sick to care for their son. When he when back to America, he took Eliot with him.

And there he lived ever since.

Eliot stopped at a gas station and bought a bag of crisps and a soda. He wished that he could walk out of the gas station and see a glowing Tube sign or a double-decker night bus instead of a barren parking lot in the middle of nowhere, Pennsylvania, but it was just another impossibility.

He pulled out his phone. Thought about calling his mother. Thought about looking up Tess in the student directory. Remembered she hated him. Slipped the phone back in his pocket.

Eliot drove slower on the way back, wishing he could ignore the GPS directions back to the city and just keep going. The night wasn't screaming so loudly in his ears, and he turned the music down so it was more melodic and less thumping. He ate his crisps and drank his soda and hated every single second of the land that rolled past his windows.

When he parked in front of his flat, the city was exhausted familiarity, and Eliot's mouth tasted of all the magic he'd tried for and ruined.

thirteen

Inside of Jessop, you were coming to life.

You were in a book in a crypt, a book forgotten by time and religion and history itself. A book that pooled dark liquid, dripped down a desk. Beads of ink split off and dripped onto carts, onto bindings and pages, spilling and congealing and growing.

Inside the boy's office, you pulled the ink of yourself into a body and stood. You gazed at your hands, every color and none all at once.

You traced your fingers across the bindings of a book. Your hand pooled on the surface, the meniscus of your body too fragile, too insubstantial, to feel the leather cover.

You looked around. This was not the burning crypt of your last memory, nor was it the damp stone enclosure of the death before. This place was warm, smelling of dust, unguarded. This place thrilled with unfamiliar magic. This place was perfect.

There was a photograph on the desk, facing the window. You went around to consider it, footsteps tracking ink, transforming to dust, blowing away to nothing. Your solid black eyes focused on the photograph. In it, there was a woman and a boy: the woman thin and frail but laughing, the boy fighting a smile, looking somewhere past the camera. Handsome. Approachable. The perfect vessel.

You trailed your finger over the woman's arm, slung casually over the boy's shoulders. Beads of your ink clung to the surface like morning dew. You tried to remember the warmth of human flesh, but you could not.

You were a boy once; you were—

No.

There was no boy; there was nothing of what you once were. You were the universe. You were history itself—nothing more and nothing less.

You cocked your head, considering the shape of the boy's face, how his muscles would play under his flesh as he moved. Held a hand in front of your body. The noncolor shifted to paleness, a smooth hand, tidy fingernails. Up your arm tracked the color. You looked at the photograph again, cloaking your newly formed skin with a black sweater. It dripped unappealingly on the floor.

Well, you can only hide so much of your nature at once. The drips became dust. The dust vanished soon enough.

Ex Libris Infernorum.

You straightened. Closed your eyes. You could sense the girl who'd freed you from your tomb, the shape of her lips reading the words that contained you, the beauty of her terror.

Tess.

A revision: *Ex Libris Tess Matheson.*

You were free. Now, it was her time to burn.

fourteen

Tess

TESS WAS INSIDE OF A PAINTING.

Maybe it wasn't a painting, but the trees were dripping sickly, dark sap that reminded her of a color of ink her father sent as free samples to buyers he didn't like. After looking closer, Tess realized the trees weren't the only things dripping. *Everything* was.

She was in a forest of some kind, with tall trees and overgrown paths and heavy mist floating through the branches. It looked like a scene from a ridiculous horror film she'd watched with her parents one night when they'd finally started letting her see R-rated movies.

She reached for a drooping branch. It looked watery, hazy, unreal. The leaves were wet when she ran a hand over them. Tess tilted her hand back, examining her palm. Dark blood was streaked across it.

"Tess."

The whispered name came from behind her. When she turned, there was no one there. She couldn't identify exactly who the voice belonged to, but she knew it was familiar. It was a male voice: a family friend's, maybe, or a teacher she'd had last year. She turned in a slow circle, searching for a body the voice belonged to.

There was nobody there. Tess was alone in the forest.

"Tess."

Her thoughts were hazy and uncertain. She rubbed her palms on her thighs, trying to rid them of the blood.

Something snapped—a branch or twig, leaves displaced. Tess turned towards the sound and squinted into the darkness. She wasn't afraid; maybe, if she thought she'd be hurt, she would be. But here, in this dream of blood and madness, she was calm. Neutral.

She could only just make out a shape in the mist ahead. A person, maybe. A figure. A haunt, even, tall and dark. The figure moved closer, towards the place Tess stood, and something deep within her knew the figure was Eliot Birch.

Until he stepped into the light.

He had dark hair like Eliot, and beautiful eyes like Eliot, but he was thinner and stronger and older. The differences were imperceptible but present, like looking at a picture of Eliot through filtered glass or a memory. He flickered or shifted or changed, out of Eliot and back in, and it was clear he was something different and inhuman.

And then, just as quickly as she'd seen him, she came to understand him. He was the universe. His dark hair glittered with the impression of gems, of onyx and obsidian and diamond, and his skin was pale and luminous as a pearl under the liquid dripping over him. He was a boy. He was a monster. He was the most beautiful creature Tess had ever seen.

Tess's religion believed in the devil, and therefore, so did Tess. But nowhere in the Bible was the devil described like this. Not tall and handsome and grinning and drenched in blood—or no, Tess realized. It wasn't blood at all. Drenched in ink.

And yet.

Tess wasn't afraid.

The devil reached his hand forward. "Will you do what I need?"

Tess swallowed hard. There was something there, in the distance, flickering between the trees. It kept catching her eye, drawing her gaze away from the devil. Heady black smoke crept through the trees.

"What are you asking of me?" Tess asked.

He nodded, coming closer. "Let me in," not-Eliot whispered.

"Where?" Tess asked. Her breath felt caught and fluttery, and the word came out as a suggestion rather than sound. There, behind him, she caught a flash of orange. The sickly scent of burning sap filled the air. Flames crackled and one of the sap-trees split off in a shower of sparks.

"Everywhere," he said. He edged closer. "In here," the devil whispered, tapping a hand against her temple. "Into your mind." With two fingers, he shut her eyelids gently. "In here," the devil murmured, and with her eyes closed, Tess could see her own room, her own dorm. "Wherever you go, wherever you belong. I will belong there too."

"I—" Tess started, but smoke invaded her lungs. She coughed, choking on the words. "And if I don't?" she managed.

The devil stepped away from her, eyes strangely depthless as his lips curled into a smile. Flames licked into the clearing at an alarming rate. Tess backed away from them, from the blistering heat, but she was surrounded.

The flames avoided the devil.

She watched, horrified, as the devil stood in a clear circle amidst the flames. He did not catch; he did not burn.

The devil lifted a hand. The fire circled around it, forming an orb that flickered just over his palm. "You will regret it, Tess Matheson. The devil knows your name."

Smiling ever wider, he drew his hand back, and launched the flames at Tess.

Tess jerked awake, breathing hard. Sweat soaked her skin and the sheets. For a moment longer, she felt the burning impact of the fire hitting her squarely in the chest.

It was just a dream. It *had* to be a dream.

She tucked her knees to her chest and put her head in her hands. When she rubbed her eyes, Tess realized that her hands were damp.

Tess examined her palms. They were stained with blood.

No, she thought, just on the edge of panic. No, she was familiar with the way that this liquid stained the crease of her palms and smeared when she ran her thumb across her open hand. This was not blood, drying on both of her palms.

There were smudges of it on her thighs, past the hem of her shorts. Fingerprints across her ribs. Splotches on her gray sheets.

Tess slid out of bed and dashed to the mirror. Her face was macabre and twisted: streaks of dark ink on her cheekbones and nose, down her chin.

She had to shower before work. She barely had time, but she *had* to. There wasn't even enough time to figure out how she'd ended up covered in ink or where it had come from.

Tess grabbed her towel and started to the bathroom. But there was Anna on the couch, typing on her laptop, and there was no way for Tess to cover everything at once.

"Whoa there," Anna said. "Is that blood?"

"No, it's ink," Tess said, realizing how ridiculous it sounded.

But Anna already knew Tess was a peculiar person with strange habits. Still, she hesitated, looking for some normal sort of explanation. "I spilled a bottle. Changing out a pen color."

"Oh," Anna said. "Totally normal."

Tess rolled her eyes. "You know, fountain pens are finicky. This *is* a somewhat normal thing."

"If you say so."

Tess didn't have time to respond. She ducked into the bathroom, shutting the door behind her, and turned on the shower. She could not be late for work again.

fifteen

Eliot

ELIOT SAT IN HIS STUFFY, OVERCROWDED, BELOVED OFFICE
with the horrifyingly bad tea and biscuits he'd bought from
the market a few days before. They were stale from sitting out
on his desk but he ate them anyway. Everything in the room
seemed dusty and staler than usual, but he didn't care. He was
comfortable with dust.

The book was on one side of his desk. He'd cleared the rest
of the grimoires and borrowed another cart from downstairs
to house them. Strange as it was, it felt unnatural to keep
the book from the basement among the others. As if it was
poisoning them.

Tess was not downstairs when he'd come in that morning.
It was the other girl—R-name-what's-her-face—behind the
desk, staring down at her phone. Eliot wasn't disappointed
that Tess wasn't there. He didn't let himself be disappointed.

After all, she wasn't willing to help him into the stacks.
Technically that was a rule, but he'd gotten around many rules
stronger than hers before. She didn't like him, but he'd been
disliked before, and it had never quite fazed him this much.
And she wanted to return the book to the basement, which he
was mostly certain he didn't want to do.

But then, there was the other side of the coin. His wild-eyed drive the night before had left him no room for doubt: something about her had infiltrated, had spread under his skin. He could not let her burrow any further.

Eliot sat back in his chair and pulled the book to the center of his desk. Earlier, he'd thought it might be another grimoire, but how could it be if it didn't have words? There was only the bookplate and the passage Tess had read last night.

He opened the book and flipped through, page by page. *Ex Libris Infernorum* remained, but the writing Tess had read was gone. This did not surprise Eliot. After all, timing was key, and that was true of books as well as opportunities.

So the writing was gone. This he could deal with.

He had a magnifying glass somewhere in his desk, and he rifled through the drawers until he found it. Eliot opened the first page and examined it through the glass.

He waited for something to stand out, for something to set this book apart from all others. Sometimes, he had to wait for a book to speak to him, for the clues to come out and start knitting together into a story, for the facts to make sense. A book was so much more than the words it contained: it was the texture of the page, the size of the paper, the type of the binding, the material of the cover.

A splotch of red dripped onto the page.

Eliot jumped back. He set the magnifying glass aside and examined the paper. It was blank. There was no red seeping onto the page. Had he imagined it? No. He could see the image over again in his mind's eye, the drip of red, like blood.

But the page was white.

He hadn't imagined the drip.

Eliot ran a hand along the paper. Was it damp? Had he missed something? Then he flipped to the next page. In his peripheral vision, he saw his magnifying glass.

A perfect circle of red liquid rested on the center of the lens.

He ran a hand along his face and looked at his palm, searching for the source. Nothing. Next, he craned his head up to the ceiling. He'd seen enough horror movies with bodies leaking blood through the ceiling. But it was blank and white, just like always. Blank as the book itself.

It wasn't blood. At least, Eliot was pretty sure it wasn't blood.

He lifted the magnifying glass and tilted it this way and that, examining the liquid. It behaved like it should, running over the surface of the lens, leaving a beaded trail of red behind. Nothing out of the ordinary, except he had no idea what it was.

More out of impulse than any real scientific process, Eliot dipped a pinky into the liquid, then streaked it across a blank space in his notebook.

He was relatively certain the drop on the magnifying glass was ink.

Eliot examined it closer. He wasn't familiar with ink, even though he used it every day. He knew a thing or two: what pens he liked to use, that he preferred gel ink, that he reserved red ink for corrections.

None of his cursory experience explained the appearance of the drop of ink.

Eliot had too much work to do to spend the day ruminating over this phantom ink, but he couldn't think of anything else. He got up and checked the window. It was shut and locked, like usual. Nothing was out of place on his bookshelf. There was nobody hiding in the nooks and crannies, nefariously waiting to drip ink over Eliot's shoulder.

He was at an impasse, which was his most and least favorite place to be. As a boy who valued answers above all else, Eliot loved having them and he loved searching for them. It was the beginning, the questioning, that he hated.

Here was the question: How did the ink appear out of nowhere?

But that wasn't the question, was it? It was less about how. There were technical reasons for the how.

It was maybe a why question: Why did it drip onto the glass?

A where question: Where did it come from?

A what question: What kind of ink was it?

There were a million questions, a million directions. The issue was settling on one. Eliot hated trying to decipher which question was the most important.

A knock sounded on the door, timid at first and then more confident on the second go-around.

He considered ignoring it, but he also realized the person on the other side could know something about the ink, and then he considered the person on the other side could be Tess.

"Come in," Eliot said, though the invitation physically pained him. Eliot didn't like inviting other people into his space. Especially since most of them saw the artifacts of his magic lined up along the wall, and it was like he was stripped bare. Unless, of course, that person was Tess, who was present enough in his mind that he might've willed her into his physical space on his own, and that made the intrusion worth it.

It was lucky, then, that the door opened and it was Tess standing on the other side. Her eyes were blazing, which didn't surprise him in the slightest. He rarely saw her when she wasn't looking at him with some kind of fervor, angry or otherwise.

"Tess," he said, stepping lightly around her mood. "Please, come in."

She did as she was told, even though she made it seem like he hadn't invited her and she was barging in of her own accord. Eliot wasn't certain how she managed this effect, but even with his invitation, it made him feel vaguely like she was trespassing.

"Yesterday. Were we on fire?"

Eliot froze. He hadn't allowed himself to think about the day before. Not yet. He loved encountering things he couldn't explain, but Eliot *hated* when he couldn't decipher the line between imagination and reality.

The truth was this: he knew Tess had no magic abilities. It was something he was able to sense in his mother and her circle of friends. Tess had none of the affectations that he connected with a witch. And yet, when she'd read the words in the grimoire, *something* had happened to the two of them. Some sort of working that didn't require magical blood.

Eliot had never heard of such a thing. He worried it was a darker power, not like the rooted earthbound magic he himself used, but he did not know how to address the question with Tess without getting into a discussion of sorcery. That was a topic he was not comfortable broaching with anyone.

"I'm not burned," he said, rather than answering the question directly. "Are you?"

"No," Tess said, but she looked disappointed.

"Then I suppose we couldn't have been on fire."

She studied him. Perhaps she didn't believe his answer.

Eliot himself wasn't sure what he believed. Had he been in pain? Madly. Had he seen the flames blistering and blackening his skin? Undoubtedly.

Was he fine now? Undeniably.

"We have to take the book back," Tess said.

After the mysterious drip on the lens, there was no way Eliot was taking the book back. It would disrupt his scientific method. Even if it meant risking the imaginary flames again. Eliot could stomach them, he thought, for the purpose of understanding. Luckily for him, the alarm on his phone went off. Eliot glanced down at the time.

"Oh!" he said. "It's time for class. First one of the term. I have to go."

"*Eliot,*" Tess hissed. "It's summer. There are no classes."

He smiled, because for once, he had a real excuse. "I'm taking summer classes at the university."

"You can't just walk out like this."

But he could. His class was only a block and a half away and really, he had more than enough time for a conversation, but he hadn't thought up a good enough way to convince Tess to let him hold onto the book yet. He blew out his candle and slipped his messenger bag over his shoulder, whisking Tess out of his office with him as he shut the door and locked it.

"You're welcome to walk with me," Eliot said, but he had the impression she wasn't at liberty to leave work so easily, and the uncertain look she cast at the girl behind the desk confirmed his suspicion. "But I can't be late on the first day."

Tess crossed her arms over her chest. Her lips twisted into a frown. He was close enough to see the edge of her contact lenses, and he wondered how she'd look with glasses on.

Foolish, Eliot, he chided himself.

"I'm not going to forget about this," Tess said. "We're taking that book back."

Eliot didn't think she'd forget. She didn't seem like the type. But forgetting wasn't something Eliot needed—he just needed to buy a couple of hours to figure out a plan.

sixteen

Tess

ELIOT STAYED AWAY FROM JESSOP THE NEXT DAY. TESS waited for him—not really, because she wasn't wasting away expecting him to appear—until Mathilde appeared from the back offices and asked why she hadn't started locking up yet. She thought about the book and how it was still in Eliot Birch's office while she shuttered the library windows and covered the display cases in velvet.

She was still thinking about him when she rounded the corner and saw a slim form sitting on the steps of her dorm: Nat, book balanced on her knees, head resting on one of her thin wrists.

"Hey," Tess said, nudging one of Nat's knees with her foot as she dug through her backpack for her key. "Aren't they weird about letting you guys out of the dorms at night?"

Nat scrunched her nose. "It's only 5:00," she said.

Tess shrugged, but her point still stood. For the underclassmen stuck at Falk for the summer, there was a program that was notoriously close to camp. Minus all the music parts of the camps that Tess was used to—so, minus all the fun parts.

She opened the door and Nat followed her up the stairs to her dorm. "Did you at least get permission to leave?" Tess asked.

"Yeah. Aunt Mathilde wrote me a note. We're having dinner."

Tess pulled down a package of ramen, plunked it in a bowl of water, and stuck it in the microwave. "And did Mathilde write the note to let you come here first?"

Nat bit her lip. She didn't say anything. Tess sighed, watching the microwave tray revolve. "Natalie, you know the rules. You aren't supposed to leave campus without express, detailed permission. You could really, *really* get yourself in trouble."

"I missed you," Nat said, voice small. Tess closed her eyes. She hated this, acting like Nat's parent when really she could barely even take care of herself.

"Listen," Tess said. "I'm sorry I haven't been able to hang out. I've been working a lot." The microwave beeped and Tess took out her dinner, draining some of the water and adding the seasoning packet. She took a scalding bite and immediately regretted it. Tess carried the bowl into the living room and settled on the floor, nudging her shoulder against Nat's knee. "Tell me what you've been doing."

Nat still looked down at her hands, playing with the frayed edge of her library book's cover. "Well," she said, "we're all learning how to play soccer. I'm not very good. And they put us in groups based on what we want to do when we're older."

"Oh?" Tess asked, swirling noodles in her bowl. It was still better than dining hall food.

Nat nodded. "I'm with the biology group. We get to go to the hospitals a lot. Watch cool stuff." Her hands didn't stop moving over the cover.

Tess's stomach clenched. "One step closer to med school, huh?" she asked.

Nat nodded. It was all she'd ever wanted to do, be a doctor.

She had a reputation for being something of an amateur nurse, patching skinned knees and escorting kids to the nurse's office with guessed diagnoses, taking care of kids with a fervor Tess never understood.

It wasn't that Nat needed Falk to succeed, but it surely made her future easier. It was worth the sacrifice, she told herself. For Nat to get the future she deserved, it was worth it.

After Nat left to meet up with Mathilde for dinner, Tess went to her room and got out her cello. She played an experimental note, feeling it in her arms, in her chest, in her stomach. As she warmed up, she let her mind wander.

She was barely paying attention when something dripped on her arm. Her first thought was that the ceiling was leaking, but a cursory glance outside revealed it was not raining and another look at the ceiling showed there was no spot of damp. Tess looked down. There on her thigh, black against her pale skin, stood a perfect circle of something dark.

For the briefest of seconds, she was back in the burning, melting forest. Goose bumps rose on her arms and legs.

It's not real, Tess reminded herself. *It was only a dream.*

Frowning, Tess set aside her cello. She rubbed the liquid away, and the smear stained the lines of her skin. Tess examined the stain on her fingers, the way the liquid filled the cracks of her fingerprint.

Another drop fell, bleeding down her arm. Tess glanced around and realized that the drops were coming from her music stand. Liquid pooled on the flat side of it and dripped through the grated cut metal. She ran a finger through it. The liquid was the same dark color as the drops on her body.

There were no excuses this time. No open bottles she could've pushed over in her sleep, no cracked or leaking pens anywhere nearby. The ink was coming from somewhere else.

With shaking hands, Tess opened her music folder. The notes on the pages were bleeding, soaking through the papers, sharps blending into flats blending into lines and notes and rests, ink running down the paper onto the carpet below.

She gasped, pushing the stand away. Another drop fell to the carpet and she went to rub it but as soon as she did—

It was gone.

Tess's fingers came away clean.

She looked back at her music. The notes were in place. The pages were dry. There was no stain of ink on her skin. There was nothing.

"Tess," a voice said, near the window. She looked up only to see Eliot Birch. Instantly, a flare of anger burst within her. Why was Eliot here, now? She took a step closer, putting her music down, and noticed his eyes. The sharpness of his cheekbones. The waviness of his body, as if she was not seeing the lines of him at all, but the suggestions of them: a blur of a sweater, a block of a tie, but not the actual realness of it. As if she was staring at a ghost.

No—not Eliot. The devil.

"I know what you want," he said.

Tess swallowed hard. "You know nothing about me." But even as she spoke the words, she knew they held no truth.

The devil laughed, terrible and loud, and the pages around her disintegrated into ink, into nothing. She saw words flashing across the white, empty walls—not in English, not in any language she knew—all of it swirling around her and breaking down and she was alone, but she was not—

She was in her room. She was in the forest. The music stand was down and pages were flying, ink bleeding down and soaking through all over again.

When she breathed in, she tasted smoke.

She reached for the devil and touched only air. He was not there. He was watching her from everywhere.

"Tess!"

She jolted awake. She was curled up on the floor, one hand resting on the body of her cello, the other pillowed under her head. Anna stood in the doorway.

"Well," Anna said, looking around. "This is…a lot, even for you."

Tess sat up. The stand was knocked over, and music was scattered all over: on her bed, across the floor, a few pages sticking out of her closet. She grabbed a sheet for inspection, heart still pounding. It was perfect, untouched.

"Holy shit," Tess muttered. She got up and clambered over her bed to the place where the devil was. "Anna, I swear there was someone here."

"I think you had a nightmare," Anna said, leaning against the doorjamb. "You were yelling."

Tess stared at Anna for a moment, then back at the destruction of the room. Music everywhere. Dust in places where there had been no dust before, streaking the walls. Her skin was unstained, as if there had never been ink on her at all.

Her knees were weak. She sat on the bed, hard. "I…I don't remember falling asleep."

Anna frowned. She stepped carefully over the wreckage and pushed aside sheet music to clear a space for herself on the bed. "You're working a lot, you know," she said, stroking a hand through the knotted length of Tess's hair, smoothing out the tangles. "Too much, probably. Is there any way you could cut your hours?"

Tess thought of it, but then she thought of being stuck in central Pennsylvania forever, and the depressing amount of money in Nat's college fund.

"No." She leaned over to pick up her cello, examining it for damage. If the devil touched her cello, she'd actually be incensed. It was flawless as ever. "No, I'll be okay."

Anna's frown deepened. "You said someone was in here." She got up and checked the windows—all locked. Not that it mattered. They were on the third floor, after all. "What did they look like?"

She could *not* say he looked like Eliot Birch. Anna would tease her relentlessly if she thought Tess was hallucinating the headmaster's son. And she could definitely not say he was the devil, no more than she could say the devil looked like Eliot. "Just a boy," Tess said.

"A nightmare," Anna said. She threw a small grin in Tess's direction, crawling back over the bed. "Or, knowing you, a ghost."

"A ghost," Tess repeated.

Anna ruffled Tess's hair. "Hey. Ghosts and nightmares can't hurt you, right? There's nothing to be afraid of."

It had to be a mix of paranormal activity, anxiety, exhaustion, and residual fear from the tunnel the other day. She shuddered, thinking of Eliot Birch and his grimoires.

Anna nudged her shoulder. "Why don't you take out your contacts, watch some TV, and go to sleep? I'm sure you'll feel better then."

"Yeah," Tess said, but she couldn't fight the growing unease in her stomach. She felt oddly like she was forgetting something. "You're probably right."

But she knew Anna wasn't right. There was no ghost in her room. And there was no way she'd been dragged into a nightmare, not like that.

It felt *real*. But that was impossible.

Tess lingered in her room for a moment. There was a piece of sheet music on her desk, and she felt drawn towards it. A page from the concerto she'd been working on, but scribbled all over. With a start, Tess realized the handwriting on the page was her own, yet she had no recollection of writing it. An uncapped fountain pen was on the desk, dripping pale blue ink onto the wood.

We are one and the same. One body, one soul, one blood. I want what you want. I am what you wish to be. Variations of it were crammed into the page, small handwriting and large, all of it hers. She traced her fingers over it, feeling the places where the nib had broken through the paper.

And there, at the very bottom, over and over: *I will have you I will have you I will have you I will have you.*

Tess shuddered and tore the paper into pieces. It fluttered around her, falling to the ground around her feet. She capped the pen.

"Are you coming?" Anna called.

Tess closed her eyes. *There is no such thing as the devil. You have not slept. You are overworked. This is all inside your head.*

"Yeah," she said. "I'm coming."

seventeen

Tess

TESS DID NOT SEE ELIOT THE NEXT DAY, OR THE DAY AFTER. With every hour of his absence, Tess grew more and more certain he was dead in his office with only that damn book watching over him. She wasn't certain if she was annoyed because his sudden disappearance made her worry about his well-being or because it forced her to remember he existed in the first place.

And besides. She couldn't get rid of the feeling that the book had... She didn't know. But something *happened* when she read it. She wasn't alone anymore. Something was watching her: in her room, in the stacks, on the streets. She'd wake in a cold sweat with words on her lips and dust on her fingers.

The book had to go back.

The master key was in Mathilde's office, in case one of the seniors lost their keys. She hated that she was breaking another rule for Eliot, even though it wasn't like Eliot had asked her to check up on him, and she wasn't sure why she was doing it in the first place. If he was dead because of the book, he probably deserved it. That's what he got for not listening to her.

Tess waited for Regina to leave for the day before she slunk back into the office. Mathilde had a staff meeting and left her office unlocked in case there was an emergency and

Tess needed the phone. The key was just where it always was: hanging on the wall above Mathilde's desk, between a key for the building and an extra for the cages.

While she was back there... If he wasn't in his office and she took the book, she needed a way to get it back where it belonged. Tess bit her lip. She hated deception, but this was necessary.

She had a house key for her old home on the lanyard in her pocket. It looked very much like the extra key to get back in the stacks.

Just until they put the book back. Mathilde would never notice.

Tess made the switch and slipped the key into her pocket. She headed to the third floor before Mathilde caught her back there.

There was no reason to knock on Eliot's door. He hadn't come in, so he wasn't here.

Except there was some flaw in that thinking, apparently, because when Tess pulled open the door and crept inside, Eliot was sitting behind the desk, reading a book. Tess squeaked, jumping back into the walkway, before her shock turned into anger.

"Tess," he said. Eliot was too surprised to fully maintain his composure. "I haven't seen you in days."

"Right," Tess said. She stormed into the office and shut the door behind her. "You *haven't* seen me in days, but I don't think that's my fault. How did you get in? How did you get *out?*"

Eliot fussed with his tie underneath his sweater. "I, uh, I've been coming in early. No worry of yours—I've just had a lot of work to do, what with classes starting and all."

Tess wasn't buying it. "And how did you *leave?*"

His voice was a little bit higher when he said, "I didn't want to disturb you, and there's that exit to the third floor of the building, which is so convenient—"

Convenient and locked, unless he had a passcode. In fact, all the library was locked if he didn't have a passcode. "But how, Eliot?"

There was that blush again, which was still familiar. "My father's passcode," he said quietly. "It gets me in and out."

Eliot Birch was a bastard. Tess rested her hands on his desk and leaned in. She wanted him to hear her and completely understand the words she was saying.

"You've been avoiding me. And I know it's about the book."

"Tess—"

"No." The book was there, balanced on the edge of the desk, as far away from him as it could be while still being within reach. Tess snatched it and backed away. Eliot reached for it, but he wouldn't touch her, wouldn't come closer, wouldn't physically take it from her. He was too kind and too British for that. "This is going back. Today."

Eliot's shoulders slumped. "Tess, please."

Even holding the book made her nauseous. She couldn't imagine how he'd stood to be in the same room as it for so many days.

"Are you okay?" Eliot asked, not masking the concern in his voice.

"I'm fine," Tess managed around the bile. She had to get out of here. She had to get the book back in its cell, where it belonged. This was not just any old grimoire. There was something dark, something deadly, something *powerful* about this book.

She spoke slowly, mostly so she didn't vomit all over his vanilla and paper–scented office. "I'm going to take the book downstairs and hold onto it. When Mathilde leaves, you and I are taking it down to the crypt, where it belongs. Understood?"

It was obvious Eliot was trying to change her mind just with his eyes, but that wasn't working on her today. She took his silence as acceptance and swept out before he could put up a fight.

eighteen

Eliot

IT HAD TAKEN ELIOT QUITE A LOT OF EFFORT TO AVOID TESS for so long, and not just because it was a pain in the arse to either slip into the library before anyone was there or to sneak in through the third floor while Tess was occupied. It also took a lot of effort, Eliot hated to admit, because he liked Tess.

The issue was the book. It felt powerful. Vital. He'd handled many grimoires, and sometimes, he could tell just by the feeling of the cover if it would be useful. This book... It was warm to the touch, like a living thing. Sometimes, sitting alone with it in his office, he *swore* he could hear it breathing.

The book might have answers. Answers he needed.

Except, as usual, there was the problem of Tess Matheson.

He wasn't eager to return the book, but after nearly a week with it, the volume wasn't yielding any of its secrets. Eliot had thrown all his tricks at the book: clarifying spells, truth magic, a very intense session of chanting Latin he'd found on the internet. Nothing had worked.

He was resigned to the fact that the book just wasn't ready. Maybe, he thought as he walked back from class to the library, it wouldn't be ready anytime soon.

So in the battle of two evils, the book and Tess's anger, he decided to return the book. It wasn't like it was going anywhere.

He had a plan working in the back of his mind, one that would take some perfecting, but he suspected it would work.

Tess wasn't the only one who worked at the library. And her cohort, Regina—whose name he'd finally remembered—seemed more willing to cooperate.

Eliot rounded the corner to the foyer outside the library. Tess was there, curled up on a bench. She had her back to him, but he recognized the back of her head and the thick, dark blond ponytail on top of it. Wisps of her hair escaped from it, sticking out around her ears and haloing the top of her head. He slowed his pace, coming around the corner quietly, so as not to disturb her.

Tess had headphones in, so she didn't hear him coming. Her back was up against one arm of the bench and her knees were tented. She held a book in her hands. It wasn't that he was surprised to see her reading—the girl worked in a library, after all—but he'd never expected to look at Tess and see a girl. Usually, when he looked at her, she made sure that he was only seeing edges: a serrated blade of animosity, a blunt peak of stubbornness, a sharp corner of hostility. She was never just a girl, like she was now. A girl reading a book, who looked tired and wilted and…well, human.

Maybe that was it. Tess had never looked quite so human before.

The realization was more earth-shattering for him than he wanted to admit. Of course she was human. Mythical sprites and the like didn't exist outside of his books, and he wasn't an idiot. At least, he wasn't an idiot most of the time.

But here was the thing: Eliot Birch spent most of his time with the occult, the unearthly, the surreal. Yet in his time in Pittsburgh, even though they discovered that strange book and secret passageway, even though he had more grimoires in his office than he even knew existed, Tess Matheson was the most otherworldly being he'd encountered so far. It wasn't about her sharpness or the exhausting way she spent most of her time tearing him apart. It was the fact that he saw her every day—when he wasn't avoiding her, at least—and still forgot she was made of the same material he was.

"Hey," he said, moving into the foyer.

Tess didn't jump. She'd been expecting him, after all. She pulled out one earbud and craned her neck to look at him.

"I expected you to come sooner," she said.

He shrugged. He'd been on his way, but then his mother called. They'd spoken for nearly an hour before Eliot realized how late he was.

"I'm sorry," he said. "I was held up."

She narrowed her eyes. The lack of an explanation wasn't enough. But Eliot wasn't explaining more. She'd have to deal with the scraps he offered.

"Well, Mathilde is gone for the night," Tess said. "So that's good."

Eliot led the way to the library doors and keyed in his father's code. Behind him, Tess snorted, like she was both surprised and annoyed the code worked after all.

The sun was setting outside but there was no way to tell from inside of Jessop. The large windows around the room were shuttered for the night, even the ones on the upper levels. Ghostly blue lights emitted from the power buttons on the computers across the room. Apart from that, there was only darkness.

"I'm going to turn on the lights," Tess whispered, even though there was no need to keep her voice down. They could shout if they wanted to. There was no one in the library—probably no one in the building, even—to hear them.

Eliot stood very still as she moved away from him. He could hear the sound of her breathing, the pat of her footsteps. There was a sort of dull electricity in the air. It reminded him of the sound from the tunnel. The not-quite-hum, not-quite-song.

The lights flickered on, buzzing and thrumming. Eliot blinked against them, letting his eyes adjust. Tess was already in motion. She crossed back to the circulation desk and ducked under it, rummaging through a drawer.

"Lock the door behind you, hmm?"

Eliot did as he was told, then followed Tess towards the back. She held the book at an arm's length, which would've been comical if she didn't look so pained by the action, then pulled a ring of keys from her pocket and unlocked the office. Eliot realized she must've taken them earlier, without Mathilde noticing.

He did not look at the haloed wisps of hair around her head, made even more luminous in the harsh fluorescent lights of the stacks.

He did not think of what she must've been doing all day, or how sometimes, he looked down from his office and watched her read with her head cushioned on one hand and her lower lip between her teeth. He did not imagine what it would be like to touch her, to sweep the hair away from the back of her neck and let his hands linger on her shoulders, on the knob of her spine.

Eliot did not do any of these things because he believed if he denied something vehemently enough, his reality would become truth.

Except Tess caught him looking, so he lowered his head

and felt his cheeks blaze pink.

They reached the bottom floor. Tess shifted the book onto her hip and fussed with the stolen keys.

"I'll take that," Eliot said, reaching for the book.

"No," she said, too quickly. She bit her lip, and Eliot was pretty certain she thought he'd run away with the book if she gave it to him.

The key slipped into the lock, and the click of the tumblers was loud enough to make them both flinch.

"I hate being in the stacks by myself, especially at night," Tess said. It was odd for her to offer information if he wasn't specifically asking for it. He stared at her for a moment before he realized what she'd said.

"I feel the same way about my office, sometimes. And my dorm."

Tess opened the cage and let him in. "Where do you live?" she asked. He recognized she was making small talk, perhaps to both block out the silence around them and also to distract them from what they were doing. It surprised him somewhat that she was willing to sacrifice her steely ignorance of him just for this.

Or perhaps she was beginning to warm to him. Doubtful, but faintly possible.

"On Dithridge." Eliot craned up on his toes and scrabbled along the back wall of the stacks for the switch or lever or whatever it was. "In one of those older houses, converted into dorms."

"Ah," Tess said, and Eliot wondered if she knew the street he was referring to—or, even worse, the other boys who occupied those dorms: kids whose parents were oil tycoons and diplomats and celebrity lawyers, kids who were considered rich even by Jessop's standards. Not that Eliot's family was *that* rich. He was associated with them because of who he was, not what he was worth.

"And you?" Eliot asked. The switch was not to be found yet, so he moved down a shelf and continued the search.

"I live in South Schenley. It's by the park."

"Everything is by the park," Eliot said. Falk was located in Oakland, a suburb of Pittsburgh. A small school by anyone's standards, Falk was oddly shoved into the spaces not occupied by the University of Pittsburgh and Carnegie Mellon. The main buildings were in an area of Schenley Park called Panther Hollow, which was awful because everything was either up or down a hill.

Eliot was still considering the nuances of Pittsburgh geography when his fingers found the switch. He flicked it, and a grating sound filled the cage. Near the cage door, Tess winced.

The books to his right slipped away, down into the floor. Darkness filled the empty space that the shelves left behind. They watched the maw open into nothing. A fierce chill crept up his skin, and he felt a sheen of sweat across his forehead. Tess looked similarly queasy.

He didn't expect it to be harder a second time around, going back into that subterranean tunnel. He didn't even think the last time had been that difficult. But now that he knew something of the book in Tess's hands, now that he knew of the darkness that pressed heavily, he wasn't sure how much he wanted to go down those steps again.

It didn't seem like Tess felt the same foreboding chill, like they wouldn't be so lucky to get out the second time. "Come on," she said, flipping on her phone flashlight. "I don't want to stand here all night."

Following her was the only option. The weak beam of the torch bounced off the stone walls. They seemed darker this time, streakier somehow, as if they'd been exposed to a patchy rain.

He wanted to point out they could've just stood at the top of the steps and tossed the book into the void, but Tess was already turning down the tunnel towards the dead end.

He couldn't turn back.

nineteen

Tess

TESS GENERALLY PRIDED HERSELF IN BEING THE TYPE OF person who didn't care what others thought of her. And yet, the thought that Eliot Birch could believe she was afraid of this fucking hole in the ground physically pained her.

The flashlight beam at the end of Tess's hand was trembling. Everything about this tunnel was too dark, too close; a sentient being. It was clingy, a living thing, like the book itself. This time around, the humming was closer, whispering: *Tell me your secrets. I've shown you the truth of me. Stay a little longer, Tess.*

Maybe Jessop was haunted after all. But haunted or not, Tess was not going to let this godforsaken tunnel get the best of her.

She just wanted to get to the end of it, toss the book, and go. The only thing keeping her from breaking into a run was the steady sound of Eliot's footsteps behind her.

If she focused on hating him instead of being afraid, she would get through with her pride intact. If Eliot saw her break, he would have yet another thing to use against her.

The tunnel widened into the room at the end, and she traced the walls with her light until she found the alcove Eliot had taken the book from.

She'd almost forgotten she was holding it, but now the book in her arms felt hot—maybe hot and wet, even, like when she'd skinned her knee as a child and the blood soaked through her pantleg.

"I'm dumping it," Tess said. She needed to get rid of it. The sensation of heat was now coupled with that humming, ringing in her ears. The heat was too much like the fire; if they stayed any longer, she feared they'd both ignite.

Tess pushed the book onto the alcove. As it fell, it opened to the first page. Tess caught a glimpse of it: *Ex Libris Tess Matheson.*

No. She was imagining it. She slammed the book shut and spun around towards the entrance, running right into Eliot. She hadn't heard him come so close. Immediately, on instinct, his hands caught her upper arms to keep her from stumbling back. Her phone slipped out of her fingers and clattered to the ground, sending an erratic shaft of light up the wall.

"Sorry," Eliot said. His voice was very, very close. When he exhaled, she felt his breath on her skin. Her breath caught. She was surrounded by him, by the pleasant scent of pages that clung to him, by the warmth in his kind brown eyes.

This was too much for her brain.

Really, the vomit shouldn't have been unexpected. The whole book situation made her queasy to begin with, and the added humming made a cold sweat break out across the back of her neck, which was usually a physical indication she was going to vomit. She shouldn't have been surprised when her stomach finally decided to stop tumbling and eject whatever was inside all over Eliot's sweater.

"*Shit,*" he gasped, jumping back, but it was too late.

Tess gagged, coughed, and pressed a hand over her mouth.

Her skin was sticky and whatever had made a reappearance from her body tasted foul.

"Are you okay?" Eliot asked. He moved closer again—*No, go away, dammit, I'm sorry,* Tess thought—and laid a hand on her elbow. "Come on. Let's get you back up."

Eliot didn't say anything about the fact he was now wearing the contents of her stomach. Keeping a hand on her elbow, he swept her phone from the ground and steered her back towards the stairs. Tess's stomach still twisted, and her head was ringing and terrible. There was that *humming,* or *buzzing,* or *whispering,* and it just sounded like it was getting louder and louder, echoing in her head.

"Let's get you cleaned off," Eliot said. She felt Eliot's hand and little else. She barely saw the steps under her feet and then she was on her knees halfway up with no idea when she'd fallen.

"Tess," Eliot said, and his voice sounded urgent now. "Come on. We have to get out of here."

She wanted to lay her head down on the stone and go to sleep. It was so cool on her overheated skin. The seven steps were too far. She could stay here for as long as she wanted, Eliot Birch and his insistence be damned. The dark wasn't so scary now that she was a part of it.

"*Tess,*" Eliot begged. "Please."

She closed her eyes. It wasn't so bad.

The ground vanished from underneath her, and she was close to the smell of her own vomit again as her head rested on Eliot's chest. Everything swayed with the gait of his walk. She looked up, watching the curve of his chin.

The devil carried her out of the stacks, his heartbeat pounding against her cheek.

No—not the devil. It was Eliot. Eliot, living and human.

He tucked her phone away somewhere, cutting off the light, until they broke through the barrier into the special collections cage and her eyelids were veiny red with the fluorescents.

"*Fuck*," Eliot hissed, and the fear in his voice made her open her eyes. At first, she was confused—had he spilled something on himself, before she threw up on him?—but then she recognized the scent permeating his clothes and her skin. She didn't get the full effect of the vision until Eliot set her down against the wall and knelt before her.

The front of his sweater was soaked black. Her clothing had black specks all over it, and when she lifted her hands, they were stained too.

"Open your mouth," Eliot demanded. Tess did as she was told, but she could only imagine what he saw: black-stained teeth, dark-streaked tongue. Because even though it was impossible, Tess recognized the liquid that stained Eliot and her—the very same liquid that had somehow come from her body.

Ink.

twenty

Eliot

ELIOT CARRIED TESS HALFWAY UP FROM THE STACKS AND dragged her the rest. There was a memory replaying over and over in his brain, one of his mother, weak from treatment, unable to get inside after a rainstorm. Tess felt too frail in his arms.

But she hadn't protested. Pale, covered in a sheen of sweat, she'd allowed him to drag her. Hadn't even questioned it when he set her in his desk chair and turned away to perform a short spell meant to ease stomachaches.

He wished he knew something stronger. Something that could reveal the truth of the ink, something that could explain what had just happened.

Eliot nicked his thumb, spilling a drop of blood into the chalk circle on his desk. He lit a candle and set it over the blood. A quick chalk marking, a bit of smoke. A few words, hushed so Tess couldn't hear him.

He glanced over his shoulder as the magic started to shimmer in his working. It was impossible to tell if she was conscious, but with her ragged breathing, at least he could hear that she wasn't dead.

The thought of it almost stopped the words on the tip of his tongue. Eliot cleared his throat, turned back to the working, and tried to focus once more.

His mind wandered anyways. Eliot was never good with people his own age. Even Henri, Eliot's closest friend at Falk, knew nearly nothing about him.

Eliot had always felt behind, just out of the circle of friendship with another person, just on the fringe of commonality. But with Tess… It was as if he wasn't *trying* to fit in or empathize with her.

She didn't pretend. She didn't pander or try to please him, really. In fact, she seemed to do anything possible to ensure that he didn't get his way.

Tess Matheson didn't take shit from him, or anyone else.

He admired her for that. Too much, probably.

In London, his mother had made him watch a new version of *Cyrano de Bergerac* that one of her artsy friends had managed to get her a recording of. There was one monologue that caught him, that *hurt* him: Cyrano could write to Roxane all of his waking thoughts, wax poetic about her virtues and faults, but he'd burn up the letters and declarations before letting her see a word of them. He couldn't face that level of vulnerability or exposure; couldn't risk it.

Eliot had never understood wanting like that. In his mind, affection was a nebulous thing. Desire was not his currency; only knowledge mattered.

He stole another glimpse at her. He was unsettled; he was horrified to think she could've been truly hurt by tonight's explorations.

The final words of the working passed through his lips, and resolve formed with their departure. Half agony, half hope. That was the line, wasn't it?

When it was done, he heard her sigh behind him.

No more time for thought or conjecture. Eliot blew out the candle and turned around. "Are you feeling any better?" he asked.

Tess blinked, looking up at him. Her eyes looked unfocused, pupils dilated. "I didn't mean to throw up on you."

Eliot fought a smile. He put the candle back on the windowsill, scrubbed out the chalk and blood with his palm. "No one ever does."

Too many words, too many thoughts, no words at all. Nothing more came out of his mouth. She shifted, sleepy and dazed, blond hair shimmering in the faint light of the remaining candle he'd left burning.

When he was overwhelmed like this, there were only quotes and lines, graced upon during his reading and filed away—between the shadow and the soul, sun dismantled. There were words he could say to her, his own or someone else's, but he could not cross that empty space between them. Not now, with her frail and weak, with the shimmer of magic clinging to the air between them.

Her eyes flicked to him. "You should blow that candle out."

Eliot smiled faintly and nodded. He blew out the flame, letting the words and lines scatter with the dying of the light.

twenty one

Tess

ELIOT WOULDN'T LET HER WALK HOME. AFTER ALL, IT wasn't every day that one vomited ink onto another person, and he wanted to take every precaution. Or he needed another favor from her. Tess couldn't tell for sure.

"Okay," Eliot said, starting the car. "I don't think I need to ask you this, but I'm assuming you haven't been eating pens lately or anything."

"No," Tess said. Part of her wanted to flip down the mirror and look at her face, but she knew she'd look like a nightmare. She had no doubt her mouth and chin were stained with dark ink, and it would be a miracle if she got into the dorm and past Anna without a discussion.

"That's what I thought," Eliot said. The streetlight flipped to yellow and he didn't even try to make it through the intersection, which was annoying. Actually, it was annoying just to be in the car. Her dorm was not a far walk, and she doubted that his was, either. It was a frivolous waste of gas to drive around like this. "You're sure this is ink?" Eliot asked.

"It's ink. I know it when I see it." She was too defensive, but whatever. For what it was worth, she did feel bad about puking on him. "We shouldn't have taken that book out of the tunnel in the first place."

Eliot snorted. "That's hardly the point."

Maybe, but it *felt* like the point. Tess couldn't deny that her recent purge felt like the result of the book. Her stomach turned at the memory of its wet heat in her arms.

Even worse, being in the car with Eliot and seeing him in this half-flickering darkness was like calling the devil and summoning him out of her dreams. She was no longer certain she could separate the two.

But if the book was gone, the devil should be too.

"Here's the deal," Tess said, exhausted of the entire adventure. "We found the book. It was creepy, and we shouldn't have taken it out of the basement in the first place. But it's back now. It's back in its tomb. So we should forget about this whole thing and move on. Okay?"

The light turned green. She stared straight ahead, focused on that green light. The car didn't move until the person behind Eliot beeped at him, and then they lurched into the intersection.

Eliot didn't say anything.

"Turn right here," Tess said, even though she would've been far more comfortable if they'd remained in silence.

Eliot turned right.

"And again here."

No answer. No words. It was as if Eliot felt his silence was response enough, as if he was already cutting the imaginary ties of the grimoire that was the only connection they shared.

Tess's block came into view. She didn't want to say anything. Maybe if they kept driving, she wouldn't have to speak another word for the rest of eternity, or until they ran out of gas.

"This is me," Tess said.

Eliot pulled over. They sat for a moment in silence, listening to the too-soft drivel of the radio. Tess reached for the gearshift and put the car in park for him.

"May I walk you up?" Eliot asked.

"I don't think you should."

The glow of the dash made him look like a demon from a children's story book, all angles and edges. She forced herself to look away from him. "When you say that we should forget," Eliot said, "do you mean that you don't want to speak anymore?"

"I'm not going to ignore you, if that's what you mean."

Eliot took a deep breath. "I don't want this to be the end."

For a brief moment, he was Eliot and the devil melded as one and she was certain, if she watched him long enough, he would look over at her with eyes black and empty.

The book is gone and so is the devil.

"Well, I don't want…" She searched for a word, but settled for waving her hand vaguely towards the outside. "*This* to continue."

He sighed. "No, not the book—not that. I fancy you, Tess. And I'd like to…keep seeing you."

Seeing her? Though their time together did tend to be heart racing and illicit, it wasn't for romantic reasons. She had no feelings for him other than general annoyance.

At least, that's what she told herself. Frequently.

Another glimpse at him, then away; quick so he wouldn't see, so he wouldn't know how often her gaze found him. He had his eyes trained straight forward at the bumper of the car parked on the street in front of them. License plate: STK8789. Silvery gray. Dented on the left, below the taillight.

Eliot Birch was soaked in ink she'd vomited onto his sweater.

And he liked her.

And he was absolutely insufferable.

And yet. The catch of her breath in the stacks. The awareness of his hands gripping hers. Tess forced it out, forced it away.

It wouldn't be hard to knock that dent out, Tess thought. The scratch through the middle would remain, but the bumper would be smooth again.

Whether she liked it or not, Eliot Birch was a Falk boy through and through.

"That wasn't a question," Tess said.

She heard Eliot's sharp intake of breath, but she couldn't look at him. To look was to reveal everything. "May I take you to dinner?" Eliot asked, softer this time, less certain, if that was possible.

Eliot was someone who, if she gave him the ability, had the power to hurt her. He was the son of someone she reviled, too charming to be trustworthy, knowledgeable in things that scared her. The *idea* of falling for Eliot scared her.

What did she want? Everything. Nothing. All of it, all at once.

Eliot Birch, with his perfect tie tucked into his once-perfect sweater, sitting in his perfect car, was everything she'd come to hate about Falk. The book did not change that. Nothing, Tess thought, could change that.

"I don't think that's a good idea," Tess said. She unbuckled her seatbelt.

A silence. She rubbed her chin, trying to wish away some of the pigment. "Right," Eliot said. "Of course."

"I should get going," Tess said.

The car door squeaked a little when she pushed it open.

Her stomach was settled now, but full of some other sort of tension: butterflies, maybe, or regret. Tess darted up the stairs to her dorm. Anna was nowhere to be found, which was good for the ruin that was her face, but bad for the ruin that was her heart.

On a whim, Tess looked out the window, down at the street. Eliot hadn't left. The headlights of his car shone against the silver of the one in front.

Tess closed her eyes. All over again, in her mind, she turned and felt him catch her. Again and again, this: his hands on her arms. The sudden, close smell of waxy vanilla, clean pages, a tinge of sweat. Looking up and seeing him staring back at her.

When she opened her eyes, the car was gone.

twenty two

In the stacks, anger dripped from the pages of books and seeped up from the floor. Your ink coalesced in the corner of the third floor, running down aisles and up stairs and over metal shelves until you came together into the hands and eyes and hips and hair. You, not-Eliot, stood tall in the darkness. There was no need for light. You knew where you were going.

You stretched out your hands, watching the ink shift underneath your skin. This form would only last so long. What you needed was a body. Flesh and blood, bones and gristle, and a fresh, beating heart.

You were a boy once; you remember your body, you remember your flesh, you remember how it felt to—

You remembered nothing. You were not that anymore.

There was only one body you could occupy without destroying it entirely: that of she who had released you. Tess. The human girl.

Others would disintegrate under your touch, fall prey to that horrible mortal decay that claimed all, in the end. You could use them, but not forever.

But the girl's body—that would be enough for you. She had called you. The touch of your hand would not stop her fragile heart. Instead, together you would be something powerful. Something immortal.

You smiled, the sharp edges of your teeth catching your lips, blood-colored ink trickling down over your chin. Freedom beckoned.

twenty three

Tess

TESS BRUSHED HER TEETH UNTIL HER SPIT WAS NO LONGER black. In the shower, she scrubbed every bit of her body twice, then a third time after washing her hair. Dressed in shorts and a soft crewneck of her father's, she applied a face mask.

She did not think of Eliot.

She did not think of tunnels.

She did not think of books.

When she wanted to, Tess was very good about tiptoeing around the edge of a subject and skirting away when her mind got too close. Refusing to think about Eliot was like refusing to think about the cost of Boston Conservatory and how much she wanted to go there or how the fields smelled at home right around July when everything was blooming.

Tess brushed her teeth again for good measure, turning around and around, trying to hum her way through a concerto around her toothbrush. Except when she spun, she caught the edge of something in the mirror. She spat out the toothpaste and faced her reflection head-on.

Something was dribbling from her nose in her reflection. Dark, brackish blood. Tess pressed a hand to her nose and pulled it back, but her fingers came away clean. Her eyes flicked back to her reflection.

Blood poured from her nose, from her eyes, from her ears. The skin of her reflection flaked away, leaving just a skull behind.

Shit shit shit, Tess thought. She pressed a hand to the mirror. The devil stood behind her. His mouth cracked into a grin.

She whirled, breath catching in her chest. There was no one there, no one behind her. She was alone in the bathroom, just as she had been before.

Maybe Anna was right. Maybe she was overworked and hallucinating. Tess sat on the lip of the bathtub, pressing her palms against her eyes. It was going to be fine. It was common for stressed-out people to break. She didn't know how to be less stressed—or how to stop seeing things like that—but maybe if she relaxed for the night, things would be okay.

She could put on a podcast, wait for her face mask to dry, and not think. Not puzzle through the day or the week. She intended to do just that, except…except. When she stood, there was a handprint on the mirror, smudged in something dark.

Tess got up to take a closer look, anxiety prickling down her spine. Fingerprints and lines of the palm, all defined against the glass, that were certainly not there moments ago.

Tess lifted her hand. The fingerprint was much too big to be something she'd left behind.

The devil was not gone.

Her phone rang, briefly terrifying her—*not alone not alone you are not alone here*—but she hastily wiped the print away and went to find her phone.

It could be Nat. And it was.

Tess put the call straight to speakerphone. "Hey, kid," she said. Her throat still felt a little rough, and her voice was gravelly. She hoped Nat didn't notice.

"Tessy," Nat said. "Did you talk to Mom about coming home for the Fourth?"

Well, this wouldn't be the relaxing conversation she'd hoped for. "I didn't," she hedged, mostly because she herself could not bear the thought of it. And that wasn't including what Nat's reaction to everything would be. After all, Nat wouldn't be ready for the shock of it: most of their furniture sold, except for the girls' rooms, which had been left untouched. The pile of bills on the dining room table, unpaid.

No, they would not be going home for the Fourth of July. And no, Tess wasn't sure how to tell Nat that.

But her sister had to find out eventually.

"Bus tickets are expensive," Tess finished, hoping this was enough. Nat wasn't oblivious; she knew a bit about the family's money troubles, even though no one had gone out of their way to explain things to her.

"But it's a holiday," Nat said.

"It'll be fine. We'll do something ourselves, here, if we have to. Fireworks. A picnic."

"It won't be the same."

No, it wouldn't be the same, but there was nothing she could do about that. Tess was already breaking, trying to save money for college and pay for her lessons and still have enough to put money into Nat's account while sustaining herself. It was a miracle she hadn't already broken.

"We'll make do."

Nat sighed and Tess hated the sound of it.

"Do you have time to get dinner this week?" Tess asked. She barely had time herself, but she hadn't seen Nat in a few days and desperately missed her.

"I can go tomorrow."

"What about next Friday? After my lesson?"

Nat sighed. "I'll miss crepe night, but I guess I can go then."

Nat and her food preferences. "We can get crepes," Tess said. "I could make them."

"Fiiiiinnnnnneeee." There was the murmur of voices in the background, and then Nat's muffled answer to some unheard question. "I gotta go. It's time for soccer."

It would've been a challenge to get Nat to play soccer at home, but at Falk, there was an endless stream of activities for the kids stuck here over the summer to participate in. And if Nat hated anything, it was being left out.

"Have fun, kid. Love you."

"Loveyoutoo!" Nat said, voice hurried and far away from the phone before the line went dead.

Tess closed her eyes. Theoretically, she could pay for the tickets, but the house they grew up in would be a shell of what Nat remembered. Tess didn't want to expose her to the fighting or the reality of their financial situation.

Tess rolled over onto her side. Her face was dry and the mask was cracking. She needed to get up and rinse it off, but it was so nice here on the couch. With her eyes closed, it was easier to forget about the devil, about Nat, about anything other than the slow rush of the air conditioner and the exhaustion weighing heavily in her bones.

She had not been here before, and she had no memory of how she had come to be here.

Tess stood in a large room. The walls were white and ceilings were high, with windows set far up into the walls. Light streamed through, but the time of day was indeterminate.

Tess turned in a slow circle. She was surrounded by shapes shrouded in sheets. Some of them were stained—maybe with blood.

"I wondered if you'd visit tonight," a voice behind her said. The devil.

She turned. He was there, amidst the shapes and stains, wearing Eliot's face and ink like blood. He hadn't been there just a moment ago, she was certain.

He moved closer, fanning out his fingers and taking hold of her elbow. His skin was cold. His fingertips grazed her ribs.

"I didn't have much of a choice, did I?" Tess snapped. She wanted to step away from his touch but fear held her in place.

"You always have a choice," the devil said.

Tess doubted that greatly, but she sensed that fighting would get her nowhere. "You know my name, but I don't know yours. What should I call you?"

"Call me Truth."

Tess nodded. She glanced around again, unsettled by the grayness of the light. She felt leached of color herself. "Where have you brought me now?"

Truth turned around in a circle, examining the place just as Tess had. She watched his face closely. It was odd, seeing the differences between him and Eliot. Though they were nearly identical, their expressions were not.

She couldn't be sure, but Truth almost looked hopeful. "I haven't brought you anywhere. You've conjured this place up yourself, but I have filled it." He glanced back at her, his eyes morphing between gray and blue. Here, in this light, he looked...well, human. Substantial. Not like the suggestion of a person, not like a ghost she could reach through, not like a demon sent to torment her.

Tess hugged her arms to herself. It was dangerous to think of him like that, as anything other than a devil.

"What did you fill it with, then?" Tess asked.

The devil walked through the sheeted objects, and Tess had the feeling he wasn't fully focused on her. He seemed just as caught off guard as she was. He stopped at one of the shapes and, with a flourish, swept the sheet off.

A blank canvas stood on an easel. Truth's face fell.

"Is that not what you expected to find?" Tess asked.

The sheet slipped from Truth's fingers. "It is exactly what I expected to find." He turned back to her, eyes ever shifting. "Do you know what hell is, Tess Matheson?"

She bit her lip. "I…" It was a question she'd considered, in odd ways: she decided she believed in it, but she also figured she'd never truly be awful enough to go there. "I imagine it's quite a bit like burning."

Truth smiled wryly. He reached for a sheet, revealing another empty canvas. Another, and another. Sheets fluttered to the ground like falling leaves. It was a forest, in a way, just like the burning forest of her last nightmare.

"Hell," Truth said, gesturing around them both, "is a lot of nothing."

She didn't think a room full of empty canvases was scary enough to be hell, but she didn't want to directly question the devil.

"I don't understand."

"Hmm." The devil shuffled through the sheets and walked along the edge of the room, looking for something. "I thought you would. Perhaps I'm mistaken." His eyes lit up, flaring blue, as he unearthed a full palette from underneath one of the sheets.

Tess watched in silence as he chose a canvas. He considered it for a moment, looking almost as if he was building up bravery. There were no brushes, so when Truth painted, he used his fingers.

Bold strokes appeared at the touch of his hand. Clearly Truth had been accomplished, as he knew intuitively how to create shapes and dimension even without tools. An image began to take shape: a forest, burning.

But as Tess watched, the edges began to soften. Paint from the top of the canvas, paint she thought was drying, dripped down. As the devil worked, the paint undid itself, dripping and pooling on the floor, moving more rapidly with every stroke until each slash of color ran down immediately.

The devil stared at the white canvas. Tess stared with him.

"Hell," the devil said, "is failure. It is unbecoming. It is undoing. It is an empty canvas, a song with the notes reversed, until nothing remains. Do you understand now?"

Tess swallowed hard.

She did understand. Hell was an empty and dusty stationery shop with eviction notices and no customers. Hell was a cello unplayed, maybe never played again.

This time, when the devil came close, she did not flinch. He ran his hand up her arm, over her shoulder. Fingertips traced her cheek. Cupped her face. Lined the shell of her ear. His head dipped close.

"You think you know hell, but I can show you the opposite. I can show you what I can give you."

She just wanted out of this moment, out of this awful studio. "Okay," she agreed.

The devil twirled her, and Tess's vision went dizzy and uncertain. She wore a gown of blood, beautiful and alive, like hot silk against her skin. It rose up, warm against her body: a high neck, as if she were being strangled, a full skirt. The studio around them faded to black, came to light once more, and it wasn't a studio at all.

Tess and the devil stood on a stage. He was still Eliot, still midnight, still darkness, dressed in a coat with tails. He no longer held her. Instead, he presented something: the most beautiful cello she'd ever seen. Shining black, like it had been carved from onyx.

"Take it," the devil said.

Tess's hands shook, but she wrapped her fingers around the neck. There was a seat behind her then, and she adjusted the cello between her legs. There was a bow—of course there was a bow—and it wasn't just the devil and Tess anymore.

He slunk behind her, daring as a promise, and swept the hair away from her neck. His breath was warm against her pulse point as he dipped low towards her.

"Play for me. For us," the devil pleaded.

How could she refuse? His hands did not leave her shoulders, fingers perched on the bare skin there as if she were an instrument under his command. Tess took a breath, drew the bow, and bent to the cello.

She'd never heard such a sound before. Her hands were moving, under her control and hers alone, but she had never played like this before. She had never dared to *dream* of playing like this. She was better than she'd ever been, better than Alejandra had ever been, better than any cellist she'd heard. Every note bled with perfection. Every caesura was a held breath, a precipice into freefall.

It didn't matter what she played—notes weren't enough to encompass the sound that swelled from between her fingers.

And through all of it, there was the devil. His fingers on her collarbones, his lips in her hair, his breath against her ear. The devil behind her, and the scent of blood surrounding her, and before her—oh, before her. There was an audience.

She gazed out at them as she played. They flickered: souls of the dead, decaying bodies, the faces of everyone she'd ever known. She should've been afraid, but she wasn't.

She finished, and one final note rung out. Tess hadn't consciously decided to end the performance. She'd just known time was coming to a close, and the devil had more to tell her. She needed to answer his call.

The audience before her sprung into a standing ovation, louder than the ovation at her last recital, louder than the competition in Philadelphia when she'd won first place for the very first time. She rose too. Rose and bowed, clutching the black cello against her body.

The applause went on forever. It went for no time at all. And Tess bowed again and again as the roses cascaded in: red and white and pink, pooling at her feet. Until the flames of the forest rose up once again, devouring the audience, consuming the roses, dissolving Tess's dress of blood until she was left gasping once more in the devil's arms.

"What...what was that?"

His eyes were black and full. "This is what I could do for you, if you only let me. This is what you could become. Do you understand?"

She pressed a hand to her chest, trying to catch her breath. Her heart pounded against her hand, desperate and wanting.

And that was the worst part of it, the wanting. She'd given

so much to be here, to be a good role model for Nat, to get them through this damned year. But in the devil's arms, she'd seen what she really wanted. The praise, the skill, the success. The black cello, melting into her body like they were one being.

"What would you give?" he asked.

Everything, Tess thought. *Don't ask. Anything. Anything at all.*

He reached a hand forward, tracing her lip with his thumb. "Don't be afraid," he whispered. "I know what you need."

His other hand pressed to the small of her back, and suddenly, it wasn't empty. Something cold and hard pressed against her skin. He brought his hand around. His palm, shielded between their bodies, opened to reveal a slender blade.

"Do you know what you must do, Tess?"

Her nostrils were full of the scent of blood, thick and cloying. When she closed her eyes, she saw her own body, stained with blood, ripped open at the throat and wrists. Her own body, once more wearing a gown of blood.

She placed her hand over his, on the blade, cold metal biting into her fingers.

"Remember," he said, and then he was gone.

Tess's eyes snapped open. She surfaced from the dream like she was breaking through the surface of water, where everything was clearer, weighted. She shot up, expecting to still be clutching the black cello. But no.

Just Tess. Empty-handed and alone as she ever had been.

Under the couch, the devil's blade waited.

twenty four

Eliot

LUCILLE HAD AN INEXPLICABLE OBSESSION WITH FAKE greenery. It draped the edge of the breakfast bar, lined the mantle over the fireplace, and webbed the walls of the foyer. It was even here, in the bathroom, carefully wound around the metal edge of the mirror to look like it had grown there naturally, as if Eliot's father's tidy home in Squirrel Hill was being invaded by the world outside.

Which was ironic, considering Lucille hated just about everything about nature.

Eliot splashed some water on his face. He'd only arrived minutes ago and he already felt like he was suffocating. Everything his father said so far was an attack: "Eliot, why haven't you applied to this college? Don't think you're smart enough? Eliot, why haven't you published anything? If you're studying words, you might as well at least try to get good at them. Eliot, why are you such a disappointment?"

Well, he hadn't said that last one, but it was clear all the same.

"Eliot, dear, food is ready!" This was Lucille, voice saccharine and pinched.

"I'm coming!" Eliot shouted. Now that he was in the hornet's nest, he had to do his best to avoid getting stung.

The house that his father and Lucille lived in was almost as nice as the country estate, but everything in the country house was passed down through the generations, and here, it was new. Eliot didn't even want to think about how much the massive dining table cost, but was grateful for the six feet of space it put between him and his father, with Eliot in the middle of one side and Lucille and his father capping the ends.

Lucille was on some kind of odd diet, so everything on the table was raw and unidentifiable. Eliot took little bits as the serving dishes were passed to him and pushed the piles around his plate.

"Did you sign up for that math class I recommended you for?" his father asked, taking a bite of some sort of puree.

Eliot kept pushing the food around. "I didn't. Not for summer term, anyway. I'm taking a literature class and a history class this term."

His father snorted. "For what purpose?"

Because I am, Eliot wanted to say. "Colleges are looking for more of an interest in the humanities," Eliot said. "A liberal arts education. Even if I were to go into math or science." Which he wasn't. Not that he was bad at math or science; Eliot was good at school in general, and if he didn't understand a concept, he just asked Henri to explain it to him.

Another snort, but nothing more was said. While he was preoccupied with his food, Eliot risked a look over at his father. He sat straight, too straight, bowing his head slightly every time he took a bite of food.

He was an objectively attractive man, Eliot supposed. His once-dark hair was shot through with gray, especially at the temples. He kept himself clean-shaven and fit, playing on a community men's rugby league and going to the gym most evenings. There was a picture of his father that Eliot used to keep on his nightstand when he was away on business, back before he realized Eliot had his mother's magic and turned against him. The picture itself was from his first publication on vectors, back when his father taught at the collegiate level. He was twenty-three in it, just a few years older than Eliot, and Eliot always thought he'd grow up to look just like him.

He was very, very wrong. Next to his father, Eliot looked like a twig. A nerdy, socially awkward twig.

"Aren't you going to eat?" he asked, waving a fork at Eliot's plate.

"I have been," Eliot lied.

Birch's eyes narrowed, just a little. As usual, Eliot wondered if his father made him stick so close to him as punishment to Eliot, and not just his mother. "Lucille spent all day cooking. Be respectful."

He wasn't sure how not eating was being disrespectful. Or how Lucille could've spent all day cooking when everything was raw.

"He's fine, Edward," Lucille said.

"He should eat. He's going to look like *that* the rest of his life if he doesn't."

"I look fine, Dad," Eliot said, too quietly to be heard over Lucille's, "He's perfectly handsome."

His father harrumphed again, muttering something under his breath, but Eliot didn't care that much. He wished he had Tess's number. If anyone hated his father, it was Tess. Maybe they could commiserate.

There were so many things left unspoken between them, things Eliot wanted to shout across the table just to see the look on his father's face.

But no shouting, no argument, would make him understand Eliot and Caroline's magic. If his father had his way, Eliot would forget about it altogether. And forgetting his magic…well, to Eliot, that was almost as bad as forgetting how to read or how to walk. It was a part of him.

"You *are* looking a little pale. Are you feeling okay?" Lucille's voice was tinged with warmth, and it made Eliot's stomach curl.

"It's because he never leaves that library," his father said.

"I'm not in the library now, am I?" Eliot snapped. His father raised an eyebrow at him. It was a challenge: *You want to sass me, boy? You want to find out what happens?* Softer, Eliot amended, "I do leave. I just have plenty of work to do, for my senior thesis."

Lucille ignored her boyfriend's eye roll, and Eliot wondered if he really was here because she wanted to see him and not because of his father. "Have you started applying to schools? Or is it too early?"

"It's a little too early," Eliot said. "August I can start, I think."

"That's wonderful," Lucille said. In another world, another lifetime, Eliot wouldn't dislike her. After all, she was kind. She spoke softly and she always smelled of roses. But in this world, he knew what she was: a woman who was dating his father while his mother was dying halfway across the world, and because of that, he could never fully forgive her.

"What do you do all day in that library, anyway?" his father asked.

A million things. Read grimoires, practiced magic, drew shapes in the dust of his office, considered the curve of Tess Matheson's cheek and how nicely it rested on her palm.

"I study," Eliot said.

"Are you seeing anyone?" Lucille asked. An annoying question from anyone, but even more so coming from her, especially in his father's presence.

"No," Eliot said. "I'm not."

There must've been something in his tone, because suddenly, his father was scrutinizing him.

"You're not seeing one of those library girls, are you?" his father asked, and it was clear by the tone of his voice that when he said "library girls," he actually meant "scholarship students."

"No," Eliot said too quickly.

Another hard look from his father. "Good. I want you to stay away from them, Eliot. If they pretend they like you, it's only because of your money."

I wish I could turn you into a toad, Eliot thought.

Lucille coughed into her napkin. Because, of course, when his father and Lucille first started dating, that was what everyone suspected of her. Knowing his father, how hard he was to deal with, Eliot still sort of suspected that of her.

None of it mattered anyway. If he was interested in Tess, which he unfortunately was, the interest was unrequited. He was a fool if he thought otherwise.

twenty five

Tess

T<small>HE WEEKEND WAS A MESS OF FOOD AND SPILLED SALSA AND</small> crabby tables, but Tess couldn't get that dream out of her head. Couldn't stop thinking about the press of the devil's fingertips, the susurration of his breath, the coolness of the cello in her hands.

Was Eliot experiencing the same things she was? Tess doubted it. If he was, he probably would've come to her already.

Maybe. But she couldn't forget about the parallel tracks of the headlights outside her window that night—or even worse, the feeling in her stomach when she'd opened her eyes and they were gone.

Awkwardness aside, she *needed* to talk to Eliot. She didn't want to—God, really, she never wanted to *see* him again after the horribleness of puking on him coupled with turning him down for a date—but the devil was not gone, even now that the book was. She could still feel the press of the blade in her hand from her dreams, and the image of the devil's pleasant smile was burned into her brain.

Monday morning, after she opened the library and sat fidgeting at her desk for nearly an hour and a half, he finally appeared. He walked through the door like he was stepping out of one of her dreams, only confident in his own insecurity.

Tess looked away when he caught her gaze, cheeks burning.

Eliot nodded to her and hesitated as if he meant to say something.

Tess opened her mouth, but no words came out. What could she say? She wasn't going to apologize, couldn't apologize, and she had no idea how to bring up the dreams without him saying anything about the book first. Eliot's uncertainty turned to a grimace. He swept up the stairs, into his office, and shut the door behind him.

Tess had barely moved. Hadn't spoken. She closed her eyes and dropped her head against the desk. So much for talking to him, for acting normal. She couldn't decide which was worse: Eliot acknowledging their mutual disasters, or Eliot coming into the sun-drenched library like a stranger.

Regina arrived at noon, just as scheduled, and said something mundane about the weather and the number of people on campus. Mathilde sent Tess to the nearby deli to grab her a sandwich for lunch, and then made her sit at the desk while Regina shelved books.

But still, Eliot's office door remained closed.

The library remained empty and quiet.

Mathilde came out of her office when Regina was still downstairs. Her grayed hair was swept back into a clip, and she looked more like Tess's grandfather, whom she'd barely known.

"Theresa," she said. "I have two matters to discuss."

Tess nodded, pushing her chair down the desk to allow Mathilde space to bring the other chair closer. Mathilde set down a paper on Falk letterhead. "As your guarantor, I received this letter in the mail."

Tess hunched over, trying to read quickly, but the only

words she caught were *Natalie Matheson* and *tuition increase* before her breath seized in her chest. She glanced up at Mathilde.

She couldn't take more shifts. Dammit, she couldn't work any harder than she already was.

"I just want you to know about it," Mathilde said, folding the letter back up and putting it in the pocket of her sweater. "Now that Natalie is moving into the high school, her tuition has increased. I've already covered it. You don't need to worry about her funding."

"But…" Tess sputtered. She gripped the edge of the desk, trying to make sense of it. "You said you wouldn't pay for it. For us to go here. Why are you… You don't… Are you sure?"

Mathilde studied Tess for a long moment, and she couldn't shake that odd feeling of familiarity. She herself had never gotten close to many members of her father's family; her grandparents died when she was young, and Mathilde, the only remaining great-aunt, only appeared in Tess's life for holidays. Asking for help was a last-ditch effort, one she didn't actually expect to pan out.

"I put myself through college," Mathilde said. "My father didn't want his daughters to go, but I did anyway. I worked hard. I didn't let anyone tell me what I could or couldn't do." Mathilde leaned back, looking away out the window, down the slope of rolling grass towards the park. "I see that in you. You work hard. You're not going to stop. But if you keep going on like this, I worry what will happen."

Tess closed her eyes to regroup. "I'm not going to burn out. It's just a few more years."

"A few years is a long time," Mathilde said—somewhat forebodingly, Tess thought. In a rare moment of affection,

Mathilde reached over and laid her withered hand over Tess's. "Let me worry about Natalie. You just focus on you, Theresa. Alright?"

Tess sighed, either in relief or the knowledge that she now owed somebody else. "Okay. You said you had two things?"

Mathilde's expression hardened. Her eyes flicked up to the offices and back to the desk, and she produced another piece of paper. "I received a remote request for one of young Mr. Birch's books. I only need the book for a few hours to scan pages and forward them on. Could you retrieve it for me?"

Tess fought the urge to groan. If only there was a way to take a key, to go up without Eliot noticing… But no. Mathilde had done her a favor. And after all, this was her job. She took the paper.

"I'll get it," she said.

Mathilde nodded. "Don't be too long," she said, and again, there was that peculiar note of warning.

Tess trudged up the stairs as if every one was one step closer to the gallows. Which, in a way, it was. She didn't want to talk to Eliot—or, rather, she didn't know what to *say* to Eliot. *Hey, I'm sorry I threw up on you, but I think I'm having PG-13 dreams about the devil?* Not likely.

She knocked twice. His voice said, "Come in." After taking a second to steel herself, she opened the door.

There was no trace of happiness on Eliot's face when he realized it was her. "Do you need something?"

Tess flung out the paper towards him. An explanation; an excuse. "I'm here for a book. Just for a bit. We need to send pages to someone."

Eliot got up, stretching out every movement and taking his own sweet time as if he was intentionally trying to prolong her discomfort. He scanned the paper, frowned, and turned to his cart of books. Tess glanced over at the shelf of weird things he had, just as she always did when she was in here. There was some new sort of chalk marking on the shelf and another on his desk. She fought the urge to move closer to investigate.

"Here," he said, pulling a book and thrusting it out towards her. She took it, catching a glance of Eliot's chalk-whitened hands. He had a few rings on—something she'd never noticed before. One, on his pinky, looked like a wedding ring. She looked away before she could remember how his hands felt catching her. Or worse, how they felt in her dreams.

"Is there anything else?" Eliot asked. He crossed his arms over his chest. Then, because he looked too uncomfortable just standing there, he turned, took a square of cloth from his desk, and began wiping away the chalk markings.

"No, of course not," she said, only because she hated that set to his shoulders and the way his jaw kept working. But of course something *was* the matter. There was ink staining everything around her, simultaneously dying the world black and leaching the color away from her life. She took a quick breath and a second to recollect, and said, "Actually, yes. I need to talk to you."

"So talk." He was intensely focused on one spot on the shelf, rubbing the chalk into non-existence and leaving only streaky smears of dust.

"Have you had any strange experiences since we took the book back?"

Eliot paused. "Strange?" His voice was tightly contained within that single word, but his hand stopped scrubbing the already erased marking. "I can't say that I have."

"Right." Tess waited, sure he would turn around and say

something, sure he would sigh and the tension in his shoulders would release, sure the one awkward moment they'd had in his car would dissolve and leave their former camaraderie behind.

Except, of course, they didn't have any former camaraderie. The only experience they'd shared was the book, and that saga was over. She had no reason to speak to Eliot anymore, besides polite nods to one another when he was coming and going.

"Okay," Tess said. "I guess that's it. I'll see you around."

She turned to go—she should've gone—but the bubble of sudden frustration was too much for her to walk away and leave it behind.

She *hated* feeling this off-kilter where Eliot was concerned. He was not meant to take up her time or occupy any space in her thoughts. He was not meant to be any more than a boy she helped with books.

She hated that she thought about him at all, let alone as often as she did.

Still facing away, she said, "You know, this whole time, I didn't think you were just talking to me for a date."

Silence behind her. She couldn't do this, have her back to him, and not see his reaction. When she turned, Eliot was by the window, forehead pressed to the pane, eyes closed.

"I wasn't, Tess." His voice was tense and even, a string tuned to the breaking point, a bow pulled across it—one long, eerie note.

"Then why are you being so rude now?"

"I'm not being rude," he snapped. "I saw something that wasn't there, and I don't fault you for not feeling the same way. All I'm trying to do is move on with my life and taking some space for myself to realign with that, and you waltzing in here is making that extremely difficult. Okay?

You rejected me. I'm not mad. I'm not upset. I am giving you your space so you don't feel awkward for being honest with me, because if I was in your shoes, I would want the same thing from you." It was more words than she'd ever heard him say at once, more words than she thought he had inside of him at any given moment. Softer, but not calmer, he continued, "All I want is some peace."

If he wanted peace, he could have it. "Fine," Tess said. "I'm sorry I bothered you." A deep, dark voice inside of her whispered, *If he wanted peace, he wouldn't wear the devil's face*, but Tess pushed that voice far down inside of her and locked it away.

She turned on her heel and went out.

twenty six

Eliot

ALL I WANT IS SOME PEACE. RIDICULOUS, ELIOT SCOLDED HIM-
self. He sounded like some sort of washed-up, unlikeable bastard, like some pathetic boy who couldn't get a date. He was
aiming for Mr. Darcy and made himself into a Collins instead.

Eliot and his overloaded satchel shuffled back home,
ignoring the note from Henri on the door—*Haven't seen you
in a bit. Emiliano's?*—and threw himself onto his bed. He
would not go to Emiliano's with Henri. He would not take
such a risk.

He would call his mother and deal with the wreckage of
himself afterwards.

The phone rang, discordant and unending. Earlier in the
summer, he'd thought his father might have something to
say about the massive phone bills Eliot's calls accrued, but he
hadn't. It was only later that Eliot learned Lucille dealt with
most of the bills; she was the only one who knew how much
Eliot was really spending talking to his mother, and she hadn't
breathed a word of it to his father.

The call went to voicemail. Fear pinged deep in Eliot's
heart. If something happened…

But no. Josie would've told him. Josie would've called.

He tried again. This time, before his thundering heart

could rise to his throat, before he could really start worrying, Josie answered.

"Eliot, dear. I'm sorry, it's not a good day. I don't think you'll want to speak to her." She said it all in a rush, each word running into the one before.

"Oh. Are you certain?"

"Dead certain," Josie said. "You don't want to hear about today, Eliot. She keeps talking about blood and magic…"

Of course, Josie didn't know the truth. He got up and paced, past the window to the bed, past the door to the window, past the window to the bed, over and over again. "Should I come home? Do you think it's that bad?"

"Eliot, love…" There was some sort of noise in the background, some sort of slip and then a wail. "I'll call you if I think that needs to happen, okay, darling? Focus on your studies."

And then Josie hung up. Eliot stared at the useless technology in his hand. It couldn't get him to London unless he suddenly developed an app for teleportation.

He threw it at the wall. The screen shattered. Immediately, there was his father's voice in his head: *You naïve boy. Don't you think of consequences? Do you ever stop and* think *before you act?*

No, he wanted to shout back. No, he didn't think, didn't ever think. He picked up his broken phone and slid it into a drawer so he didn't have to look at it anymore, didn't have to face the reality of his own carelessness.

He sunk down against his bed, tucked his knees against his chest and bowed his head down. Tried to breathe. Tried to think.

He was twelve, on the edge of thirteen, when they noticed something was wrong. Things were forgotten, misplaced. Once, he'd found his mother sitting on the kitchen floor, crying because she'd lost dinner. They'd found a perfect Sunday roast, fully cooked, sitting on a dusty shelf in his father's office with no explanation for how it had gotten there.

The diagnosis followed, just days after the incident with the roast: anaplastic astrocytoma. A brain tumor.

There was a surgery that Eliot barely remembered, and days spent curled next to his mother in hospital beds as specialists came and went. Long afternoons spent barely paying attention to lessons while her endless tests marched on, one after the other, all with the same results.

Nothing was working.

When he went home for the weekends, Eliot noticed more spell books in the house, caught the scent of magic lingering in the garden. Visitors came and went, claiming to know his mother from her Oxford days. Eliot realized, despite being fearless, she was afraid to die.

It wasn't a surprise when his parents decided to turn from the NHS, to find experimental treatments. And eventually, her cancer started to become almost manageable. It was fine, through most of his freshman year at Falk; even fine into his sophomore year. But last year, things once again took a turn for the worst.

No matter how much Eliot begged, no matter how much he pleaded, his father did not let him return home. He had to sit here, in America, while she was dying. While the cancer came back, while she forgot who she was, while her magic slipped away.

He had to watch, and he had to suffer.

Sometimes, Eliot wondered if the whole thing was set up to punish him for a thousand unchangeable indiscretions. Because he looked more like his mother and acted more like her too; because he told the truth when he shouldn't have. Because he had his mother's magic and his father's disappointment. Because he was weak.

In the end, none of that mattered. He couldn't forgive his father even if there were reasons.

Eliot allowed himself the barest moment to pretend that it wasn't real. And then he picked up his wallet, shoved his phone into his back pocket, and went out to get his screen fixed.

twenty seven

Tess

"TESS."

His voice was there the instant she closed her eyes. At first she thought it was the devil but no—no, it was not. It couldn't be.

Tess stood in the middle of her father's ill-fated stationery shop, half memory, half nightmare. There was the door to the back room, where they kept stock. There was the desk where the register stood, where her father used to run figures and design new pens and pick colors for marbled papers. There was the window seat where she spent her afternoons in between school and cello lessons.

But it was not all as she remembered.

Tattered, water-damaged paper and notebooks laid strewn across the floor. The window over her seat was shattered, glass spilling over the moth-eaten cushion. The lettering on the window flaked away, spelling M THES   TATI   NERY CO   NY.

She trailed her fingers along one of the shelves as she crossed the shop. Someone rustled in the back room, adding to the horrible familiarity. There could be two people in that room, and both options were bad: her father or the devil.

"Tess," the voice said again.

The door opened. Her father stood, silhouetted in the entry.

When she left, there had been no final blowout. It had been anticlimactic, if anything. Tess had never directly fought with her father about what he had caused, what he had done. Because in the end, if she examined her own choices, she feared she would've sacrificed just as much for what she wanted.

She understood why her father kept throwing money into the shop even when it was failing, even when there was nothing left, even when it dragged the family into ruin with him.

"You came back," her father said.

But she hadn't. Not by choice, at least. If she had her way, she'd never come back to this place where everything fell apart.

She clenched her fists and immediately realized something was wrong with her hands. Tess looked down.

Her calluses. They were gone.

Hard calluses marred her fingers for the last few years, created by her cello strings. They peeled every so often, but never all at once and never like *this*. Her hands were unfamiliar and useless, as if she'd never picked up a cello.

She looked back up at her father. He was frowning at her, brow furrowed.

"Where's my cello?" she asked, too frantic.

Her father's expression clouded. "You sold it, Tess. You stopped playing. You gave it up. Don't you remember?"

"No." She staggered back, catching herself on a shelf. This was it: The end of what she could handle. The absolute bottom. Tess could handle her father's failure, the embarrassment of losing everything, the pain of keeping Nat and herself afloat, the agony of just getting through the day. She could bear it because, at the end of the day, she could become someone else in the music. Tess could feel the weight against her knees, rest the curve of it against her heart like a second heartbeat, and become someone else.

Her father looked away from her. "You did what you had to do. We all have to sacrifice our dreams eventually."

Before Tess could answer, the bell above the door chimed. She turned to see Eliot Birch walk into the shop, and her heart swelled with something like relief. Eliot would know what to do, or he would say something right. But no, this was not Eliot. It was never Eliot when she wanted it to be.

"You've done this," Tess hissed, because it was too familiar. It was the empty studio all over again, the burning forest. It was another illusion. "What did you do?"

"Who are you talking to?" Tess's father asked.

She turned between the two of them, taking in her father's confused expression against the devil's growing smirk.

"Dad. Why did I stop? Why did... *How* did this happen?"

"You already know what—"

"Tell me."

They stared at each other, unveiled. Both failures. Both empty. It was everything Tess had always feared.

"It doesn't matter," Mr. Matheson said finally. He went to the register and opened the drawer with a creaky *whoosh*. Tess didn't have to see to know it was empty. "The why isn't what matters. You decided you weren't going to be me. You decided you weren't going to throw everything away for a dream. You grew up. And you did it without bringing everyone else down with you."

He slammed the register shut. Tess winced.

"Why am I seeing this?" Tess asked the devil, who skulked by the front door.

"Because you need to see it."

She bit her lip. This place was too awful, too painful. It represented everything destroyed and lost. "You were supposed to protect me from this," Tess said, surprised by the catch in her own voice. She angrily swiped at the tears in her eyes.

But when she looked up, her father was gone. It was only Tess and the devil. Tess and Truth.

She lashed out, sweeping a row of marbled papers off the shelves. While they fluttered down to the floor, she tipped over a table and kicked down a display case, relishing in the shattering of the glass. This place deserved to be destroyed.

She turned on Truth, on this *useless* devil. "Why did you show me this?" she yelled, hating the shrillness in her voice. Falk, the library, Emiliano's… All of it was supposed to make her feel more powerful, give her something of her future back. She'd never meant to come here again.

Truth did not move from the doorway. She hated him for his silence. Tess pushed over another case, cutting her useless hand on the cracked glass.

She turned on him, clutching her bleeding hand to her chest, breathing too hard. "*Tell me.*"

"This is your story."

Tess closed her eyes. The fight went out of her. He wouldn't lie to her, not about this. Not when she knew deep in her soul that it was true.

She was weak. She was a failure. She would give up.

"This is your story, but it doesn't have to be. Let me unwrite it."

"How?" she asked. Her voice cracked on the word.

He came closer and ran his fingers over her cheekbone. She could smell the ink on them, just as strongly as she could smell it everywhere around her, and bottles shattered and bled from shelves in her peripheral vision. "You can be more than this, if you do what I ask. If you give in to me."

Tess's brain was foggy. She couldn't remember exactly what it was he'd asked of her, or really, if he'd asked anything at all. Somewhere, in the back of her head, pumping in the vessels of her heart, she heard the mournful cry of a cello.

"I don't remember," Tess said, but even now, the images were returning. Blood on her skin, blood on the floor. A revision: "I can't."

"You can't?" the devil asked, moving closer. His lips were there, inches from hers, and his breath smelled like orchids. "You can't, or you won't?"

He reached for her hand and she expected to feel the cold metal of the blade on his palm when he twined his fingers through hers, but his hand was empty. Of course. He'd already given her the blade, the weapon of her own destruction.

"I can't," she said again, but that wasn't the truth. She could. She knew where the blade was. In her mind, she saw how it had fallen out of her open palm. It glittered against the floor under the couch like broken glass.

She could. She *wanted*.

"Eliot," Tess said, because his face was so very close.

The devil's eyes went dark. "That's not my name," he said, "and you'd best remember that."

Of course it wasn't. He was Truth. He was the devil. He was eternal death. He made her believe he was everything that wasn't this failure, this emptiness, this calamity.

She was standing in the ocean. She was on the edge of a precipice. She was falling from some great height and crashing and drowning and flying and there was something damp on her wrists now, not just the damp of inky muck, but the damp of something hot and new.

This was the only way out. This was the only salvation. She was not her father, and she would not allow herself to become him.

This was not her story. Not anymore.

She reached up with her bleeding hand and tangled it in the devil's hair. Tess had only a second to see the shock flutter across his face before she brought his face down to hers.

When Tess kissed the devil, she tasted death on his mouth.

twenty eight

SHE KISSED YOU, AND SHE TASTED LIKE MORTALITY. SHE kissed you, and she tasted like light. Your hands skimmed over her arms, raising goose bumps. If she was real, if she was not just a dream stuck in your nightmare, you would be able to seize her from the inside. You would be able to take her heart in your fist.

But this was not the reality. Instead, you felt her body, soft against yours. You felt the hitch of her breath. When you kissed her, you felt as inhuman as you ever had.

You clung to the image of Eliot Birch, pulled over you, cloaking the horror of your own body. You relied on his boyishness to charm her as her unwoken body stumbled through the apartment, searching for a knife that had come from your hands.

You were a boy once. You were a boy and you remembered, and you knew what it was to have flesh and bones and blood and not be trapped here, like this, wanting but never having.

When you were a boy and not the devil, it wasn't so bad to feel this way; to have the clawing of want digging talons into your throat.

"Tess," you breathed against her lips, relishing her name despite yourself. In the duality of her mortal body and her dream one, you felt the press of the knife, cold and metallic. You traced a path and felt a rush of blood.

This was not something you could want.

You were not human. You could not want the things you used to, the things you bargained for. There was a boy once, a boy whose name you once knew, and he made a bargain and he gained everything and lost even more.

And now, you shouldn't have wanted to touch her skin; you should have wanted to inhabit it. You shouldn't have wanted to feel her heart pounding against your hand; you should have wanted to stop it. But the wants of the boy you once were and the wants of the devil you became mixed up and grew distorted.

You were a boy, and the only way to get back to anything other than this torment was to kill her. Leave her dead and drained, this girl who released you, and take her body for yourself.

You shouldn't have wanted to give her everything knowing you'd take it all away.

In the past, there was a long-forgotten bargain, meaning-less against the swell of time. There was a boy whose name you'd neglected to hold close. You remembered his face but you could not pull the ink of you into the shape of him. You remembered the feeling of his skin, the tightness of his mus-cles, the tug of being inside of something real.

There was a boy, and there was a book, and you were not meant to remember either. Half-open eyes, an inhalation of breath, her hand on the back of your neck, and you almost felt like a boy again. Almost allowed yourself to shift back, to believe, and that was enough to lose control of her.

But the dream was shifting, changing, as pain came to her mortal body. Underneath you, her brow furrowed. She bit her lip. She pulled back, pulled away, and you were left with nothing.

twenty nine

Tess

THERE WAS BLOOD ON HER SHEETS.

Tess wasn't sure when she'd woken up, but she had the impression of kissing the devil and then she was here, in her own skin, with pain burning on one wrist and metal biting into the opposite palm.

She tried to swipe the sleep out of her eyes but only succeeded in smearing her vision with blood.

She dropped the slender blade and rubbed the blood away from her face with a dry section of her sheets. From the waist down, they were smeared with inky muck that might never come out no matter how much she scrubbed them.

A gash marred her left wrist, jagged around the edges, still oozing blood. She wanted to throw up, but the pain was almost a blindness and she knew that she needed to treat the wound fast.

But why treat it? The devil whispered in the back of her mind. *You know what you need to do.*

Tess closed her eyes and pressed the heels of her palms against her eyelids. A drop of blood skimmed her cheekbone and rolled down her face like a tear. She didn't want to do it. She didn't want to surrender, to give Truth any part of herself.

She closed her lips against a scream and tasted the death he'd breathed into her mouth.

She wrenched out of her tangled sheets and pressed her wrist against her shirt to staunch the bleeding. Every tiptoed step between her bedroom and the bathroom was head-pounding agony.

Tess stripped and got into the shower to wash away the blood and corruption. The cut on her wrist was deeper than she'd imagined, dirty with ink. If she went to the hospital, there would be too many questions. She'd have to just wrap it herself, then, and hope for the best. Anxiety gnawed a hole in her stomach, but her head was feeling a little better, she wasn't nauseous, and there hadn't been *that* much blood in her bed. Perhaps she'd be fine. Perhaps it would heal on its own.

She rinsed the gore from the wound, then washed one-handed, her wounded wrist raised over head, so as not to disturb the scabbing blood on her wrist. Dripping wet, sitting on the edge of the tub, Tess clumsily wrapped gauze around it and secured it with half-damp tape that barely held. It wouldn't last long, but she couldn't do better. Hopelessness mingled with exhaustion.

Now that she wasn't bleeding out, it was harder to keep her creeping horror at bay. Tess stared at her hands, examining the clinical patch of white gauze against her skin.

Movement in the corner of her eye caught her attention. There was something dark dripping down the shower walls, coming from the shelf where they kept their shampoo and conditioner bottles. Tess squinted at it, trying to decipher if it was errant blood.

No. It was ink. Of course it was, she thought, stifling the sob that threatened to choke her. Ink from the labels of the bottles, running down.

She wasn't alone. Not here, not in her dreams, not in the library. She was *never* alone anymore.

The ink pooled in the remains of the water, seeping up the edges of the bathtub. She wanted to feel afraid. She wanted to feel anything other than exhaustion.

Tess couldn't remember how the cut was made. She was deeply certain she'd done it herself, intentionally or otherwise, but she just couldn't *remember*.

That was the scariest part of it all: there was no agency on her part, no sense of will. There had never been a decision to slice, no memory of getting the knife from under the couch. She remembered the taste of the devil's lips and then the searing heat of her wrist. There was no in-between, no middle.

She wanted out.

Tess dropped her head to her hands. All she could smell was her own blood. But the scent of blood reminded her of a story her father used to tell.

When Tess was much younger, he would sit in bed with Tess and Nat on either side of him and read them folktales. Her favorite were the ones about vampires—how they stole in at night, the fear that surrounded death, the image of garlic between pointed teeth. And this: The protection that came from a revoked invitation. If a vampire was not invited in, it could not enter.

Tess closed her eyes. She wanted to be home, in her bed, in the small room she shared with Nat. She wanted to be in the farmhouse where she knew every creak like it was the sound of her own breathing. She wanted to be where the smell of ink was light and familiar, not deadly.

But this was no vampire. This was no children's story, meant to frighten her when the lights were out.

Except…vampires weren't the only creatures who could be expelled. She did not know anything about her religion, even though she'd been born into it, but she did remember enough scary movies to know about exorcism.

Could she exorcise the devil? She didn't know. There weren't any other options.

A hazy memory came to her, shattered and distorted by waking: *Wherever you go, wherever you belong, I will belong there too.*

But not anymore.

"I don't give you permission," Tess whispered. "I don't want to be a part of this story. I don't want you in my head. I don't want to die."

It couldn't be enough, but the plea was all she had.

When she opened her eyes, blood had already soaked through the layers of bandages. This whole thing was hopeless. She'd never escape the devil. But behind her, the ink had settled in the bottom of the bathtub. It didn't move.

"Holy shit. *Tess.*"

Tess whipped around, and the tape on her wrist gave way. Sleepy-eyed Anna was there in the doorway, dark hair pulled into a braid, dressed in pajamas. Her eyes flew wide when she saw the blood.

"Tess! Oh my God! Are you— Did you—"

And then Anna was crying.

It was so sudden that Tess could only sit there, naked, exposed, confused. Anna slid to her knees next to the well of the bathtub and grabbed Tess's wrist as the bandage unfurled. She didn't even seem to mind that Tess was naked, even as Tess scrambled for a towel with her free hand.

"Did you do this to yourself?" Anna asked, and her voice was low and furious and horrified.

"I didn't...I didn't mean to." How could she tell the truth? How could she be honest with Anna? She turned her face, expecting pity or horror. But all she got was this: Anna throwing her arms tight around her, burying her face in the back of Tess's shoulder blade, nestling into her wet hair.

"Please don't hurt yourself," Anna whispered against Tess's skin. "I care about you too much. So many people love you too, too much."

Even though it hadn't been intentional or wanted, even though she hadn't done it on her own, Anna's words broke something inside of her. She wept as Anna recovered the soft black robe from her room and dressed Tess in it, and even more as they sat at the kitchen table and Anna bandaged the wound properly after Tess wouldn't go to the hospital. And she wept as Anna made tea for both of them and said nice things about her: how good she was at the cello, how much she loved her sister, how well she was doing with the world on her shoulders.

Finally, through snot and tears, Tess said, "I didn't mean to." She wiped her nose on a tissue Anna handed her and insisted, "I really, really didn't. I think I... I've been having dreams. Bad dreams. And sleepwalking."

To her surprise, Anna wasn't insulting or suspicious. Her dark eyes were full of concern. "You didn't do it intentionally?" Anna asked.

"No," Tess said, wiping away more snot. God, if only she wasn't so leaky, if only she could speak right, if only she could tell Anna the truth. If only she could call Eliot.

"I'm afraid," she admitted, because it was as close as she could come to telling the truth.

Anna reached across the table and laid her hand over Tess's. It was hot from the mug of tea, and dandelion-fluff light on hers.

"Afraid of what?" Anna asked.

Afraid of the devil. Afraid of the library. Afraid of the book. Afraid of growing up. Afraid of her future. Afraid of disappointing Nat and Mathilde and her parents. Afraid of failing.

Afraid of everything.

"I'm afraid to go to sleep," Tess said.

"Sleep in my bed," Anna said. "I won't let anything happen to you. I promise."

She wasn't sure how to say yes—but she was exhausted and terrified. And she'd been at Falk for months, thinking she'd only found enemies, and had come home to Anna every single day. They'd laughed together and commiserated together and stayed up late and eaten ice cream and talked about home and boys. And through it all, Tess hadn't realized just how much she had come to count on Anna until now, when she no longer had to be alone.

"Okay," Tess said. "Let me get dressed."

thirty

Eliot

AVOIDING THE LIBRARY WAS INCONVENIENT AND ANNOYING, but avoiding Tess Matheson was even worse.

Eliot hadn't seen Tess since she'd blown into his office like a hurricane on Monday, and now, on Wednesday night, he had the realization that he'd have to go back eventually.

But maybe, if he went when the library was technically closed and keyed in with his code, he wouldn't have to see Tess's face and be reminded of the way her mouth looked when she smiled.

The sun was setting when Eliot parked in the faculty lot. He had an invitation for dinner from his father on his voicemail—"Eliot, Lucille wants to see you again this weekend. She says you're spending too much time by yourself. That builds character, being alone, but she's insisting. Call me back. We will have dinner on Sunday"—and he had no desire to begin to think about a response.

As expected, Jessop was dark and quiet, and the reading room was blissfully empty. With Eliot's luck, he figured he'd accidentally arrive when there was an event keeping the library open late, or even worse, right as Tess was leaving.

Eliot stalked across the library, not realizing until he was halfway up the stairs that he was tracking footprints behind him.

He stopped, noticing the trail of dark liquid on the tiled floor. It started from the circulation desk, from what he could tell. There was a laptop left behind on the desk and a bag in the shadows underneath it.

Eliot crouched down, closer to the trail up the steps, and dipped his fingers in the liquid. When he brought his hand closer to his face, he smelled the bite of copper. Blood.

Blood from the circulation desk, disappearing up the stairs. Eliot's heart clenched with fear.

Tess.

He raced up the stairs. The blood didn't stop at the second-floor landing. Eliot had a horrifying suspicion as he continued up another floor.

On the third floor, the trail continued down the walkway and then curved into a door. *His* door.

The keys to his office were heavy in his hand. He didn't know what he would find on the other side of that door—God, he didn't even want to look—but it was not going to be good. And worst of all, there was a chance it was—

No. He could not allow himself to think Tess was there.

He had his phone with him. He could call the police, tell them he'd found blood in the library, that he needed help. But there were his bloody footprints all through the library. Eliot was alone. If there was something heinous on the other side of that door, he did not know how to answer any questions for why he was here, and more specifically, why he was here by himself.

Eliot did not have an alibi.

He could not call for help. He had to know what was on the other side of the door. Because if it was it was something explicable, like a wounded animal or some odd side effect of a spell he'd miscast, then he could use a spell to clean up the blood and act like nothing had happened.

And if it wasn't...

All he could hear was Tess's voice in the back of his head: *Have you had any strange experiences since we took the book back?*

Eliot crept forward. The key was warm from being pressed into his palm, and he was sure when he opened his hand, there would be a reddened indent in its shape.

Three steps away. If Tess was in there, he didn't know what he'd do.

One step away. He didn't know who he was amidst the cloud of fear within him.

He unlocked the door. This old building creaked incessantly, and his door was no exception. The sound was like a scream in the silence of the library.

At first, as his eyes were adjusting, he thought it was fine. The trail ended near his carpet, but then shapes began to form. His desk. The hump of his chair. A stack of books, dangerously close to the edge of his desk.

And there, a black shape in the middle of the burgundy rug.

A body.

thirty one

Tess

IT WAS NEARLY 9:00 WHEN TESS'S PHONE STARTED RINGING. She was greeting a table but she could feel it there, buzzing in the leftmost pocket of her apron, whirring against her thigh.

The call was from an unknown number. Tess ignored it and switched her phone to Do Not Disturb.

At 9:30 she checked her phone again. She had thirteen missed calls now, all from the same unknown number.

"Hey, Lou?" Tess said, catching her manager's arm. "Mind if I step outside for a minute?"

"Sure," Lou said.

Tess went out back and moved a few feet away from the two kitchen guys who were sitting on crates, smoking cigarettes. She hadn't even fully unlocked her phone when the call screen came up. The same number again. A Pittsburgh number, judging by the area code.

"Hello?"

"Tess, thank God." To her surprise, it was Eliot's voice on the other side. At least, she thought it was. His words were shaky, uncertain, breathy.

"Eliot? What's going on?" And then, because it just occurred to her: "How did you get my number?"

"It's in a binder. On the front desk. Tess, I need your help."

THE DEVIL MAKES THREE

"Why are you at the library?" She checked her watch. Obviously, Jessop was closed, and it had been for hours. But then again, Jessop's hours of operation had never mattered to Eliot before.

"I needed—oh, that's not the point. What are you doing?"

"I'm at work," she said.

"Can you get away?"

Tess frowned. No, not really. But deep down, she knew Eliot wouldn't be asking her, wouldn't even be calling, if it wasn't an emergency.

"I can try." Tess bit her lip.

"Please." Eliot's voice was shattered glass and exhaustion and fear.

After their tense discussion the other day, Tess was certain he wouldn't call her—wouldn't even speak to her, probably—unless there was an actual emergency. She'd find a way to get out of work. "I'll be there as soon as I can."

Even though, just days ago, he'd been asking for space.

Why am I doing this? But there was the sound of Eliot's voice, terrified on the other side of the line. Tess sighed.

It took a faked family emergency in an only half-faked shaky voice, but Tess managed to escape work and made her way to Jessop as dark deepened the shadows of the city.

The lights were off in the unshuttered upper library windows when Tess finally reached the building. She would've missed Eliot, sitting there on one of the benches in the lobby if he hadn't quietly said her name.

He was silhouetted in a thin pane of moonlight. His hands were splattered with something dark, and for one weary moment, she wondered if they were stained with ink.

"Didn't you have anyone else you could call?" Tess asked.

He looked up, clearly caught off guard. "No," he said. "No, I... Who would I call?"

Tess bit her lip. If she even began to answer that question, he'd know how closely she paid attention to him. "What's going on?" she asked instead. There was something so lost, so forlorn about him. She lowered herself to a crouch in front of him and laid a hand on his knee.

"There's a body in my office."

She couldn't have heard him right. Tess stared at his face for a long moment, waiting for the catch, waiting for the joke. It didn't come. "Excuse me?"

"A dead body. I went in to get some papers and there is blood everywhere and a dead body in my office."

Tess blinked at him. Surely, he was lying. Surely, this was some kind of prank. But if it was, Eliot was far crueler than she could've imagined.

"Show me."

When he looked up, his face was pale and his eyes were red. "Tess, I don't want to go back in there."

"Then why did you call?" Tess snapped. And then, realizing the full gravity of the situation: "Did you call the police?"

"No."

"What the hell, Eliot?"

He closed his eyes again, pressing his palms against them, like he could push away whatever he'd seen if he only tried hard enough. Only then did she realize the dark smudges on his hands were blood.

"What was I supposed to do? I was alone in there, with no way to prove I had nothing to do with it. How would that look? I don't... I don't..." His voice was lost in a choked gasp.

"Okay, okay. Let's go look. We'll figure out what to do from there." She wasn't sure why she needed to see it so badly, but it was almost like if she saw it, she could sort through some sort of plan. Or know he was telling the truth.

Eliot nodded. He stood shakily and led the way towards Jessop.

"You should use your code again," Tess said, and she felt a flare of guilt for it. But if they did file a police report, it would show that Dr. Birch's code had been used to access the library both times.

Either he didn't think of the same thing, or he already knew he was complicit. Without protest, Eliot keyed into the library and opened the door.

Tess could smell the blood.

She switched on the light after Eliot shut the door behind them. The fluorescents buzzed to life, bringing the dark blood into rusty red color. And the look on Eliot's face did not lie: there was a nauseating amount of blood.

"Okay," Tess said. She was a naturally calm person, and this looked like the type of situation that would require her to keep her wits about her. She thought of her mother cleaning up dead birds from the yard after a rainstorm when Tess was eight. She could be that calm, that detached, even though they were talking about a human body now. "So this looks pretty bad."

Eliot didn't answer. He started towards the third floor, and only then did Tess notice the footprints. "Hey. Eliot, watch where you're walking. I think these belong to…" She trailed off. Whoever had done the crime? The victim?

"No," Eliot said miserably. "They're mine." He lifted up one foot, revealing the faded red tracks on the bottom of his shoe. "I didn't realize I walked through it."

Tess sucked in a breath. The evidence against Eliot was piling up by the second. He must've realized how bad things were looking for him, because he stopped his ascent and anxiously rubbed his face. The only thing he succeeded in doing was streaking half-dried blood over his cheeks.

If this was a situation that required the police—and she was thinking that it would be—then Tess made a mental note to have Eliot wash the blood from his face before they arrived.

"Okay." She couldn't spend any more time dwelling on this, or else she would lose the calm she was trying so hard to maintain. "Show me the body."

thirty two

Eliot

ELIOT HAD NEVER BEEN SO CERTAIN THAT HE WAS HAVING A heart attack. His heart was thudding so desperately that he was sure it would burst out of his chest and beat away through one of the library windows. And then there were the pauses between, the moments of silence, when his panic was so thick he thought he would choke on it.

Every step drew him closer. Every heartbeat, every move, every furtive glance from Tess.

If he opened that door again…

No. He could get through this, these horrible seconds, and up to his office. He would open the door and Tess would know what to do and who to call and *this would end*. He was Eliot Birch, shy and quiet, friend of books everywhere. He was not a murderer, even though there was a body in his office, and of course the authorities would know that. Of course.

Except, they would see the books in his office: human sacrifice and demonic rituals. They would see endless papers on reanimation, on healing, on death. And maybe, they would see Tess as more of a cover than anything else.

They reached the top of the stairs. The smears of blood were drying and cracking now. He could hear Tess's breathing behind him, quiet and even, and it was the only reason he kept going. Around the corner, up another flight of stairs. Every step was another skipped heartbeat, and he wished that he could reach back and take Tess's hand, because he didn't know how he could drag his leaden feet any further.

His office door loomed before him. When he closed his eyes he could see the body, just as clearly as when he'd flicked on the lights and realized what he was looking at. The girl was there on the middle of his rug, crumpled on her side. Her arms were outstretched in front of her, and her eyes were wide open. The blood came from her wrists and throat, brutally torn open.

The door was in front of him.

He could not open it.

He couldn't reach his hands to twist the knob.

Tess said, "Eliot."

He could not open it.

Tess's fingers were warm when she threaded them through his. With her other hand, she reached forward and twisted the knob. The door creaked open.

Eliot closed his eyes. He did not want to see.

Beside him, Tess's breathing was still measured and even. Her hand remained firm. There was no hitch when she saw the body, and she didn't pull him closer into the office. He could not look.

But Tess could. Because she was infallible, because she was fearless. Eliot felt like he was going to vomit.

"So, uh, is it behind your desk or something?"

"What?"

"The body," Tess said, and her voice was too calm, too steady for the ruin of the girl in his office.

"No," he said. He had to look, but to look would be to instantly get sick. "It's right in the middle…"

"It's, uh. Eliot."

Eliot opened his eyes. The door to his office was open, and Tess must've flicked on the light. The burgundy carpet was stained dark with blood, and he could make out three points where it was completely soaked. But that was all. The books were still stacked haphazardly on his desk. His chair was pulled out and angled, and there was a sweater draped over the back from last week.

There was no body.

"Fuck," Eliot whispered. And then, because once wasn't enough to encompass it all: "Bloody fucking hell." His hand went limp in Tess's.

The calm was stripped away from Tess's voice. "You said there was a body. There isn't a body. What's happening?"

He'd been holding his breath. The edges of his vision started to shimmer a little, and he knew he had to take a breath to keep standing, to stay aware in this reality where there was no body.

"There was a body, Tess. Right there. You see the shape of her on the carpet, don't you?"

Tess released his hand and moved farther into the room. Eliot didn't want her to go in, but it wasn't like he could keep her. She already thought he was lying as it was. There was a reddish stain on her gray, long-sleeved Emiliano's T-shirt, and he focused on it as she knelt down and examined the bloodstain.

"Did you take a picture?" Tess asked.

"Why the *fuck* would I do that?"

She glared at him, and he tried to regain his composure. "I'm sorry. No, I didn't." He ran a hand through his hair and took another breath. "She was here. And it wasn't just any girl.

It was the one you work with."

Tess's head snapped up. "It was Regina?" Her voice had an edge of panic to it.

Regina. He'd been avoiding thinking her name, as if doing so would lessen the gore of her corpse. When Tess said it, a new wave of nausea rolled through his stomach and he fought desperately to keep his composure.

"Yes." He had to convince Tess he was telling the truth. The fact that she'd left work for him, that she'd come all this way just to find the body missing, felt like a cruel prank. "Her laptop. She left her laptop and backpack here. It's on the desk."

Tess got up and pushed past him. He watched through the door as she leaned over the bannister, looking down at the circulation desk. He already knew that Regina's laptop, still half-closed, was there.

Tess didn't move. She just kept staring at the laptop, at the trail of blood.

"What do we do?" Eliot asked.

She didn't speak for a long time. The buzzing in Eliot's ears calmed down a little, but he still wasn't sure about his heartbeat tripping along. Tess turned back to him, and her face was twisted with confusion. She went back into the office.

Eliot couldn't quite move yet, so he just watched her. She ran her fingers along the edge of the books and examined them, as if searching for dust—or blood. And then she turned and examined the splotches on the floor. With her face twisted as it was, she looked like she was trying to will the body into existence or coax answers out of the yarn of the carpet.

Then, to his surprise, she crouched down again and pressed her fingers directly into the wettest spot.

Eliot's face instinctively wrinkled in disgust. Excess liquid oozed from the carpet, pooling around Tess's fingertips, staining them dark red. She lifted her fingers to her nose and smelled them, as if to confirm that it was, in fact, blood.

Her eyes flicked to his, dark and confused, but not surprised.

"Eliot," she said carefully. "This is ink."

And then, terribly, awfully, it was gone. The ink on Tess's fingers dried and flaked away to dust. Eliot ran out of the office and to the stairs. There, all those bloody footprints, all those pools of inky blood, vanished.

A low, eerie wind swept through Jessop, leaving nothing behind.

thirty three

Tess

THEY WERE THE ONLY PEOPLE AT THE COFFEE SHOP. SITTING across the table from her, Eliot looked irreparably shaken. He'd bought an English Breakfast tea for himself, chai for her, and croissants for both of them, which sat untouched on the middle of the table.

She glanced at her phone, faceup on the table. For her own sanity, she'd tried to call Regina dozens of times. Every call went straight to voicemail.

Something had gone terribly, absolutely wrong, but to fully process it was to be terrified, and to be terrified was to be defenseless. Tess could not let terror distract her; she could not let her guard down.

"Tell me what happened," Tess said. Again she found herself looking at Eliot, studying him—always, always looking too much at Eliot. She tried to look at the wall, at her phone, at anything else.

Eliot sighed. "I went to the library to get something from my office—"

"You know, if you get caught using that code, you could get in serious trouble," Tess pointed out, because the day was already long enough and she had to work in the morning and exhaustion weighed heavy in her veins.

"I know," Eliot snapped. He took a moment to collect himself, and softer, said, "I'm sorry." Tess didn't apologize back, even though he left her a pause to before continuing, "Anyway. I needed something from my office. So I went in and the blood was there—I'm telling you, it was blood—and I went upstairs. The trail led right to my office door. I opened it and she was there, in the middle of the rug."

"Not cut or anything? Not bleeding?"

Eliot winced. "She wasn't hacked to pieces, if that's what you mean. She had... I can't say that they were stab wounds. They were like... I don't know. Like something had torn her open."

Tess shuddered. "Like an animal? Like, her abdomen was ripped open?"

"No. Wrists. And throat. Not like it was neatly slit or anything. She looked like it had been *torn* open. The edges were all rough and—" He couldn't finish. He gagged once, pressed his hand against his mouth, and closed his eyes. Eliot was silent for a long time while he regained control over his stomach. Tess waited, feeling a little bad for asking for details—but she still wasn't sure she could believe him.

Except.

Her fingers found the edge of the gauze wrapping, still there around her wrist, where Anna had secured it that morning. She figured she'd be able to stop wrapping it next week, maybe, when the wound wasn't quite so vicious.

As she toyed with the tape on the gauze, something dawned on her. The explanation of Regina that Eliot had offered was familiar to her: blood everywhere, wrists and throat cut. It was the same image she'd seen of herself in the dreams.

"Almost like she'd cut them herself," Tess said quietly.

Eliot looked at her. "I don't know how she'd be able to. But yes, maybe."

Tess closed her eyes. This was too much, especially for a night like tonight, when she'd already been awake for her fill of hours for the day. "So her body was there, in your office, bleeding out, and now it isn't."

"It seems that way."

"And she was definitely dead. She didn't just walk out herself."

"No. I would say she was, at the very least, 100 percent dead."

"Do you think… Do you think the book has anything to do with it?"

Eliot frowned. "I came to that conclusion too. All of this that's been happening—not to me, but it seems that things are happening to you—it all feels too coincidental, lined up as it is."

Tess nodded. "Should we get the book back out?" she asked, even though the thought of going back into that hellhole underneath Jessop made her hands go clammy and her mouth dry as a bone.

"No," Eliot said quickly, and it was clear that he had the same reaction. His left fist clenched, and he took a short sip of his tea before continuing. "I don't think… The book has what it wants. It has blood. Nothing more will come of this."

But Tess could remember the curl of the devil's lip and the icy coldness of his breath. She didn't think this would be the last of it, not by far.

Don't betray me again, Theresa.

But somehow, she had.

thirty four

Tess

TESS AWOKE THURSDAY MORNING ON HER MATTRESS, dragged onto Anna's floor, to the lingering smell of some sort of pastry, bastardized by the Crock-Pot. Anna's bed was empty.

She hadn't dreamt since the night of her injury, whether it was because she'd ordered the devil away or started sleeping in Anna's room. Either way, she was happy about that, but there wasn't much else to be glad about.

Anna was humming to herself in the kitchenette. She turned when Tess came in and handed her a bowl of warmed-up cinnamon roll. "Your phone rang a few times this morning," Anna said, adjusting the towel on her head. Her mouth was arranged in a straight, concerned line. "Everything okay?"

"It should be," Tess said, even though it was anything but okay. She grabbed her phone and was unsurprised to see the contact ID: *eliot bitch*. "Just a sec."

Tess ducked into her mostly abandoned room to call him back. Despite the awkwardness still remaining between them, if he was calling her, it was probably for a reason.

"Hello?" he said.

She was ashamed of the relief that rushed through her at the sound of his voice. "You okay? You called me."

"Yeah. Are you?"

A weighted, flawed question, but one she deserved considering she asked first. Maybe technically she was okay. Maybe, but probably not. "I'm fine."

There was a brief silence on the other line. Tess figured Eliot was thinking the same thing she was: How could either of them be okay?

"Are you on the early shift today or..." He left the question open ended, most likely because the question ended *or is it Regina?*

"I am," Tess confirmed.

"Right. Well, I remembered you sometimes got there before Mathilde, and considering everything, I figured you wouldn't want to go in by yourself. Or, at least, it would be nice not to. Could I... I could walk you there?"

He was rambling in a way he usually didn't, reminding her of tense shoulders and too-bright headlights and the heat of her own shame.

But why did this have to be shameful? The truth was she didn't want to go in alone. She could hide her fear, yes, but she wouldn't be alone in the library anyways—something dark would be lurking there along with her.

Maybe it was weak, but having Eliot there would make her feel better.

"That would be nice," she managed. A glance at the clock; she was still early, but not by much. "Can you be here in ten?"

<hr />

Eliot had never looked so casual as when he showed up on Tess's doorstep. He had on a white T-shirt and jeans, with none of his usual charm. There was a colorful design on his right arm, edging under his sleeve, and it took Tess a moment to realize it was a tattoo.

The revelation that Eliot had a tattoo was shocking. She couldn't imagine him putting something so permanent on his body. She tried to conjure up an image of Eliot in a chair, arm extended as someone tattooed him. Maybe there was a story behind the ink, and he'd told it while wiping away tears. Maybe it was at a hole-in-the-wall shop in London, clogged with cigarette smoke and smelling of beer and rain. She couldn't even really make out what the tattoo was, with most of it hidden under his sleeve and his arms crossed over his chest, and there was no way she was going to ask about it now.

"Hey," he said.

"Hey."

What else was there to say? She should've told him about the dreams, about the devil and his promises, but in this moment, seeing him in the sunlight with his hair tousled and his eyes soft with worry, she didn't want to think of any of that.

"You can come in. I just need to finish a couple of things. Mine's at the top."

He followed her up the three flights to the dorm she shared with Anna. Anna had just left for her own work study job for the day, so they were alone. Being here with him, in her territory, made her feel nervous and uncertain. Did he notice how sparse their dorm was, filled only with the necessities Falk had provided? The dorm didn't feel like her, besides her room, so that was where she took him, even though her mattress was missing and things were a little messy. It was better than the bare bones of the shared spaces, the spaces that had no trace that she'd ever existed there.

Eliot took a seat in her desk chair and Tess sat on her steamer trunk to finish packing her bag. She tried to put space between her and Eliot, but in her room, everything was cramped and close.

Eliot reached forward and Tess thought he was going to touch her until his hand met the smooth, black case of her cello. "Ah," he said, running a hand reverently down the case. "You play, right? Re— I heard you were good."

Something about the statement was shocking, and Tess allowed it to distract her. All her life, she'd been known as Tess the musician. It was so much of her identity that she didn't know who she was without a bow in her hand and the weight of her cello between her legs. But here was Eliot, someone who she suspected knew the darkest parts of her, and he hadn't known the first rule of Tess Matheson: music above all else. She felt like she'd been plunged in cold water.

What definable things did she not know about him? And why, suddenly, did she want to know all of them?

He's the enemy, Tess reminded herself. *He's the one who started this.*

"I've been playing since I was little," Tess said, even though it felt like a simplification. She didn't just *play.* "I actually have a lesson later tomorrow and I haven't practiced in a few days, which is just awesome." She tried to smile, to show she was joking, but the whole thing felt fake.

"You can play now," Eliot said. "I won't mind. I'd like to hear you."

She'd played for hundreds of people. Thousands, maybe, though not all at the same time, of course. And yet, the idea of playing in front of Eliot Birch, alone in her room, felt like it would be the same as showing him the gashes on her wrist, the same as telling him the truth about her parents and her situation.

And worse—she hadn't touched her cello since the dreams. She didn't know how to take it, to play and know that it could never feel like it had when she'd played with the devil's hands on her shoulders.

"We don't have time," Tess said, getting up and swinging her bag over her shoulder. "Don't want to be late, do we?"

For once, he didn't argue.

They walked to Jessop in silence. "I'm just going to grab a few things," Eliot said, cautiously eying the upper balconies, "and then I'll be right back. Shout if you need me."

She wouldn't.

It was kind of cute, Tess thought. How he was suddenly pretending to be brave in front of her.

There was a new delivery of magazines, so Tess started shelving them. She was still sorting them alphabetically when she heard the back door open and the clicking of keys as Mathilde came through the office.

"You're early," Mathilde said.

Tess glanced at the clock. "Only a few minutes," she said. "I had nothing better to do." It wasn't quite true. She could've played for Eliot, if she'd really wanted to.

"Did someone come in with you? I thought I heard a voice."

Tess waved towards the third floor. "Dr. Birch's son came in to do some work or something. He's in his office."

"Ah." Mathilde leaned against the cart that Tess was trying to organize. "I hope he hasn't found what he's looking for."

"What do you think he's looking for?" Tess asked, fighting to keep her voice steady.

Mathilde's eyes clouded over, and Tess had a sudden prickle

in her spine. "Something he shouldn't be," she said. There was something going on here, and Mathilde definitely knew more than she was letting on. Was Tess caught?

"If he has any other book requests, I'll handle them. There are dangerous books here, Theresa." She sighed, and for a moment, she seemed to be as tired as Tess felt.

"Of course," Tess said. She couldn't think of anything else to say, anything that could illuminate more clues without condemning her for what she and Eliot had found.

But worse, eventually Tess would have to say something about Regina. If what Eliot saw was real, then Regina was not going to come for her shift and then it would be undeniable. They'd need help.

Tess eyed Mathilde. Perhaps…

Upstairs, Eliot's office door opened. Almost simultaneously, someone entered the library behind her. Tess turned to see who it was—a teacher, probably, or an old man asking to use the bathroom—but she nearly lost the cinnamon roll she'd eaten for breakfast when she saw Regina standing near the heavy wooden door of the library. Regina, looking exactly as she had the day before.

Except.

Except she had a very, very thin red line on her throat. Tess had to squint to see it. If she hadn't been examining her so closely, she was sure that she wouldn't have seen it. And there, as Tess focused, she noted her irises. Not brown, as they had been before. But black, shimmering and dotted, as if her irises contained the universe. Somewhere a few floors up, she could feel Eliot's eyes on Regina, too, and imagined him frozen on the stairs just as she was behind the circulation desk.

Mathilde was the only one who wasn't shocked to see the

newest arrival. "Regina," she said. "You're early too. Aren't you meant to come in at noon?"

"I forgot something last night and it couldn't wait," Regina said. Her voice was off, just a little. Again, it was so subtle Tess wouldn't have noticed if she hadn't already been on edge. There was a rasp to her tone now, as if she was getting sick—or as if she'd been screaming.

"Well, if you're here, feel free to help Theresa with the shelving," Mathilde said. She started towards the back office.

Tess couldn't move. She needed to say something, do something, but she could only stare. Finally, she managed, "You left your laptop here." It sounded like an accusation. She wanted to say, *You disappeared. You didn't answer your phone. You were missing. Eliot saw your body.*

"I was in a hurry," Regina said. She didn't move farther into the library or towards the desk. Regina didn't say anything about what Eliot had seen.

Tess should've made an excuse to get away and get to Eliot, but she still felt frozen. And judging by the silence from the stairs, Eliot hadn't moved, either.

"Is everything okay?" Tess asked, struggling to keep her voice even.

"Oh," Regina said, moving closer to her. Fear prickled down Tess's spine and she edged back. "Everything is just wonderful." Her lips quirked up in slow motion, like a demon mimicking human expression, but her eyes didn't change. Slowly, slowly, her lips parted to reveal her teeth.

When Regina smiled, her mouth was full of blood.

thirty five

Eliot

"I'm telling you," she grumbled. "I'm telling you her mouth was bloody."

Tess and Eliot were in the courtyard. It was more comfortable out here, safer even. They sat cross-legged, facing each other. Tess pulled out fistfuls of grass and rained the pieces down on her legs.

"I'm not disagreeing with you," Eliot said. He was tired if he was anything. "I think you did see blood. But I also agree with your assessment the other night. All of this has to be a hallucination."

She pulled up another fistful of grass. "I don't see why we would be hallucinating, though. You and I both... We both saw the blood in your office. We can't deny it, Eliot. This is happening."

Eliot shrugged. Uncomfortably, he thought of what he'd first told Tess he was studying: death and resurrection and magic. Did she think he'd caused this? At the beginning of the summer, he'd thought that there was some tidy solution to death. Now, he worried he'd found it, and it terrified him. "I don't know what we did wrong."

Tess closed her eyes. "I have to tell you something."

She looked so worn, sitting there, covered in grass. So hopeless. Something tugged inside of Eliot, and he hated it. Tess glanced down at her fingernails, stained with chlorophyll and dirt. "I've been having dreams. I think they're about the devil, but he calls himself Truth."

Eliot didn't say anything for a long time. And then, finally, shakily: "Can you tell me about these dreams?"

Tess nodded. Her eyes were distant, as tired as he felt. "They started really soon after we found the book. I don't remember exactly what he asked me, but I remember he talked to me in a forest. And when I woke up, I was stained with ink."

"And you only spoke to him once?"

Tess colored. "No," she said. He felt something stirring inside of him, something like hatred—or even worse, even more inexplicable, something like jealousy. "I dreamt of him a few more times. He wanted to give me... It doesn't matter. He wanted me to be happy, I think. Or successful. In order to make a trade. And the devil... I don't know how to explain it, Eliot."

Eliot shivered. There was something she wasn't telling him. He could see it in her eyes, in the set of her shoulders, in the shakiness of her chin. He reached forward and set a hand on her knee. "You can trust me."

Cautiously, Tess rolled up her sleeve. "In the dreams, I think he had some control over my body. And he gave me a knife. I don't know if it was real or what, but...I cut myself. I woke up covered in blood."

"Covered in blood?" Eliot repeated. He couldn't think of it. And even more, he couldn't look at her, because if she caught him looking, she'd see the emotion on his face and know the truth of what the thought of her in danger did to him. "Couldn't it have been ink? Like what we found the other day?"

He was uncertain for the approximate three seconds it took Tess to finish rolling her sleeve, flip her wrist over, and remove the patch of gauze she wore. The edges of the cut were a little purple from bruising, and she really should've gone to get stitches, but it was healing okay enough.

He couldn't bear it.

"Tess…" Eliot looked away quickly. If she saw his face, she'd know. If she saw the horror in his eyes, he'd be revealed. "Did you do that?"

"I don't know," Tess said, and the thought of someone else in her room with her while she was sleeping, harming her, was equally horrifying. "I told you. I just woke up like that."

Eliot rubbed his eyes, as if he could buff away the worry he couldn't show. "Okay. So something is happening here. And I don't think we can just act like it's going to go away."

"What do we do?"

"I don't know. But Tess, if anything tries to hurt you again… please call me. Tell me. Or someone else. As long as you're not by yourself." She was blushing, looking off to the right. Strong and stubborn as always. The edge of a blade—a blade growing less sharp by the second. He laid a hand over her wrist, both hiding the gash and protecting it, and she looked up to meet his eye. "Don't try to do this alone."

And he wasn't even sure how he could say such a thing, because he'd done everything else in his life before this alone, and judging by the look on her face, Tess had too. He didn't know how to give his fear, his anxiety, his worry to another person, but maybe he could take some of hers.

"Okay," Tess said.

It was getting late in the afternoon, and Eliot glanced at his watch. He wanted her to ask him to stay, even though they both knew she wouldn't.

"Class?" she asked.

"Unfortunately," Eliot said, standing.

Ask me to stay. Ask me to skip. I'll do it. We can sit in this courtyard for the rest of the day, the rest of the night, forever.

He had the terrible urge to tell her about his magic. He'd never considered telling anyone before; after all, that was the root of the destruction of his parents' marriage. Before the affairs, before the illnesses, the truth was unavoidable: Caroline Birch had magic, and her husband could not understand.

"I'll walk with you," Tess said quickly, surprising him. She pulled her sleeve down to cover her wrist and brushed the grass off her legs. Eliot reached a hand down and tugged her up.

She was quiet as they crossed the park towards Forbes Avenue. He felt the compulsion to make small talk, but what was the point of that?

"We should do some research," he said instead. "To figure out what the devil is. Or demon. There has to be something, in folklore or religious texts or—"

Tess snorted. "We'll probably find some bullshit about witches or something. Nothing useful."

Eliot winced. "Tess, we accidentally summoned some demon by reading a book," he said mildly. "It tried to kill you. Perhaps multiple times. You can't tell me you don't believe in that sort of stuff anymore. You're living it."

It was the closest he could come to a confession. *I'm a witch,* he wanted to say. *I could heal you, if you'd let me.*

But she just sighed. "Okay. Research. Do you think there would be anything in those books you requested?"

Eliot considered it. There was some folklore there, a bit about demonic traditions, but it hadn't been the intent of his borrowing spree to get books about the devil. "We could check," he said anyway. "Maybe there's something. A spell, or..."

Tess nodded. "We can give them a look. Until then, call me if anything gets spooky, okay?"

Eliot nodded. They reached his building and Tess looked away, over at the flagpole decorated with people walking to the sky. It was an art installation Eliot had never fully understood. It didn't help that somebody was always stealing the figures.

"I'll see you later?" Eliot asked, readjusting the strap of his bag.

"You bet," Tess said. He wanted to take her hand or push the stray hair away from her face, but he could not. He settled for a half smile instead and watched her walk away.

thirty six

Tess

MATHILDE AGREED TO WRITE A NOTE TO GET NAT OUT OF
the dorms for dinner Friday, after Tess's lesson. Earlier, after
failed attempts and making a huge mess, Tess had realized that
it was practically impossible to make a crepe in the microwave.
Instead, she settled for store-bought crepes, spread them with
Nutella, and decorated them with carefully cut strawberries.
She was just scattering powdered sugar on top when Nat
texted her to say she was there.

Tess scrambled down to let her in. It was drizzling, and
Nat's shoulders were spotted with rain. "I hate walking in
this," she complained as she trudged up the stairs behind Tess.

"I thought Mathilde was driving you down?"

"She drove me to the corner and dropped me off," Nat
said. As soon as she was through the door, she wrung out her
hair—an overreaction, Tess thought, hiding a smile. Though
Tess loved her, Nat was something of a drama queen.

"I pulled off crepes," Tess said, grabbing the plates and
bringing them over to the couch.

Nat smiled. "Not really crepe night quality, but they'll do."
Tess shoved Nat's arm with her elbow. She fell giggling to
the couch.

This felt…maybe not normal, but like something that *could*

be normal. The two of them again, just hanging out.

Tess grabbed her laptop while Nat started on her crepe. She wished they could afford Netflix, but it wasn't a necessary expense and she didn't know anyone else who had an account they could mooch off of.

Instead, she turned on a YouTube ballet series they both liked. Neither of them danced, but there was something about the drama of it that made it addictive.

Tess settled back with Nat on the couch. For once, there was quiet in her head. She didn't have to think about the devil, or Eliot, or work. Some vague part of her knew she could share her troubles with Nat, but that wasn't her place, really. Tess was the one who shouldered everything, who listened to Nat's problems.

She wouldn't make it a two-way street.

Nat watched one of the dancers spin. A bit of Nutella was smeared on her chin. "If you could do anything, what would it be?"

"Like a superpower?"

"Nah, like a talent. And don't say cello. You already do that."

Tess snorted. "Um. Probably something practical. Like accounting or coding." If she was good at that, then she could get a well-paying job or freelance to keep herself afloat while navigating the professional musician situation.

"You're so boring," Nat groaned.

Tess elbowed her again. "Why is it boring to be practical? What would you do?"

Nat put her empty plate on the ground and flopped back on the couch. "I don't know. Maybe I'd be a good painter." Tess didn't think too deeply into that, because to think of painting would be to think of the empty studio, and she was not going to let the devil ruin this moment of peace.

"You could be good at painting," Tess said. She fought the urge to ruffle Nat's hair. "If you practiced."

"Practicing is boring. I just want to be good."

Tess rolled her eyes. "The world doesn't work like that."

Or does it? There was the ebony cello in her hands, the crowds in front of her. There was the devil and his bargain.

Tess squeezed her eyes shut. No. The devil had killed Regina—any bargain he offered, even if it allowed her to succeed, was just a preamble to death.

She needed to talk about something else. "What do they have planned for you this weekend? Is there still that soccer tournament?"

"That finished last week," Nat said. She wiped her hands on her jean shorts and pulled out her phone. "The arts festival is downtown this weekend."

"Are they taking you?"

Nat smirked. "Sort of."

Tess didn't like the sound of that. "What do you mean, 'sort of'?"

Nat's grin widened. "Pinky promise you won't tell anyone?" She held her hand out to Tess, pinky extended. Tess hated agreeing to something before she knew exactly what she was agreeing to, but she wasn't going to figure out what Nat was up to unless she did. Begrudgingly, she linked her pinky with Nat's.

"Okay, so. They're taking us to the Warhol and the Point in small groups, then four of us are signed out to go meet Nya's mom and we'll be dropped back at campus before 11:00."

"Okay…so you're hanging out with Nya and her mom?"

Nat's eyes shone with glee. "No, of course not. Nya's mom

lives in Toronto. But her older sister lives in the city and got us all signed out! So we get a full day of freedom downtown."

Tess stared at her. She didn't like this, not only because it was a horrible idea and *ridiculous*, but because it broke at least six rules. "Nat. Dude. You're thirteen."

Her smile faltered. "So?"

Tess threw a pillow at her. "*Natalie*. You can*not* go roaming around a strange city by yourself. Do you even know how to get back?"

"I won't be by myself. I'll be with Nya and Alexa and Haylee."

"Who are also thirteen," Tess muttered.

"And we'll take the bus back," Nat finished. "Also, Haylee and Alexa are fourteen. So."

Tess's head fell back against the back cushion. "Whatever. You should absolutely not be going around by yourself. This isn't the mall in fucking Lancaster. This is a city with like drunk people and creepy men and predators, and you don't know your way around. What bus do you take back? Do you even know that?"

"Google maps is a thing."

She needed a moment so she didn't say anything awful, so she didn't snap. Tess grabbed the plates and took them to the sink.

It didn't *matter* that someone had signed them out or that they were going in a group. Besides the danger level of what Nat was doing—and Tess was pretty sure she wasn't just being overprotective; Nat was a young thirteen and Tess was just looking out for her—there were other factors to worry about.

Nat looked sullen when Tess came back in and down beside her. "What if Falk finds out?"

Nat rolled her eyes. "They won't."

"But what if they do? You don't know they won't." Tess tucked a knee to her chest and locked her hands around it. "If someone says something or if one of the other girls on the floor finds out. If someone posts on social media. Do you know what happens if Falk finds out you all snuck out?"

Nat didn't answer. Tess recognized her own stubbornness on her sister's face: the line of the mouth, the set of the chin, the look in her eyes.

"You'll get kicked out of Falk," Tess finished, since clearly Nat wasn't going to answer. She struggled to keep her voice level. "No scholarship. You'll go back home. None of this will matter." Control. Tess had to remain in control of herself, of this. "Is that what you want?"

Again, silence. Nat pulled at the frayed edge of her shorts, breaking off blue-white threads of denim.

"Is it?"

"You do what you want, all the time. And they haven't kicked *you* out."

Tess rolled her eyes. "I submit my work schedule to the dorm sisters every month. They know when I'm coming and going, and I'm here before curfew when I'm not working. Besides, I'm not thirteen."

"You're not an adult, either."

"Maybe not, but at least I can take care of myself."

Nat got up without a word and started for the door. Tess scrambled after her. She couldn't risk this. If Nat got caught and got herself thrown out of Falk, there was nothing more Mathilde could do, and it wasn't like Tess had a reason to be here without her, and she couldn't just go back with their parents.

She couldn't. And she wouldn't watch Nat risk everything. "I'll tell Mathilde."

Nat stopped, one hand on the door. "You wouldn't."

Would she? Maybe. It was a violation of Nat's trust, but this was a situation Tess couldn't afford. Maybe they wouldn't kick her out, but…

"If you don't promise me you'll come back with your group tomorrow and you won't violate rules, I will tell Mathilde."

Nat glared at her. Her eyes welled with tears, because Nat's emotions were hardwired to her tear ducts and Tess knew she hated it.

"You're not my parent," Nat seethed.

No, she wasn't. But at the same time, she had to be. Tess crossed her arms over her chest. "I'm sorry," she said. "But you know I can't let you do this. Promise me."

Her eyes were awful, burning things. "Fine. I promise."

Tess nodded. The fight drained out of her. She just felt empty. This wasn't a battle she was supposed to be having, not one she'd prepared for. She wanted someone else to tell her what to do, what to say.

"I hate you," Nat said simply. She'd said it before, yelled it during fights over trivial things like hoodies and favorite blankets, but she'd never spoken it like this. Level. Honest.

As if it was true.

Tess couldn't stop her as Nat left, slamming the door behind her. She groaned, rubbing her eyes. Nat wouldn't go through with it, but it sucked all the same. Tess sat on the couch a few minutes longer, thumb on her left hand rubbing a callus on her right.

It wasn't fair. She hated making choices Nat didn't like, even if it was better for both of them. But if her parents wouldn't take care of Nat, then it fell to Tess, and she was not going to sacrifice her sister's future for anything. Not even for her love.

thirty seven

Eliot

AFTER ELIOT LEFT THE LIBRARY ON FRIDAY AFTERNOON, HE went to his usual spot where he met Brooks, the security guard who ensured Eliot could get where he wanted. It was on Pitt's campus, on one of the benches in the shadows of the trees that lined the walk between the Cathedral and the chapel.

He stopped at a food stand to grab two orders of dumplings, General Tso's chicken, and an order of fried rice.

Brooks was waiting, as he always was, with a Diet Coke and two sticks of string cheese. He handed one to Eliot.

"Weather's nice," Brooks said.

Well, this was a topic Eliot excelled at. He could talk about the weather endlessly. "It is. Looks like we're due for a warm weekend."

"Good time for a barbecue," Brooks remarked. He took the General Tso's from the bag Eliot handed him. Eliot ripped open a soy sauce packet and doused his dumplings.

Though this lunch was a regular occurrence, Eliot had a particular topic to bring up with Brooks today. He'd been a security guard at Falk for nearly fifty years, since before the school acquired Jessop. And he was a talker. If Eliot could just get him onto the subject, he'd open up easily.

Eliot cleared his throat. "So. I've been spending a lot of

time in Jessop, and at night especially, it's creepy. My friend Henri said it's haunted. Have you ever heard that?"

Brooks frowned. "I don't like to go in Jessop at night. Don't know how you spend so much time there."

"Why don't you like it? Have you seen something?"

Brooks shrugged. He wasn't being his usual talkative self, which meant… Well, Eliot wasn't sure what it meant, as he wasn't a detective and also was not generally great when it came to people. He pushed the dumplings around with his chopsticks.

"I think it's cursed," Eliot decided on.

"That would explain the fire," Brooks agreed.

Eliot frowned. He thought he'd heard of a fire at one point, but he wasn't sure. It reminded him of the first time with the book, and the sensation in his office he'd fought to forget. The certainty that he was burning, watching Tess's flesh blacken and flake away from her bones.

They'd both been on fire. But what did that say about Jessop?

"When was there a fire?" Eliot asked.

Brooks sighed, like he still wasn't entirely happy with this conversation. "Oh, probably…thirty years ago? Give or take." The corner of his mouth lifted, which Eliot recognized as something he did when he had a particularly good piece of gossip. "Right after Ms. Matheson started working there. She lived through it. Creepy, isn't it?"

Something about this jarred Eliot. "Was she involved at all?"

Brooks shrugged. "Doubt it," he said through a mouthful of chicken. "Unlucky, though. But not as unlucky as the guy who died in it."

Now *this* was a surprise: someone had died in Jessop. "Do you, uh, happen to know anything about that?"

Brooks shrugged, putting his empty containers back in the plastic bag. "It was a long time ago. And none of my business. You know I don't like that library."

Eliot nodded. "No one really does," he said. No one but him, and maybe Tess. But she probably bore a sense of duty rather than any real affection. He sighed. It was impossible to explain how magic felt stronger in Jessop, how he felt more himself. But it was also impossible to forget that within its walls, he, too, had burned.

———

That night, Eliot forced himself to return to Jessop. *If it hasn't invaded your mind yet, maybe it can't*, he convinced himself as he keyed himself into the library.

He climbed the stairs to the third floor, muscles tense to aching. While he walked, he ran through spells. He was not strong enough to cast many without artifacts to compel the magic, like his mother was. He needed all manner of herbs and blood and earth and runes in order to get his magic working properly. His mother, on the other hand, could say a few words and hum a tune and set everything right again.

Magic was fickle that way. Eliot tried not to let it bother him too much. Instead, he made a study of it. By analyzing his own magic, he could understand it a little better.

He paused in front of his office. He couldn't shake the image of the body on his carpet. When he'd spoken to Tess, he'd tried to brush it off, to make it seem like nothing, but it *wasn't* nothing. This was a fixture from his daily life, a girl he'd seen in classes for years, even if he hadn't really known her. And now something had happened to her, something terrible, something that he couldn't understand yet.

And it was all his fault.

Eliot sunk to his knees in front of his office door, trying to control his breathing. He took his chalk from his pocket and drew a few quick marks. Sliced his thumb with one of the multitudes of small pocketknives he kept perpetually in his bag or in his desk or in his wallet, just in case. Ignored the brush of pain and smeared some blood in the middle. A few more lines and the spell was done. Magic thrummed in his veins. It was a protection charm. Perhaps not strong enough to stand up against the devil, but it was *something*.

He went into his office. All was as he'd left it, which was to say, all was a mess. He sighed, dropping his bag onto one of the chairs, and went to the carrel of books.

He'd requested every book that could hold spells. Then, his devotion had been single-minded: find something to heal his mother. Now, when he skimmed the titles, he found them lacking. There were history books mixed in, ones that told of dark magic rather than gave him instructions for it. About two dozen of them, scattered amongst the more instructive grimoires. Eliot pulled them and stacked them on his desk.

Demons. Dark magic. The devil. These were the things he searched, muttering under his breath and dead to the world around him as dawn broke; as something grappled at the door of his office and found itself forbidden.

thirty eight

Tess

Tess finished her Sunday shift at Emiliano's by roll-ing silverware until her fingers were aching. By the time she grabbed her bag and said her goodbyes to her coworkers, the sun dipped low over the horizon.

She walked out the back, relishing the sultry summer air as it rushed around her. Emiliano's was always either too hot or too cold, never just right, and today was one of those days when she felt like she was wasting more energy shivering than actually doing her job.

Tess had barely gone a block when she saw her.

Regina stood across the street. She was unable to cross, with four lanes of one-way traffic separating her from Tess, but it was enough to be jarring. Tess hesitated for a moment, watching her. She couldn't even be entirely sure Regina's eyes were on her. She stood against the wall of the Subway, face slack, staring off into the distance. There was no smile on her face; there was no expression at all.

Something was not right. A sense of urgency prickled in Tess's skin. She needed to get home to safety, and fast.

Tess turned around and started for home. In the sum-mertime, South Oakland was deserted. Tess found herself walking faster than usual, eager to put distance between her and Regina. It was nearly a twenty-minute walk to her dorm, fifteen if she was really booking it.

And Tess was *booking* it.

She remembered what Eliot said about calling him, but this wasn't an emergency. Regina was just...there. It wasn't like she was doing anything malicious.

Unless...

Tess looked over her shoulder.

Far back, far enough that she would've had to run to catch up, Regina was following her.

Tess ran.

It wasn't like she was unaccustomed to running, but she was unaccustomed to this blood-pumping, terrified sort of running. She was gasping for breath and aching before she even reached the end of the block, but there was no way in hell she was stopping.

Tess slowed, risking a look over her shoulder. Regina was still the exact same distance away—which didn't make sense, since Regina wasn't running. In fact, Tess couldn't be sure, but it didn't look like she was moving her legs at all.

When Tess saw Regina at work the morning she went missing, she'd been wearing jeans, rolled at her ankles, and a pair of sandals. Now, Tess saw the flesh of her ankles and feet, bloated and discolored, straining against the crisscrossed braided leather of her shoes. Some of the puffy skin was cut and cracked, and days-old lines of dried blood clotted over the straps.

No, her feet were not moving. The only parts of Regina that were moving were her smile, slowly growing wider, and her eyes, blinking at intermittent intervals, more to dispel the flies that gathered around her head in a halo than to fulfill any biological need.

She's floating. Shit shit shit, she's literally *floating.*

She refused to dwell on this. She could not slow down. She could not stop. She could not break.

Just a few blocks more. Every time she turned, Regina was there—maybe getting closer. Maybe. Gaining ground on Tess little by little, inch by inch.

Tess hit her dorm and nearly slammed into the door. The cold metal of her key ring slipped through her fingers and clattered onto the concrete steps. She swore under her breath. Regina had rounded the corner of her street and was coming closer, closer, closer.

Tess ducked down and scraped her keys up. The short, gold one. She fumbled for it and somehow managed to turn it and wrench the door open. It locked automatically behind her, but she wasn't going to press her luck. Tess darted up the stairs to her dorm. One more lock, one more key.

Two floors below, the main door of the apartment opened. Regina floated on the other side.

"No no no fuck no," Tess gasped, twisting the key in the lock. She slammed the door behind her and hit the deadbolt home, then locked the doorknob.

But how had Regina gotten past the first door?

At the worst possible moment, her heart was flooded with memories and grief. Clearly, this thing inside of Regina was not Regina. Though they weren't friends, not really, Tess couldn't just... She thought of Regina training her, of her laughing in the stacks. Of her smile when she'd write test answers under the hem of her skirt, so she could flip it up to check her responses. Of the annoying way she popped her gum. The things that made Regina a teenager, a girl, a human.

And what was she now? A body? A devil?

Tess sat down against the door and dropped her head to her hands. She had to think, and quickly.

On the other side of the door, the scratching started.

"Tess." The voice was half whisper, half hiss.

Tess didn't answer. She couldn't. Her blood was frozen.

And still, the whispering on the other side of the door, now turning into a whimper. "Tess, please let me in? I'm so scared. I need to talk to you. Tess."

She pressed her hands against her ears, trying to block out the sound of Regina's voice. There had to be something she could do. When she'd banished the devil the first time, what had she done? Ordered him out. But that had done nothing to stop Regina from getting into the building, and she didn't want to test if the protection only extended into the apartment—no, she could not just open the door and find out.

On the other side of the door, the whispering became more urgent. Tess couldn't listen to it. It sounded too much like Regina for her to tune it out completely. To listen was to be convinced. To be convinced was to be killed.

Think think think.

She got up and peered through the peephole. There, on the other side, was the horror of it: Milky, deflated eyes, still colored with those shimmering black irises; green-tinged skin; cracked lips, ripped at the edges. She was coming apart at the seams, the edges of a gash opening back again on her throat, black blood leaking over her collarbones. Tess could *smell* her through the door, rotten meat and decay.

"I can save you," not-Regina crooned from the other side of the door. "I can change everything."

Tess squeezed her eyes shut, backing away from the door. She had to do something. If she did not deal with Regina, someone else would have to, and she wouldn't risk endangering anyone else. Fear, thick and dark and heavy, threatened to choke her.

"Go away, Regina," Tess tried.

"I won't hurt you," the body on the other side of the door promised. "I can't leave you. Let me in, Tess. Please, let me in."

She took a deep breath. Tried to calm herself. That surety, the same that arose whenever she played the cello, rooted itself against her breastbone. Tess reached for it, let the calm spread from her heart, through her veins, to her brain, to the tips of her fingers.

She thought back to mythology, to the devil, to vampires, to all the horrible and false things she could think of, all come true and out to get her. Tess considered what she was capable of. No longer trembling, she made up her mind.

"I can give you what you want. I can change your story," Regina said, her voice melting into the devil's and back again.

"I know," Tess said. Carefully, knowing how the old building creaked, she took a step back towards the kitchen. "I know."

thirty nine

Eliot

ELIOT SAT IN FRONT OF HIS FATHER'S HOUSE FOR A SOLID five minutes, debating if it was worth it for him to just run. Except, if he kept showing up to his father's house like a good boy, maybe he could take the weeks between the end of his summer classes and the beginning of the school year and go back to England.

Finally, he got out of his car and went up the path. Lucille was there at the door, waiting for him, and he wondered if she'd been there the whole time he was sitting.

"You look like you haven't slept, darling," Lucille said, reaching to touch the bags under his eyes. Eliot moved away.

"I've had a strange week," Eliot said.

Lucille pressed her lips together, but she didn't ask further. "Well, dinner is about ready," she said. "Have a seat in the dining room, why don't you?"

Lucille disappeared into the house, calling for his father. Eliot went to the dining room, set once again for their not-so-cozy party of three. He sat on the side and waited.

All things considered, he didn't dislike Lucille. Even though his father himself was a rubbish bin of a human being, the women who were attracted to him were lovely.

Lucille cared about Eliot, which was something he couldn't

hate her for. It was awkward, of course, especially the first few times, when she'd tried to get too close too quickly. But she realized, somewhere along the line, that Eliot was happiest when treated like a museum: visited occasionally, remarked over, but easily forgotten and left at the end of the day. He preferred to be regarded from a distance.

And there was another thing he respected about her: she never tried to replace his mother. Even though his father had tried to force her into the position of Eliot's mother, even though it disappointed him when Lucille didn't melt into that role.

Everything would've been fine, Eliot thought many times, if it hadn't come down to timing. If his father had just waited until his wife was out of the picture. After all, Eliot thought bitterly, it wouldn't be long.

But his father had never been very good at waiting.

Lucille came back in, carrying a steaming bowl of pasta. His father followed behind her, drink in hand, cheeks ruddy. He had an envelope in his hand, marked as airmail.

"Something came for you," he grunted, tossing the envelope onto Eliot's plate. The return address was to their home in Hertfordshire, and for a brief moment, Eliot's heart leapt. Had his mother written him something? But, then, why would she send it to his father? Why wouldn't she call?

"Someone sent it to the house," his father said, adding ice to his drink from the side bar. "That satanic nurse of your mother's sent it here."

Eliot kept his features carefully composed. He liked Josie—even though she was not magic in the slightest—and she took good care of his mother. Perhaps that was what his father faulted.

While he was occupied with his drink and Lucille went back for the bread basket, Eliot opened the envelope. It encased another one, this addressed to him. He recognized it from Annika, one of his mum's uni friends—one of his mum's more *talented* uni friends. Eliot had taken a few lessons with Annika in her Oxford garden. She provided his mother with most of her more difficult to find or dangerous herbs.

As he broke the seal of the envelope, it expanded. Eliot recognized the trick, used to mask illicit items to get through the postal service without getting stopped in customs or costing more in postage.

There was a note inside. Eliot glanced up, noted that Lucille was now quietly telling his father why he shouldn't pour more whiskey into his glass, and went back to the letter.

It was only a few lines long. More would possibly appear when he was alone.

This is your mum's regular order for the summer harvest. Please write if you need anything more specific.

Eliot frowned down at the note. He had the abrupt and awful feeling of something ending, something he couldn't stop. Annika had addressed this to him. She knew his mother would not be needing these things anymore. Perhaps she'd never practice magic again.

"Well?" Birch asked, settling in. Eliot accepted the serving dish from Lucille, pushing the envelope into his pocket with his other hand. It shrank back down to a manageable size. "What is it?"

Eliot cleared his throat, stalling. Annika went to Oxford with both his parents—meaning his father knew vaguely what something from her would contain.

"Just a letter," Eliot said, pushing pasta onto his plate.

"From one of mum's old friends."

There was too much of a pause. Eliot glanced up from his food. His father's mouth was set into a thin, hard line. "Not one of her...degenerate friends, I hope."

Eliot clenched his jaw. If Eliot's suspicions were correct, the "degenerates" Birch spoke of were other witches, which certainly meant his father was drunk and volatile. That was the only time he would speak of anything related to magic or his mother. At the other end of the table, Lucille was intently focused on her napkin.

Don't make it worse, he reminded himself. *Don't antagonize him.*

But Eliot was so *tired*. "I quite like Mum's uni friends, actually." It wasn't much, but it was enough, and Eliot knew it the second the words left his lips.

His father's eyes flared. "Before I met her, she was running around with any satanist she set her eyes on. Why, if you knew her in her Oxford days, you wouldn't idolize her the way you do. Believing in this and that. Teaming up with a coven, worshipping the devil."

Eliot set his fork down. "I would appreciate if you didn't talk about her that way. Considering she raised me."

His father laughed, low and condescending. Of course, Eliot saw now, he wanted to pick a fight. This wasn't his first drink of the night, and he was primed for battle. "One day you'll realize that I'm not the villain in this story."

But he was.

He'd become the villain when he had an affair—or many, though Eliot only knew of the one; when he outlawed magic in the house; when he shattered Caroline's vials and burned her books and held her bleeding wrists above her head as she begged him to stop, as Eliot could only watch from the corner and scrub out the chalk markings on the floor and watch her lie about what they'd been doing. He'd become the villain when he'd seen her magic and tried to take it away.

"Edward," Lucille said, very quietly. "This isn't the best conversation for dinner."

"No. This is my son, and I'll speak to him as I choose." His father's cold, dark eyes turned back to Eliot. "I know how you see me. I'm the evil one who drove you away from your mother, who brought you here, who's ruined your life. But you're wrong. I've given you everything you've ever wanted. I've given you security and education and money, without asking questions, without asking for anything. And what do I get in return?"

Eliot's nails dug into his palms. He tried to feel for his magic, to pull it close around him, but any power he had had retreated to somewhere deep inside of him.

"I get a son who hates the sight of me. A son who tried to curse me."

Lucille looked between them. Eliot refused to meet her eyes. His father sneered and took a sip of his drink, gearing for another round.

"I want to go back to the UK," Eliot said. He wasn't sure how the words had escaped him, if he'd even said them at all.

His father laughed, short and harsh. "You're not going back. You think I'm going to let Caroline take anything else from me? You think I'm going to let her ruin you more? She's already turned you against me. Filled your head with fanciful bullshit. Told you you were magic. It's time to grow up, Eliot. Be a man. You can't follow your mother around forever."

Eliot wanted to be anywhere else. At the head of the table,

Lucille was hiding her face. Eliot stood up from the table. "If you want me to stay, you'll stop talking to me like that."

His father rose too, taller than Eliot, broader than Eliot. "I will speak to you however I want."

It was as if Eliot was drowning. He could see his father, but he couldn't breathe, and he couldn't get out of there. It would always be like this. His father held all the cards, always. It didn't matter how much Eliot tried to grow up, tried to grow away.

It's not you it's not you it's not you, he tried to repeat, over and over again in his mind. It was a mantra from his younger days, back when he was a child, back when he idolized his father and everything began to change. *It's your magic he hates. It's not you.*

But Eliot was too old for that. He and his magic were one and the same. By hating his magic, his father hated *him.*

"You're just like her," his father sneered. "That *bitch.* You do what you need to get what you want. Even now, look at you, trying to manipulate me, to get your way. That's always been you. Selfish, never realizing what a life I've provided for you."

Someday, he'd be past all of this. He'd be out of this dining room, out of this house, out of this city.

"Edward, please—"

"You have no reason to hate her," Eliot snapped.

"She taught you to hate me," he said, turning a look of utter disgust on Eliot.

His father wasn't finished. "I lost my position because of you. The respect of the community. I know that's what you did, you son of a bitch." He slammed his glass down. Amber liquid splashed over the table. Lucille flinched again. "You tried to fucking curse me. She put you up to it, didn't she?"

Eliot could taste the words on his mouth, corrupted

infatuation charms he'd tried years ago and never worked. Maybe it was about conviction after all. Maybe he was right, and Eliot had ruined everything himself.

Lucille stood, moved closer to Eliot. As if he was a child in need of protection. He shot her a look to stay put. He wished he could say something, anything, to make it stop. But he'd learned the best thing was to stay quiet and wait for it to be over.

"You think you're special," his father continued. He stalked around the table, glass in hand, getting in Eliot's face. "You think because you're like your mother, you're better than everyone else." Eliot paled, risking a glance at Lucille. He didn't know if she had any idea of what he could do—and how she'd react if she *did* know. "You're an abomination. A freak." He waved at Eliot, drunk and angry. "And your mother is just the devil's bitch."

"I hate you," Eliot said. It was a surprise. He'd never said it before, not out loud, not like this. And the response was immediate.

The back of his father's hand cracked against his cheek, whipping Eliot's head to one side. He staggered back, falling into the china cabinet. At the end of the table, Lucille gasped his father's name.

He felt dizzy and strangely ashamed, like he'd been caught in a private act. Eliot raised his hand to his cheek and felt moisture there. Blood, where his father's ring had broken his skin.

"I think," Eliot said, trying to maintain his calm, trying to keep his head, trying not to cry, "that that's my cue to leave. Thank you both for this evening."

He turned and left, feeling numb all the way down the walk to his car. His head was buzzing and his cheek stung and in the house, he heard the beginning of an argument between

Lucille and his father.

When he got into the car, he rested his head on the steering wheel. How had it escalated so suddenly, out of nowhere? What had Eliot done to incite his father's wrath? And what was he going to do now?

He was no one without his magic. He could not give it up. Not for anyone.

And then, his phone was ringing.

He whipped it out of his pocket, cursing under his breath, committed to not answering, even if it was his mother.

But it wasn't his mother. It was Tess.

forty

Tess

ONE STEP, CREAKLESS AND SILENT. TESS HELD HER BREATH and waited. She wasn't sure if Regina would think she was escaping and come flying into the room, using whatever strange trickery she had to get through the locked front door. If that happened, she would be out of luck and probably dead.

Another step.

"Tess," Regina pleaded. "I can tell you everything. I can give you everything you've ever wanted."

Tess took a deep breath. "I'm sure you can." Her voice came out as barely a whisper.

The door rattled. "Why are you moving away? Where are you going? Why won't you let me in?"

Shit. Tess froze halfway across the living room. The door-knob rattled again. The scratching resumed. But Regina did not even try to break down the door, even after she'd proven so easily downstairs that locks meant nothing.

Maybe the apartment *was* safe. But she could not hide in here forever.

Almost without thinking about it, she started to hum. It was a simple thing: just her lines from the piece she'd been working on, Barber's "Adagio for Strings." She closed her eyes and focused, just as she did every time she picked up her cello.

Tess blocked out Regina's voice and the awful scratching. Every one of her steps was timed to a beat until her heart was no longer racing. Until she was flooded with calm. She kept on humming, eyes closed, until she bumped into the far wall. She knew this apartment, every corner of it, and her hand found the knob of the drawer where they kept the knives.

Tess selected three. The sharpest ones. Two, she slipped into her belt. One, she gripped tightly in her hand.

She squared her shoulders and hummed louder. Anna was visiting her parents until Monday. It was just her, alone in the apartment as darkness fell. Her and Regina. Her and the devil.

She took a step. Adjusted her grip. Regina called her name, growing more desperate. Tess hummed louder.

There are many different kinds of fear. The kind that prickles your stomach, like standing on the edge of a cliff looking down, considering the possibilities. There's the kind that makes you freeze, like getting a text from a parent to call them immediately or watching the car in front of you stop suddenly without knowing if you have time to brake without smashing into them. There's the tickly, fun kind of fear too, the kind that comes from ghost stories and scary movies and campfires.

And then there's the kind of blunt-edged, dulled fear that slows everything down, grinds everything to a musty halt in the middle of a haze of panic. It's a fear so deep that no other thoughts, no other emotions can exist alongside it. It's a numbing fear.

This was the kind of fear Tess felt.

If the thing was still living, Tess thought, trying to be logical, she would have to kill it. Some part of her registered her odd detachment and wondered if she was going into shock. But shock would not keep her alive. Logic might.

Step by step, she made her way to the door. Blood loss did not kill the thing that now inhabited Regina, judging by the amount of blood in the library when Eliot had discovered her body. So she should not attempt to slit its throat. But there was the brain, maybe—going for an eye and stabbing through, or something of that sort. Fragmentary images of it all swirled in Tess's mind, and she had to take a moment to let the nausea pass after imagining popping one of those milky eyeballs like she'd seen once in a movie.

Keep humming, she thought. *Keep humming and keep moving*. Another step forward. On the other side, Regina's voice had grown hoarse. The scratching was also dulled, sounding like it was skin against the wood and not her nails. Tess shuddered, imagining bloody, broken tips on the end of Regina's fingers.

So not the eyes, then. The thought of stabbing her in the eye was too much for Tess, and might not even work. The heart, Tess decided. If she could stop the heart, maybe she could stop the thing that was not Regina anymore. And for good measure, just like she had with the devil himself, she would tell Regina that she was not welcome.

She was right back in front of the door. Tess allowed herself ten seconds. To prepare herself, to check her grip, to make sure when the door swung open, she was ready.

Ten. A deep inhale. A prolonged note.

Nine. Switching the knife to her other hand to wipe the sweat on her palms against her jeans.

Eight. Time to lean forward, to check that Regina was right outside the door.

Seven. Seeing that swirling, blood-vesseled eye staring through the hole back at her. A sharp gasp, but reassurance. She was close enough.

Six. Transferring the knife back to her right hand, grip tight. Her fingers felt less shaky when wrapped around the matte black handle.

Five. *This is for Nat. If you don't get rid of her and she kills you, all of this will be for nothing.*

Four. *This is not going to be what kills you.* Maybe this was bravery, after all. Just fear layered on top of fear until the only option left was action.

Three. A deep breath. Maybe the last one ever.

Two. A hand on the doorknob. Sliding the deadbolt with her other hand. The climax of the piece. The best part.

One. *My name is Tess Matheson. I am stronger than the devil. And I am not going to die today.*

Tess threw the door open. It crashed against the wall. The ruin that used to be Regina was there in front of her, stinking and terrible. Before it could move, before it could react, Tess raised the knife over her head and was plunging it down, down, down.

The knife went in just over Regina's breast and scraped between two ribs—grated to a stop. She couldn't push it in any further.

Her hands were covered with the blood that sluiced from Regina's body. Cold and thick, like she'd been dead for hours. Days.

Regina gasped and a lone trickle of blood ran down the corner of her mouth. "Why?" she asked.

Tess was hyperventilating too much to answer. All she could think was *I just stabbed someone. I just stabbed someone. I just stabbed someone.*

She pulled herself together, choking on bile. "I forbid you," Tess managed. Regina's expression faltered. Tess wondered if there was any part of her left inside of this body, or if she was entirely the devil's now. "I forbid you from this home. From Nat's. From my family. I forbid you and I renounce you."

Regina blinked those horrible eyes and turned, knife still in her chest, and walked away down the hall. She didn't look like she was in pain or anything; she just turned and left. Tess was too stunned to call after her.

She did not dissolve into a deluge of gore, as Tess had expected, or fall at her feet. She just...went.

Tess slumped against the wall as it all caught up to her. Her hands were awful, smelling of rot and coated in blood. Something was trailing down her face, and she couldn't be sure if it was blood or tears.

But she'd survived. She choked on a sob, on a breath, on a broken-off bit of humming. And she remembered the one person she *hadn't* remembered to protect. The one person who the devil knew about. The one person the devil knew he could use against her—because of course, this whole time, he already had. Tess's heart caught in her throat, beating too fast.

Eliot.

forty one

Eliot

"What is it?" Eliot asked, because of course she wouldn't just be calling him for no reason.

"Eliot." There was a long pause, and he wasn't sure how to read it, but something in her voice had his foot on the brake. He frowned into the gathering darkness.

"Tess, what's going on?"

"Where are you right now?" Flatness. That was what it was. Her voice lacked any intonation at all, as if she just had to get the words out to keep herself from screaming.

"Driving home from my father's. What is it?"

Another pause. "Regina's body...attacked me. Or...followed me home. She is dead and decaying, and she came to my apartment, and I stabbed her in the heart, and I thought she'd come after you next."

A prickle of fear slipped over Eliot's skin. He shot a cursory glance into the mirror, as if Regina's body would be grinning at him from the backseat. "What are you saying?"

There was a clatter, either of Tess dropping the phone or throwing it, and then a long string of curse words half-muffled by something. Maybe the sound of vomiting followed, but Eliot couldn't be sure.

"Regina's body," Tess said, back again. "Decaying. Disgusting.

But something is inside of her, Eliot. Something is *possessing* her. And I don't think I killed it. Not completely."

Eliot's mouth was dry. He checked the rearview again, the hair on his neck standing on end. "What do we do?"

"Come here," Tess said wearily. "I just… We have to figure out what happens next, and I know my dorm is safe. I need to clean this up before someone notices."

"Okay," Eliot said. He wasn't sure if he was terrified or confused or if he even believed her in the first place. "But let's run through this one more time. Tell me everything that happened."

The description took the entire drive. Tess broke off at points into deep silences, broken only by Eliot saying her name. With every word and every description, he grew more and more certain the apprehension growing in his stomach was, in fact, terror.

Eliot careened into a space in front of Tess's building and threw the car into park. She wasn't speaking now, and all he could hear was her quiet, uneven breathing. He thought she'd been crying, but he couldn't align an image of her with tears in her eyes with the fierce edginess that usually lived there.

Which was why it was all the more startling when he really did see her.

The lock on the front door was broken—probably the work of the devil, but Eliot didn't want to think too much on that, because to do so would be to realize the danger of the situation. A trail of blood led to the back dorm on the third floor. The door to her flat was a ruin of blood and wood splinters and tiny bits of flesh clinging to the scratched away paint. A small pool of blood stained the carpet.

Eliot knocked softly. "It's me," he said.

The girl that opened the door barely resembled Tess. Dark circles stained the space under her eyes. Her nose was red and puffy, and her eyes were watery. Before, he'd always thought she was slender, but now she just looked gaunt. Blood speckled her shirt and stained her hands.

Without even thinking, he reached for her.

"Wait," Tess said, grabbing his upper arms. She stared intently into his eyes, searching.

"What is it?"

"I…" She trailed off, looking away. "Tell me one book I originally took you into the cage for."

Eliot searched his brain. "Uh. *The Book of Shadows?*"

Tess exhaled, and the relief was clear in the way she folded into him, allowing him to tuck her head underneath his chin and envelop her completely, like he was hiding her.

"It's you," she said. "It's actually you."

"Of course it's me," Eliot said, stroking her hair. "Who else would it be?"

Tess didn't answer.

She was shaking so hard. He felt her heart thundering in her chest. She clutched him so, so tightly, and it was all he could do to tighten his own grip, to surround her, until he was certain that the only thing she could sense around her was him.

"Did she hurt you?"

Tess paused, and Eliot's heart thundered. If the devil hurt her…he would find a way to kill it himself. It would not escape Eliot. He'd use every bit of magic he could find.

"No," Tess said. "No. I'm fine."

They stood there for a long time, long enough that Eliot's arms hurt from holding her so tight. Tess pulled away, dry-eyed, looking resolved. "I need to shower. And then we'll figure this out."

He nodded. Her words broke the spell between them. Tess stepped away, and Eliot went to look at the ruin of the door.

"Yeah, that's going to be an issue for the damage deposit," Tess said ruefully, coming out of her bedroom with a towel slung over one arm. "I have no idea how to explain it to Anna."

"I'll fix it," Eliot said. Tess frowned at him, but just ducked into the bathroom.

forty two

Tess

TESS STARED AT HER REFLECTION IN THE MIRROR. SHE WAS streaked with blood and gore, covered with the stuff up to her wrist on her stabbing hand. Her fingers were sore from holding the knife. She had a flicker of a memory; a reflection from before, one she'd dismissed as an illusion. Now, looking at the splatter of blood across her face, she wondered if it was a warning.

Carefully, she removed the other two knives from her belt and set them on the porcelain sink. She turned on the shower, and then the sink while she waited for it to warm. Steam clouded her reflection as she carefully washed her hands once, twice, a third time. Scraping under the nails. Lady Macbeth, hands gloved in blood that would not wash away. She didn't realize she was sobbing until she could no longer breathe.

Tess pulled off her clothes and got into the shower, curling into a ball on the floor, letting the water fall. In the steam and the hiss and the pounding of the water, she let herself cry. She ached past her muscles, down to her bones, either from adrenaline or fear or exhaustion.

Worst of all, every time she saw Eliot hanging around Jessop or annoying her elsewhere, she felt the tug of Truth. Even though she knew they were not the same, even though she could tell them apart—mostly—she felt the pull of the devil when she saw Eliot's face.

Perhaps that was what the devil wanted. Perhaps he'd put on Eliot's body because he knew what Tess wanted, even before she'd known herself. Even before she'd considered him as anything more than a nuisance.

No. He was still...still... She didn't know. He was still an unknown, still a variable she couldn't account for. Still a line of accidentals she fumbled over every time.

Eliot could *not* see her like this. He could not see any trace of this when she got out of the shower and went back out. If he saw this, he would know the truth of how much Regina had scared her, and she could not let that happen.

And worse. She could not let him see how afraid she was when she realized Eliot was unprotected, when she thought there was the chance Regina could come after him too. She pressed her hands to her eyes, trying to suppress the remaining panic. Any of it, all of it. Because, for the first awful time, Tess realized it meant something to her for Eliot to be safe.

She brought her fist to her mouth and bit down hard. She couldn't be like this, sobbing in the shower. She couldn't be weak. And Eliot could never know of any of this.

Mechanically, she stood. *I won't let it hurt him,* Tess thought. *I won't let it hurt anyone. If someone is going down, it will be me.*

forty three

Eliot

ELIOT DIDN'T HAVE HIS RUE OR THISTLE OR HIS FAVORITE herbs, but he checked the kitchen for anything he could use. He set it all up: chalk runes for tidying and freshness and cleanliness; lemon peel for purifying; spearmint, for cleansing and renewal; a drop of his blood. Under his breath, the spells for a clean house and a fresh slate.

"Eliot." He looked up. Tess was done, a sure sign he'd lost track of time yet again. She was wearing her glasses, and her hair was down and dripping over her shoulders. "What the hell are you doing?"

"I..."

But it was too late. The root of his spell had already been laid. The wood of the door groaned, blood flying away in huge drops and dissolving into dust, settling in motes that glimmered in the hallway lights. The wood splintered and doubled, regrowing into a smooth, white surface. Everything smelled clean and light, like happiness or the soil after rain or the fog he missed more than anything. Like magic. A faint shimmer hung in the air, over Eliot's body, over the door. His palms tingled with magic, skin already healed.

Maybe he'd wanted to be caught. After all, how did he expect to explain his ability to set her dorm to rights in the space of a single shower? The truth was, he *hadn't* been think-ing. He'd only wanted to make things right. Perhaps, after all of this fuss, he just wanted her to know the truth.

He sat back on his heels. Watched Tess's face. She swal-lowed hard, one eyebrow raised, and crossed her arms over her chest.

"I suppose I have to tell you something," he said carefully. He couldn't look at her, couldn't see the hatred growing in her eyes, like it had with his father, when he knew the truth. "I...I have magic. Am magic. I'm a witch." He snapped his fingers, one of his *only* tricks, and a spark flew from his fingertips.

Tess laughed, and the sound was a bit too hysterical for his liking. She clapped a hand to her mouth. Finally, she said, "I hate to say it, but...that's the least surprising thing that's happened."

He blinked at her. Nobody but his mother's coven and his father knew about his magic. His mother loved it because it was a part of her, too; Birch hated it because he'd never have it and never understand. He figured that would be how whoever else he told reacted.

But Tess almost looked delighted by the fact. She came over, took in the setup, and ran her fingers across the newly fixed door. "Huh," she breathed. "Think you could fix the front door, too?"

Eliot fought to hide the surge of relief inside of him. "Of course I can." He hovered behind her, watching her inspect his handiwork, and he felt an odd sense of belonging in this ramshackle dorm with Tess's wet hair and the smell of magic in the air.

"Have you...used magic on me before?" Tess asked. He

worried at her tone. She sounded less thrilled. Or maybe afraid.

"I have," Eliot said carefully. "Not maliciously. When you were ill when we took the book back. I just wanted to make sure you were okay." He shrugged. "And my office is enchanted, for safety."

"Eliot—" she started. She turned, catching him off guard, stumbling into him, and he grabbed her arms to keep her from tripping. Her fingers locked around his upper arms, one thumb brushing the bottom edge of his tattoo.

His breath caught.

All at once, it was too thick and too much, the things he'd been thinking and pushing away, the things that had been flooding his deepest thoughts. Freckles dusted across her nose and over her cheeks, constellations he could spend ages exploring. He wanted to trace the tip of his finger over the curve of her lip, to consecrate his magic with the warmth of her breath.

Moving carefully, like she was a fragile and beautiful thing he could destroy, he lifted a hand to her chin, tilting her face up towards his. Magic glimmered in his fingers like he'd called a spark to them.

He grazed his thumb over her bottom lip, watching intently as her lips parted, as her eyes flicked down and then back to meet his gaze. Eliot leaned down, brushing his nose against hers, feeling their foreheads touch. A centimeter, and he'd be kissing her. A breath, and he'd finally know the shape of her lips, finally be able to escape them haunting his dreams. He shifted towards her and nearly—

She closed her eyes. "I, um. I can't get the smell of ink... of *her*...out of my head." Tess turned, angling her head down, pressing her cheek against his palm. "I just. Yeah. Need to get out of here."

Tess's hands fell away and she broke out of his grasp, sending him a rueful smile as she ducked into her room.

forty four

Eliot

H<small>E</small> <small>SMUGGLED</small> <small>A</small> <small>PIZZA</small> <small>OUT</small> <small>OF</small> <small>THE</small> <small>DINING</small> <small>HALL</small> <small>AND</small>
bought a two liter of soda from the corner shop. They laid
on their bellies in Schenley Park, eating pizza until there was
nothing left but grease spots, passing the soda back and forth
between them. Tess had a little bit more color, but he couldn't
stop noticing the unhealthy look about her, now that he'd seen
it. He wanted to put her to bed or feed her more or take care
of her somehow.

But he knew Tess was not the type of person who would
tolerate being taken care of. Even now, that fierce look was
coming back into her eyes, clear through her glasses. That
light hadn't been fully extinguished after all. It had only been
burning low for a spell.

"Why did you want to come to the park?" Eliot asked. He'd
offered to drive her to his dorm, or they could've stayed at the
dining hall, but Tess insisted on the park. It was nice to be in
an open space, he thought—to not be so close to her wet hair
and the honey scent of her skin; to put some distance between
them and what didn't happen at her dorm.

"It feels safe," she said.

Darkness softened her edges just enough that she didn't
look so feral. He'd never thought of her like this, wearing

shorts and a T-shirt, spread out on the grass, looking at stars. He'd never seen her wear her glasses before, either, and it made her look sleepy and secret.

"There's no..." she said. "I don't know. I can't feel the devil here."

The words sent a shiver down his spine. He swallowed thickly, wishing it wasn't true. Because she was right. A small miracle existed in the park: he couldn't feel the fear or the danger that had been a dull hum over the last few weeks, ever since they'd found the book.

And another miracle: when he turned his head to look at her, he found her looking back.

"What are we going to do?" Eliot asked.

Tess's eyes slid shut. "Let's not talk about it. Not now. I can't stomach it."

Eliot wasn't going to argue with her about that. He couldn't really stomach the discussion now, either, but they had to have it eventually. "Okay."

"You said you were at your father's house. How was it?"

Eliot thought about lying. Saying it was tolerable, or even smiling and remarking that it was good, or saying something pleasant about the food. "It was..." He faltered. After all of this, he couldn't find it in himself to lie about this. Not to Tess. "God, it was terrible."

For a moment, the only sounds were from the park, and the Oakland nighttime: cars accelerating, crickets, a train going through Panther Hollow. And then, Tess said, "Did he hit you?"

Eliot was about to ask how she knew, but Tess had a peculiar way of reading him. She rolled enough so she could reach him and gently traced the outline that his father's signet ring had cut into Eliot's cheek. It stung when she touched the raw area, but not as much as it sparked when her skin met his.

"It doesn't matter, does it?" All of a sudden, it was hard to swallow.

"It matters to me," Tess said quietly. She moved her hand down, away from his cheek, and Eliot immediately missed the feel of it until she moved it to his arm and started tracing figure eights on his bicep, under the curl of his tattoo. "That day in the stacks, when we were looking for your books. You said Falk was only bearable. Did you mean only the school specifically, or being in America, or did you mean something else?"

Eliot sighed. The worst part was he could see himself telling her the truth, clear as he could see the stars above them. "I guess you could say all of the above."

She didn't stop the figure eight patterns, sending shocks into his skin with every turn of her finger. "Why?"

He bit his lip. There were a thousand answers, but only one truth. "My mother might die before the end of summer."

Her hand stopped. "Eliot. I'm so sorry."

He hated condolences, so he brushed it off like errant blades of grass, shedding the sadness her pity aroused in him. "No, it's fine. Everything is okay." But it wasn't. He knew that this summer would be the last summer, the end of it all. The end of his childhood, the end of her magic, the end of his mother. There were stories he could bear. And there were stories he couldn't, but he'd have to.

Tess flipped over onto her side to face him, and he could feel her eyes boring into his face. He couldn't look at her. To look would be to cry, to weaken, to break. In the grass, her hand found his. Like in the tunnel, she took his hand and entwined her fingers through his.

"You don't have to be fine," she said.

He turned his head. Her glasses were knocked off her nose since she was lying on her side, giving her a strange, endearing, extra eye effect. And the ferocity was gone. She was not a blade or an edge. She was a girl, looking at him like he was a boy, looking at him like he mattered.

So he told her everything.

He told her about his mother, and how thin she'd gotten, how he could encircle her wrist with his thumb and pointer finger. And about her voice, like a bubbling creek or a flute, and how she'd used to tell him fairytales when he was little as they walked through the woods that surrounded the country house. He told her about his magic, how sometimes it felt as tight and vibrant as a bowstring and sometimes it was loose and hard to shape. About how he felt alive when he used it.

He even found himself telling her about what really happened with his father when things went wrong.

It had been a Thursday. He wasn't sure how he knew that, after everything else had faded behind a veil of memory, but he knew it had been a Thursday. His hair was wet, because he'd had swim lessons at school that day, and he was eleven. He'd asked his mother very nicely if he could go by himself from their London flat to his father's university, taking the train, not talking to strangers. Back then, he admired his father nearly as much as he admired his mother. She'd tucked a phone into his hand and told him he could, only if he didn't bother his father at his work, only if he called her when he got there.

Things had been...strange at home lately. His mother's friends had started helping her with Eliot's lessons; lessons that left him feeling tired and charged in a way he never had before. Lessons on magic and runes and blood. Lessons his mother told him not to tell his father about, no matter how excited he was, no matter how much he loved him.

Eliot loved to visit his office. It made what his father do feel magical, almost like his mother's workshop. Dr. Birch was a professor at one of the universities, esteemed for his writings on astrophysics, which Eliot thought was a sort of magic in itself. He had a dedicated group of mentees. Eliot had even met some of them, but none stood out so much as a PhD candidate called Shel. He was never sure if Shel stood for Shelly or Shelia or Shelissa or if she was simply Shel, with her brown curly hair and her nice blue eyes. She called Eliot "Eli," like his mother did always and his father did sometimes.

He'd been to his father's office before, thousands of times. He had a particular way he walked down the hallway, even though he was now eleven and far too old for such things: skipping the white tiles, walking in only the black, edging around the mathematics hall until he reached his father's door.

It was his office hours, which usually meant his father was behind his desk with the door open. But not today. The door was closed, and there were voices coming from inside. Soft, whispery voices, and quiet laughs, like pleasant secrets were being told.

Eliot knocked softly. Nobody answered, but that had never stopped him before.

Except this time, when he opened the door, it was his father and Shel. His father *with* Shel.

Eliot froze for a moment, only a moment, long enough for Shel to look up, see him and scream, try to cover herself.

And Eliot ran. He ran until he was well and truly lost and the phone in his pocket kept ringing and ringing and it was his mother, he *knew* it was his mother, but he couldn't talk to her. Eliot was old enough to know what was going on. Old enough to know that it would hurt her.

He went to Hertfordshire, to the country house, where he felt safe. Eliot used the key under the ceramic frog to get in and ran to the place where he and his mother practiced. He pulled down one of her books, the ones she told him never to touch without her, and he opened to the glossary and found a section on infatuation spells.

His mother's jars of herbs were carefully labeled, and Eliot pulled down all the herbs mentioned in the grouping of spells. Long words and short, familiar and unfamiliar.

He made a pile of them. Basil and blue vervain and five finger grass and coltsfoot, dill and hibiscus and jasmine and lavender and mandrake, mistletoe and orris root and peppermint and raspberry and willow bark.

Eliot drew every symbol, cut his thumbs until the blood flowed, and when that didn't work, he cut lines on his arm. He cried, muddling the words of the spells. He did not feel the rush of his own magic; he knew it was not working.

And then, after his parents had spent hours looking for him, headlights cut through the haze. His mother ran around the house, calling his name, and Eliot couldn't stop crying long enough to answer.

His father heard him and froze in the doorway, eyes glazed over with fury. His mother came in after, one hand pressed to her mouth while she took in the ruin of the scene and put the pieces together. Eliot sat in the middle of the floor, surrounded by smoking herbs and scorch marks, arms bloody up to his elbows.

"Caroline," his father said very, very quietly. "What have you done?"

That was the first time Eliot saw hatred in his father's eyes. None of his spells worked. When he most needed it, his magic failed him.

He remembered something now, relaying the story to Tess. Eliot closed his eyes, tried to push the memory away, but it was useless.

"You promised me," his father had seethed, "that he would know nothing of this."

Eliot felt nauseous. Tess didn't let go of his hand. She examined his face as if she could peel the years away, strip him down to that eleven-year-old boy he once was, reaching for magic that would never work.

"Did you tell your mom what happened?" Tess asked. She hadn't spoken at all, as he relayed it.

Eliot rolled onto his side, still holding her hand. His arm was starting to cramp but he wouldn't let go, not for the whole world.

"Of course I did," Eliot said. "She wrapped my arms, and when my dad went away to be furious somewhere else, she healed me with magic. And I told her. She yelled at me, which was something she never did, but she was terrified when I was lost. And she sent me to bed after forcing me to eat this god-awful soup.

"My dad came in after my mother went to bed. He smelled like alcohol and firewood. He sat down on my bed and said, 'Eliot. What you saw today must remain our secret. But more importantly, you must swear to me, *promise me*, that you'll never do that sorcery again. You never should have learned of it. It will ruin you.' And I laid there, hearing the hatred in his voice, knowing it was directed at me. And I couldn't help but think, *how can he love me if he hates what I am?*"

"But…" She only said that, that one word, and he warmed to her immediately. She didn't have to say anything else. Tess understood what his father didn't.

"I told my mother," Eliot said to the grass. "I told her what he said, and she didn't seem surprised, which was the worst part. She just…fell a little bit. Curled into herself."

His father had never called him Eli again. Not after that. After Eliot betrayed him. Eliot couldn't help seeing how they were all tied up: his father's betrayal, his mother's magic, his own. How they were the same thing, in the end.

"Did your mother leave him?"

Eliot sighed. "She would've, if she didn't get sick. And they were separated, when Dad first came here. But no. Regular treatment and magic weren't working for her illness, so they are trying something experimental, and she can't pay for it without my father's money. And it just…looks better if he stays married to her. So they separated but didn't divorce." He didn't know what else his father had to gain from staying with her. Maybe he did it just to control Eliot. If he took Eliot away from his mother, maybe he could strip away his magic.

"But how did your father come here?" Tess asked. "Why would he leave, if he had a good job?"

Eliot sighed, running a hand through his hair. "That's kind of my fault too. When I told my mom, it got back to Shel. She got scared and reported the affair to the university. My father was let go. I can't say he was blacklisted, entirely, but he was never able to get back in with a uni. So when he was offered a job at Falk, the choice was clear. And he left and took me with him."

"As punishment?"

Eliot's mouth tasted sour. "Maybe," he said, but he wasn't sure who Tess was thinking was getting punished: him or his mother.

It didn't matter. They both were, in the end. "And here we are."

After a pause, when all that was left was the sound of crickets filtering back into his ears and the laughter of students somewhere on Pitt's campus, Tess said, "I wish there was something I could say that would matter."

It was a strange thing to say, Eliot thought, but it wasn't necessarily untrue. Usually, when he mentioned any part of this story, or anyone knew it, there were I'm-sorrys and condolences and it's-not-your-faults all around, until the sympathy was so thick around Eliot that he was suffocating.

But here, now, he could breathe.

He wanted to kiss her.

He was not going to.

"Why are you here?" he asked.

Tess sighed, and her hand felt uncertain in his now that it wasn't there simply to offer comfort. He squeezed hers a little, trying to reassure, and held his breath until he felt a faint squeeze back.

"It's boring," Tess said.

"I doubt that." Nothing she said could bore him.

"My parents will lose the house if my mom doesn't find a job, and my dad threw all of our money at his failing business," Tess said all in a rush, like a confession.

"Is this a sudden change in status?" Eliot asked. "The no-job thing, I mean."

Tess sighed. "She was a teacher, but public schools are getting funding cut and— It's boring, honestly. It's just, teachers are getting laid off, and she happened to be one of them. And my dad runs a pen company, but all the money from that was paying for his stationery store. So."

"Ah," Eliot said.

"They're good parents," Tess continued, pulling more grass. "But they're…naïve. They don't see the consequences of things. They forget a lot. They don't see how hard it is for… I don't know. To get into college and pay for it. They don't really get what it's going to take for Nat and me to be stable adults, and so I took matters into my own hands. I couldn't play the parent at home anymore. So I talked to Mathilde, and now we're here."

"And do you like it here?" Eliot asked, though he suspected he knew the answer.

Tess's lips twitched upwards. "I'll be honest. I'd like it better if your father wasn't here."

Well, he couldn't argue with that.

Her hand in his was distracting, and he couldn't stop looking at her lips, tracing the shape of them with his gaze. He wondered what it would be like to not feel this much, to not cling to every word she said.

"You have a tattoo," Tess said after an extended moment of silence. "What is it?"

Instinctively, Eliot's hand went to his upper arm, where his tattoo went from his shoulder to the middle of his bicep. "That," he said, like he was embarrassed, but really, he wasn't. It was personal. Nobody had ever asked about it before, because very few people had seen it in the months since he'd had it done. "My mother has the same one."

It wasn't an answer, not really, and the curious look from Tess was enough to let him know she wasn't going to let that slide.

"My mother was an English professor," Eliot said. "That's why my name is Eliot. Both for T. S. and George, her favorite poet and her favorite author."

"'Let us go then, you and I, where the evening is spread

out against the sky, like a patient etherized upon a table,'"
Tess quoted immediately.

Eliot cracked a smile. "Right. Exactly. Mine is in her
handwriting, and hers is in mine. It's a teapot with a George
Eliot quote: 'Only in the agony of parting do we look into the
depths of love.'"

"And the teapot?" Tess asked. "I don't see how that fits."

"It's a joke, between my mother and me. There's that line,
about measuring life in coffee spoons, and she used to say that
she measured her life in pots of tea instead."

His voice was choked, soft, fragile. Like his heart. Eliot
sat up and lifted his sleeve to show her. Sure enough, there
it was: the quote, written in elegant script too perfect to be
human, that instantly made him homesick. Surrounding the
quote was the teapot, simply outlined and delicately shaded
on his arm, decorated with scrolls and flowers on his mother's.

Tess shifted forward and pulled her hand free from his. She
traced the edge of the teapot. Eliot watched her, mesmerized,
as her mouth turned up into a smile and her eyes sparkled into
a laugh.

"What?"

That giggle, that perfect sound, escaped once more. "I just
realized that you literally have a teapot tattoo. You're the most
British person I know."

He couldn't look at her and not smile. She was so close, so
warm, when she ducked her head and bit her lip. And God,
above all, he wanted to kiss her. But he didn't, and even still,
he was happy.

When blood flooded Tess's cheeks and he felt the answering
warmth on his own face, he felt magic singing through his veins.

forty five

TESS DIDN'T GO INTO THE LIBRARY WITH HIM. SHE WAITED for him to emerge, grim-faced and laden with grimoires. Back at her dorm, he set the books across the bare box spring of the bed like an offering. Her mattress was still in Anna's room.

"Okay," Eliot said, voice pitched low. Tess curled up in a carpeted corner and watched him, seeing the scholarly tilt of him slipping back into place. "These are the closest things I could find. I marked the pages that might be useful, but I haven't actually read much."

He passed her a book. "Can you hand me a pen?" Tess asked. "They're behind you. On the desk."

She didn't miss Eliot's frown as he passed her a clear demonstrator pen from her desk. "Fancy," he said, but his voice sounded uncertain.

"Something wrong?"

He shook his head. "It makes me nervous. Ink. Like it could attack me at any moment." He said it all quickly, as if waiting for her to judge him.

Tess took the pen, twisting it in her hands, considering. "I mean, our track record over the last few weeks has not been good."

Eliot shrugged.

She turned back to the book he'd handed her. The issue

with working at a library and having a good memory was that she could remember pulling almost every single one of them, could glance at the spine and place them on the shelves in her memory. This one was from a grouping of astronomical books, and she could guess before opening it that it would be useless.

"We should organize them by call numbers," Tess said. Eliot looked up at her, confused. "Listen. The system the library uses groups stuff with similar topics. So if we have a lot of books about astrology, they won't be helpful, but the folklore and witchcraft ones would."

Eliot frowned.

"Or you could use magic to find what we need," Tess said. The words tasted odd on her tongue. No, it did not surprise her to find that Eliot was some sort of…something. Maybe she was just desensitized to magic. She'd grown up with ghosts, she now courted the devil. Eliot's witchcraft felt strangely right.

"That's not how it works," Eliot said, rolling his eyes. But a small smile teased at his lips, and Tess had the impression her casual mention of it was welcome. Like, for the first time, Eliot didn't have to hide anymore.

She took the books and examined their spines, grouping them. Once she found two piles that looked satisfying, focusing mainly on dark, forbidden magic and a history of it, she divided those books between her and Eliot.

While they read, she couldn't help sneaking glances at him. Eliot was clearly in scholar mode, small frown permanently etched onto his face, brows wrinkled, eyes a little squinted. She thought of the devil in the dream before she'd woken up covered in blood. Of the caress of his hands on her skin.

Would that be how Eliot felt, if he touched her the same way?

"I think I found something," he said, halfway through his

third book. Tess was still on her first, too easily distracted. She got up and sat next to him, reading over his shoulder.

"There's a grouping of folklore about a book. It's called the *Höllenzwang*. In the lore I've come across, it contains a demon. The reader of the book releases him. To put him back, the reader has to read the text backwards."

Tess thought it over. She recalled reading the book, the slipperiness of the words on her tongue. "It sounds plausible," she said. "What do you think?"

He frowned. "It doesn't say anything about ink devils or hauntings or dreams. I don't really know, to be honest."

Tess nodded, considering. "I feel like it's the only option we have. I mean, I think I ended Regina…"

"About that," Eliot said, voice a little higher. He turned and pulled another book onto his lap. "I don't think this fits exactly, but it's about demonic possession. But Tess… It's not an elegant solution."

Tess could tell from his tone she was not going to like this. "What is it?"

Eliot's eyes were flat, focused on the closet doors. "Decapitation."

"Decapitation," Tess repeated. Just the word made her feel sick. She looked down at her hands and tried to imagine removing someone's head.

You have to do this, she thought. *You have to do this and you have to read the book backwards and you have to set yourself free.*

She felt the resolve forming inside her. It was terrifying and sickening and awful, but if this was what it took to survive…

How far could she go? Far enough to end it. Far enough to take her own life back.

"Okay," Tess said. "Okay."

forty six

Tess

TESS TOOK EXTRA CARE DRESSING IN THE MORNING. SHE braided her hair into two tight plaits and dressed in a pair of army green shorts that she felt good running in, a loose black tunic shirt, and tennis shoes. After a moment of thought, she tucked a knife and a flashlight into her bag before dashing out the door.

Eliot wasn't in the library yet so Tess would have to occupy herself with work until he arrived. It was strange to Tess that he was still so comfortable coming into the library, even after everything that had happened to them. She certainly was not. Didn't he feel the press of sinister evil on his heart when he walked through the door?

It was nearing 10:00 and she was staring off into space when she realized that someone was pressed up against the far window of the library, smiling ghoulishly inside.

Regina.

The knife still stuck out from her ribcage. She was caked in blood, speckled with mud. Leaves and sticks tangled in her hair. She looked greenish and dead, decaying.

Tess froze in the middle of the floor. As she watched, Regina raised one hand and waved at her, like a small child.

How had no one *seen* Regina? Now, she was in a thicket

of trees that bordered one edge of the building, but she'd had to walk there to find them… Unless she could just appear and disappear, but that felt more impossible than Eliot's magic.

She grabbed a cart and wheeled it back into the office. Her heart was pounding. Tess didn't think Regina would attack Mathilde. No, it was Tess herself who was the devil's target. "Do you mind if I shelve some books?" Tess called, willing her voice not to shake. If she could get into the stacks, where Mathilde could not hear her, she could call Eliot. Maybe. If there was reception.

"I'll watch the reading room," Mathilde said, taking her cup of tea with her. Tess had a moment of fear that Mathilde would walk out into the reading room and see Regina at the window, but when she turned to look, Regina was gone.

Fear blossomed like a dark orchid in the pit of her belly. She had to reach Eliot. She had no doubt she was emotionally strong enough to decapitate Regina herself, but it was also a matter of being *physically* strong enough.

Tess unloaded the cart of books into the dumbwaiter and pressed the button. Her hands were shaking and she wanted to run, but if Mathilde looked back right now, she needed to seem productive. Once the elevator was on its way, she dashed up the stairs into the stacks.

She fumbled for her phone to call him. The line rang once, beeped sadly, went silent. Tess pulled the phone away. *Call dropped*, the phone mocked. She tried again. Same result. But there would be service higher, in Eliot's office. And maybe she could wait for him there.

The floors in the stacks were shorter than those in the library, so the third floor of the library, where Eliot's office was, was really the fourth floor of the stacks. Tess hit the second floor and quickly turned up to the third. She was just reaching it when she splashed through a puddle on the stairs.

There shouldn't have been a puddle.

There was no reason for there to be a puddle.

The puddle was ink.

She couldn't stop. Tess carefully proceeded up the last two steps and stood on the third-floor landing, listening. There was a steady *drip, drip, drip* somewhere, but she couldn't find the source of it. Slowly, slowly, she rounded the corner into the main area of the stacks.

From what she could tell, the floor was empty.

The stacks were a monstrous creature all on their own. Floor-to-ceiling shelves full of books, spaced with four feet between them. No way to see into the aisles unless you were already rounding the corner. It was not hard to hide in here.

She knew she should keep going—dart around the shelf to the stairs, run up to the fourth floor, get to Eliot's office *now*—but if there was something here on this floor, the worst thing would be to let it get behind her.

Tess wished she'd had the foresight to bring her knife with her into the stacks, but here she was. Alone and defenseless, without service to call Eliot.

She grabbed a heavy book from the closest shelf to use as a shield. Somewhere farther down, the floor creaked. That feeling of not being alone was confirmed by that simple shift, that tiny sound. The hair on her arms stood on end.

And still, somewhere, there was that *drip, drip, drip*.

She crept down the narrow aisle, peeking around each corner before she passed a new shelf. One aisle. Empty. Two. Empty. Three. Empty.

Tess glanced over her shoulder, just to be sure. Nothing.

As Tess began to round the corner to peek around the fourth shelf, she heard a thud. Maybe not a thud—maybe a shuffle. A shuffle and a drip, and it was enough to make Tess's heart seize up in her chest.

Regina was in this aisle. She had to prepare to round the corner and see Regina's dead eyes looking back.

But it wasn't really Regina, Tess reminded herself.

As she counted away seconds, steeling her nerves, she wondered if people ever got used to dead bodies. After all, there were people who did this for a living. Stumbled across them, half-decayed. Cleaned away whatever remained when a person became a collection of unsavory biological matter.

Tess did not know how to be the kind of person who turned the corner, saw Regina's animated corpse, and didn't recoil.

But she had to get it over with, sooner rather than later. Tess rounded the corner.

Now that there was no glass separating them, Regina's body looked even worse. Her eyes were milky and looked soft, like they were going to liquidize and run down her cheeks. The thought was enough to make Tess gag. Her skin was mottled, cast in greenish and purpling hues. Dried blood flaked away from her hands. Her skin looked both too tight and too loose, and under her tank top, her stomach was bulging. Tess recalled some awful episode of a police procedural she watched with Nat once, an episode in which the gases from decay had caused the corpse's midsection to erupt. A maggot wriggled out of Regina's pierced button nose and fell squirming onto the library floor. Tess stepped back.

"Tess," Regina said, and there was a guttural edge, like her vocal cords had been slashed. Her voice didn't sound anything like her. "Why did you have to make things difficult?"

It took Tess a moment to recognize the voice that not-Regina was slipping into, but the hazy, dreamy quality of it snapped the similarities into place. Regina was speaking with the devil's voice.

The smell of rot filled the aisle, and Tess had no idea how she hadn't smelled it before.

"I didn't make things difficult," Tess said, wishing for a weapon. She could turn and run, but there was no running away from this. The devil would only follow her, and there would be nothing guarding her back.

Regina reached out with her broken, bone-tipped fingers. Tess hadn't seen the full extent of the ruin of them after the devil had spent so long scratching at her door the night before. Now, the flesh flayed away from her bones in blackened strips.

"I could've given you everything."

Tess didn't know what the devil was offering, but it wasn't safety. She held the book tighter, protecting her chest.

"I'm not yours," Tess said. Maybe if she did what Eliot had told her to last night, she could drive the devil away. "You are not welcome in this place. You are forbidden."

Regina's mouth trembled, then twisted into a smile. Wider, wider, wider it went, too high at the corners, too open, and dried blood stained the cracks between her teeth as if there was no moisture in her mouth and hadn't been for days. As if she was already just a skull.

"Oh, you silly child," the devil said. "Don't you understand? You're in my realm now."

Tess didn't have time to wonder what that meant. The devil turned Regina's hands and lightly touched her ruined fingertips to the shelves on either side. To Tess's horror, something brackish and black trickled from the books, pooled on the shelves, poured down to the floor. It corrupted the other books it touched until the whole section of shelf was bleeding dark, heavy liquid. The liquid collected in the middle of the floor, just in front of not-Regina's feet. And then, Tess heard the drips, the flowing of the liquid, from the other shelves up and down the floor.

Ink.

All the ink was running out of the books and collecting on the floor. Already, it was edging towards her, moving like a sentient creature. Not spreading, like it had before. And it wasn't just flat black—it was every color at once. Shimmering and vivid, changing. It was not the harmless ink her father bottled and sold. This ink was real and alive, containing some part of the devil within it, controlled and ready for more blood.

Tess shuddered, realizing what the difference was. This ink was the same universe as Truth's eyes in all the dreams she'd had before. Everything and nothing all at once; terrible and beautiful and coming for her soul.

None of the folklore said anything about *this*.

"No, no, no." She couldn't let it touch her. And as the ink collected, she knew she had to get rid of not-Regina, once and for all.

Her only weapon was embedded deep within the corpse's side.

Tess had to think quickly. The knife was there—all she had to do was claim it. It was now or never. And in her head, she heard Eliot's instruction: cut off her head. Decapitate the body, and it would be over.

Tess lurched forward while Regina's hands were still pressed against the shelves and her head was tossed back in that horrifying laugh.

The knife came out easier than Tess had expected, sliding out of the body with a horrible *schlick* noise, and Tess almost fell backwards.

The laughter cut off abruptly, and the devil's head snapped upright, then cocked at a horrible angle. Around them, the ink continued to drip.

"And what are you going to—"

The devil was cut off by the knife as Tess regained her balance, lurched forward, and cut Regina's throat. Forcing through her own revulsion, she grabbed a fistful of Regina's hair and forced her head back against the stacks.

Just do it and it'll be over, just do it just do it just do it.

Regina's flesh was soft with decay. Tess used all her might, sawing through the muscles of her neck. Blood poured from the wound—not a spurt, as Tess expected, because the heart was not beating. Had not been beating for days.

The devil let out a cry of rage, one hand grabbing for Tess's as the other clawed for her eyes. But Tess squeezed her eyes shut and kept sawing. As the devil thrashed, the gore splashed onto her, room temperature blood that tasted of rot and horror.

She hit bone and the devil sagged against the shelves. The attempts to pry her hands off were weaker. Though the devil's spirit tried to keep after her, Regina's dead body was too weak.

Tess dragged the body down onto the ground and knelt next to it. Her hands were slick, covered with tepid blood and bits of rotten flesh. Blood sluiced from the wound, great black tides of it rushing over Tess's fingers, thick and sticky and slick. She found the notch between two vertebrae and cut there, then through the last bit of skin. It made a horrible cracking sound as her knife hit bone.

Dead eyes stared up at her, neck and jaw a mess of gore.

"The devil knows your name, Tess Matheson," a voice whispered in Tess's head. And then the body exploded into a bomb of brackish, hellish ink.

Tess choked and gagged on it, spitting out what had gotten into her mouth. She wanted to puke, but she didn't even think that would get the horrible taste out of her mouth.

Around her, ink dripped from the shelves. When it hit the ground, it turned to dust. There was nothing of Regina left except for the blood on Tess's hands, coating the knife, and awful, charred bones. Tess wiped the knife on the carpet, smearing streaks of blood and bits of rotted flesh. Even though she waited, it did not fade away.

She was free, for now. But she knew, sooner rather than later, the devil would be back.

Tess ran.

forty seven

Eliot

WHEN ELIOT CAME IN, TESS WAS MYSTERIOUSLY MISSING and only Mathilde was in the reading room, stationed behind the circulation desk. A slight, dark pinch of worry tweaked in his stomach. Either Tess was here and occupied, which was likely, or she hadn't shown up for work in the first place.

He could've asked Mathilde, but something about revealing he knew Tess to her boss felt forbidden. So he called her phone. There was no answer. That didn't confirm or deny his suspicions, but it did send his heart beating into overdrive.

He called her again, thinking she might've had her phone on silent or was in the middle of a task. Again, she didn't answer. Which, Eliot considered, was beginning to feel like a pattern. Maybe Tess was just terrible at answering her phone.

Eliot sat behind his desk, tapping his chin with one finger, staring at his phone. He had a few options. Mathilde was still down there. Even though speaking Tess's name to her felt strange, he could do it.

There was also the option of going to her apartment, swinging by to make sure she wasn't in there—and if she was, that she was okay.

If she wasn't at her apartment, then he'd have to worry for the rest of the day. And if she *was* at her apartment, then going there would be as bad as publicly declaring his feelings for her.

But she had to be safe. And if he sat here all day, hiding in his office like a coward while Tess was hurting somewhere...

The thought was enough to force Eliot into action. He put his sweater back on and rolled the sleeves to the elbows. He was considering putting his tie back on, too—which felt like a waste of time, considering the importance of the mission—when his door flew open so wide it hit the wall and nearly shut again.

When he turned, he was relieved to find Tess heaving the doorway. And then, immediately disturbed to see that she was covered in blood.

"What happened?" he gasped.

She stepped inside quickly and shut the door behind her. "Mathilde can't see me," she said. Eliot wanted to say if that was the case, then maybe she shouldn't have opened the door so aggressively, but he couldn't sass her when he saw how hard her hands were shaking.

When he shut the door behind her, he realized that she smelled horrifically of death. She must've seen him screw up his nose because she said, "I know. It's terrible."

There was an extra sweater in this office somewhere, and he rifled through drawers until he found it. It pained him a bit to hand it over to her, but she clearly needed it more than he did, and he had more than enough sweaters. Even if Tess kept ruining them.

She wiped her face on it, smearing the cheerful blue fabric with dark streaks of ink and gore. Long scratches ran down her cheeks, trickling blood.

"What happened?" Eliot repeated.

She told him, starting from seeing Regina at the window

and ending with the explosion in the stacks of not-Regina's body.

He wanted to say something that could comfort her. Clearly, she was a mess, and not just physically. Even though Eliot knew the truth of what Regina was—she'd been dead for days; there was no way they were going to get her back to normal once the devil had claimed her—he wasn't the one who had to face the reality of ending her.

The night before, it had been so easy. To pull her into his arms, to take her hand. But now, in the light of day, he couldn't imagine crossing the space of the desk, reaching out, bridging the gap between them. Her hand was inches away. She was so close. The distance was impenetrable.

"Let me heal you," Eliot said. It was something. A small thing, but something.

Tess looked at him for a moment, uncomprehending. And then she nodded.

He felt oddly self-conscious, taking down what he needed for two spells: one for cleansing and one for healing. He felt Tess watching his every move as he drew the runes and cut his thumb, drawing a bead of blood.

"Does it ever scare you?" Tess asked. "Using the magic."

Eliot shook his head. "Usually, I feel worse when I know I can't."

He performed the magic carefully, overenunciating every word and double-checking his symbols. He didn't want to mess up. Not on Tess. But soon enough, her skin was clean and the cuts on her cheeks were healed, leaving no trace behind. He didn't miss her lifting the gauze on her wrist and peeking at the wound there. Even that was healed.

There was a leftover smudge of dust on her cheekbone.

Without thinking, Eliot set his tools aside and reached forward to rub the streak away with his thumb. Tess's eyes flicked to his. He knew he was still touching her, that his fingers were curled under her chin; he knew he'd been caught taking care of her again.

Eliot let his hand drop.

"I think…" Tess started. She stopped and bit her lip, and then her face twisted in revulsion, like she could taste the memory of ink on her skin and instantly regretted it. He had the sudden stirring panic that she was going to say something bad about him and the way he couldn't stand to be far from her, but a little softer, she continued, "I think we need to ask Mathilde for help."

Eliot hadn't been expecting her to say this, so it took nearly half a minute for him to gather his thoughts enough to make a coherent answer. "Do you think she would believe us?"

Tess looked at him, really looked, and for the first time, he saw that she was breaking. "Eliot, someone *died*. Their body exploded and is all over my fucking skin and the devil tried to kill me, multiple times." Softer, creakier, she finished, "I can't do this anymore."

He couldn't fight the notion that he'd failed somehow, like he'd been meant to protect her and had found the task impossible.

But he wasn't meant to protect her. Tess wasn't someone he could protect.

To be honest, he was a little afraid of her. She *had* just decapitated someone.

So Eliot said, "Okay." If Tess thought she'd believe them, then Eliot had to have faith in that. He thought back to his conversation with Brooks the Friday before. There'd been a fire in Jessop, one Mathilde had been around for.

Maybe, then, she knew about the vault and the book. Maybe she'd know what to do.

Tess led the way out of the office, down the stairs, to the circulation desk. He followed her like a foot soldier trudging behind a celebrated general, resolutely certain of his imminent death.

Mathilde saw them coming, and her eyebrows flew into her hairline at the sight of Tess's disheveled hair and twisted clothing.

"Theresa," she said, standing. "What did you get into?"

There was no lead-up, no prelude. "I think we summoned the devil," Tess said.

forty eight

Tess

THE THREE OF THEM SAT AT A PICTURESQUE WIRE TABLE IN the park plaza. It wasn't close to peak lunchtime, so not many people were milling around the space. As soon as Tess admitted what they'd done, Mathilde had insisted on them getting out of the library and locking the door, even going so far as to disable the keypad access.

"Start from the beginning," Mathilde said when Eliot was settled with a cup of tea from the stand in the park.

"We found a book," Eliot said, not making eye contact with Mathilde. Tess got the impression that he was afraid of her, or at least intimidated.

"Found where?" Mathilde asked.

Tess and Eliot exchanged a look. There was no point hiding the truth. Judging by the set to Mathilde's mouth, she already knew exactly what they were going to say. And maybe that meant she knew something about how to fix the situation. Eliot nodded to Tess, like he felt the same way, urging her to speak. Slowly, Tess said, "In the basement of the library. Uh, the basement under the basement."

"The sepulcher," Mathilde said.

Sepulcher. Grave, she knew, from a particularly fraught reading of Poe's "Annabel Lee" in a ninth grade English class.

It felt ridiculous to associate the word, usually linked with some far-fetched, horrific fairytale, with Falk or Jessop.

Ridiculous, but accurate.

"We did some research. We think it's called the *Höllenzwang*. Do you know about it? What it is?" Eliot asked, apparently already thinking ahead while Tess's brain was still sputtering around in circles. He was leaning forward in his chair, elbows on the table, eyes urgent. This was clearly his scholar-on-a-mission mode.

"Tell me you didn't read it," Mathilde said wearily, already knowing they had.

Tess bit her lip. "Technically, I did," she said, oddly wanting to take the blame away from Eliot, even though it was mostly his fault. If anything, this made her great aunt look even more distressed.

Mathilde shook her head. *Boys like that scare me*, her aunt had said.

"You know what it is, then. How did it get there? What is it? Why was it hidden instead of destroyed?"

Mathilde stared at her hands, eyes distant. "I couldn't destroy it. I couldn't bring myself to do it. I always thought, if the book stayed intact, then maybe he would come back, when the devil was gone."

Tess didn't need to look at Eliot to know that he was staring at her, eyes full of questions. "He? Who is he?"

"My husband, Harry," Mathilde said. Tess tried to keep her face flat, but inside, she was shocked. She'd never known Mathilde was married, couldn't imagine her being with anyone other than herself. "He's the one who found that damned book in the first place."

"What happened to him?" Eliot asked. But Tess already

suspected she knew the truth. If he'd tangled with the devil and he wasn't here now, there was only one true answer.

Mathilde stretched her wrinkled hands out, as if she was seeing them as they were forty years before, smooth and without age spots, wearing her wedding ring. "Harry was ambitious. Here was the goal: to find a book that held God, a book that held truth. He'd heard of it before, in whispers when he was at university; a book that held some monster and the secrets of the universe. No one knew exactly what it was: some called it Faust's book, some said it was made from the tree of knowledge of good and evil, some said it was the seventh book of Moses. Others said it was just another grimoire."

"But grimoires aren't that powerful by themselves," Eliot said, eyes flashing. Something caught in Tess's throat. Even the subject of it felt forbidden, ancient, unknowable.

"If you don't have magic, maybe not," Mathilde said. She sounded lost to time as she spoke, there in body with them at the table, but mentally in some moment long past. Tess didn't know what to make of it. "He went all over searching for it. Jerusalem. The remains of Mesopotamia. The catacombs of Sicily, the mausoleums of France, and then, finally, the tombs of England. Because the English took everything, didn't they?" She made eyes at Eliot, who sat back in his chair and took an extended sip of his tea.

"Did you go with him?" Tess asked.

"No," Mathilde said. "He said it was too dangerous, and I was needed here. It was right after Jessop was acquired from the university, and I was just starting my job here—exploring the library, ordering the books. The sepulcher was there then, but it was cleaned out and patched over, so nobody could access it. It was Harry's idea to install the door, so he could keep the most precious of the books down there, out of sight."

Tess shook her head, trying to put the pieces together. "Okay. So he found the book when he was in England, didn't he? And then he...what? Brought it back?"

"He didn't know it was dangerous," Mathilde insisted. "There was no way to know what it was. But this is what we learned: there was a demon in the book, or a devil. There was something older than us, stronger than us. Something that wanted us dead."

Eliot nodded, listening but not judging. Tess envied him that ability. Because, right now, she was definitely judging. "And then he read it and the devil killed him. Right?"

"No," Mathilde said softly. "No, he didn't read it." Her eyes were softer than usual and blurred with tears when she looked up and met Tess's eye. Tess wasn't sure she'd ever seen her like this: so vulnerable looking. Not like butterfly wings. No, now she was a dewdrop on a leaf, only there for a moment, destined to disappear. "I did."

Tess blinked, a fierce relief rifling through her. If Mathilde read the book out loud and was still alive, then there was a way out of this. She looked at Eliot, certain she'd see the same delirious relief on his face, but his brows were drawn together and his lips were turned down into a frown.

"How did you get out?" Tess asked, trying to lead Eliot to the same conclusion she had. That there was a way out in the first place.

"Harry and I thought... We thought if we set the book on fire, if we burned it all down, we could be free."

"The fire," Eliot said, sitting back in his chair, running a thumb over his chin. Tess had heard of it, in passing: a great fire years and years ago that had nearly taken the entire building down with it, but left Jessop smoldering.

"I thought the fire happened before Falk bought the library," Tess said.

Mathilde shook her head. "No. It was soon after, so soon after. We thought…we thought if we could get rid of the book, we could get rid of the devil."

And that worked so well, Tess thought.

"But clearly, that didn't contain him," Eliot said.

Mathilde shook her head. Tess could barely align this—the story, the horror of it—with the reality of sitting in the park in summertime, midday, as the world continued around them. "He has to own you, to have your heartsblood. Only then can he be free, with you as his servant, until you face the same fate as the demon did, trapped in the book. Me, then. You, now. The reader. You don't understand what he's capable of. He won't stop until you're his, Theresa. He can't harm you himself outside of your dreams, but he can take others. If you give in, he's free. He'll never be contained again.

"We thought we could burn it all, but the devil got in Harry's veins, started to possess him. Harry's last act was to set the fire and burn with it so I could get free."

"And the book survived the fire," Eliot said.

Mathilde swallowed, and she was so thin that Tess could nearly see the saliva traveling down her throat. "It did. In the morning, I had to go into the smoldering library and deal with the devil by myself."

"I'm so sorry," Tess said. "But Aunt Mathilde, I have to ask you. How did you get the devil back in the book? Because clearly, you did."

Mathilde sighed unhappily. "I did. The original reader must read the text backwards. Tess, in this case. That will trap him, little by little. But it won't happen easily, I assure you." She took Tess's hand and squeezed it. Veins stood prominent, blue against the pale marble of her skin. "He can't touch you, not unless he's acting through someone else. He alone has no power over you so he will ruin everything around you. He will kill everyone you love. And in the end, he will get inside your head, and try to destroy you from the inside out."

Tess didn't want to hear any more. She wanted to pull her knees up, to turn away, as if she could curl herself up and tuck her body away like an egg in a shell. Across the table, Eliot looked as stormy as she had ever seen him. It took a moment for Tess to identify what it was. He looked like he was going to lose a battle, but he would fight it anyway.

"He took Regina," Eliot said wearily. Tess shot him a quick glance, uncertain, but he just shook his head. "That's why... why we had to tell you. Tess dealt with her earlier."

Tess did not like the connotations of what he meant when he said she'd dealt with her. She didn't want to think about it ever again.

Mathilde looked between the two of them. "You dealt with her? Properly?"

"Yes," Tess whispered. "But what do we do? Who do we tell?"

Mathilde only shook her head. "I will figure out how to handle it," she said wearily. "But if he's taken one person already, no doubt he'll be searching for another vessel."

The words hung in the air. Tess turned them over, terribly aware that nothing was safe. "But you did it," Tess said. "You bested him."

Mathilde's eyes were cold and hard as flint. "I did."

They didn't need it to be easy. They just needed it to be possible.

forty nine

Eliot

TESS AND ELIOT DECIDED TO STAY TOGETHER. THE LIBRARY would remain closed, Mathilde insisted, until nightfall, when the three of them would return to finish off the devil once and for all: Mathilde for her knowledge, Tess to read, and Eliot to…to…be the muscle. Not that he had much in the muscle department. But he was here in this mess since the beginning, and there was no way in hell he would let Tess finish this herself.

Tess's roommate was home when they got to her dorm. She was a girl Eliot recognized from many of his classes— Anna Liu. He thought she was here on scholarship and on an accelerated track. They nodded to each other when Tess shut the door behind them.

"Eliot," Anna said. "I didn't know you and Tess were, uh, friends."

Something about this made the back of his neck burn. Sure, what he and Tess had was unconventional, but it was odd that she hadn't even said anything to her roommate about him.

When he looked over, Tess was blushing scarlet too. "Oh, we have a project to work on. Don't we, Eliot?"

"Right," he agreed, although the excuse was unconvincing. What project would they be working on during the summer?

Anna raised her eyebrows, but before she could say anything

else, Tess was pushing Eliot through the kitchenette, towards her bedroom. "I'll catch you later!" Tess said.

With the door shut behind them, she seemed more comfortable. "Well, sorry about that," Tess said. "I forgot she was coming home today. Otherwise, I would've said we could go to your place, but I wasn't sure…" She didn't have to finish the sentence. Even though the devil hadn't made an appearance, there was no way to know that his dorm was safe.

But there was another revelation, one that seemed even more disconcerting to him. She didn't want other people knowing that they were friends.

He sat down on her desk chair and tried his best to not look like he was sulking. She folded cross-legged on her bed. "What's wrong?" Tess asked.

There were a million answers to choose from, so it was definitely not a good idea when he said, "Nothing."

Tess's frown deepened. "Eliot. You can tell me."

But he couldn't. He could tell her everything about his fears of the devil, how much he missed his mother, how badly he wanted to leave this place and never look back. But never, not in a million years, could he sit here in her room and tell her that now, after all this time, he cared about her. Deeply.

"I don't want you to get hurt in all this," Eliot said. It was one form of the truth anyway.

"Are you afraid?" Tess asked.

Eliot closed his eyes. "Not for myself," he said.

There was the sound of creaking, and a few soft footsteps, and warmth on his cheek. When he opened his eyes, Tess was there in front of him. Her hand was on his cheek and her face was inches away, so close he only needed to shift and he'd be kissing her.

He would not make the first move. Eliot Birch was a lot of things, and forward was *not* one of them.

The only thing he could do was reach out and rest one hand on her waist. With his other, he brushed the hair out of her eyes. "I don't know what I would do," Eliot said, knowing how much this would reveal, "if I walked into Jessop on any given day and you weren't the one there to insult me. If I had to know that I would never see you again."

It was too much. It wasn't enough. It was all he could offer.

"Nothing is going to happen to me," Tess said. She leaned in a little and this was it, Eliot knew, this was it, and maybe he'd been wrong about her feelings changing because now she was leaning towards him and—

And the timing was wrong. She knew it as well as he did, judging by the look of her. He sat back, putting space between them.

"Tess," Eliot said, and her back tightened, like she knew what he was going to ask. "Will you play for me?"

She turned, surprised. "What?"

He nodded to her cello, leaning against the wall. "Your cello. I want to hear you play. Will you?"

She shrugged like there was nothing better to do, even though he had a million ideas—ideas he would never say out loud, of course. "You don't want to hear me play," she said.

He sensed an odd bit of hesitation, and her fingers were tracing circles in her thigh. She didn't look at him. "But don't you love it?" he asked. "Are you nervous I won't think you're good?"

She laughed, not a real laugh, but a sad and lilting thing that oddly reminded him of a dreary pigeon. "I—"

"Just play, Tess," he said. "It'll distract you."

She didn't look happy about it, but she didn't argue for

once. It took her a moment to unpack the cello, take out the bow, run it across the strings. He waited for her to take out a stand or some music but she didn't. She sat there, screwing up her nose at the cello for a moment before she touched the bow to the strings and began to play.

Before that moment, that second, Eliot thought he knew her. After all, he cared for her, didn't he? He knew about her parents, about how much she loved her sister, about her drive and ferocity.

What he didn't know was that she could take the entire world in the palm of her hands and reflect it with her fingertips. He didn't know that she could stop both time and his heartbeat all at once, fold him into nonexistence between notes. He didn't know that she could be even more entrancing to him.

Which was to say, when she took a breath at the end of the song as if she'd been holding it the entire time, he realized he didn't know her at all.

It was like finding the correct answer, like reading a spell and watching it unfold. It was like nothing at all he'd ever experienced before and everything he'd ever wanted. He was so, so tired of wanting her this much.

He knew he should've said something when she finished, though her eyes were still closed and she was curved over the body of the cello. And when her eyes slid open and found him, peaceful as he'd ever seen them, he definitely should've spoken.

But Eliot, who always had words dancing in his head, could think of nothing to say.

When she played, it was a lot like watching magic.

"Would you like to hear something else?" Tess asked.

There was only one answer. "Yes."

fifty

Tess

SHE'D FINISHED PLAYING AND PUT AWAY HER CELLO, AND they went for food, and then they each went to their separate dorms to get dressed for the night's activities.

On her walk back, she tried to call Nat. Her sister didn't answer—hadn't answered her all week, since their argument. But if she hadn't heard from the school, then at least Nat hadn't snuck out and gotten expelled.

She tried Nat one final time. Nothing.

When she returned, Anna was waiting for her. "So. What's going on with you and Birch?" she asked, ready to launch a full-out assault. "And why am I just hearing about it now?"

Tess bit her lip. She couldn't keep it from Anna forever, could she? "He liked me, but I think I scared him away."

Anna snorted. "Good girl." But then she caught the look on Tess's face and frowned back. "Or…is that a bad thing?"

"I don't know," Tess hedged, running her fingers along the edge of a tea towel. But she *did* know.

"You like him, don't you?" Anna asked.

Like wasn't the word for it, Tess thought. She marveled at his compassion, so carefully hidden away most of the time. She was proud of his intelligence, even though she had no claim to shaping it, even though it had nothing to do with her.

Her heart flipped a little bit every time she saw his face, even though he was either smirking or saying something ridiculous about 99 percent of the time.

This was dangerous territory.

"I think I do," Tess said.

Anna leaned back on the kitchen table. "I mean, he's nice, when he talks. Which isn't often, but that's just from class. And his accent is good." She shrugged, ducking into her room. "Could be fun."

So Anna wasn't fully on board, yet. But if they succeeded tonight, if the sun rose to find both of them alive and breathing, then there would be time to bring her around. Time for all of it.

Tess and Eliot met outside of the doors to Jessop. Both wore black, not because of any previous agreement, but because, at least in Tess's mind, it felt like the best color in which to do something illicit.

"Are you ready?" Eliot asked.

No, but she had to be.

The library did not look like it had endured the horror of Regina's body this afternoon or like it held any danger for them this evening. But, as they both knew far too well, looks were deceiving.

"Mathilde?" Tess called, letting the heavy door shut behind them.

Her aunt appeared in the door of the office and walked towards them. She stopped at the edge of the balcony overhang, shrouded in late evening shadows. "Good. I was waiting for you," Mathilde said. She glanced behind her at one of the large windows, where they could see the sun beginning to set. "First, we must shutter the windows. I don't want anyone to see what is happening and come investigating. We are the only ones who should be in here, beginning to end. Nobody else needs to be endangered."

Tess and Eliot exchanged a glance. "We always shutter the windows at night," Tess agreed quietly, even though she hated the idea of losing what little moonlight leaked through the windows. Neither of them particularly wanted to be here in the first place, and remaining in the library in the dark seemed even worse.

They worked their way around the room, closing each shutter until the only light that remained was the dim reddish tint from the emergency exit sign. Mathilde remained under the balcony and away from the light, arms crossed over her chest, until she became nothing but a dark suggestion of a person.

"Good," she said when they finished. "Now, follow me."

Tess could feel Eliot's eyes on her, dark and uncertain. And even though she felt the same way, she couldn't look back at him. To look back was to confirm there was a reason to fear. Mathilde was here, a supervisor, a guide, a source of knowledge. They would be fine.

Soon enough, all of this would be over.

Tess rubbed her thumb across the silvery scar on her wrist, all that remained of the gash after Eliot healed her. She needed this to be over.

In a single file line, Mathilde, Tess, and Eliot went into her aunt's office. It was fully dark back here with no light leaking in from the reading room, and Tess was relieved when

Mathilde stopped to take two flashlights out of her desk, one for herself and one for Tess. The emergency lights were always on in the stacks, so even though the shadows were heavy and thick, the darkness was gray instead of black.

She was surprised when Mathilde led the way up instead of down. Eliot must've been, too, because she sensed him pausing for a moment before following them, a little slower than before. By the looks of it, they were taking the path through the stacks to the upper floors—but that made no sense. All three of them knew that the devil's book was in the subterranean tunnel under the basement, and unless Mathilde had moved the book when they weren't there, then going upstairs would do nothing to rid themselves of the devil.

Tess's internal clock chimed dimly. This whole thing was taking too long, stretching too far. They'd already been at the library for almost half an hour, and she could feel the tension inside of her stomach build with every second that passed.

"Mathilde?" Eliot's voice was quiet behind Tess, as if the darkness made him feel unable to speak at his full volume. Mathilde, who was halfway around the landing to the second floor and rounding the stairs to the third, turned back. There was something weird and foggy about her eyes, something dark about the way she held her hands around the flashlight.

"What is it, boy?" Mathilde asked, and Tess's warning bells flared a little higher. There was something hostile in the way Mathilde called Eliot "boy." It wasn't like she'd simply forgotten his name. The word was a spat insult, an insinuation of guilt for some terrible crime. And beyond that, Mathilde's voice had taken on a gravelly tone that made Tess's skin crawl.

Eliot bumped into her, and she hadn't realized she'd stopped moving. Her hands were at her sides, and she didn't know that Eliot shared her fear until his icy cold fingers moved to touch hers.

"Why are we going up?" Eliot asked. His voice was solid, strong, but he wrapped his hand around Tess's and squeezed. She had a knife in her belt, but she wasn't ready to reach for it yet, let alone use it.

"I shut and locked the fire doors to the first floor," Mathilde said. "To contain everything in the basement. So we have to go down through the elevator staircase." Her mouth twisted into a smile, and it was so unlike any smile Tess had ever seen on her great aunt's face. A chill ran up her spine. She squeezed Eliot's hand back. If only she could speak to him without Mathilde hearing, lean over to whisper in his ear, *There is something very wrong here.*

"But why would we go all the way up, instead of down?" Eliot asked. His hand was moving, creeping up the back of her shirt, skimming the skin along Tess's waist, and she was about to grab his wrist with her free hand when she realized he was feeling along the waist of her jeans for the knife he knew was there.

"This way is better," Mathilde said. "He can't get out, then." That smile stayed on her lips, that ferocity in her teeth. Eliot's hand was a centimeter away from the knife, almost there, gracing the edge of it—

"Theresa, come here and hold the light."

His hand stopped. Tess had to move forward, to make it look like nothing was happening. His finger tapped twice quickly on her overheated skin. It was both an urging to stay safe and a reminder that she was armed.

"Okay," Tess said. She'd only moved a few steps forward

when Mathilde turned off the flashlight, tossed it aside, and lunged.

Before Tess could think, before she could react, Mathilde's icy cold hands were around her throat. The flashlight dropped out of Tess's hands, going out when it hit the ground, plunging them into the gray darkness of the emergency lights.

There was a shout, and she wasn't sure if it was from her or Eliot. She couldn't breathe around Mathilde's hands. Her hands flew up to Mathilde's, trying to pry them off, but they had too tight of a hold.

The whites of Mathilde's eyes went black.

It was the devil's voice that said, "You're mine now."

fifty one

Tess

"TESS!" ELIOT SHOUTED.

Mathilde pushed Tess back against the bookshelves, pinning the knife between the shelf and Tess's body. The old woman was crushing her throat, both hands closed around it, gleeful murder present in her inky eyes. Dark spots bloomed on the edge of Tess's vision.

Deep down, sickeningly, Tess knew that the devil wasn't only trying to strangle her. He was trying to break her.

If she could angle her back, slide out from behind the shelf, maybe Eliot would be able to grab the knife from her belt, but she could barely move. All she could do was pathetically paw at Mathilde's hands as the life ebbed out of her.

The devil's voice pressed against her on all sides, so present and loud in her fading mind. Laughing.

She felt Eliot slam into her, coming between Mathilde's arms and her neck, bending the frail woman's arms despite the devil's borrowed strength. Mathilde cried out, losing her grip, and Tess staggered back against the shelf.

Tess blinked hard, trying to focus. She dropped down to her knees as air rushed back into her lungs. Everything was still wavy, a little bit unclear. Mathilde and Eliot struggled above her. Mathilde's hands reached for Eliot's throat, but she was too short to reach it with him holding her back, and Mathilde was too wiry for Eliot to get a good grip on her. And over the commotion there was the roar of the devil's voice, but Tess couldn't quite figure out what he was saying.

It took a moment to realize her hands were wet and ink was dripping down from the shelves, pooling on the floor around her.

"Eliot!" she cried, but her voice was a soft rasp, not nearly loud enough to overpower the devil's. Weakly, she pulled the knife from her belt and crawled through the thick ink towards Eliot and Mathilde. She didn't care that the ink was all over her hands, running up to her wrists. The devil couldn't hurt her on his own.

She could slit an Achilles tendon, probably, or stab an artery, if she could get close enough. They'd fought their way to the dumbwaiter, with Mathilde's back to it. Sludgy ink poured down the shelves, coating Mathilde and melding into her skin, forming a cover over her. It looked sturdy, rough and hard to break, like a shield.

The door to the dumbwaiter was open at Mathilde's waist level, and Tess had an idea. She gripped the slippery shelves, hoisting herself up. If they could incapacitate her, then they could cut off her head before Eliot was harmed, before the devil could do any more damage.

Not-Mathilde was too distracted by Eliot to notice Tess slinking down the shelf towards her. She wiped her hands off on her jeans, trying to rid them of the ink.

Mathilde pushed Eliot back against the opposite shelf, and his head made an awful noise as it cracked against the metal. Ink darkened his hair and made blacker spots on his already black shirt. A line of blood trickled down from his temple, from a cut in the shape of Mathilde's nails.

The space between Mathilde and the elevator was just what Tess needed.

Tess moved behind her and grabbed Mathilde by the chin and hair, forcing her to bend backwards, bringing her head down. She slammed Mathilde's neck on the lip of the open dumbwaiter. Eliot didn't even need a look from her to recover and crush the door to the dumbwaiter down as Tess took her hands away.

The bones of Mathilde's neck made a sickening crunch as they were crushed beneath the dumbwaiter's sliding door. Tess turned away, unable to see the inky body and blood oozing from the torn bits of flesh and align them with her aunt.

And still, she could hear the devil laughing.

"Tess," Eliot said, and his voice was as ragged and gory as Mathilde's body. "I need the knife."

Numbly, she handed it to him.

She turned away, but she could still hear the noise. The awful *schlick* of the knife cutting through her aunt's neck, the *thump* as the head detached and fell into the dumbwaiter.

Tess flinched when her aunt's body exploded in a deluge of ink. The bones clattered to the ground, looking as scorched as Regina's had.

Her butterfly aunt, her frail companion, the only person who'd been able to save her.

Neither of them moved. They should've, she knew, before the ink all around them began forming something sinister.

But she couldn't move her feet. She couldn't come to terms with the fact that Aunt Mathilde had been here, seconds ago, and now she…wasn't.

She was dead.

But dead, in Tess's mind, had never meant ceasing to exist. It had never meant exploding into nothing, leaving only bones and memories behind. Death meant a funeral and a gathering of relatives and a body and mourning. Death was not this messy, gory thing that she couldn't understand, this skip from existing in one second to dissolving in the next.

Tess knew they had to move, that they had to keep going, but she saw a scrap of lavender fabric that had been torn away from Mathilde's sweater, and Tess found herself on her knees without any memory of falling.

Eliot's face loomed in her vision, too close and real. His ink-smudged hands moved to her face, cupping her cheeks, and she saw his lips moving but she couldn't hear the words he was saying.

Two deaths. Two people that she'd known, that she'd spoken to, and now they were gone. Because of her.

Mathilde had held her as a baby, been at her first birthday party, held her hand when she'd crossed the street, watched her grow up. And now she was nothing but the ink soaking into the knees of Tess's jeans.

She closed her eyes, squeezed them against the memories. She felt Eliot's hands but all she could hear was her aunt's voice: *Boys like that scare me. Because they want to know everything.*

She pulled away from his hands, from his comfort.

"I never wanted her to die," she choked out, skidding away from him. Her back hit one of the shelves of books and ink dripped onto her shoulders. "She shouldn't have been— This shouldn't have…" She couldn't speak. Words were lost in the strangling ache in her throat.

Eliot crouched in front of her. Shame flickered across his face. "Tess…"

"Get away from me," she said. She could barely speak, hyperventilating, suffocating.

"Tess," he said, stronger now. "That wasn't Mathilde. You know that."

She choked on a cough. There was too much ink, too much death, and she was falling apart. She was shattering, splintering, exploding. She'd never get out. Neither of them would. They were going to die in this goddamn aisle, decay into ink, dissolve into nothing.

He gave her a hard shake. "*Tess.*"

She clutched his arms, nails digging into his skin. "Don't let him take me."

He looked like a monster. He looked like a savior. Ink stained his cheekbones, sinking into his pores, darkening his eyelashes. Eliot took her shoulders, held her steady. "He's not going to take you."

Eliot pulled her up to her feet. She wasn't sure how, but she was conscious of him dragging her, of her putting one foot in front of the other, stumbling up the stairs and then up another flight. And then they were back out in the dim reading room, on the balcony of the third floor, and Eliot was pulling her into his office.

She collapsed into a chair as soon as it was underneath her. This whole day, this whole month, was a horror show. And now that Tess knew what the devil could do, she had no idea how they were supposed to beat him.

He knelt on the carpet in front of her. Eliot's hands gently probed the skin around her throat. His hands were dark with ink and clammy, a reminder of what had happened to them back there—and what they'd done.

When he was satisfied with his analysis, he tilted her chin

down towards him, forcing her to look him in the eyes.

"Are you okay?" he asked.

No, she was not okay. She was so far from okay that the thought of answering him made her feel a little hysterical, but her throat hurt so badly after the first giggle escaped that she trapped the rest of them behind her lips.

Eliot didn't blink, didn't flinch away. His eyes were gentler than she deserved. She had to look away from him.

"There was nothing you could have done," Eliot said. "The devil got her before we were even here, Tess."

Tess closed her eyes. She knew he was right. He had to be. She didn't know how or when, but Mathilde was gone before she and Eliot had come back for the evening. Like Regina, by the time they'd removed her head, she'd already been dead.

"What will we do now?" Tess asked, and her voice was still too soft and too rough. She tried to clear her throat, but then it only burned.

Eliot sighed, running an inky hand through his hair. "Well, we have to go back in the stacks," he said. "And down to the tunnel. I don't think Mathilde was lying to us about how to get rid of him."

"Reading it backwards," Tess said.

"*You* reading it backwards," Eliot emphasized, picking at the carpet. She wondered if there was accusation in his voice, like he was afraid she wasn't brave enough to complete the task, or if he was simply reminding her of what needed to be done.

"I know," Tess snapped.

Eliot looked wounded, like her words were as sharp as the ink-and-blood-coated knife he still held in his hand.

She wished she could say something, but how could she pick up the fractured pieces of herself and make them complete enough to comfort him?

Finally, Eliot said, "I did what I had to."

"I know," Tess whispered, and then quickly, "I would have done the same." Immediately, she was ashamed of the response. As if that made her death sting less. As if that made her lack of existence bearable. "I…I don't know how to feel about it," Tess admitted, because it was the truth.

Eliot nodded as if he understood, or at least, as if he was trying to. "I'm sorry, Tess. I'm so, so sorry."

She took his sympathy, swallowed it like a bitter drink, allowed it to absorb. "She took Nat and me in when we needed her."

Eliot laid one of his hands on her knee, fingers stretched. "She deserved better. You deserve better. And there's only one way to avenge her."

Tess nodded, just barely. The truth bubbled inside of her, acidic, corrosive.

"The sooner we finish this, the better," Tess said.

The thought of entering the stacks again made her heart shrivel up inside her and her stomach turn to lead. Tess didn't want to go back. She wanted to run far, far away without returning to this godforsaken library ever again.

Something vibrated against her. She nearly jumped out of her skin before she realized it was just her phone in the pocket of her jeans. With shaking hands, Tess pulled it out to see Nat's name on the caller ID. She had to answer.

Tess tried to clear her throat, but there wasn't much she could do to help the hoarseness of her voice. Ignoring Eliot's look, she half turned away from him to answer the call.

"Hey, Nat," she said, trying to sound bright and failing miserably. If she was going to risk her life going into the stacks, she wasn't going to allow this conversation to be awful. Tess would even apologize for their fight, even though she wasn't at fault.

"Tess." The fear in Nat's voice was thick and piercing. "I don't know how to say this, but I think your bookshelves are… bleeding."

Tess's blood turned to ice. She glanced at Eliot, and it seemed that he could hear too, because he was looking back at her with that expression caught somewhere between misery and terror.

"Where are you?" Tess asked.

Nat's voice was a shaky whisper. "Your dorm. I talked to Mathilde about our fight and she signed me out. Um. So I could apologize. I came to see you and Anna let me in and…" There was a pause, and Anna's voice in the background, and then Nat was back. "We're in the bathroom. With the door locked. We don't know what to do."

"What do you mean?" she asked. Eliot moved closer, pressing his ear to the phone with hers so he could hear Nat's response.

"There's stuff. Coming from your books and papers and… I don't know. It's everywhere. On the table and floor. Did you— Wait." There was a shuffling noise, and Tess thought her fingers would break from how tightly she was gripping the phone. Then, hollowly: "It's seeping under the door."

Tess took a ragged breath. Ink, she could deal with. Besides, she'd forbidden not-Regina—and the devil with her—from going after Nat. Nat was safe, and ink was everywhere, so this was probably just a distraction. A scare tactic to get her away from the stacks, away from the book, so the devil could take her.

"Get out of there," Tess snapped, and the force of her voice surprised even her. "I don't think it can hurt you. Not now. But you need to get out. Do you understand me?"

A pause of silence, and Tess could hear Nat's uneven breathing but nothing more. If the devil took Nat… If they had to…to… No. She couldn't think of it. Eliot's hand was on her back, then, as if he could ground her.

Regular ink wasn't going to hurt them, but the kind that looked like the universe. That ink, the kind that looked like the devil's eyes—that was the dangerous kind. The kind that took over Regina and Mathilde.

"Put Anna on, okay?"

A brief shuffling sounded, and a few sniffles that made Tess grab for Eliot's hand. He squeezed back fiercely. And there was Anna's voice, strong and clear. "Tess, it's all over the floor. We can't get out without stepping in it."

"Do you have shoes? Anything to cover?" Eliot asked, leaning in to be heard.

"No," Anna said.

"We've touched it enough, and we're fine," Tess said slowly. "You're going to be fine. You just need to get out of there."

"I'm not going to sugarcoat this," Anna said wearily, "but the ink…burns? Nat didn't touch it but I did and it definitely stung."

Tess and Eliot exchanged a look. All Tess could think of was Anna, the night she'd found Tess bleeding in the bathroom. The warmth of her body in the morning, nestled next to Tess, with the sunlight playing on her shoulders.

"Get out of there *now* and nothing will happen to you," Tess said, feigning surety. "We'll handle it. Just get out of there, away from the ink, and it will be okay."

"Listen, Anna," Eliot said. Tess angled the phone so he

could speak into it. "Don't touch anything that has ink on it. Posters, signs, any paper. Keep on walking until you're at the park. Can you do that?"

"Yes," Anna said.

"Can I talk to Tessy, please?" Nat asked.

It was that squeaked "Tessy" that was enough to break her out of her trance. She pulled the phone back. "Natalie, listen to Eliot. Go with Anna. Wait for us there. We'll be there soon."

"I'm scared, Tess."

That small admission was enough to undo her. Tess breathed in through her nose, out through her mouth. The devil could not have Nat. He could take Regina. He could take Mathilde. Fuck, he could even take Tess. But she would not let him take Nat.

"You have to be brave, Nat. It will be okay. Go with Anna."

"Okay," Nat whispered, and Tess could hear the edges of tears in her voice. "I love you. And I'm sorry."

Tess's voice caught when she said, "I love you too." She hung up the phone. Inches away, Eliot was watching her.

"It's hurting them," she said quietly.

Eliot closed his eyes for a moment. She watched him take a deep breath and release it slowly. "Then we have to be fast, don't we?"

Tess leaned down and rubbed her hands on the carpet, smudging the burgundy with gore. She got up from the chair and reached a hand down to Eliot. He looked at it for a second, and then his eyes flicked up to hers. "Are you sure you're okay?"

She wasn't okay. She most certainly was not okay. But she was not going to let anything hurt Nat. Not anything that she could prevent.

fifty two

THERE WAS A WAY INTO THE BOY.

When you as the old woman gripped his arm, you felt the call of it even through his shirt. *Master master master*, the ink called, *we serve as always serve you want you help you let us in.*

Just before the woman was bested and your vision cut, you saw what you needed, imbedded into the skin, a way to take him even through the protection of his magic.

You were a boy once yourself, before you were a devil. Sometimes, you remembered being a boy, not pulled into the shape of others, not commanding skins that did not belong to you. You remembered what it felt like to touch, to feel, to consume. To live. You wanted that, above all. To feel that way again.

It was easier not to remember what you sacrificed. There was a book and a boy, and then you were the boy and the book was not you, was not consuming you from the inside out and turning your soul to ink.

Freedom, the book begged, the first time you traced your paint-stained fingers against the cover. *Give me freedom and I'll give you eternity.* So the bargain went, hammered and defined, and there was no need for the book to kill to get what it wanted then. Either because you were weak or because you wanted.

Now, you were not so lucky. Tess did not want the way you wanted; she was not willing to bargain the way you were. It was like the other reader, all those years ago, who would not cave to your demands even as you burned the world around her.

You could've formed your ink around the shape of her, pressed your half-formed palms to her shoulders, carved her body through what little power you still had, and yet she would not have bargained.

You saw it in her. You *admired* it in her, even as it tore you apart; even as your ink craved to feel the warmth of her skin once more.

She would not bargain for much, but she would bargain for the boy—which turned your glimmer to ash and curved your ink around the words *jealous* and *sacrifice*.

If all else failed, there was another place you could find yourself welcome: Tess's threshold had been blessed, but the boy's purifying magic had swept it all away. He had gotten rid of the wards that prevented you from entering. You dripped from music notes and novels, from homework and cookbooks and fast food advertisements.

There were fates worse than death. There was grief endless as time itself. It was time Tess learned that.

fifty three

Eliot

BACK TO THE CAGE, WHERE IT ALL BEGAN.

The pale glow of the emergency lights cast ghostly shadows as they made their way back down the stairs. It reminded Eliot of the dim lighting of his mother's sickroom. He hated it. It didn't help that they were making their way through an inch of murky ink that covered the floor like a swamp.

The devil was everywhere here.

They heard his laughter in every corner and his whisper from every shelf. He had no body to inhabit now, but that didn't stop him from throwing up illusions in the shadows or making the aisles slick and hard to cross.

He ran through incantations in his head, as if that would help. Healing. Purity. Goodness. Strength. If he had his mother's magic, he would've been able to cast spells now, but he was useless without a great many objects. And even if he could summon magic, it was too difficult here, away from any natural sources of power.

They held hands, more out of safety than anything else. It was good to be tethered to her, Eliot thought. The dark smudges on her face and bruises on her throat made Tess look even more threatening. She was a forgotten warrior, a lost god, fierce and terrifying.

Eliot caught a glimmer out of the corner of his eye and turned to face it. He almost slipped on the stairs to the basement, but caught himself quickly on the railing. When he pulled his hand away, it was black with ink. A ray of light shone across it, revealing a glimmer of—something. Before he could be certain, the shimmer was gone.

A pinch of fear started in his stomach. He quickly wiped away the ink from his bare skin, but when he did, he saw that his hand was already blistering. Eliot gritted his teeth against the pain. There was some sort of reaction happening, and magic fizzled in the back of his brain. He reached for it, his own magic, and it eluded him.

"Tess," Eliot said. "Is the ink hurting you?"

She glanced back at him, over her shoulder. "No," she said, and something changed in her voice. She leaned in, scrutinizing the ink that surrounded them. "Why? Is something wrong?"

"I'm fine," he said. Maybe the ink was burning, Eliot thought horribly, because it was finally infecting him.

Eliot shoved his blistering hand into his pocket and released a shaky breath. He thought of his mother, lips pursed together, suffering without telling him how much. If she could be strong, so could he.

He followed Tess through the muck of the basement to the cage. The metal of the grated gate was twisted in places, as if the ink was eating away at it as it dripped between the bars.

It looked like the entire library was melting.

Tess set to work on the lock. Somewhere in the library— upstairs, maybe?—there was a distant roaring. To Eliot, it sounded like the ocean.

Above them, one of the emergency lights flickered and burned out.

Tess swore under her breath. The key wasn't fitting or something, but Eliot couldn't look.

Somewhere, the roaring, whooshing sound grew louder. Eliot looked up, wondering if it was the building's air conditioning kicking on. Only then did he notice the ink running down the stairs, rushing heavier than it had before.

"Tess," he said, and his voice was thin and his mouth dry. "I think there's—"

He didn't have time to get the words out. The rush of ink increased to a torrent, to a tsunami. She turned into his chest, clutching his shirt. He only had time to lock his arms on the grate on either side of her, pressing his face into her hair before the ink swept down the stairs like the ocean had been unleashed upon them.

Before that moment, he'd never thought of what darkness tasted like.

The taste was rot and corruption and bile and horror, death and sadness and hopelessness all in one, mixed with the chemical taste of ink and mustiness of dust. The wave passed and he gasped for air, coughing against Tess's hair, and then, all too soon, a second wave came. He rocked unsteadily on his feet, and it felt like the ground was sucking out from under him. Tess's nails scratched into his chest, and he wondered if he was suffocating her or if her head was even above the level of the ink.

The ink was in his nose, in his throat, thick and hot like blood.

Protect Tess, he thought; what a foolish, terrible thing, to think he could protect anyone from this.

Another break came, and he quickly swiped the darkness away from his eyes. Ink coated the lights, making them glow even dimmer, but he could see that they were both up in murk to their waists—and more importantly, there was no sign of another wave coming.

"Now, Tess," he said into her ear, because the devil's laugh was deafening in the room full of horror.

She turned in the cage he made with his arms and chest, going back to the lock. He still felt the knife, desperately gripped in his left hand, the same hand that had held hers on the way down. It was slick with ink, clutched against the bar, but he could not drop it. The knife was their only protection.

A small click sounded, quiet enough he shouldn't have heard it. "Okay," she said. "We're in."

She swung the gate open, and they waded into the cage. Eliot mourned all these precious books lost, now soaked in the devil's ink. Who knew how much knowledge was leached from these pages?

"Where was the latch to open the shelves?" Tess asked.

Eliot fumbled along until he found it. With a low, moaning noise, the grate began to open. Already, he could feel the ink in his veins, seeping in, taking hold.

"Tess," he said. He couldn't see her face in the darkness, and maybe it was better that way. He pressed the knife into her hand, felt the slick heat of ink against her palm, and then her fingers closed securely around the handle. He pressed his mouth to her ear so only she could hear him. "You have to be the one to read it. If anything happens to me, you have to... You know what you have to do."

She pulled back, and he wondered what she was looking for on his face—and even worse, what she would find there.

He picked up her left hand, the hand that held the knife, and guided the blade. Gently, he pressed the knife to his throat, just enough to pierce the skin below his Adam's apple, drawing a drop of blood. His heart stuttered.

Was he here, looking at his own death?

"If something happens, you have to," he said.

"Eliot—" she started.

He shook his head. "You know what will happen if he takes me. You know that I won't…I won't be able to fight it." Eliot leaned down, close enough to make out the different colors in her eyes, even with the dim lighting. "You have to survive this, Tess. With or without me."

Another hesitation, but she was less certain this time. Her forehead bumped into his when she nodded.

"Good."

As soon as his hand released hers, the knife fell away from his throat. The door was fully down now, and the level of ink decreased as it rushed down the stairs to fill the tunnel. They had no flashlight. They'd have to find their way in the dark.

He was about to reach for her hand when she grabbed him by the chin with a force that surprised him. He was scared for a split second that they were wrong, that the devil had gotten into her anyway, but then she jerked his head down to hers.

When she kissed him, it was full of sweat and fear and beauty.

Her nails dug into his chin, but then he wrapped his arms around her and she released him only to wrap her arms around his neck.

Eliot gasped a little when she pulled away. He felt unsteady, and it had nothing to do with the blistering that was rapidly traveling from his ink-burned hand to his shoulder.

"If I don't kill you tonight," Tess said fiercely, lips inches away from his, "I'm doing that again."

fifty four

YOU WERE ALREADY INSIDE HIS VEINS WHEN SHE KISSED THE boy. She was sweet, human and pure, like honeysuckle on your tongue.

fifty five

Tess

TESS AND ELIOT WALKED SHOULDER TO SHOULDER DOWN the final set of stairs into the darkness. She kept a firm grip on the knife in her hand. The sound of the sepulcher was in her head, but this time, it didn't sound like a buzzing at all. It almost sounded like music.

Eliot was right. She needed to get the devil back, to protect Nat, even if that meant…

But how could she bear hurting him?

"I'll keep a hand against the wall," Eliot said, but his plan faltered as they reached the bottom.

The sconces along the wall were lit. Not with fire, but with a dark, bluish light, like souls were guiding their way to the room at the end of the tunnel.

Tess looked at Eliot. They hadn't seen the glow from the cage. In this light, both of them looked ghoulish and uncertain. Tess saw the ink streaked all over Eliot's skin and swiped at it with her sleeve, exposing some of the pale skin of his throat.

"I will be very grateful for a shower," he said. She would've smiled if his voice hadn't been so shaky.

In the back of her head, the devil whispered, "Come to me, my love."

Tess squeezed her eyes shut. *No*, she thought, *I am not*

yours. I will never be yours.

At the end of the tunnel, the devil laughed.

Next to her, Eliot yelped. His hand slipped out of hers. When she looked over at him, he was scratching frantically at his left bicep.

"What is it?" Tess asked.

"It's— Bloody hell." Unable to reach the skin under his shirt, he pulled it off as if it was on fire.

Tess choked on a breath. It was his tattoo. The ink was spreading through his veins, slowly migrating from his upper arm, up his shoulder, heading towards his throat, with another line snaking towards his heart. Eliot scratched at the tattoo, leaving lines of blood where his fingernails broke the skin. Ink dripped from it and the migration of the ink slowed for a moment as dark streaks of it mingled with his blood.

When he met her eyes, the fear there was unmistakable.

"I don't want him to have me," Eliot said, and his voice was barely a whisper above the rushing ink. A little stronger, he said, "You can't let him have me." A muscle ticked in his jaw, and she could barely hear him when he said, "I can't feel my magic." He sounded like he was already dead.

Eliot's eyes darted to the knife, then back to her face.

"No," Tess said. She couldn't do it. She did not come all this way to cut off Eliot Birch's head, to feel the spurt of blood soaking her if he was still *Eliot*, or to watch him erupt into darkness if he belonged to devil.

His hand closed around hers. He drew her hand and the knife up to his neck, and she thought she could hear his heart thudding between them. He rested the tip of the knife against his throat, where there was a red nick on his skin from where the blade had been only minutes before.

"Do it, Tess," he said through clenched teeth.

In the space between one breath and another, she tried to imagine leaving this tunnel alone, without Eliot. Leaving him here in pieces. She could see it, horrible and real: walking into Jessop on any given day without him there to smirk at or say something so blindingly ludicrous that she wanted to throttle him. Going through her days without him insisting on feeding her or requesting books she didn't want to find or offering small, inexplicable kindnesses. Going through her days without *him*.

This was the awful truth. Eliot Birch was the most stubborn, insufferable, privileged boy she had ever met, but he was also the only person she wanted to see most days. The only person who made her forget her anxieties, her terror, all the shit she'd dragged herself through to take care of Nat.

And now, here in this sepulcher, she was going to kill him.

No. She closed her eyes. There had to be another way. If she could free him from the ink, buy them a few minutes...

Maybe she could get the ink out of his body. It was a terrible thought, a foolish thought, but it was the only one she had. She thought of how the ink stopped when he broke his own skin scratching, as if it could be drawn out of his skin or cut away.

"How much do you like your tattoo?" she asked.

Eliot blinked. "Pardon?"

"I'm going to cut your tattoo off." She was not going to make it to the other end of the tunnel without him. It wasn't a matter of whether or not she technically *could*—Tess knew she was strong enough to get there, read the book, and defeat the devil—but she was not going to leave Eliot behind.

Eliot looked at her, stunned. But then he took his hand off

hers, off the knife. He tore the ink-soaked bottom off of his shirt so only the dry part remained. He balled it up and stuck it in his mouth, between his teeth.

Only then did he turn to the side, facing the wall, offering his mangled tattoo for her to mangle further.

Tess took a deep breath, but it wasn't like her hands were going to get any steadier than they were right now.

She put the knife to Eliot's arm and began to cut.

fifty six

Eliot

IN HIS MEMORY, HE SAT IN THE CHAIR. THE TATTOOIST, AN Essex geezer with an accent thick enough to threaten years of Eliot's education, prepared the gun. Across the room, Josie watched over the pages of a magazine. She didn't approve of the adventure, but she couldn't stop it.

His mother held his hand. She was in her wheelchair with a blanket across her lap. Bandages covered her arm, where her tattoo had been finished minutes before.

She rubbed a balm into Eliot's palm out of sight. One for numbness and courage. Eliot smirked. "You don't think I have the pain tolerance for this?" he asked.

"I *know* you don't," his mother said. She kissed his temple.

His tattoo hadn't hurt. Her magic guaranteed that.

This time, the pain was inescapable. This time, the pain was everything, blotting out every fear or memory he'd ever had. This time, his mother was not coming. This time, his screams were absorbed by the fabric of his T-shirt. This time, the only one who heard him was the demon, and he only laughed.

fifty seven

Tess

Tess scraped and scraped until Eliot's arm was a mess of blood without a trace of ink. As if pulled away by the skin, the angry tributaries subsided as well.

I'm not going to let him have you, Tess thought. *I'm not going to let him have you. I'm not going to let him have you.*

He didn't relax when she'd finished. When she looked up, she realized he was still looking away from her, eyes squeezed shut. She tucked the knife back into her belt and tugged for the material in his mouth.

"Eliot," Tess said. Her voice echoed in the stones of the tunnel. He unclenched his jaw, releasing the shirt. Tess took it and tied it around his arm to staunch the bleeding. Nothing more could be done until they were safe, back above ground.

"I'm sorry," she said. "I didn't want to kill you."

"Bloody hell," Eliot said, eyes still shut.

She wanted to give him time to recover, to breathe, but now, they had work to do. She switched sides so she was closer to the arm that wasn't injured and seized his hand again.

"We have to keep going," she said. He didn't answer, but his jaw set a little tighter. "Can you do magic? To heal yourself?"

He shook his head, a muscle in his jaw ticking. "No. Not without... I need things for it. I can't just do it."

They made their way to the room at the end of the tunnel. Tess expected to find the devil in there, waiting for them. Instead, there was only the book, there in the alcove in the wall.

As soon as Tess laid her hands on the book, Eliot moved beside her. "Is this what you want?" he asked in a voice that was not his own.

This was not Eliot. He did not bear the wound she had just given him, was not smeared with blood. She looked in his eyes to verify what she already knew. The devil stood beside her.

She turned to tell Eliot, but...but... No. Tess turned around and around in a circle, but Eliot was gone. She couldn't find him. She was in the room, and the devil was beside her, but everything else was blank. This was a dream, a blank space of fog and confusion.

The studio.

No, not the studio.

Tess turned again. She was alone in the room—but no, she wasn't, because there was the devil, standing against the wall, like he'd been waiting there all along. And for all she knew, maybe he had.

The sepulcher. The end of it all. The center and end of everything.

"Where is Eliot?" she asked. She clutched the book against her chest. It was too precious, too necessary, to let out of her sight.

"Eliot is dead," Truth said. When she looked up at him, it was as if he *flickered*, like one second he was there, and the next second it was Eliot, with his mouth twisted into a scream. She could tell the difference between them now, better than she ever could before. Where Eliot's eyes were warm and brown,

Truth's were black, terrible, dotted with stars. His skin was too pale; his bones were too lean. He was both dead and alive, clinging to the edge of something vital that Tess's mortality could not understand.

"No, he isn't," Tess said. She was certain he wasn't. Because she'd saved him, hadn't she? Everything from the last few hours was very fuzzy and getting dimmer by the second. She longed desperately to go to sleep, but the floor was covered in something dark and slick.

Eliot is dead.

But no, he wasn't, Tess thought, and panic bubbled within her. None of this mattered if Eliot was dead. None of it made sense if Eliot was dead.

The devil held out a knife.

She almost took the knife, but along the long, flat blade, she saw an image, as if it was a screen. She saw Eliot, reaching for her, and her own hands, plunging a knife into his heart. Pulling it out. Stabbing him again and again as blood gushed around her, as it stained her skin and she could taste it, hot and coppery and—

"He gave himself up," the devil said. "You killed him. He sacrificed himself for you."

No. If Eliot was dead...

Everything flickered again, too quickly, and she almost thought she heard her name.

Tess's brain was foggy. She was supposed to do something now, she knew—but what? It was like the dreams all over again. She shifted the book to one hand and rubbed her forehead with the other. It was wet with blood. She had no idea if it was hers or not.

Was there a book in her hands?

Or was there a knife?

Was Eliot dead or alive? Who was Eliot, and who was Truth?

The devil leaned close, so close she could smell the dust on his breath, the time on him. "Do you remember what I can give you?" His hand, his knife hand, traced the blade over her lips, and she tasted blood. Down the sensitive skin of her neck went the blade, grazing but not cutting, down her chest, to her stomach, then diagonally to her heart.

Tess reached for the knife where the devil held it, poised against her breast.

A shimmer in the image. Eliot's voice. "The *book*, Tess! Read it!"

Eliot. She wanted Eliot.

But the devil could give her everything. It came in flickers: the studio, the black cello, the audience. What did she want? Eliot. She wanted freedom. She *wanted*.

She wanted to be free of this book and its devil.

The book. She looked down. The book was in one hand, the knife in the other. "I'm sorry," she said to the devil, and his smile faltered—but was it a smile or a grimace? "I think I must…"

"No," the devil said, leaning close to her ear. His tongue flicked out and caressed her earlobe, sending a shiver down her spine. "The knife, Tess."

"The *book*, Tess, the fucking *book*!"

Eliot. But Eliot was dead, wasn't he?

The book was Eliot, and Eliot was the book, and the devil was Eliot too. Devil or demon or specter or monster, haunt or magic or horror or Eliot himself.

The devil reached forward and took the book from Tess's

hands. "You know why it had to be you, Tess. Don't you?"

She squeezed her eyes shut. "I don't know what you're talking about."

He reached forward, tracing the curve of her cheek. His fingers were burning hot against her skin. She wanted to lean into him; she wanted to pull away. Tess did not move.

There was only this. Only the devil, only time, only death. Eliot Birch was dead, and the entire world was burning.

He opened his book with one hand to show her the insides. There were those lines of gold, glowing in the bluish darkness of the tomb. "I knew as soon as you touched the cover. I knew what you wanted, what you would do. Tess, I've been waiting for you since the beginning of time."

Tess was shaking her head. She tried to back away but the devil caught her, keeping her close. "I'm not evil," she insisted.

The devil's lips curled into a smile; it wasn't Eliot's knowing smirk, but something darker, something that sent a shiver running down Tess's spine. Even though his skin was hot as an open flame, she was so, so cold.

"I'm not evil either," he said. One hand locked around her wrist, holding her knife-hand steady. "I'm only the truth, after all. I'm the motivation behind everything you do. I'm the deepest part of you. I am yours and you are mine."

She wanted to deny it. Wanted to flee, to leave Eliot and the devil and Jessop behind—but. The truth echoed through her, as if this was the very first time anyone had truly known her.

The devil stepped closer. All pretenses faded. His face was open, honest. "I'm the only one who understands you. I know what you want, more than anything. What you need. I could make you greater than you could ever be on your own."

She heard the sweet tune of a cello in the back of her mind. Tess didn't doubt him. He could give her everything. All she ever wanted, all she'd worked for.

"Make it so," the devil said. "Stay mine, forever." He pulled Tess's hand up, and light glinted off the knife. "Stay with me."

She sensed something stirring, something awful and unnamed, as she looked at the devil. There, in his eyes, Tess saw herself. Her own human inadequacy; the realization she would never be enough to matter, never be good enough.

Tess hesitated, looking at his face. She saw grief and longing and something else she didn't expect to find, not so raw and open, not in the devil's face.

Want.

"Oh," Tess breathed, as reality swirled around her.

It echoed every human desire she'd held in her heart, every wish to be better and more and flawless. She saw her hands, rife with calluses but practiced. *Perfect.* She saw his brushstrokes. She saw him, a boy, a devil.

They were the same. Too late, Tess understood. She was not looking at someone who'd failed or fallen. She was looking at herself, her own story. She saw the devil looking back, and in his gaze, she saw her own image.

fifty eight

Eliot

Eliot was in hell. There was no other explanation.

The moment Tess touched the book, the room had flooded with ink, sweeping him up and slamming him against the wall. The viscous fluid burned as it solidified into a webby prison, keeping him secured against the wall.

But when it all settled, Tess was there. Unharmed. Her face was utterly, impossibly blank.

Ink spun around the room, forming a man. Fear choked in Eliot's throat. He knew this devil. It was him. It was a fallen god, a debauched angel.

It had Eliot's own face and eyes like the universe.

And then it wasn't Eliot at all. The figure shifted, reformed, and he was looking at his father. He raised a hand and slapped Eliot across the face. Eliot tasted blood in his mouth.

"Do you think your magic is enough to save you from this?" he sneered. "You are weak. You have always been weak."

Another reformation, and his mother stood before him, whole and healthy. She took his chin, fingernails digging into Eliot's skin.

"Mum," Eliot gasped, pulling against his restraints.

But her smile was twisted, a mockery of the mother he remembered. "You thought I loved you. You are a fool, Eliot.

Just like your father." Her nails dug in deeper, and Eliot felt the wetness of blood trickling down his chin.

"Don't leave me," Eliot begged. "Don't leave me here."

His mother only looked at him. "No one can save you." She turned and left the room. Eliot knew, in some part of him, that it wasn't truly his mother, that it was the devil—but she was right all the same. No one could save him.

He strained against the ink that bound him, screamed everything he could think at Tess. But none of it was enough. None of it would ever be enough.

He couldn't hear what they were saying, but the devil took Tess in his arms.

He screamed and strained and bled. His throat was hoarse and painful. And through it all, he thought of his mother.

If he died before her, she would know, somehow. She would wake up in her gauzy bedroom, in her mind or out of it, and she would know deep within herself that Eliot was not in this world anymore. Just as Eliot was certain he would know the minute her soul released, the moment she left him.

She could not save him.

But worse: he could not save her. Over and over, it echoed, cutting off his screams and leaving him gasping as the ink burned trails into his skin.

He could not save her, he could not save her, he could not save her.

Eliot could not save himself.

Magic or not, witch or not, he was absolutely *useless*. He was going to die; Tess was going to die; his mother was going to die. He had power filling his veins and no way at all to use it.

He would hang on this wall for the rest of eternity, and someday, someone would come down to this godforsaken tunnel and find his bones.

"Tess," he pleaded, but there was no use. He could barely see her through the ink dripping into his eyes. He could only barely make out the shape of her, a fallen angel, tucked into the devil's arms.

There had been no one there to protect her, either. No, Tess had to protect everyone else.

Tess had to protect everyone else.

Realization flooded through Eliot. He fought his bonds, scraping his bare skin on the rough stone behind him. "Tess!" he shouted. He didn't know how to get through to her, how to make her hear. But he had to. "Natalie!" he shouted. "You have to do it for Natalie, Tess!"

He had no way to know if it was enough. For a moment, just a moment, he thought she might see him. And then the ink crawled inside of his mouth, choked his voice, turning his words to garbled cries of nothing.

Eliot Birch had always been a failure. He could not save anyone, and now he could not even save himself.

fifty nine

SHE SAW HIM THERE, IN HER DREAMS, WATCHING HER SLEEP. She saw him in her nightmares. She saw the hell that was his past, all of it at once: the waiting and the torture and the wanting to be more, more, more, and never quite getting there. The apple and his mother's braid and pigment and ink; fear and loathing and desire and wanting, more than anything, the wanting.

She could not forgive him. She could not excuse what he'd done, what he'd become. But she could accept that this devil was not mindless. He was not full of violence.

He was human, once. And he was terrified.

Tess pulled her non-knife hand loose and trailed it up his arm, rested her hand on his shoulder. "I see you," she said, and it was a realization.

The boy in front of her—because that's what he was, after all—did not look like Eliot. Pale skin, hair the color of a raven's wing, green eyes, and a sharp nose. Broader in the shoulder than Eliot but shorter. Maybe her age, maybe older or younger, maybe timeless.

"I see you," she said again.

"You can't," the boy said, and his hand was shaking on hers, shaking on the knife, and the silver of it glimmered with ink.

She shifted her hand down, flat-palmed against his chest.

Everything was coming clearer now: his shirt, open to the middle of his chest, stained with paint, ragged; the ends of his hair, falling over his shoulders; a scar across his chin.

He had no heartbeat.

He was trying to kill everyone she loved. He'd killed Mathilde and Regina, was going after Nat and Anna and Eliot, and he had nearly killed her. She welcomed the pulse of dark magic across her fingertips, prickling like a jellyfish sting. Tess pressed her fingers in harder, watching as the boy winced. He shifted, tucking the book under one arm. Ink congealed on its surface, staining his shirt.

"Why did you do it?" she asked, even though she didn't need to. The deal came clearly now, through the magic between them: twenty-four years, endless talent, the adoration of the entire world. And the panic of being trapped, the terrible reality of losing your own body and becoming nothing, of being reduced only to ink and magic and nightmares.

It was a tempting offer. Twenty-four years of perfection was enough to become unforgettable.

The boy lifted his hand to his chest, covering hers. He almost felt real. Solid.

And this: Tess realized with an odd sense of wonder that, all along, she had the strange magic to turn the devil back into a boy.

"I never wanted to," he said. His eyes slipped shut as his fingers slotted between hers, hand getting warmer, squeezing tight. "I only wanted to be free."

Magic swelled between them, not through the boy-devil, not through her, but like a thousand voices shouting and demanding and fighting. Reality swirled around, too close and too loud.

Nat.

She didn't know how she'd forgotten her in the deluge of ink, or if she really existed in the first place, but she remembered her now and she was certain that Nat was being pursued by the magic and *her sister needed her.*

She could hear Eliot now, too, shouting from somewhere far away, almost louder than death itself.

"Stop the magic," Tess pleaded. "Save them. Stop the ink. You have to. You have to be able to."

The panic settled, terror close and hot through the deluge of ink that threatened to swallow them both. "I can't," he said. "I can't control it."

Her fingers tightened as she realized the truth of it. If he couldn't do it, then she couldn't either. "I'll do whatever you need," Tess said, growing desperate. She readjusted her grip on the knife and an edge cut into her palm. There was the book between them, ink flowing from its pages, and Eliot screaming, and Nat dying, and she could not slip from this nightmare into reality if they ceased to exist.

The boy-devil leaned close, close enough that she could smell the blood on him. "Free me from this torment," he begged.

Tess met his gaze and absorbed the terror, the desire, the exhaustion. Possession, she realized, was not the only freedom.

The magic was thick in her ears, pounding like a second heartbeat. Ink poured between the boy-devil's fingers, over her hands, prickling her skin. She tasted the metallic bite of it on her tongue.

His eyes were turning black, going dark. This was the devil: all human emotion covered, swallowed, smothered.

"*Free me,*" he pleaded, a terrified boy.

She could not let the humanity leave. To want was human;

to possess was unnatural.

Tess arched up, rolled onto her tiptoes, and knotted her knife hand in the devil's hair. He gasped in surprise, some clarity returning to his eyes, flashing for the briefest moment through the magic.

She kissed the devil. It was nothing like kissing Eliot. It was like praying to a false god.

His surprise lasted only a moment, but that was all Tess needed. She seized the book, gripped it, and turned away from him.

Tess was alone in the room.

Nat.

She opened the book and began to read.

"Him before comes that ink all trusts knowledge seeks who he but, himself only trusts guidance for inward looks who he For. Ignorance their of burden the in burn good the Let. Forsaken and damned the to belong Earth the May." And then, slower, for good measure, "Mih erofeb semoc taht kni lla stsurt egdelwonk skees ohw eh tub, flesmih ylno stsurt ecnadiug rof drawni skool ohw eh roF. Ecnarongi rieht fo nedrub eht ni nrub doog eht teL. Nekasrof dna denmad eht ot gnoleb htrae eht yam."

A great whooshing sound echoed in Tess's ears, as if she were in the middle of a tsunami, and then a release of everything.

Silence.

sixty

Tess

WHEN TESS WOKE UP, SHE WAS LYING IN DUST.

A piercing light shone behind her closed eyes. Her body shook violently. Tess did not want to see what she had wrought, did not want to take in the death around her, did not want to open her eyes to find Eliot's body. But the shaking would not stop, as if a great earthquake was tearing through Jessop and would swallow her with it.

And if she'd failed, maybe that was best for everyone.

When she opened her eyes, she found Eliot looking back. The shaking stopped abruptly but his hands remained on her shoulders, fingers digging into her flesh. He was pale from blood loss and still smeared with an impossible amount of ink, but he was there. Alive.

"Hell," he breathed, as if he'd been expecting her to be dead too. And then, softer, rawer, "Tess, you beautiful creature, what took you so long?" He couldn't say anything more, because she grabbed the back of his head and covered her mouth with his.

Something was pressing into her back, though. Tess broke away and sat up, dully noting the inky flood had mysteriously disappeared and realizing she'd been laying on the knife. She picked it up. The blade was still dark with gore.

"What is that?" Eliot asked.

"I think…" Her brain was still foggy, but she remembered the way the devil had held it so reverently, and looked down to see that her own knife was still secure in her belt. "I think it's his. The devil's."

Eliot grabbed the knife and examined it for a moment. Standing slowly, unsteadily, he walked to the alcove where the book rested. Without any further thought, he raised the knife high.

"Wait," Tess said, holding out a hand. Eliot stopped, looking over at her. He began to say something, but she wrapped her hand around the hilt of the knife. She felt the bite of steel on her wrists, felt the splash of Regina's blood, saw the awful deadness in Mathilde's eyes. "Let me," she said.

Eliot watched her for a moment, then nodded.

Tess took the knife, handle warm and slick with Eliot's blood. She ran one finger over the black leather cover, a reverent thing.

She remembered how the devil's lips felt against hers, and the fear in his eyes just before. When she closed her eyes, she saw the red flesh of an apple, cradled in a child's hand.

Tess brought the knife down.

It seemed like an indecent act, stabbing the book. It bled as if it was a living thing, spurting blood and ink against Tess's hands, and Eliot watched with one hand pressed against his mouth.

A breath, and a boy, there inside her head like a dream: a flash of green eyes, and a deep sigh, like some great energy within her had been released. She saw a boy and a book, a boy and a devil. A boy with magic he didn't understand, who was never meant to die.

Nobody was there, but she sensed the brush of fingertips

on her cheek and—

Thank you.

The knife clattered out of her hands.

While the book bled, something in her throbbed. It *wanted.*

You're my master now.

Tess clenched her hands into fists at her side. The ink flexed oddly against the book and receded.

When she turned back to Eliot, he was breathing hard. "Shall we get out of here?" he asked.

"Yes," Tess gasped.

The stacks looked as if the horrors of the night had never occurred. There was a faint smell of darkness, but no stains of ink where the books had flooded. Everything looked… normal. Horrifyingly, world-shatteringly normal.

As if Mathilde and Regina had never died, or had never existed at all.

"I thought I killed you," Tess confessed.

His smile was sad and soft in the dim glow of the emergency lights. "Not yet. But I'm sure there will be time for that later."

She waited in Mathilde's office while he went upstairs to cleanse the stacks of their blood and fingerprints—in case this became a crime scene. When he skittered back down the stairs, his face was grim.

"The bones are… They look burned," he said. "Both Mathilde's and Regina's." He ran a hand through his hair, looked over at the wall, where a framed picture of Mathilde and Tess's father hung. "I thought there was something we could do."

"She's gone," Tess said. The truth of it was hollow in her stomach.

Tess's phone didn't start ringing until they'd cleared the

reading room, where service returned. Eliot dashed up the stairs to get another shirt from his office while Tess answered.

On the other line, Anna was sobbing.

"Anna? Anna, what's wrong?"

Anna's breathing was ragged and frantic, and for a horrifying moment, Tess wondered again if they had failed. "We tried to get out," she managed. "But...I don't know how it happened, Tess. I don't— Nat didn't— Oh God, oh *fuck*."

Emotions left her. She could only stare straight ahead. "What happened?"

"She's dead, Tess. Nat is dead."

It was the end of everything. The end of the world.

sixty one

Eliot

NAT'S BODY WAS CURLED AT THE BASE OF A TREE, IN A COPSE near Tess's dorm. The yellow glow of a streetlight only barely illuminated her calf. From this distance, as Eliot threw the car into park and dashed out after Tess, she looked like she was sleeping.

Anna sat next to her, shaking.

"What happened?" Eliot asked. Tess froze a few feet away, staring.

"I don't know," Anna muttered, swiping her nose. "We need to call an ambulance. The police. Someone."

Eliot glanced back at Tess. She hadn't moved. Her face was empty. She was in denial or shock, unable to deal with this. Unable to process.

Eliot did not blame her.

"How long has she been gone?"

Anna looked up at him. She had not faced the terror that plagued both Tess and Eliot for weeks, but her expression reflected everything Eliot was feeling. "I don't know. I called as soon as… When I couldn't detect a heartbeat."

And it had taken four minutes for Eliot to speed from Jessop to here. Maybe it was enough.

"Go to her," he instructed. "Tess can't be alone." Anna

nodded, probably relieved to have something to do. Or still in shock.

He couldn't look at Tess. Behind him, he heard a wretched sob. If she hadn't fully broken before, she would now.

He had a small kit with him, always. Eliot unpacked his herbs and candle and knife. He could not save his mother.

But maybe, he could save Nat. And to save Nat was to save Tess too.

Eliot did not allow his hands to shake as he straightened Nat's body. She was still warm, nearly feverish. A thin sheen of sweat cooled on her arms. He searched for a pulse. As Anna said, there was none.

Eliot opened Nat's eyes. Ink ran from her tear ducts and the whites of her eyes were stained black. When Eliot shifted Nat's jaw, more ink poured from between her lips.

This was not a job for CPR or medical intervention. Medicine could not replace what the devil had claimed.

There were no spells for this. No cures written or recorded.

Once, someone had told him that magic was about conviction. Once, Eliot had believed he could save anyone if he tried.

It was the summer his mother was going to die.

Eliot took a deep breath, flicked his thumb, and lit the candle. He drew his blade across both of his palms, drawing blood. He rolled salt in his hands until the fine grains were sticky with blood, and ignoring the sting, smeared it on Nat's cheeks.

Purity. Safety. He hummed under his breath, willing the ink out of her body. Willing the devil's magic purged.

More ink ran down her face, down her cheeks. Vaguely, he could hear Tess's sobs increasing behind him.

Conviction.

I will not let you remain dead, Natalie Matheson.

Eliot took the candle and passed the flame over Nat's lips three times. *I recall you back here. Return to me.*

Conviction.

This was it. This was the summer.

Eliot dug his bloody fingers into the earth, calling forth all of the magic he could muster. It filled him like spilled gold in his blood. This was power like he'd never had before, power like he'd never imagined. His skin shone with the force of the magic he gathered.

Eliot let the failure slip away, the anxiety, the terribleness of it all. He was not a failure. He was Eliot Birch, and he was going to do something impossible.

He pressed his hands to Nat's chest, pushing into her sternum. Her eyes flew open as Eliot pressed the magic into her, as he coaxed her back from whatever fiery place the devil had taken her to. Nat gagged on the last of the ink that surged from her mouth.

She choked and sputtered, but Eliot did not stop. He pressed the magic deeper, forcing it into every vein and capillary. Her back arched against him, body seizing. But there, at the edge of everything, he felt the tug of her soul.

It was hard to explain. He felt as if he'd found a loose thread in a sweater. Eliot reached in and pulled. It was as she had been, unchanged, untainted. There would be no improvements in this Nat, no healing, nothing left behind in hell, but she would be whole again.

"Eliot!" someone shouted, Tess or Anna. He couldn't feel himself; he had no body at all. He was only magic, roots and earth and the fabric of the universe.

Someone was shaking him. He'd let go of Nat and fallen

on his side, breathing hard. He opened his eyes to find curious, fearful eyes peering down at him from a face that was familiar and not familiar at the same time.

Eliot could barely catch his breath. "Natalie, is it?"

Nat blinked down at him. Full and alive, she looked eerily like Tess. "You're bleeding," she said.

"You're alive," Eliot answered. He sensed the magic leaving, swirling away, shaking the very foundations of the ground beneath him. He closed his eyes and faded with it.

sixty two

Tess

NAT.

Tess stared at her, alive, kneeling over Eliot.

Nat.

Vibrant, heart beating, Eliot's blood smeared across her cheeks and collarbones. The sobs choked her, now from relief rather than horror.

"She was dead," Anna said. "I swear it."

"I know," Tess said. There were no words, no feelings to encompass her relief and terror and the mix of all of it. She stumbled up from her knees, closing the last few feet between them, and threw herself at Nat.

"You're impossible," Tess said into her hair. "I love you so much."

"We need to get him inside," Nat said, pushing away and picking up Eliot's arm.

He was not hurt, just sleeping. He breathed deeply and evenly, a small smile on his face. Tess was full of too many emotions, too many things.

She could not process any of it.

The three of them carried him upstairs, into the dorm. Anna picked the lock of one of their old roommate's rooms and dragged the stripped mattress into the living room. They laid Eliot on it, arms extended. Tess wrapped bandages around his cut palms and skinned shoulder while Nat showered in the bathroom.

Tess made her leave the door cracked open. She couldn't stand to have Nat out of earshot.

"Will you finally tell me what's going on?" Anna asked. She'd rinsed most of the ink from her body, but specks of it still splattered her clothes. Tess shuddered.

"How much do you want to know?"

"Everything."

Tess considered this. There was too much, all from the beginning, and no guarantee that Anna would believe her. But she'd seen the ink, the horror of it. She'd watched Nat die and later return. She'd witnessed Eliot's magic.

So Tess told her. She told her everything.

As dawn light broke gray and misty outside the windows, Tess was by Eliot's makeshift bed, waiting for anything to happen. Waiting to stop feeling so empty.

Regina was dead. Mathilde was dead. Nat had died; that had been the worst of it, even for the brief minutes she had to endure it.

She did not know how to come to terms with the fact Nat had been gone, or understand how Eliot had brought her back. After Nat went to sleep, Tess settled next to him, holding vigil, waiting for him to wake.

Finally, Eliot's eyes opened, slowly and painfully.

"Hi," she said.

"Hi." He took in the room, the twinkle lights Tess and

Anna had hung a few weeks back and the discarded towels Nat had left hanging on a chair. "Are you okay?"

"I'm fine," Tess answered. "How are you feeling?"

"I'll survive." He grimaced when he moved to take her hand. "And how's Nat?"

"She's fine. Asleep, with Anna," Tess said. "Um, I told Anna. About all of it. She called in an anonymous tip for the police to investigate Jessop."

And maybe things were better that way. Because the fear of some false, mysterious serial killer that explained both of the deaths was better than the truth getting out, better than speaking of the devil.

"Interesting," Eliot said.

Tess felt strangely shy in front of him, now that things were back almost to normal and everyone was safe. She didn't know how to thank him for saving Nat. She didn't know if she could ever thank him enough for it. She wanted to duck her head into his shoulder and hide.

Eliot cleared his throat and examined the gauze on his hands. "I wanted to say thank you. You didn't have to save me, you know."

"I know," Tess said. "I'm sorry about your tattoo."

Eliot sighed. "It was nice, wasn't it?"

She didn't need to look at him to know he was joking, but she did anyway. After everything they had endured, every emotion she'd tried to ignore, looking at him now without hiding was a privilege. There was something soft in his face, maybe because of the exhaustion, or maybe not. Maybe it was something else, something that made her cheeks burn red.

Eliot sat up and studied the wrapping around his shoulder. "Did you request all of those grimoires to practice necromancy?" she blurted, because she knew what was coming, and she wasn't ready.

Eliot sighed, ran a hand through his hair, and winced at the pain.

"Do you want the worst answer, or a pleasant one?"

Tess shot him a glare. "I kissed the devil to save your life, Eliot."

He frowned up at her. "You kissed him?" Tess pretended to poke him in the ribs and he hurriedly said, "Kidding, kidding." He snatched her hand and wrapped it in both of his. "The truth. I was looking for a way to help or heal my mother. Don't look at me like that; it's not possible. But it's the only thing I had left."

"Could you?" Here it was, the truth she was afraid to confront. She didn't know how to understand the ramifications of it. "You...you saved Nat. You brought her back. I think you know how much that means, how much I can't thank you enough for it."

"I know."

"And could you save your mother like that?"

He drew her hand to his lips and pressed a kiss against the side of it. "No, I don't think so."

Tess bit her lip, fighting an inexplicable sense of guilt. "Why not? You said you wanted to heal her, to raise the dead. That's exactly what you did to Nat."

Eliot shook his head. "I felt it when I brought Nat back. I wasn't changing anything or altering her at all. If I brought my mother back, I'd bring her back as she was. Sick. She's gone, Tess. Even if I tried to keep her here, she would not be herself. There is no magic to restore what she's already lost. Nothing is going to save her. The only change now will be that she'll have her peace."

There was nothing she could say to make it any better. She didn't know how to deal with it, or how to align this wet-eyed Eliot who wouldn't look at her with the one she'd faced hell with only hours before.

He needed softness. She did not know how to be soft. She did not how to offer comfort at all. But for him, she'd try.

She leaned over and pressed a kiss to his forehead. "I hope she finds peace," she said. It wasn't enough, but it was all she had.

"Tess," he said, and her name didn't sound like the other times he'd said it. It was a declaration, a caress, a truth. He cleared his throat again. "I know that eventually I'm going back to England and you're going to be a famous musician and my father is terrible and everything is a mess and you think I'm a douchecanoe"—he couldn't not smile when he said it, and that smile made her smile, damn him—"but I don't think I'm going to find another human being like you in this entire godforsaken universe, and I don't think I ever want to."

That last part, that 'ever want to,' burrowed somewhere deep within her, and she had to look away so he didn't see the pinpricks of tears that suddenly burned in her eyes. "What are you saying?" she asked.

"I'm trying to say I'm in love with you, and I'm doing a terrible job of it."

Her eyes snapped back to his. "You are doing a terrible job of it," she said, but her voice was as watery as her eyes, and when she saw him smiling—damn him and his smile—she knew, again, that she was smiling back.

"I hate you," she said around the lump in her throat, because she wasn't going to cry in front of him, not now when they were both alive. He let her know that he understood by reaching out with his good arm and tugging her towards him over the center console, knotting his fingers into her hair as she clutched his shoulder and held him tight, because his mother was dying and her family was on the edge of poverty and three people had died because of them and he'd brought one back and she'd probably never be able to afford conservatory and he couldn't go back to England, but right then, right there, it didn't matter.

They were free.

sixty three

Eliot

THE COFFEE SHOP IN SQUIRREL HILL WAS NEARLY DESERTED when Eliot arrived, expecting to see his father. Instead, Lucille was there, in the back corner, nursing a black coffee.

"Hello," Eliot said, barely able to hide his surprise. He slid into the seat across from her.

"Hello," Lucille said. She wasn't wearing her usual makeup, and her eyes were softer than usual, bluer. She pushed a cup towards him. "I got you English Breakfast."

"Oh. Thank you." He took a sip and found it too hot, so he sat the cup between his hands. He had no idea what to say.

When his father called him the night before, asking about the police's inquiry into Jessop, Eliot had told him he didn't know anything. And then, when he told him to meet him at the coffee shop this afternoon or else, there was nothing else Eliot could've said.

He'd wondered if it was so his father could interrogate him. But if Lucille was here alone, probably not.

Lucille's eyes now traced over the scab on his cheek, down to his shoulder, where the gauze from his bandaged arm peeked out from under the sleeve of his T-shirt. He should've healed it before, but he was still too exhausted from saving Nat.

"When are you done with classes?" Lucille asked.

Eliot frowned. He wasn't in the mood for small talk. "Two weeks. Why?"

Her expression cleared a little, as if she'd made a guess and been correct. She pulled something out of her purse and slid it across the table. When Eliot opened the folder, he saw flight confirmations. Round trip to London. Departing in two and a half weeks, returning the day before school began.

"How did you…" Eliot couldn't finish the question.

Lucille spoke quickly, as if making a confession and wanting to get it over with. "I don't want to replace your mother. Ever. But I don't think it's fair, the way this is going, the way you're sandwiched between them, and I hope you don't only see me as the other woman."

Eliot stared at her, shell-shocked, uncertain what to say.

"I hate seeing you hurting, Eliot," Lucille said. "And this situation is shit. I'm sorry I fell in love with your father when I did, and I don't want to ruin your life. So here. Go be with your mom. Because you deserve to spend as much time with her as you can."

Eliot couldn't speak. There was a lump in his throat, choking him, and if he kept looking at the flight confirmation, he was going to cry. "How did you do it?" Eliot asked.

Lucille smiled, just a little. "I gave him an ultimatum," she said softly.

An ultimatum. Just like his father had given Eliot. Eliot could imagine it now: Lucille, a force to be reckoned with, throwing china and laying down the terms. Either Eliot could go to England or she would leave. A risky bet, but one that had paid off.

He was out of his chair in half a second, throwing his arms around her, and she was laughing into his hair. "Thank you," he repeated over and over again.

"It's going to be okay, Eliot," Lucille said. She pulled away, and he could see that she was crying too. "But don't tell him I told you it was my idea."

Maybe, just maybe, he could make it through this.

"I won't," Eliot said.

sixty four

Tess

GETTING A MOVING VAN TO MATHILDE'S HOUSE WAS PROV-
ing to be a giant pain in the ass. Nestled on the line between
North Oakland and Shadyside, it was surrounded by narrow
one-way roads that her mom kept missing. Tess, Anna, and
Nat sat on the porch, waiting with frosty glasses of tea.

This was an odd day, one Tess had been waiting for with
trepidation since Mathilde's will had been read. She left the
house and all of her possessions to Tess's father, her only
remaining family. The money she'd saved over the years and
inherited from her husband Harry was split between Tess,
Nat, and her parents, with trusts set up to put the girls through
college. In the city, it would be easier for her mom to find a job,
and her father could continue the pen company from home.

And now, the day came for Tess's parents to join her and
Nat in the city. They'd sold their house and the stationery
store. It was time for a new start.

There were more conversations to be had, discussions
between Tess and her parents. Maybe they weren't at war anymore, but she didn't know how to trust them. Living together
once again would be a constant negotiation.

"Do you think you'll make it to the vigil?" Anna asked.

"I'm not sure. What time is it supposed to start?"

"Um, 8:00, I think."

Tess nodded, not looking at Nat or Anna. "I'll be there." The vigil in honor of Regina had been set up by the school in a rare moment of compassion. There would be therapists, too, for anyone who wanted to talk—and police officers, for anyone who had leads.

Tess rubbed her eyes. It was hard not to be exhausted after two weeks of interrogations, investigations, and uncomfortable discussions. Luckily, Eliot's sweep of the stacks was thorough enough that neither of them had been named as suspects after the bones were discovered. In fact, the official opinion was that Tess was meant to be a victim of whoever murdered Mathilde Matheson and Regina Heigemeir.

Of course, they knew better.

"Oh!" Nat yelled, jumping up. "There they are!" She dashed into the yard to intercept their mom and the moving van. Her father pulled in afterwards, driving the family car.

Anna's hand landed on her shoulder. "Hey. Are you okay?"

Tess bit her lip. She hadn't seen her parents in months. Besides discussing Mathilde's death and assuring her parents she was safe, they hadn't spoken much.

"I have to be, don't I?"

Nat launched herself at their parents the moment they were out of their vehicles. Tess watched as they hugged her, squeezing her tight, kissing her hair.

Anna nudged her arm. "You can do it."

Tess sighed, but Anna was right. Nat and their mom went to the back of the van to start unloading. Her mom looked up, straight at Tess.

She got up and forced herself down the stairs. "I'm so sorry," her father said when she stopped just in front of him.

"I'm sorry that you had to go through this without us." She respected that he didn't pull her straight in for a hug, that he gave her space. He smelled like metal and ink—but not the dusty kind that had clotted in her dreams. He smelled new and clean, like home.

Tess examined his face. "How could you have helped? You ruined everything." His face fell. She sensed they were all quiet, her mom and Nat and Anna, listening to her. But it didn't matter. This was something she had to face. "I didn't tell you and I couldn't tell you, but you ruined all of it. And I need you to know that."

He nodded. His jaw twitched, something he did when he was disappointed. "I know," he said. "I know, and I'll never make it up to you, and I'm sorry, and I know."

"I don't forgive you," Tess said, rigid. "I can't forgive you. Not right now."

Her dad took this in and nodded. "You don't have to. What do you need from me?"

She hadn't expected—hadn't known— She was ready for a blowout, a clash, the fight that they'd never had at home. She wasn't prepared for this immediate peace.

Tess was *exhausted*. She was tired of holding it together and pretending and being angry. When she looked at her dad, she no longer saw failure. She saw his humanity. The mistakes that made him real.

She would write her story her own way, without the devil.

She threw herself into his arms and of course he caught her. She couldn't be mad anymore, not now, because it was okay and her parents were here; because she'd never given Mathilde the chance to get closer to her, and she'd regret it forever. She would not make the same mistake again.

"Stay," she begged. "Stay, and don't hurt me again."

"Okay," Dad said. And then Mom was bringing Nat in and Anna joined from the porch, even though she hadn't been formally introduced, but it didn't matter. They were alive and Tess and Nat were safe. She allowed herself to be comforted.

Just as she did dozens of times a day, Tess closed her eyes and thought their names. *Mathilde. Regina. Harry.* And then, even though it was too late, even though there was nothing else to do, *I'm sorry, I'm sorry, I'm sorry. I will not forget.*

Eliot's car pulled in front of the house, half on the street, half on the curb in regular Pittsburgh fashion. He was outside, leaning against the driver's side door, scanning an article on his phone. He kept snapping his fingers, calling a flame to them, and extinguishing it with the flick of his hand.

"C'mon," Tess said, skipping a greeting and sliding into the passenger's seat. "You have a flight to catch."

His bags were in the backseat, toppled over like fallen gravestones. For a boy who had more money than the king, Eliot sure had some beaten-up luggage. This was all Tess could think as they drove to the airport, hands entwined on the center console. Eliot was driving now, one-handed, wearing sunglasses that made his smile look even shinier, but Tess would take his car back.

He left her hand for just a moment to turn down the radio. "How was moving?" he asked.

Tess sighed. "Depressing as hell. Everything is just as Mathilde left it. Obviously."

"It'll be better," Eliot said, squeezing her hand.

She looked at him, admiring the peak of his nose, the curve of his ear. "I'm going to miss you. You know that, right?"

That smile burned across his face, slow and true. "You won't have to miss me for long. I'll be back for school. How was your first lesson?"

Tess shrugged. Alejandra had set her up with a musician from the symphony, insisting that they'd still chat once a week, but that it was better to have a teacher in person.

"He's strict," she said, feeling the calluses on the tips of her fingers stinging.

"Which isn't a bad thing," Eliot said. He took the exit to the airport, and Tess's chest tightened. She was afraid of what would happen when he got on the plane and flew away for the rest of the summer. Here was the truth: Eliot's mother was going to die. He knew it. She knew it. No spell, no grimoire, no devil was going to bring her back, no matter how much Eliot tried.

And another truth: Tess did not know how to be soft for him. She was still uncomfortable with vulnerability, and though she'd opened up to Eliot before, she was not certain how to make him feel better when she was never fully okay herself. She did not know how to comfort him, how she'd put him back together when he shattered, if there was even a point in trying. Even in breaking, Tess only grew harder.

Eliot pulled into short term parking. It seemed too brief, too strange for her to just drop him off, so they'd compromised by agreeing she would come into the airport. She stood by while he printed his boarding passes and waited for his check-in to work, with no shortage of snide asides about the lack of efficiency of the Pittsburgh Airport.

Things would never be the same between them, after this

summer. Tess was sure of it. He would think she was too rough, too cruel—she was the girl who'd killed Regina, the one who'd hurt him. Despite the cracks and all they'd been through, she couldn't be certain what version of her Eliot saw.

"But actually," Eliot softly raged. "Why can't they just fly direct? Why the hell do I have to go to New York, or Chicago, or Iceland? *Iceland,* Tess."

She didn't answer.

Softly: "Tess?"

Eliot had taken off his sunglasses and was watching her carefully.

"I need a minute," she said.

Eliot went to check his luggage, and she watched as he laughed with the airline attendant. This was Eliot, as he always had been: secure and brilliant and rich. And here she was. Lost.

She'd been different, since the devil. Not by huge amounts; it wasn't like her eyes turned into the universe and she inhabited other bodies, but different enough that she noticed. She felt colder, like she'd lost some small human bit of herself in the crypt.

When she talked to Eliot like this, she thought he noticed, too. And more terrifying to that stony part of Tess that wanted to remain locked away: that he noticed, and it didn't make him care about her less.

But then he was back, and she couldn't put on a fake smile to say goodbye to him. It was all she could do to hug him back when he wrapped his arms around her.

"What's wrong?" he whispered into her hair.

She couldn't lie to him. "You're going to go to England and come back and this will all be over, like it never happened. And when you come back, things will be different. You need someone who… I don't know. I don't need you to remind me who I am, ever. I'm like a rock. An unaffectionate rock. I don't know how to make things better. And you're *magic*. What am I supposed to do about that? In school, you'll go back to being you and I'll go back to being me and one of us is eventually going to leave."

He pulled away to study her face. She was being ridiculous, she knew, so she tried to hide in his chest once more, but he held her chin and kept her steady.

"You're wrong," Eliot said, clear and quiet. "I'm going to go to England and think about you every day. And we will field all the gasps of horror on the first day of school when everyone realizes the talented, brilliant Tess Matheson is dating Dr. Birch's gargoyle of a son. You're right that you're a rock. You're a boulder, if anything. The world crashes around you, and you stay standing. At least one of us is strong."

Tess couldn't help laughing. "You're not a gargoyle," she said.

He leaned down and kissed her, once, twice. Whispered: "I'm never going to ask you to be weak for me."

She hugged him as tightly as possible and breathed in the scent of him. Dust and pages and sage. A slight hint of vanilla from those candles he was always burning.

"I'm going to miss you," he said.

"Get on your plane, Birch," Tess responded. She kissed him again, sweetly this time, and watched him get in line for security.

She was halfway back to his car when her phone buzzed. A text from Eliot.

I'll be back before you know it, you witch-hunting fuckface.

Her smile was instant and radiant. She looked over her

shoulder, as if she could see through the walls and lines to where he stood, but she didn't need to see him to know that he was laughing too.

epilogue

Everyone on campus knew the Jessop Library was haunted. It wasn't just the uncatalogued grimoires or inexplicable noises that made students take longer routes across campus to avoid the building entirely. It was also the murders that took place there over the summer, murders that hadn't been solved—that might never be solved.

Tess Matheson was not afraid of these ghosts.

After all, she was the one who created them.

On the first day of school, the first day that the library had been open in weeks, she reported at exactly 7:30. The new librarian was a young woman named Jackie. Tess had met her the week before in the park, and the two of them had coffee and tentatively discussed a schedule for the school year. It would be Tess's responsibility to train any new student employees and make sure the work was getting done.

In a way, she hated being here, but not just because of what happened. She also hated the library because she knew deep down that she belonged to it, and it belonged to her.

There was power thrumming in Jessop's walls. The ink knew her when she entered the halls. The words knew their master. There was nothing for her to fear here.

No, in Jessop, she was not afraid. She was fearsome.

She said hi to Jackie in the back office and stashed her backpack under the circulation desk. There was part of a schedule on the desk, names crossed off and scribbled again, and she squinted down at the written names to decipher who would be working. There'd apparently been some finagling this morning because more than one name was crossed off the list, leaving a mess of blotted ink.

Above her, someone cleared their throat. Immediately, annoyance flooded through her. She hated when people did that to get her attention.

Tess looked up. Navy and crimson tie immaculate over a white button down, capped with a navy sweater. Khakis pressed to perfection. A smirk that she knew far too well.

"Eliot," Tess said.

He'd gotten in just the day before and she hadn't been able to see him—hadn't been sure what to say. They hadn't spoken much since his mother's funeral. Tess cared enough about him to give him time away from her edges. He looked tired and a little sad but also…lighter. Untethered.

"What are you doing here?"

He crossed his arms over his chest. "Well, if you must know," he said, obviously fighting a smile, "I work here."

Tess raised an eyebrow. He tapped on the schedule clipboard. And there it was: three names crossed off on the morning timeslot next to Tess's, and then, scratched above them in Jackie's handwriting, *Eliot Birch*.

"You've got to be kidding me," Tess said. She wanted to wipe that grin off his face. Or kiss him. She hadn't decided which yet.

Eliot shrugged, but he was already grabbing one of the carts, laden down with books that hadn't been shelved in the time Jessop was closed. "Are you going to tell me where these go, Matheson?"

She was going to kill him, one of these days. But then she caught sight of the spines: the books on the carrel were from the first floor cage. All of them had come from Eliot's office in the first place.

"Ask Jackie for a key," Tess said, settling back in the desk chair. She already knew how many books were on the carrel because she and Regina had pulled every single one of them, and there was no way she was putting them back.

He frowned. "Aren't you going to help? There's like, a hundred books here."

One hundred and forty-seven, to be exact, Tess thought. "Nope," she said, opening a book from her bag. "This one's all on you."

He sighed, but he took the cart back, like he was told. Tess watched him over the edge of the book, not even bothering to hide her smile anymore. It was true. Eliot Birch was insufferable.

But at least now he could get his own damn books.

In the comfort of the library, in the sanctuary of Tess Matheson's body, you opened your eyes.

acknowledgments

IT IS IMPOSSIBLE TO CONTINUE WITHOUT NOTING FIRST that I am absolutely an emotionally driven sap who has very little room for logic. As such, without the people listed below, this book never would've been more than a Word document.

Thanks to my agents, Dr. Uwe Stender and Amelia Appel, who have been with me through years full of ups and downs. This book would have never existed without your careful notes and unending encouragement (and ignoring me every time I said, "It's done, it's over, let's forget it ever existed"). Special thanks to Brent Taylor and the entire team at TriadaUS for being so lovely and supportive.

For Lauren, my endlessly patient and enduring editor, who guided me through every step of the process. I hope you know you are stellar, but I could also be biased. Huge thanks to Will Kiester, Tamara Grasty, Mary Beth Garhart, Meg Palmer, Lizzy Mason, Lauren Cepero, Lynne Hartzer, and the rest of the team. Special thanks to Melia Parsloe for creating such a beautiful cover.

My parents, sister, and family have supported me unquestioningly throughout my writing journey. Thanks for tolerating my secrecy and acknowledging when we weren't allowed to talk about things publishing related. Quick sound-off: Jane and Vic, my parental units; Lex; Grandma Peg; Dana and Tony; Kim and Craig; Susan; Lindaly and Win Sr., Jeanna,

Justin, Win, and all family; Stacy, Doug, Jacob, and Squid; Jeff, Britt, Chris, and Taylor; and all others. Special loving memory to my grandparents who did not see this book get published: Hengust and Vito; and Jean, who kept every bit of writing I ever did and wanted so much to be here.

To Becca and Kat and Rebekah and Erin, who encouraged me even when I was awful. And for Evi, who read the early drafts of everything. To Mike and Kali, thanks for tolerating me. Also thanks to Dan C., Katina, Joe V., Rachel, and my much-loved Burgatory crew. Thanks to all other CP's and betas who read sections of this and offered wonderful feedback.

To all of my writing friends: thank you for being incredibly supportive, and also for just letting me complain a lot. Special thanks to Tasha S. and Carly, Bibi C., Kelsey R., Julia B., Hannah C., Chloe G., Hannah W., Claribel O., Kim V., Emma T., Alechia D., Kat D., and Daphne. Love and thanks to Pennwriters and crew, B Street 6, and everyone I might have left out in my haste.

Special love and thanks to the lads, Kish and Michael. Thanks to RHUL Group 3, Shakira, Paul, Gema, Fabia, Steph, and Maddy. For encouragement and teaching, thanks to Dr. Anna Whitwham, Dr. Eley Williams, Dr. Adam Roberts, and Dr. Prudence Bussey-Chamberlain at RHUL, and Siobhan Vivian, Nancy Garcia, and Robert Yune at Pitt.

Thanks to Matt, who tolerates me on a daily basis, and the entire Moss/McKenzie/Mutchell/Bird conglomerate.

To anyone who I've forgotten, you have my thanks as well, and will probably get a sobbing apology for not including you. And a special thank you to anyone who has picked up this book and read it through. To you: it's about you, always, and I am forever in your debt.

about the author

Tori Bovalino is originally from Pittsburgh, Pennsylvania, and currently lives in London with her cat, Sir Gordon Greendige II. She holds a BA in English and anthropology from the University of Pittsburgh and an MA in creative writing from Royal Holloway, University of London. She is currently a student in Royal Holloway's creative writing and practice-based PhD program. Tori is obsessed with good chai, oversized sweaters, and talking about Pittsburgh. She is active on Twitter as @toribov.

Read on for an excerpt of
Not Good For Maidens, a new
novel from Tori Bovalino

not good for for maidens

tori bovalino

PROLOGUE

May

Boston, Eighteen Years Earlier

MAY HAD WAYS OF COPING.

She ate. That was an improvement. She ate, and sipped the water that Laura kept pushing toward her. She looked out the window of the brownstone, watching the people down below. She kept looking for the city walls, but of course, they weren't there. The walls, the people, the market—they were all a world away.

May coped, and she slept, and she ate. She held her tongue until her voice was rusty in her mouth, until her vowels were unfamiliar and her accent heavy against Dad's. But silence was better than screaming, and if she opened her mouth, May was not sure what would come out.

She smiled when their father brought a new candy every day from the shop on the corner, presenting them with an endless rotation of American snacks that turned her stomach. She let Laura fret over her because it hinted at forgiveness awarded or forthcoming, even though it tugged at that deep guilt May couldn't shake.

When she was alone—which was rare, with Laura's fretting— she hummed to herself. She knew the songs, all of them, by heart.

Backwards and forwards and all the way around.

Are you going to Scarborough Fair?

No, May thought, staring down at the street as their father rounded the corner with a shopping bag hanging from one hand. *No, I've been to Scarborough Fair, and I'd not like to return.*

Sometimes, in the moments May forgot about it all, she woke up searching for something within herself she'd lost, only to realize all over again that it was gone.

Thirty-two days after they arrived, Laura knocked softly at May's door. "Are you in there?"

"Yes," May said. Where else would she be?

Laura came in. She was wearing a dress, green, that she didn't have in York. She must've bought it here, but May couldn't remember her leaving to get it. Perhaps she'd gone when May was sleeping. Laura looked better now. Less thin, less tired.

"I'm going out tonight," she said, nudging a fallen silk scarf on the floor with one foot. May had gotten it in Leeds four years before.

In their past life, in the times before, this would've been an enticing bit of information. May felt it tugging in her mind, that spark of something that would've interested her. It only lasted a moment in the current fog of her brain, the dimmest of embers in a pile of ashes.

But it was a fog she didn't like Laura to see. "Oh?" May said, remembering that she had to say something.

Laura nodded. "With a boy. He works at that bookshop on Newbury."

There was a pause, a pause May was probably supposed to fill. She stared at Laura blankly. Maybe she was meant to ask his name. May had never been to the bookstore on Newbury— Laura had invited her, but May didn't like to leave. She felt the age of the city pressing against her skin. Not York old, not by a longshot, but the closest this country had.

All she could think was: *Don't stay too late, don't seek the market, you don't know if there's a market.*

Laura's smile faded. May had failed, she knew. She should've pretended, should've asked something. Anything.

"Are you okay with me going?" Laura asked. "I can stay."

Stay here, in her green dress, with Dad and his questions and haunted May? Stay here when she wanted to go, after she'd sacrificed everything for May? It would be a travesty, probably, to keep Laura inside. No matter how much she wanted to ask her to stay. No matter how much the idea of a house without Laura scared her.

She dreamt of her sometimes, in the haze of the market: Laura, brave and valiant. Standing tall, stained with the juice of cherries and shining with sweat, blood leaking out of a gash across one arm. Laura, always the stronger sister, always with the greater will; Laura, come to save her yet again.

Laura, who had given up the entire world for May.

"You go," May said. She tried on a smile, but her teeth felt dry and the corners of her mouth cracked and Laura looked even more wary. "Go and have fun." She turned back to the window so she didn't have to watch Laura leave.

Coping was an odd thing, May thought, as she watched Laura flit out onto the street in her green dress, into the arms of a kind-looking brown-haired boy with a mediocre silver car. Coping was pretending to listen to Dad as he chatted over dinner and nodding in the appropriate places, and returning to her room and the window seat as soon as she was able. Coping was watching the people on the street but not seeing them, not really processing, because she was trying too hard to see the horns and warts and pale green skin glamoured to look human; not thinking of the magic she'd lost or how Laura must resent her. It was not running through the spells that were once so familiar to her she practiced them in her sleep, not calling Mum every day to see what she was missing, what she'd given up, what she'd thrown away because of May's mistakes.

Coping was not thinking about the market, not thinking about the market, not thinking about anything other than the market.

When May slept, it felt less like she was slipping from consciousness and more like she was falling out of present time, back to somewhere else.

Well, not just anywhere else. Most times, her mind went back to the beginning. To York, her home, where the pavement smelled like rain and fog, where she knew the streets by heart. She closed her eyes and imagined standing in the shadow of the Minster with a girl by her side, unbloodied. In her imaginings, she and Eitra walked the velvet night, through misty rain and clear darkness, fingers entwined.

In her imaginings, Eitra did not die. May had that thrill of magic back, even if she could not use it. They were home, home, home, in the place where May could not return.

But in the end, May opened her eyes, like always. In the end, she was always banished, always alone, and Eitra was always dead.

An indeterminate amount of time later, long past dark, May watched the silver car pull back up to the curb. The boy got out, went around, and opened Laura's door. They kissed on the street outside.

May tasted a rush of goblin blood in her mouth.

She swallowed it down.

Minutes later, the door opened and shut, and Laura came in silently to sit on her bed. Her cheeks were flushed and her hair askew, and there was no point telling her that the buttons of her dress were not done correctly.

It was a detail she noticed, May realized, despite the fog.

"You look like you haven't moved," Laura said.

May shrugged.

Laura sighed, slipped off her shoes, and shimmied out of her dress. She pulled the pins from her hair and grabbed a spare shirt from May's drawer.

"Come to bed," Laura said.

May nodded. She slipped under the sheets, still in her jean shorts and tank top that Laura made her put on that morning. Laura smelled of cigarette smoke and lipstick, but it was okay. In a way, it was the first time she'd smelled normal since . . . since before.

Laura ran her fingers through May's hair, combing through the tangles. "You're here," she murmured. "You're safe. You'll never go again, May. Do you hear me? You'll never go to the market again."

May bit her lip. Because, though she was an ocean away from the market, though she may never see the walls again in her life, she knew the truth. She was a part of the market. Some part of her would always be there. Some part would never leave as her blood clung to Eitra's skin, as they decayed into flowers and moss together. Maybe, in her time away, some part of her had become the goblin's property, even if Laura had gotten her out.

When she closed her eyes every night, she fell into the same nightmare of the goblins grabbing Eitra's arms and legs and holding her down, pushing her into the grass of the park as she struggled against them. In her dream, May never closed her eyes fast enough, or perhaps she forced herself to watch.

Maybe she watched because she hadn't in real life, when it had really happened. She'd only heard the snick of the knife, had only imagined the hot splash of Eitra's blood, and heard her sharp scream cut off.

But in her nightmares, her eyes were open. In her nightmares, every night at the witching hour, May watched Eitra die all over again.

She'd never left the market. She'd never leave the market. And when it was time, when it came again, the market would take her back.

That was the truth of coping: it was just delaying the inevitable.